ALL THE WRONG PLACES

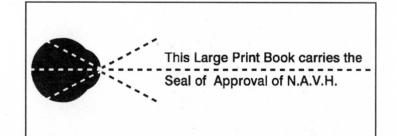

This Large Print Book carries the
Seal of Approval of N.A.V.H.

ALL THE WRONG PLACES

JOY FIELDING

THORNDIKE PRESS
A part of Gale, a Cengage Company

Farmington Hills, Mich • San Francisco • New York • Waterville, Maine
Meriden, Conn • Mason, Ohio • Chicago

LIBRARY OF CONGRESS CIP DATA ON FILE.
CATALOGUING IN PUBLICATION FOR THIS BOOK
IS AVAILABLE FROM THE LIBRARY OF CONGRESS

ISBN-13: 978-1-4328-6148-3 (hardcover alk. paper)

Published in 2019 by arrangement with Ballantine Books, an imprint of Random House, a division of Penguin Random House LLC

Printed in the United States of America
1 2 3 4 5 6 7 23 22 21 20 19

TO WARREN, WITH LOVE ALWAYS

CHAPTER ONE

"So, tell me about yourself," he says. He smiles what he hopes is a sweet smile — neither too big nor too small, one that hints at a wry, maybe even offbeat sense of humor that he thinks would appeal to her. He wants to charm her. He wants her to like him.

The young woman sitting across from him at the immaculately set table for two hesitates. When she speaks, her voice is soft, tremulous. "What do you want to know?"

She is beautiful: late twenties, porcelain skin, deep blue eyes, long brown hair, just the right amount of visible cleavage. Exactly as advertised, which isn't always the case. Usually the photos they post are a few years old, the women themselves older still. "Well, for starters, why a dating app? I mean, you're gorgeous. I can't imagine you'd have any trouble meeting guys, especially in a city like Boston."

She hesitates again. She's shy, thoughtful as opposed to self-absorbed. Something else he likes. "I just thought it would be fun," she admits. "All my friends are on them. And I've kind of been out of the dating scene for a while . . ."

"You had a boyfriend?"

She nods. "We broke up about four months ago."

"You broke up with him?"

"Actually, no. He broke up with me."

He laughs. "I find that hard to believe."

"He said he wasn't ready to be tied down," she offers without prompting. Her eyes fill with tears. Several escape without warning, clinging to her bottom lashes.

Instinctively he reaches across the table to wipe them away, careful not to disturb her mascara. "You miss him," he says.

"No," she says quickly. "Not really. It's just hard sometimes. It's more being part of a couple I miss, our friends . . ."

"Were you together long?"

"A little over a year. What about you?"

He smiles. *She's trying,* he thinks. Even though he can see her heart isn't really in it. Still, some women never even think to ask. "Me? No. It's been a while since I've been in a serious relationship. But we were talking about you."

8

She looks toward her plate. She hasn't touched her food, and he spent hours preparing it, letting the expensive steaks marinate all afternoon, wrapping the large Idaho potatoes in tinfoil for baking, arranging the watermelon and feta cheese salad just so on the delicate floral china, wanting to impress her. *Maybe she's a vegetarian,* he thinks, although there was nothing on her profile to indicate that.

He should have asked when he suggested dinner. "Tell me about your childhood," he says now.

She looks surprised. "My childhood?"

"I'm assuming you had one." Again, the sweet smile hinting at greater depths.

"It was pretty ordinary. Nothing much to tell."

"I'm guessing upper middle class," he offers, hoping to stimulate the conversation. "Comfortable lifestyle, maybe a nanny or a housekeeper, parents who loved you, made sure you had everything your little heart desired."

"Not really. Well, maybe at first," she agrees tentatively. "Until I was about six and my parents got divorced. Then everything changed."

"How so?"

"We had to move. My mom had to go

9

back to work. My dad remarried a woman we didn't like. We were always being shuffled back and forth."

"We?"

"My brothers and I."

"I like that you say 'I,' " he interrupts. "Most people would say 'me.' They have no respect for grammar. Or maybe they just don't know the difference between the subject and the object of a sentence. I don't know." He shrugs, sensing her mounting discomfort. Not everyone is as concerned with grammar as he is. "How many brothers do you have?" he asks, aiming for safer ground.

"Two. One's in New York. The other one's in L.A."

"And your mom? Where is she?"

"Here. In Boston."

"Does she know where you are tonight? Well, how could she?" he asks, answering one question with another. "Don't think she'd approve of your agreeing to have dinner in a stranger's apartment, would she? Are you always this adventurous?" He cocks his head to one side, a gesture some have called charming, and waits for her response.

Another hesitation. "No."

"Should I be flattered? 'Cause I'm feeling kind of flattered here, I gotta admit."

She blushes, although whether the sudden redness in her cheeks is from embarrassment or anticipation, he isn't sure.

"Is it because I'm so good-looking?" He says this playfully, accompanied by yet another smile, his sweetest one so far, and although she doesn't respond, he knows he's right. He *is* that good-looking. ("Pretty boy," his father used to sneer.) Much better-looking than the picture he posted on the dating site, which in truth isn't a picture of him at all, just some shirtless model with handsomely generic features and washboard abs whose photograph he saw in a *Men's Health* magazine.

Good-looking enough to make a woman silence the nagging voice in her head warning her to beware, to follow him out of the crowded bar where they'd agreed to meet and go with him to his apartment near Sargent's Wharf, where he's promised a gourmet feast.

"You're not eating," he says. "Is the steak too rare for you?"

"No. I just can't . . ."

"Please. You have to at least try it." He cuts a piece of meat from his own plate and extends his fork across the table toward her mouth. "Please," he says again, as blood drips from the steak to stain the white table-cloth.

She opens her mouth to receive the almost raw piece of meat.

"Chew carefully," he advises. "Wouldn't want you to choke."

"Please . . ." she says, as the cellphone in his pocket rings.

"Hold on. I'll just be a minute." He removes the phone from his pocket and swipes its thin face from left to right, then lifts it to his ear. "Well, hello there," he says, lowering his voice seductively, his lips grazing the phone's smooth surface. *Finally,* he thinks.

"Hi," the woman on the other end of the line responds. "Is this . . . Mr. Right Now?" She giggles and he laughs. Mr. Right Now is the name he goes by on the multiple dating sites to which he subscribes.

"It is. Is this . . . Wildflower?"

"It is," she says, more than a trace self-consciously, not as comfortable with pseudonyms as he is.

"Well, Wildflower," he says. "I'm so glad you called." He's been anticipating this moment for what feels like forever.

"Are you still in Florida?" she asks. "Is this a bad time?"

"No. It's perfect. I just got back into town

about an hour ago."

"How's your mother?"

"Much better. Thanks for asking. How are you?"

"Me? I'm fine." She hesitates. "I was thinking maybe you were right, that it's time we give this another try."

"No maybes about it," he says, eager to nail her down. "At least on my end. How about Wednesday?"

"Wednesday is good."

"Great. Are you familiar with Anthony's Bar, over on Boylston? I know it's usually crowded and it can be pretty noisy, but —"

"Anthony's is great," she says, as he knew she would. Crowded, noisy bars are always a woman's preferred place to meet.

He smiles at the woman sitting across the table, notes the tears now wriggling freely down her cheeks. He checks his watch, making no move to wipe the tears away. Anthony's Bar is where he met her less than two hours ago. He is being rude and insensitive.

"Say six o'clock?" he says into the phone.

"Six is good."

"No more last-minute cancellations?"

"I'll be there at six on the button."

"No!" his dinner companion shouts unexpectedly. "Don't . . ."

He is instantly on his feet, his hand sweep-

13

ing across the table to slap her hard across the face. It connects with such ferocity that the chair to which she is securely tied, her hands handcuffed behind her back, teeters on its hind legs and threatens to fall, causing the noose looped around her neck to tighten. He watches as she gasps frantically for air. Another minute of flailing uselessly about and she will likely lose consciousness.

He's not ready for that. He isn't done with her yet.

"What was that?" the woman calling herself Wildflower asks.

"What was what?" he asks easily in return, walking around the table to steady the chair, then covering the frantic woman's mouth with his free hand. "Oh. Probably just the TV. Some guy getting the shit kicked out of him. Excuse the language."

A second's silence. He can almost feel Wildflower smile.

"Are you going to tell me your real name?" she ventures.

"I'll tell you mine if you tell me yours," he replies flirtatiously. A lie. He never tells any of the women his real name. "Although I gotta say, I kind of like Wildflower."

"Then suppose we leave things the way they are for now."

"Till Wednesday, then," he says.

"Till Wednesday."

"Looking forward to it."

He returns the phone to his pocket and removes his hand from the woman's mouth. "If you scream, I'll stick this steak knife in your eye," he says calmly, brandishing its serrated edge in front of her face. The noose around her neck is now buried inside her flesh. He doubts she has enough air to scream, even if she were so inclined. Still, he'd underestimated her before.

She'd been so easy. Almost too easy. Mesmerized by his beautiful exterior, she'd gone along with his every suggestion, agreeing to leave the dark, crowded bar to enjoy a home-cooked dinner in his apartment, then eagerly sitting down at the small, round table with its white linen tablecloth already in place, not comprehending the danger she was in until her hands were handcuffed behind her and the rope was literally around her throat.

She'd tried so hard, been so compliant, going along with his silly game of pretending they were on a real date, answering his stupid questions, even offering up a few of her own, undoubtedly hoping to save her life. And even when she recognized this for the pipe dream it was, when the phone call convinced her that she was simply one of

15

many, that there was nothing special about her, and that he was already moving forward, who'd have thought she'd have the gumption to try warning his next victim? He admires that.

Not that it matters.

He resumes his seat at the table and calmly finishes his meal, careful to chew each piece of meat thirty times, as his father used to insist. He hopes she won't do anything stupid, something that will make it necessary to finish her off quickly. He wants to take his time with her, show her he's more than just a pretty face.

He smiles, hoping to convey that she has his full attention. She deserves that. But even as he lifts the last piece of steak toward his lips, his imagination is already leaping ahead.

To Wednesday.

And the woman who will be his crowning achievement: Wildflower.

CHAPTER TWO

Three Weeks Earlier

At just after seven A.M. Paige Hamilton woke up to find her mother sitting on the side of her bed in her pajamas, her normally youthful features betrayed by a series of worried lines that made her look every one of her seventy years.

"Mom?"

"How was your date last night?"

"You woke me up to ask about my date?"

"How was it?

"Not good." Paige pushed herself up on her elbows, recalling last night's unfortunate rendezvous as she shook her shoulder-length brown hair from her eyes. The man had been at least twenty pounds heavier and five inches shorter than his profile on Match Sticks indicated. What was the matter with these guys? Did they think that women didn't have eyes, that they wouldn't notice the discrepancy?

17

"That's too bad," her mother said. "You thought he sounded promising."

"Mom . . . what's going on?"

"I don't want to worry you."

"Too late for that."

"I'm sorry."

"Don't apologize. Tell me what's wrong."

Her mother's sigh shook the double bed. "I think I might be having a stroke."

Paige was instantly on her feet, dancing abstract circles on the hardwood floor. "What are you talking about? What makes you think you're having a stroke?" She searched her mother's face for signs of anything off balance. A drooping eyelid, a twitching lip. "You're not slurring your words. Are you dizzy? Are you in pain?"

"I'm not in pain. I'm not dizzy," her mother repeated. "You have such a lovely figure," she said, as if this were a perfectly normal thing to say under the circumstances.

Paige grabbed her pink silk robe from the foot of the bed and wrapped it around her naked body, trying to make sense of what was happening.

"I didn't realize you slept in the nude," her mother continued. "I always wanted to do that, but your father preferred pajamas, so I followed his lead."

"Mom! Focus! Why do you think you're having a stroke?"

"It's my vision," her mother said. "It's kind of weird."

"What do you mean, it's kind of weird? How weird?"

"I'm seeing all these flashing lights and squiggly lines, and I remember reading that a change in vision is often the first sign you're having a stroke. Or maybe a detached retina. What do you think?"

"I think I'm calling nine-one-one."

"Really, darling? Do you think that's necessary?"

"Yes, Mom. I really, really do." Paige grabbed her cellphone from the night table and pressed the emergency digits. "Try to stay calm," she advised her mother, although *she* was the one on the verge of hysteria. She'd lost her father to cancer two years ago. She wasn't ready to lose her mother, too. At thirty-three, she was much too young to be an orphan. "What are you doing?" she asked as her mother pushed herself off the bed.

"I should probably get dressed."

"Sit back down," Paige said, listening to the phone's persistent ring against her ear. "Don't move." She threw her free arm into the air in frustration. "What's the matter

19

with these people? Why aren't they answering the phone? I thought this was supposed to be an emerg—"

"Nine-one-one," a woman's voice said, interrupting Paige's tirade. "What is your emergency?"

"My mother's having a stroke."

"Well, it could be a detached retina," her mother qualified.

"We need an ambulance right away." Paige quickly gave the dispatcher the address of her mother's posh Back Bay condominium. "They'll be here in five minutes," she said, crossing to the en suite bathroom and throwing some cold water on her face, then applying deodorant before grabbing the first thing she saw in her closet and pulling it over her head.

"That's a pretty dress," her mother said. "Is it new?"

Paige glanced at the shapeless floral sundress that Noah had always despised. She quickly reminded herself that Noah's likes and dislikes were no longer her concern. "No. I've had it a while." She retrieved a pair of lace panties from the top drawer of her dresser and stepped into them, pulling them up over her slim hips.

"You don't wear a bra?" her mother asked.

"Well, I don't really need one," Paige said,

deciding that attempting a normal conversation was her mother's way of assuring her that everything would be all right, that even if her retina was detaching or, God forbid, she was having a stroke, she would be fine.

Except things weren't fine. They hadn't been fine in a while.

"I never used to need one either," her mother said, almost wistfully. She looked down at her more than ample chest. "And then suddenly, I get these. Now! When nobody's looking. When nobody cares."

In other circumstances, Paige might have laughed. Now she could only fight back tears. "*I* care." She sat down beside her mother and hugged her close.

"You're a good girl." Her mother leaned her head against Paige's shoulder. "I love you more than anything in the world. You know that, don't you?"

"I know." Paige felt a pang of guilt. Not because she didn't love her mother. She did. It was just that she'd always been more of a daddy's girl, her father's outsized personality having tended to overshadow everything in its path, even when he was on his deathbed. "I love you, too."

"Don't you worry." Her mother patted Paige's knee. "I'll be okay."

"You promise?"

21

"I promise."

Paige smiled, knowing such promises were futile. Hadn't her mother made the same promise when her father was first diagnosed with the cancer that would kill him barely a year later?

"Don't worry. Your father will be fine," she'd assured both Paige and her brother, although it was doubtful that Michael, older than Paige by almost four years and a successful cardiologist in Livingston, New Jersey, had been as gullible.

Her mother looked toward the bedroom door. "I should at least put on a robe."

"I'll get it," Paige said. "Don't move."

"Bring a change of clothes for when they send me home," her mother called after her as Paige marched toward the master bedroom down the hall. The July sun was already streaming through the automatic blinds in the living room, sending streaks, like bolts of lightning, across the beige marble floor.

Her parents had moved into the two-bedroom condominium five years ago, downsizing from their six-thousand-plus-square-foot home in the suburb of Weston. ("Who needs such a big place anymore?" her mother had asked at the time. "You kids are long gone and the dog is dead.")

Had her mother always had this sardonic sense of humor? Paige wondered now. Why hadn't she noticed before?

The condo, located in one of Boston's most prestigious neighborhoods, was spacious and modern, with floor-to-ceiling windows in the living-dining area as well as the library that had doubled as her father's office and the small family room off the large kitchen. The two bedrooms were located off the main hall in the opposite wing of the apartment. Each room afforded an equally stunning view of the city.

Paige cut across the ivory silk-and-wool carpet that covered the master bedroom floor, slamming her hip against one of the four posters of the king-size bed as she hurried toward the walk-in closet. *Well, more a room full of closets,* Paige thought, wondering if her father's clothes still occupied the half that had been his, or if her mother had finally packed them off to Goodwill. Robert Hamilton had been such a natty dresser, whether wearing a suit and tie or more casual attire. *And those socks,* Paige thought with a smile. Years before it had become fashionable, her father had sported a huge selection of colorful, wildly patterned socks that were a perfect complement to his equally huge and colorful personality.

Tears clouded Paige's eyes and she brushed them aside. She missed her father so much.

Was she about to lose her mother, too? Was everyone she loved destined to abandon her?

"God, you're a selfish bitch," she muttered, retrieving her mother's blue terry-cloth robe from a hook inside the closet, then selecting a pink cotton dress and some surprisingly racy underwear from the built-in dresser — had her mother always worn bikini panties and push-up bras? — and carrying everything back to her room.

Not that the second bedroom had been meant for her. Originally, it was intended as a guest room, for whenever Michael and his family came to visit. But Michael's busy schedule had precluded such visits happening often, and his wife had preferred staying in a hotel, so the room had stayed largely empty and unused. But then Paige's father had died, and six months ago she'd lost her job, and two months after that, her live-in boyfriend had left her for another woman — well, technically, *she* was the one who'd had to move out — so Paige's mother had suggested that she move in with her. "Just temporarily," she'd stressed. "Until you're back on your feet again."

24

Was that ever going to happen? Paige wondered now, entering the bedroom to find her mother standing beside the window, staring down at the tree-lined street ten stories below. "Mom, what are you doing? I told you to stay still."

"I'm just admiring the day. There isn't a cloud in the sky."

"Can you see all right?" Paige asked. "What's happening with your eyes?"

"Still lots of fireworks. It's kind of like one of those sound-and-light shows. Only without the sound." Her lips curled into a weak smile.

"You're scaring me."

"I'm sorry, darling. That's the last thing I want to do. I'll be fine. I promise."

The phone rang as Paige was helping her mother on with her robe. Paige listened to the concierge's worried voice, then hung up the phone and took a deep breath before attempting a smile of her own. "The ambulance is here."

CHAPTER THREE

"Joan Hamilton?" the man asked, entering the small, nondescript office and shutting the door behind him, his eyes darting between Paige and her mother. He was young and pleasant-looking, with a full head of dark, wavy hair. He wore a white coat over slim khaki pants and a navy-and-white-checked shirt.

"That's me," Paige's mother said, lifting her hand into the air and wiggling her fingers. She'd changed out of her pajamas into the clothes Paige had brought along.

"I'm Dr. Barelli." The doctor sat down behind his desk, smiling at the two women sitting across from him. "How are you feeling?"

"I feel fine," Joan Hamilton said. "A little foolish. My eyes are . . . well, they seem to be . . . fine."

Dr. Barelli opened the folder in his hands, scanning its contents as Paige and her mother watched him expectantly. Not that there was anything else to look at — the pale green walls were bare except for a generic reproduction of a boring landscape; the furnishings were minimal and strictly utilitarian; the desk was void of personal touches or family photographs; the window behind it overlooked a brick wall. Probably some sort of communal space, used for quick discussions and consultations. Still, the room was a welcome respite from the endless corridors and plastic chairs Paige had been sitting in since they'd arrived at Mass General. If she never saw another ancient edition of *Star* magazine, it would be too soon.

It was approaching one o'clock in the afternoon. They'd been at the hospital almost five hours. Her mother had undergone a multitude of tests, including an MRI and a retinal scan, as well as a series of examinations to determine whether her heart was operating as it should. Technicians had drawn so much blood, Paige marveled that her mother had any color left at all.

"Well," the doctor began, looking up from his folder and smiling again. The smile sent creases up his cheeks to his eyes. "It's all good news, from what I can see."

27

"Good news?" Paige and her mother repeated simultaneously.

"Your blood tests are normal, boringly so, if you don't mind my saying. Your blood pressure's a little high, but nothing to be overly concerned about. Both your retinas are exactly where they should be. Your vision is excellent for a woman your age. As is your brain function and just about everything else that we tested for. In fact, you just might be the healthiest person in this place."

"Well, isn't that lovely," Joan Hamilton said.

Paige gasped with relief. "But . . . her eyes . . ."

"Classic ocular migraine," the doctor explained.

"A migraine?" Joan repeated. "But I didn't have a headache."

"You're lucky," Dr. Barelli said, dark eyes sparkling.

"I don't understand," Paige said.

"Your mother experienced the aura that often accompanies migraines. They involve lots of squiggles and flashing lights, usually starting small and then building in intensity before petering out, usually in twenty to thirty minutes."

"That's exactly what happened," Joan

28

Hamilton agreed.

"They're not uncommon, especially as you get older. And the good news is that they're not serious. More of a nuisance than anything else. You might not have another one for years," the doctor continued, speaking directly to Paige's mother, "or you might have one tomorrow." He went on to say that although there were many theories as to what caused them, no one really knew for sure, and that while medication could be taken, the auras usually disappeared before such medication could take effect, so it was preferable just to wait them out. "Of course, if you're driving, I'd advise pulling over."

"That's it?" Paige asked as her mother rose to her feet.

"That's it." Dr. Barelli extended his hand across the desk for the women to shake.

"An ocular migraine," Joan said, almost proudly, as they waited for the elevator. "Who knew?"

"You must be starving," Paige said, speaking for both of them as they stepped onto the street moments later. She'd been surviving on black coffee since they'd exited the ambulance and, as far as she knew, her mother hadn't had a thing to eat or drink since last night.

"I'm famished," her mother agreed. "Let's

go somewhere nice for lunch. Do you have time?"

Paige checked her watch. She had a job interview at three o'clock, her first one in more than two weeks, so it was important she not be late. Normally she preferred being early, but she'd learned the hard way that being early wasn't always a great idea. She closed her eyes, seeing herself tiptoe down the narrow hall of her old apartment toward the bedroom she shared with Noah, hearing the all-too-familiar laughter behind the bedroom door. "There's a neat little café over on Charles Street," she said loudly, trying to block out the sound of that laughter.

"Why are you shouting?" her mother asked.

"Sorry," Paige said, hailing a nearby taxi.

Unfortunately, the small café was crowded with tourists, drawn to the street's reputation for quirky fashions and charming antiques shops, and they had to wait for a table.

"Dr. Barelli was very cute, didn't you think?" her mother said when they were finally seated and their order taken.

"A little young."

"They're *all* young. *You're* young."

Paige's cellphone rang before she could think of a suitable response. She reached into her beige canvas bag and extricated the phone, grateful for the interruption. Her mother meant well, but Paige wasn't in the mood for one of her patented *you're a smart, beautiful girl, there are plenty more fish in the sea* pep talks. "Chloe, hi," she said to her oldest and best friend.

"Can you come over?" Chloe said, wasting no time on unnecessary pleasantries.

"Is something wrong?" Paige pictured her friend pushing her straight blond hair away from her pale blue eyes and chewing on her full bottom lip.

"Only everything."

Shit, Paige thought, understanding the source of Chloe's problems without having to be told. "I have a job interview at three. I can come over after that."

"Great. See you then."

"Something wrong?" her mother asked, repeating her daughter's question as Paige returned the phone to her purse.

Paige shrugged. *"Only everything,"* she heard Chloe say.

"About the doctor . . ." her mother began. "I just meant —"

"I know what you meant, Mom," Paige interrupted. "But it's not like I've locked myself away in some tower. I'm putting myself out there. I'm on a dozen dating

31

sites. I've gone out with six guys in as many weeks . . ."

"Maybe you're being too picky."

"Maybe," Paige said, too tired and hungry to argue. Was it being too picky to expect a man to be . . . honest? Were *all* men liars? "What about you?" she asked, turning the tables on her mother.

"What do you mean, what about me?"

"It's been two years since Daddy died. Have you ever considered . . . ?" She could barely finish the thought, let alone the sentence, the idea of her mother being interested in any man other than her father too ridiculous to contemplate.

"Don't be silly, darling. I'm an old woman."

"Seventy is hardly old. Not anymore. And you look fantastic. Dr. Barelli said you're in great shape."

"For a woman my age," Joan Hamilton qualified, although there was something in her tone that said the idea of her dating again might not be so preposterous after all. She patted the side of her stylish blond bob.

"Maybe *you* should go on Match Sticks," Paige said, feeling increasingly uncomfortable and wondering why she was persisting. She looked around the restaurant's small, dark interior for the waiter, wondering what was taking so long with their food. "Oh, God," she said, suddenly burrowing down in her seat and covering the side of her face with her hand. Could this day get any worse?

"What is it?"

"Don't look."

Her mother immediately twisted in her chair to look behind her.

"I said *don't* . . ."

"Sorry, darling. It's an automatic reaction when someone tells you not to look," Joan Hamilton said sheepishly. "Did she see us? Is she coming over?"

"Oh, yes," Paige said, sitting back up and watching her cousin approach, reminded of the expression "it's like looking in the mirror." Except she was pretty sure that expression was intended to be ironic, whereas looking at her cousin actually *was* like looking in the mirror, so striking was their resemblance. Which probably wasn't that surprising, considering that their fathers had been identical twins and the two girls had been born within days of each other.

"Well, hello, you two," Heather said, bending down to kiss her aunt's cheek, seemingly unaware of the stiffening of Joan's shoulders. "Fancy meeting you here."

Paige wondered whether the cliché was

33

deliberate or if her cousin couldn't help it, never having had an original thought in her life. She cursed herself for having forgotten that the office where her cousin worked was only blocks away.

Or maybe she hadn't forgotten. Maybe she'd been daring fate and fate had taken up the challenge, raising an invisible middle finger in response.

"No hellos?" Heather asked. "Okay, well. Have it your way. How goes the job hunt?" She smiled at Paige, as if she were actually expecting an answer.

Paige fought the urge to punch her cousin in the nose.

Heather shifted her weight from one foot to the other, tucking her shoulder-length brown hair behind one ear. "Well, okay, then. Nice bumping into you two. Guess I'll see you at the party."

Oh, shit, thought Paige, watching Heather wiggle away on four-inch heels.

"Don't you have a skirt like that?" her mother asked.

"I'm not going to that stupid party," Paige said.

"Oh, darling. It's your uncle's eightieth birthday. I know it won't be easy, but how can you not?"

"Because I can't," Paige said. It was hard

enough for her to be around her uncle in the best of times, to have this living, breathing replica of her father still enjoying life when her father was in the ground. How dare her uncle get to be eighty when his twin brother, superior to him in every way, hadn't been as fortunate! How could her mother bear to look at the man?

Of course, that wasn't the only reason Paige didn't want to go. Maybe not even the main one.

"You could always bring a date," her mother suggested as the waiter approached with their food.

"Two Cobb salads," the young man said as he deposited their bowls on the table.

"Maybe someone from one of those sites you're on . . ." her mother said.

Paige stabbed at her salad with her fork and said nothing.

CHAPTER FOUR

She'd come home early.

That was her second mistake.

The first had been not calling to alert him.

Of course, Paige hadn't realized at the time that alerting Noah was necessary. Or had she? Hadn't she been at least a little suspicious? Wasn't that the real reason she hadn't phoned to tell him that Chloe and Matt had returned home an hour earlier than expected from their weekly date night — Chloe had obviously been crying; there was a suspicious-looking red mark on her cheek — and that she was on her way home?

Chloe's usual babysitter had canceled at the last moment and Chloe had called in a panic — Matt was already waiting at the restaurant and he hated any last-minute changes in plans — and asked Paige if she could come over. "I'd ask my mother, but she's . . . well, you know . . . my mother."

Paige had said yes, she'd be delighted. She

loved Chloe's two young children as if they were her own and enjoyed spending time with them. Besides, she would do anything for Chloe, whose mother was a total disaster, a woman incapable of seeing anything beyond the tip of her own nose. It was a miracle that Chloe had turned out the way she had, which was, simply put, one of the sweetest people Paige had ever met.

Maybe too sweet.

Too sweet for a man like Matt, that was for sure.

Too sweet for her own good, Paige worried.

Noah hadn't objected to Paige bailing on their plans at the last minute. In fact, he'd seemed relieved, saying he hadn't been especially keen on the movie Paige had suggested anyway, and that he could use the time to prepare for the case he was working on, then get to bed early, hopefully catch up on some much-needed sleep. "It's shaping up to be a very busy week," he'd said.

Paige understood this was code for "no sex tonight," even though it was the weekend and their sex life had been less than stellar of late. "I've just got so much on my plate," he'd apologized the last time he'd blamed exhaustion and overwork for turning down her romantic overtures. Paige had smiled and said she understood. But she didn't really. As a lawyer hoping one day to make partner with the large downtown firm that employed him, Noah had been exhausted and overworked since the day they'd met. It had never stopped him from being an eager and avid lover. But something had changed in the last few months, something she couldn't quite put her finger on.

Or maybe she knew exactly where to put her finger.

And whom to point that finger at.

Maybe that was the problem.

Which was why she hadn't phoned to alert him she was on her way home, why she hadn't bothered shouting her usual hello when she entered the foyer of their small apartment, why she hadn't even glanced into the living room to check if he was there as she'd tiptoed down the hall toward the closed bedroom door. Nor had she hesitated when she heard the giggles emanating from the other side, knowing even before she pushed open the door and saw the naked body straddling Noah's whose body it would be, whose startled face she would find.

"Are you kidding me?" Paige had shouted as her cousin scrambled to her feet, tripping and almost falling as she struggled into her underwear. "I don't believe this."

Except she *did* believe it. In truth, Paige would have been shocked if the woman she'd discovered straddling her boyfriend had been anyone *but* Heather. Her cousin had always coveted whatever Paige had, be it clothing, hairstyles, or men. When Paige signed up for modeling lessons as a teenager, so had Heather. When Paige learned to play guitar, Heather had immediately signed up for lessons. When Paige bought a new pair of rhinestone-studded sneakers, Heather had run right out and bought the exact same ones.

When Paige later grumbled about these things to her father, he'd smiled and reminded her that "imitation is the sincerest form of flattery." His brother had been the same way with him. "But he was never as good," he'd added with a wink. "And everybody knew it."

So no one was surprised that when Paige went into advertising after graduating college, Heather had followed suit, joining a larger if less prestigious agency, where she'd languished in an entry-level position for years before finally being promoted to one of six junior account managers. Paige, also to no one's surprise, had risen quickly through the ranks of her smaller boutique firm to become director of strategic planning.

And then, out of the blue, her agency had been swallowed by a larger New York company. They'd brought in their own people, and Paige had found herself unceremoniously spit out, along with most of the original senior management.

"That's so awful," Heather had commiserated, managing to sound sincere despite the slight gleam in her eye. "After so many years. You must be devastated."

"I'll find something else."

"Of course you will."

Except it turned out that there weren't a lot of options available for directors of strategic planning. In fact, there were none. The few jobs Paige interviewed for were for less senior positions, and while she would have happily taken any one of them, especially as one month stretched into six, she was repeatedly deemed "too qualified." Meanwhile, Heather had begun spending more and more time at Paige's apartment, dropping over with supposed leads about potential jobs, bringing over take-out dinners she'd pick up at Eataly on her way home from work, listening with rapt attention as Noah talked about his day, laughing at even the feeblest of his jokes, and being so obvious in her attempts to flatter and impress him that Paige and Noah would sometimes joke about it after she'd left.

Turned out Noah liked obvious.

Turned out they'd been sleeping together for more than a month before Paige discovered them.

"I can't even say he left me for a younger woman," Paige had wailed to Chloe. "She's two days older than I am. And we're practically twins, for God's sake, so it can't be her looks."

"Well, it certainly isn't her personality," Chloe said.

"Oh, God," Paige wailed.

"What?"

"She must be great in bed."

"You think?"

"What else could it be?"

"It can't be that. She doesn't have the imagination."

"Well, she must have something I don't," Paige argued.

"No. Noah's just an idiot."

"Okay," Paige agreed. "Let's go with that."

Heather and Noah had been living together now for almost four months, and their relationship had caused an undeniable rift between the two families. Paige hadn't

41

spoken to her cousin since the night she'd found her with Noah, despite Heather's halfhearted attempts at reconciliation. Out of loyalty, her mother had turned down all invitations to dine with her brother-in-law and his wife.

And now Ted Hamilton was turning eighty and a big party was being held in his honor at the Ritz-Carlton Hotel a week from Saturday night, and her mother felt obligated to go and wanted Paige to come along. "You could always bring a date," she'd suggested, knowing Heather would be there with Noah.

"Yeah, right," Paige whispered, pulling out her phone as she exited the Prudential Building onto Boylston Street, checking for messages and finding none. She hailed a cab and settled into the backseat, giving the driver Chloe's address in Cambridge and silently reviewing the job interview she'd just left, going over the questions she'd been asked and the answers she'd given, knowing that it hadn't gone as well as she'd hoped, that her answers had been tentative at best, her confidence shattered after six months of being unemployed.

She just wasn't as sharp as she'd wanted to be, as she *needed* to be, if she was to secure another position. Plus, she looked less than professional in the shapeless floral shift she'd thrown on so carelessly this morning. At the very least, she should have gone home to change. She wasn't even wearing a bra, for God's sake. Even Heather would have had the good sense to dress in something more appropriate.

What was it her father had said when comparing her to her cousin? "You have the confidence without the attitude. Heather has the attitude without the confidence."

Now Paige had neither.

And Heather had Noah.

And she would most certainly be showing him off at her father's party.

"Shit," Paige said, louder than she'd intended.

"You say something?" the cabbie asked as they were approaching the Harvard Bridge.

"No, sorry," Paige apologized, returning her attention to her phone. She clicked onto Match Sticks and scrolled through the ever-expanding list of possible suitors. *Stud Muffin,* one prospect boasted beside a picture of a regrettably shirtless man biting into a giant chocolate chip muffin. Paige swiped left, watching his image disappear. *Romeo,* read the name beside a dough-faced, middle-aged man who claimed to be a fan of long walks in the rain. "Really?" Paige whispered, swiping left again. There were people who actually enjoyed walking in the rain? *Romeo* was followed by *Chaucer, Luther,* and *Just Plain Alan.* "Just plain no," Paige said, swiping left each time. Maybe her mother was right. Maybe she *was* too picky.

"Hold on. Who's this?" she asked, stopping on a picture of a man calling himself Mr. Right Now. Paige laughed. At least this guy had a sense of humor. And he was exceptionally handsome. Assuming he looked anything at all like the picture he'd posted, he'd be the ideal revenge date to bring to her uncle's party. "No," she said, imaginary alarm bells ringing in her head as she recalled last night's fiasco. "You are definitely too good to be true." She clicked off the site and tossed the phone into her purse.

What had become of meeting a potential romantic partner at work or through mutual friends, or even picking up someone at a bar? Had the ease and expediency of today's technology rendered even such basic human contact obsolete? "Ah, the good old days."

"You say something?" the cabbie asked again.

"Lots of traffic," Paige improvised.

"Always is."

Paige nodded, watching the long line of cars inching their way across the Charles River toward Cambridge. Maybe expediency was only part of it, she thought. Maybe everyone was just lonely. She leaned back against the brown vinyl seat and closed her eyes, surprised to find Mr. Right Now waiting for her behind her closed lids. Too lonely to wait for a chance encounter at work or count on a suggestion from a friend. Too lazy to head out to a bar, too afraid to risk rejection face-to-face.

So maybe she'd revisit Match Sticks later, maybe even swipe right on Mr. Right Now's picture and wait to see if he'd return her interest. Was there any chance he was as good as advertised? "Yeah, right," Paige whispered. "Dream on."

CHAPTER FIVE

Chloe was waiting by the front door when Paige's cab pulled up in front of the narrow two-story house on Binney Street. She was wearing white shorts and a vintage Rolling Stones T-shirt boasting a giant tongue festooned with the stars and stripes. Her blond hair was pulled into a high ponytail, making her look more like a teenage baby-sitter than the mistress of the house. But even from the street, Paige could see that something was wrong. Chloe's lovely features were contorted in pain, her beautiful eyes vacant and refusing to settle, her perfect lips trembling and twisting from side to side.

"Come on in," she said, ushering Paige inside the tiny foyer and closing the door.

"What's up?" Paige followed her friend into her small, all-white kitchen. "Are you okay?"

"Not really," Chloe said. "I mean, I'm not

46

sick or anything."

"The kids?"

"They're fine." She pointed toward the staircase at the back of the house. "They're in my room. I said they could watch cartoons. Do you want something to drink?"

"Maybe some water."

Chloe was immediately at the sink, filling her a glass. "Ice?"

"No, it's fine. Chloe . . ."

"It's Matt," Chloe said, handing Paige the glass of water and motioning for her to have a seat at the table.

"Did he . . . did he hit you?" Paige held her breath as she lowered herself into one of four white plastic chairs grouped around the small, round table.

"No. Of course not."

Chloe had always denied Matt was physically abusive, despite occasional evidence to the contrary. Paige sipped at her water and waited for Chloe to continue.

"But you won't believe what he's done."

I'll believe it, Paige thought. "What has he done?"

"You won't believe it," Chloe repeated.

"Tell me."

"No. I'll show you." Chloe retrieved her laptop computer from the counter beside the stove. "Check this out." Her fingers

47

danced expertly across the keyboard. Seconds later, a picture of a smiling couple appeared — all gleaming teeth and twinkling eyes — underneath the logo: PERFECT STRANGERS.

Paige knew instantly that it was a dating site. They all looked vaguely the same. Different name; identical goal. *You may be strangers now,* the site promised, *but who knows? You could be perfect for each other.*

"What am I looking at?" Paige asked.

"Wait for it," Chloe said.

Let us help you discover if a perfect stranger could be THE ONE. Sign up now, Paige read before a few more clicks sent the words careening into cyberspace, replaced by a spreadsheet of postage-size photographs of men, accompanied by brief profiles.

Chloe scrolled quickly down the list, dozens of eligible men appearing, then disappearing from view. She stopped on the profile of a man with light brown hair, dark, brooding eyes, and deep dimples bracketing his lips. "See anyone you know?"

"Shit."

"No kidding," Chloe said.

"Maybe it's not him." Paige's voice was unconvincing, even to her own ears.

"Matt and I have been married for eight years. I think I recognize him by now."

"Maybe it's just someone who looks like him," Paige argued.

"Think so? Wait here." Chloe marched from the room.

"Damn it," Paige said, leaning in to get a better look at the picture, knowing it was Matt despite her protestations. "You miserable piece of crap. What's the matter with you?"

"Here," Chloe said, returning to the kitchen and slapping a photograph on the table in front of Paige. "Think it's just a look-alike now?"

Paige found herself staring at a larger image of the same photo.

"It was taken last summer at Pete and Sandi's cottage. Matt liked it so much, he had it printed out. The smug bastard. You want to know how I found out?"

Before Paige could answer, the house exploded with the sounds of Chloe's two children racing down the stairs and into the room. Chloe immediately closed the laptop.

"Mommy!" six-year-old Josh shouted, his mouth a carbon copy of his mother's.

"I'm first!" cried four-year-old Sasha, proud inheritor of her father's big brown eyes and deep dimples.

Those damn dimples, Paige thought. They were a dead giveaway.

"Take it easy," Chloe said calmly, both children scratching at her thighs. "Have you said hello to Paige?"

"Hi," said Josh, throwing the word carelessly over his shoulder.

"Hello," said Sasha, always the more formal of the two. "We have a magic trick."

"It was just on TV," Josh said. "You want to see it?"

"I'm first," Sasha protested, tears threatening.

"Can you show us together?" Chloe asked.

Josh and Sasha exchanged glances, Sasha being the first to concede. "Okay," Josh said, looking from his mother to Paige and then back to his sister. "You ready?"

The children raised their right hands into the air, waving them up and down purposefully, as if they were wands. "Be a pear," they intoned solemnly in unison. "To be amazed."

"What?" Chloe said, a slow smile spreading across her cheeks.

"Be a pear," they said again, even more seriously. "To be amazed."

"Be a pear?" Paige repeated.

"I think you mean, 'Be prepared,' " Chloe told them.

"No," insisted Josh. "Be a pear."

"To be amazed," Sasha said, completing

50

the thought.

"Okay," Chloe said. "I'm a pear."

"Me, too," said Paige.

Satisfied, the children ran, shrieking with satisfied laughter, from the room.

"Am I wrong," Paige asked, "or did they forget to show us the trick?"

"I think changing us into amazed pears was enough," Chloe said, chuckling, and then immediately bursting into tears. "Oh, God. What am I going to do? My poor babies . . ."

"The kids will be fine," Paige said. "Right now, it's you I'm worried about."

"How could he do this?"

"Because he's a man," Paige said, picturing Noah in bed with her cousin, "and men do stupid things. Tell me how you found out about this."

Chloe sank into the chair next to Paige. "After Matt left for work this morning . . . he had a closing on this mansion in Newton that he's been trying to unload for months . . . anyway, it doesn't matter; who knows if it's even true? . . . Anyway," she said again, stumbling over her words and pausing to catch her breath, "maybe ten minutes after he left, the phone rings and I pick it up and this woman says, 'I think you should know that your husband's on a

51

bunch of dating sites,' and then hangs up. I didn't know what she was talking about. So, I decide to ignore her — I mean, she's obviously some crackpot, right? — and then, of course, I decide to check, 'cause I can't help myself, and I go to my computer and join Perfect Strangers, 'cause I'm an idiot and it's free. And I scroll through and . . . bingo! There he is. My darling husband, father of my two children, on a dating site. And not just that one. A whole bunch of them," Chloe continued. "Perfect Strangers, Tinder, eHarmony, Match Sticks . . . You name it, he's on it." She shook her head. "How could he not think I'd find out? Half my friends are on these sites. *You're* on these sites!" Chloe stared at Paige. "Did you know about this?"

"Me? No. Of course not! I would have told you. You know that."

"Would you? After the last time?"

Paige had told Chloe about seeing Matt with another woman when Chloe was pregnant with Sasha. And Matt, all righteous indignation, had talked his way out of that one, made it sound as if Paige was either mistaken or jealous. And in a classic case of shooting the messenger, it had almost cost the two women their friendship.

"Just look at these jerks," Chloe said now,

raising the screen of her laptop again and scrolling rapidly through the seemingly endless series of pictures. "Did you know they have a site specifically for cheaters? Which is probably the most honest one of the bunch. Look at *this* guy," Chloe exclaimed, stopping on a picture of a man calling himself Surfer Dude. "And *this* one, *Mr. Right Now.*"

Paige's eyes zeroed in on the familiar photograph. Mr. Right Now stared back at her, almost daring her to look away.

"He's another one who's on all the sites." Chloe laughed, a harsh, hollow sound. "As if any man who looks like that needs a dating app to meet women. What am I talking about?" she said in the next breath. "Matt's just as handsome as he is. Shit."

Paige looked back at her friend. "What are you going to do?"

"I'm not sure," Chloe admitted. "Maybe I should give one of these guys a tumble. Give Matt a taste of his own medicine."

"I don't think that's a very good idea."

Josh came bounding back into the room. "Who's that?" he asked before Chloe had a chance to close the screen.

"No one," Chloe said, snapping the laptop shut. "What's up?"

"Do we believe in God?" the boy asked.

"Do we believe in . . . ? What makes you ask that?" his mother said.

"This boy at camp today. He was talking about God and heaven and stuff. Do we believe in that?"

"This probably isn't a great time to ask me."

"Why not?"

"I'm just not sure what I believe anymore," Chloe answered, clearly too tired to pretend.

Josh's eyes narrowed. "But we *do* believe in the tooth fairy," he said warily.

Paige smiled as Chloe fought back tears. "We absolutely believe in the tooth fairy," Chloe said.

CHAPTER SIX

Her mother was in the family room, reading a book and watching the evening news, when Paige entered the brightly lit apartment. Joan immediately jumped to her feet, eyes smiling in anticipation. "How did the interview go?"

Paige plopped into a nearby chair, staring vacantly at the giant TV screen on the opposite wall. "Not great."

"Oh." Joan's smile vanished. "I thought that since it was so late, it must be going really well, that you might still be there."

"No. It was actually over pretty quick. I went to Chloe's. Sorry. I should have called."

"No, of course not. I forgot you were going over there. How's she doing?"

"Not great," Paige said, as she'd said earlier.

Her mother knew better than to pry. Both women turned their attention to the TV, where a photograph of a pretty young woman with long, dark hair now filled the screen. "Twenty-eight-year-old Tiffany Sleight has been missing for five days," the announcer was saying. "She disappeared after telling colleagues she was meeting a friend after work and hasn't been seen since. Anyone having information is asked to call police at . . ."

"Wasn't there another girl who disappeared about a month ago?" Joan asked.

Paige shrugged. It seemed that women were always disappearing. Sometimes she wished she could be one of them. Just *poof* — and she'd be gone.

Be a pear . . .

Joan grabbed the remote from the leather ottoman in front of the sofa and muted the sound. "Well, enough of that. Are you hungry?"

"Not really."

"I made lasagna."

"Maybe later."

"Do you want to go to a movie? There's a new one with that handsome actor . . . what's his name? Chris somebody . . . You know the one . . ."

"Matt's cheating on Chloe again," Paige said.

"Oh, dear. You're certain?"

Paige reached into her purse and removed her phone, getting up from her chair and guiding her mother toward the blue velvet sofa, then sitting down beside her. She clicked onto Perfect Strangers, scrolling through the various photographs and stopping on the picture of Matt. "See for yourself."

Her mother sighed. "What's with these men?" she asked. "Are they asking to be caught?"

Paige knew her mother was thinking of Noah.

Joan shook her head. "You showed Chloe this?"

"She showed *me.*"

"Poor thing. How's she handling it?"

Paige shrugged. The shrug said, *Not well.*

"Just look at all these men," Joan marveled after a silence of several seconds. "I had no idea." She took the phone from Paige's hands. "Oh, this one looks nice," she said, stopping on the picture of a man calling himself Samson. "Hair's a little long, but great smile. Very nice teeth. Maybe you should . . . what *do* you do when you want to meet someone?"

"You swipe right."

"Like this?" her mother asked, absently flicking her index finger across the screen.

"Mom! What are you doing?" Paige grabbed the phone from her mother's hands.

"What did I do?"

"You told him I liked his picture."

"Meaning what?"

"Meaning that if he's interested . . . oh, my God . . ."

"What?"

"He's interested."

"What? How do you know?"

"He was on his computer," Paige explained. "See?" She pointed to the screen. "It indicates here that he's on his computer, so he saw right away that I swiped onto his picture and he swiped back."

"This is fascinating. Now what? He phones?"

"He *messages*," Paige corrected. "It's a process. You message for a while; then if you like the messages, you agree to a phone call; then maybe, eventually, you meet for a drink."

"Why don't you just meet right away?" her mother asked. "Then you don't waste all that time writing."

"Because . . . oh, my God," she said as her phone beeped to indicate an incoming text. "He wants to meet for drinks."

"I like this man," Joan Hamilton said.

"Then *you* go out with him."

"Don't be silly, darling. It's *your* picture he liked. Write him back."

"This is ridiculous. No." *When did you have in mind?* Paige typed.

How about tonight? came the quick response. *Eight o'clock? Murphy's on Somerset?*

"Perfect," her mother said. "It's practically around the corner. Say yes. Come on, darling. You've had a hard day. First me and my eyes, then your cousin, then the job interview, then Chloe. You deserve some fun."

"He's not going to be fun."

"You don't know that. Come on. Nothing ventured, nothing gained."

"Can I quote you on that?"

"Yes, you may. Go on — tell him yes."

See you at eight, Paige typed. "I must be out of my mind."

"For heaven's sake, darling. Why else are you on these sites? How many of them are you on anyway?"

"I don't know. A few," Paige said. *More than a few,* she thought, dropping the phone to the cushion beside her. What did people do before dating sites? "How'd you meet Daddy?" she asked, burrowing into her mother's side.

"You know. Your father must have told that story a hundred times."

"I've never heard *you* tell it."

"Well, that's because I could never tell it as well as he could. Besides," she added, "I didn't want to contradict him."

"What do you mean? It wasn't the truth?"

"Let's just say that it contained a few embellishments."

Paige pulled away from her mother's side. "Such as?"

"Well, you know how your father always claimed that we met when I interviewed for a job as his secretary and he told me flat-out that he couldn't hire me because he intended to marry me?"

"That wasn't true?"

"It was . . . and it wasn't," Joan qualified. "The reason he didn't hire me was because I was a lousy typist." She smiled. "But he did keep my number, and about a week after our interview, he called me up and asked me out. And a few weeks after that, he showed up at my door and told my parents we were getting married, said he'd known from the first moment he laid eyes on me that I was the one for him." Her smile widened, bringing her whole face into play. "Over the years, the story . . . well, let's just say it . . . evolved. Like when they

60

say a movie is based on a true story. They change a few of the details, compress the time, so that what you get is essentially the truth, just more dramatic. And your father was nothing if not dramatic."

"You must miss him so much," Paige said.

"I do," her mother said simply.

"I still can't believe he's gone."

"I know," her mother agreed. "When I started having that thing with my eyes . . ."

"You mean this morning? Your ocular migraine?"

Her mother nodded. "I turned to your father . . . well, where your father would have been . . . on his side of the bed . . . and I started to say, 'Robert . . .' I wanted him to assure me that I was just being silly, that I wasn't having a stroke . . . as if he was still lying right there beside me. But, of course, he wasn't. So then I *was* sure I was having a stroke because, clearly, I was losing my mind . . ."

"Oh, Mom."

"Oh, darling. You look so worried. Please don't worry. I'm fine. The doctor said so. It's just that . . ."

"Just that . . . what?"

"Well, this morning got me thinking. No, that's not true," she corrected immediately. "I've been thinking about it for a little while

61

now, if I'm being honest."

Paige had never cared for the phrase "if I'm being honest." Whatever followed was rarely good. "Thinking about what?"

Joan Hamilton took a deep breath. "It's just that life is such a precious thing, sweetheart, especially when you get to be my age. You can't take anything for granted. We just never know how much time we have left."

"Where are we going with this, Mom?"

Her mother took another deep breath, followed by an audible exhale. "Well, at lunch you said . . ."

"What did I say?" Dear God, what had she said?

"You asked me if I'd considered dating . . ."

She had?

"And you suggested that I go on that site of yours . . ."

"I wasn't serious," Paige protested, her voice louder than she'd intended.

"I know you weren't." Her mother smiled, her lips trembling with the threat of tears. "Of course you weren't."

Neither woman spoke for several long seconds.

"Forget I said anything. I'm being silly."

"Oh, God, Mom. I'm so sorry," Paige

cried. "I didn't mean . . ."

"I know you didn't. Let's forget the whole thing."

"Are you lonely? Is that it?"

"I'm fine."

"Look. I'm going to message that guy back, cancel tonight. We'll go to the movie with that actor you like, then we'll come home and finish off that lasagna."

"No, darling," her mother said. "Absolutely not. You have your life. I want you to live it."

Paige burst into tears. "Oh, God. I'm such a brat."

"You're not a brat. You're a beautiful, sensitive girl whom I love more than anything in the world." She grabbed Paige's hands. "I'm not looking for a husband, darling. I've had the great love of my life. No one could ever replace your father; you know that. And if the thought of my dating makes you so unhappy, well, then, I won't do it."

"No," Paige said. "That's not what I want." She wiped the tears from her cheeks and reached for her phone. "I don't want you to be lonely. I want you to be happy."

"What are you doing? Don't you dare cancel your date."

"I'm not canceling. I'm going to take your

picture, and then we're going to create a profile for you, give you a fake name . . ."

"What's the matter with my real name?"

"Nobody uses their real name on these sites."

"They don't?"

Paige shook her head.

"What name do *you* use?"

Paige grimaced. "Promise you won't laugh?" She waited for her mother's nod. "It's Wildflower."

"Oh, that's so pretty," her mother said.

Paige felt surprisingly pleased by her mother's approval. "So what name do you want to go by?"

Joan gently pried the phone from her daughter's hands. "There's plenty of time to do all this another day. Right now, you're going to go wash away those tears, put on some fresh mascara and a bit of lipstick, maybe change your dress, and get ready for your date. Go on now. Get moving. That's an order." She grabbed the TV remote and clicked the sound back on, wandering aimlessly through the channels. "Oh, there's that poor girl again," she said as once again the picture of Tiffany Sleight's smiling face filled the screen.

And then, with another click of the remote, *poof,* she was gone.

CHAPTER SEVEN

Paige recognized him immediately.

He was standing near the crowded bar, laughing at something the male bartender had said, and only occasionally glancing toward the entrance. Surprisingly, he looked just like his picture on Perfect Strangers. Not traditionally handsome perhaps, but not *not* handsome. Medium tall, casually but nicely dressed in dark pants and a striped shirt, longish curly brown hair. Hence the moniker Samson, she supposed. Nice smile, as her mother had pointed out, although from this distance it was impossible to judge the state of his teeth.

Paige had slouched into Murphy's Bar behind half a dozen already inebriated young men, and quickly made her way to a table in the corner, head down, hoping to have arrived before her prospective date, wanting to check him out before he spotted her. "That way, if the guy is a dud," Heather had once told her, "you can slip out before he even knows you're there."

Except Paige would never do that. Unlike her cousin, who'd had no qualms about standing up online suitors when she'd been a regular and enthusiastic user of dating apps, Paige understood all too well the pain of being rejected. Didn't everyone deserve at least a chance? Okay, so a guy was five feet six, not six feet five — it could have been a typo; people inadvertently transposed figures all the time. So what if he was closer to sixty than forty and the muscles he'd proudly displayed in his online photo had long since turned to flab? She didn't have to marry the man. She didn't even have to go on a second date. Maybe he'd have a great personality. Maybe he'd make her laugh. Maybe the evening wouldn't turn out to be a complete waste of time.

Except they usually were. The men she'd met rarely lived up to even a fraction of their online potential, and the ones who did were generally only interested in one thing. Paige chuckled, wondering from what depths she'd dragged that old expression.

Not that she wasn't interested in the *same* thing. It's just that it had been a while — four months, one week, and two days, to be exact — and she needed at least the pretense that a new lover was interested in more than just a one-night stand. Although, who knows? She might feel differently a few weeks from now.

"What'll it be?" a perky blonde in a low-cut white blouse and thigh-high black skirt asked, and Paige jumped at the sound of her voice. "Sorry. Didn't mean to scare you."

"Sorry," Paige apologized in return, an automatic reflex. She seemed to be sorry for everything lately. "Gin and tonic?"

"Coming right up."

Paige glanced back at the bar. The man calling himself Samson was now hunched over the long glass counter, his back to her. She watched him peek at his watch, and immediately did the same. Five minutes after eight. She knew what he was thinking: that he'd give her another ten minutes before messaging to see if she was on her way, then settle with the bartender if he didn't receive a reply, and be out the door. What was she waiting for? she asked herself. *Get up and go over there. Get this miserable day over with.*

She was half out of her uncomfortable wooden chair when the front door opened and a man who could only be described as tall, dark, and drop-dead gorgeous walked in. God, he was good-looking. Maybe even too good-looking, she thought. Even better-looking than Mr. Right Now, although cut from the same type of cloth. The kind of man searching for his own reflection when he stared into your eyes.

He caught her gaze and smiled, quickly crossing over to where she stood. "Waiting for me?" he asked, a shy grin pulling at his lips, the intensity of his gaze sending tingles up and down her spine.

Paige was torn between conflicting impulses. One was to slap the smile right off his too-handsome face, and the other was to grab his arm and hightail it out of the bar before he realized his mistake.

Could she do either? she wondered, sensing movement beside her and turning to see the man she was supposed to be meeting approaching with a drink in his hand.

"Wildflower?" he asked, hesitantly.

"Samson?" she asked in return, feeling the other man already inching away.

"I thought it was you," Samson said, handing Paige the glass of gin and tonic she'd ordered. "I believe this drink is for you."

"Thank you," Paige said. "Do you think we can dispense with the aliases?"

"With pleasure." He extended his hand.

"Sam Benjamin."

"Paige Hamilton," Paige said, shaking it.

"Pleased to meet you, Paige."

"Pleased to meet you, Sam."

"I hope I wasn't interrupting anything. No, that's not true," Sam corrected immediately. "I saw you talking to that rather handsome fellow, and I thought I'd better get over here before I lost my chance."

Paige smiled, relieved that the "rather handsome fellow" had quietly taken his leave. Men that handsome had always made her nervous. Chloe's husband, Matt, was that handsome, and look what a bastard he was.

Sam Benjamin might not be the stuff of daydreams, but he was certainly presentable, and much more attractive up close than from a distance. His voice was deep and soothing. His smile seemed genuine. Even if his hair could benefit from a slight trim, his teeth were admirably white and straight.

"Should we sit?" he asked, signaling for the waitress as they took their seats at the small, round table. "A Molson's Golden? Thank you." He turned his attention back to Paige. "So, what do you do, Paige Hamilton?"

"I'm in advertising. Well, I *was,*" she

qualified. "I got let go a few months ago, so I'm currently . . . what is it they say . . . ?"

"Unemployed?"

"Between jobs," she corrected, smiling. "That sounds a little more optimistic. You wouldn't by any chance be the head of an advertising agency in need of a good strategic planning director, would you?"

"I'm a dentist."

Paige laughed.

"Something funny about being a dentist?"

"My mother said you had nice teeth."

"Your mother?"

"She liked your picture. It's a long story," she said, answering the quizzical look in his eyes.

"I like long stories."

"Maybe another time."

"Another time," he repeated. "I definitely like the sound of that."

The waitress approached with his beer.

"Thank you," he acknowledged, ignoring the tall glass she put on the table to sip directly from the bottle. "Sorry. I always prefer my beer this way."

"No, I get it," Paige said. "I like my soft drinks directly from the can. That way you get more fizz. Not so good for the teeth, I guess," she added. "All that sugar."

Sam smiled. "We could all use a little

sweetness." A slightly awkward pause. "So, you're new to online dating?"

"Oh, God. Is it that obvious?"

"No, not at all," he assured her. "Well, maybe a little . . ."

"You're right. I *am* new to this. Well, relatively new. A couple of months."

"Newly single or just curious?" he asked.

"A bit of both, I guess," Paige said, continuing without prompting. "I was with someone for three years. Till he decided he'd rather be with someone else. My cousin, actually." She monitored Sam's face closely for his reaction, saw his right eyebrow lift only slightly.

"My wife left me for her personal trainer."

"Oh," Paige said. "I'm sorry."

"Don't be. It's been almost two years. She's happy. And aside from the initial blow to my ego, I'm happier, too. And the kids are good, which in the end is all that matters."

"How many children do you have?"

"Two six-year-old boys. Dustin and Caleb. Identical twins."

"My father was an identical twin," Paige said, feeling an immediate kinship.

"Was?"

"He died two years ago."

"And his brother?"

"Going on eighty." Paige tried, and failed, to keep the bitterness out of her voice. "There's this big birthday party for him a week from this Saturday."

"That must be hard for you."

"It kind of pisses me off," she admitted, taking a long swallow of her gin and tonic. "Which I guess makes me not the nicest person in the world."

"I don't know about that," Sam said. "After my mother died — and she died pretty young, sixty-two — I couldn't even look at old people without wishing them all sorts of horrible deaths. *How did you manage to survive when my mother never got that chance?* I'd be thinking. My sister caught me staring at this old woman in an elevator once and she said the look on my face was one of pure evil."

Paige chuckled, taking another sip of her drink and returning it to the table with more force than she'd intended. *What the hell,* she decided, throwing caution to the wind and looking Sam directly in the eye. He might not be anyone's idea of a revenge date, but . . . "On that note," she began. "That birthday party I was telling you about . . ."

Sam reached across the table to take her hand. "Yes," he said. "I'd love to go."

CHAPTER EIGHT

He spots her the minute he steps through the door.

She is sitting by herself at a table in a corner of the crowded room, trying not to be conspicuous, and when she half-rises from her chair, he thinks she might be the one he came here to meet, the woman he knows as Lulubelle. He walks toward her, realizing even before he reaches her side that it isn't her.

She's a pretty girl. Not beautiful, at least by his standards, although she might be considered beautiful by others with less exacting tastes, less developed sensibilities. But there is something compelling about her, something that tempts him to veer from his original game plan and abandon Lulubelle. Something in her eyes, he realizes. A spark that tells him she is smarter than most of the women he meets, that she would make a nice change of pace, a more worthy adversary. Winning her trust without the normal weeks of online foreplay would be a true test of his prowess, his ability to seduce.

And besides, a little spontaneity never hurt anyone.

Except, of course, in this case, it will. It will hurt a lot.

"Waiting for me?" he asks, careful to keep the question on the charming side of arrogant.

She sways toward him.

But before she can answer, an unwelcome voice intrudes. "Wildflower?" the interloper asks.

"Samson?" She turns away from him as if he no longer exists.

The fake names confirm they've met through a dating site, undoubtedly one of the many he's on. It should be relatively easy to find her profile, he thinks as he begins drifting from her side.

"Do you think we can dispense with the aliases?" he hears Wildflower ask.

"Sam Benjamin," the man responds, a name as nondescript as the man himself.

"Paige Hamilton," comes the reply.

Paige Hamilton, he repeats silently, approaching the far end of the bar and making a mental note to check for her presence on Facebook and Instagram. He looks back in her direction, waiting for her to notice his absence, annoyed — even angered — that she seems totally captivated by this extraordinarily ordinary-looking man.

He wonders if her snub is deliberate and considers marching back to her table and throwing her drink in her face, then smashing the glass over her head and watching the blood slowly dribble down her cheeks. That would teach her. But then he catches sight of heavily ringed fingers waving at him from the other end of the long bar, and he is quick to regroup, to return to his original plan. He's spent weeks cultivating this relationship. It would be a shame to miss out on the payoff.

Paige Hamilton, also known as Wildflower, will have to wait for another day.

His back stiffens and his shoulders straighten as he strides, newly resolute, toward the pretty, but plump, brunette at the end of the bar. He is an arrow sailing toward its target — fast, focused, and deadly.

"Oh, I'm so sorry," the woman apologizes as he draws close. Her face goes from pink to red, so that it almost matches the color of the dress her large breasts are spilling from. "I thought you were someone else."

"Lulubelle?" he asks, his voice dripping

warm honey. Her name is accompanied by the same boyish grin he used on Paige Hamilton, the one he spent the better part of the morning perfecting. The grin is one of many in his repertoire. He can call on them at will, but still, it's important to stay diligent, to not take such things for granted. *"Practice makes perfect,"* as his mother used to say. Just one of the endless platitudes that fell from her stupid mouth every day. You could hardly blame his father for using his fists to silence her.

"Mr. Right Now?" Lulubelle asks in return, her initial embarrassment disappearing into a wide smile, the kind of smile that says she can't believe her good fortune. Unlike Wildflower, there is nothing going on behind those big, bovine eyes.

"Call me Eric," he says, although that isn't his real name. It's not even a name he particularly likes. Still, it's one he hasn't used before, and it's important to keep things fresh. While he is meticulous in certain aspects of his planning, he likes to keep other things somewhat looser. It keeps him on his toes, gives the whole charade a certain frisson. So he never picks out a name in advance, choosing to wait for whatever name drops from his lips unbidden. He's learned to enjoy tiny surprises such as these.

The women — unlike Wildflower — rarely surprise him.

"I'm Lulu," she says. "Well, it's really Louise. But no one ever calls me that."

"You didn't recognize me," he says, waiting for the compliment he knows will follow.

"Your picture doesn't do you justice," she obliges him by saying.

"Ditto," he says, lowering his chin while lifting his eyes, a move meant to suggest both shyness and sincerity. It's a lie, of course. The picture Lulu posted next to her profile — *loves Drake and all things Star Wars* — was clearly taken several years and twenty pounds ago.

"Well, I've put on a little weight since that picture was taken," she admits, acknowledging the obvious.

"I like women with a little meat on their bones," he assures her. Another lie. He isn't happy about her extra weight. It speaks to a lazy mind, a lack of willpower. He prefers his women slim and in good shape, like Wildflower. But Lulu will be punished for her dishonesty soon enough. He leans toward her, catching a whiff of her perfume. Miss Dior, he recognizes. Not bad, though he prefers anything Chanel. "What are you drinking?"

"White wine spritzer?" she asks, as if she isn't sure.

Something else he hates, this habit of turning a statement into a question. Either she's drinking a white wine spritzer or she isn't. Where's the ambiguity? Such habits point to a lack of confidence. And confidence in a woman is something he's always admired.

It makes watching such confidence dissolve that much more fun.

He orders a wine spritzer for her and a glass of expensive Shiraz for himself, then clinks his glass against hers. Once again, he steals a glance in Wildflower's direction, hoping to find her eyes searching the room for his, eager to reconnect. But instead he sees that she is still fully engaged with Mr. Sam Nobody and seems to have forgotten all about him. He stiffens, deciding that he will have to remind her.

"Eric?" a voice asks.

It takes several seconds to realize the voice is Lulu's. "Hmm? What?"

"I said, what are we toasting?"

"How about the start of a lovely evening?" he responds, recovering quickly.

"I'll drink to that." She takes a sip. "So, Eric," she begins. "Your profile says you're an entrepreneur?"

"That I am."

"You mean like on *Shark Tank*?"

"Exactly like on *Shark Tank*," he concurs, silently thanking the TV show for popularizing the idea of entrepreneurship, making it seem less vague, less in need of explanation.

"So, like, people come to you with their ideas and you invest money . . . ?"

He tries not to blanch at her repeated use of the word "like." Another lazy habit he intends to cure her of later. "Yeah. That's about it. You wouldn't believe some of the crazy ideas people come up with."

"Like what?"

"Oh, this one guy came to me with his plan to manufacture a line of scuba equipment for dogs."

Lulu laughs. "Really? That's ridiculous."

"That's what I told him." He takes a sip of his drink. "He actually has a patent for it."

She looks appropriately fascinated, which fuels his disgust. A fucking patent for canine scuba equipment! Is she really that stupid?

"So, like, where did you make your money? If you don't mind my asking."

"Don't mind at all," he says, having anticipated the question. It's the one they can all be counted on to ask. Women are so transparent. Money and good looks — that's all it takes to have them eating out of your hand. He laughs to himself — that part will come later. "I had a small business that I sold to a big company for an obscene amount of money, invested that money well and made even more, and presto, an entrepreneur is born."

"Wow," she says.

The word bangs against the side of his brain like an unpleasant echo, and he takes a deep breath, suppressing the urge to throttle Lulu to death in front of all these people. "How about we discuss it over dinner?"

"Dinner?"

"I don't know about you, but I'm starving. And I know a great place where we can go and really get to know each other. Plus, the chef is a great friend of mine."

"Really? What place is that?"

"My place," he says with his most charming smile yet, the one that generally overwhelms even the worst skeptics.

"Your place?" A quiver of hesitancy registers on her face.

He feigns embarrassment. "At the risk of sounding a little presumptuous . . ."

Lulu cocks her head to one side, emphasizing her double chin, and waits for him to continue.

"I actually went out this afternoon and bought a couple of steaks. Not that I was taking anything for granted. Just that I was so smitten with your photo. And you've turned out even better than I'd hoped . . ." He almost gags. "We can go somewhere else, if you'd prefer. Somewhere more public."

Another second's hesitation. "No, that's all right," she says finally, the offer to go elsewhere banishing her reservations. He breathes an imperceptible sigh of relief. "I'd hate to see a couple of good steaks go to waste."

"Great." He downs the last of his drink and deposits it firmly on the bar, then waits for Lulu to finish hers.

She swallows the last of it, then hands the glass to him with a smile, before reaching into her counterfeit Louis Vuitton bag — he prides himself on always recognizing a fake — and removing her cellphone.

"What are you doing?" he asks, blocking his face with his hand as she raises the phone to snap his picture.

"Sorry. It's not that I don't trust you," she demurs. "But a girl can't be too careful these days. We did just meet. If I'm going to go anywhere with you, especially your apartment, then I need to take a few precautions. And I'll need to see some ID."

"You're joking, right?"

"I know it sounds silly, but it's something I always do. I take a picture, get your address, email it to my friends so they know where I am . . ."

"And if I refuse?" he asks playfully, hoping his charm will outweigh her demands.

Lulu manages a weak smile. "Why would you refuse?"

"I guess I'm just not used to my integrity being questioned." His anger resurfaces. He is actually offended by her request.

"Well," she says, returning her phone to her fake leather bag, "suppose you think it over while I use the little girls' room."

Before he can say anything, she is walking away, her every step announcing that she is the one in control. He'd like to follow her inside the *little girls' room,* drag her big ass into the nearest stall, and force her stupid head inside the toilet bowl. How dare she question him! Someone who looks like her, who might generously register a six on a scale of ten, who could never hope to attract the legitimate interest of a man as handsome as he is — she has the nerve to ask for his identification! No, not ask —

demand! "You've gotta be kidding," he mutters, looking around the room, as if seeking confirmation from the other patrons.

He sees Paige Hamilton, aka Wildflower, still engrossed in conversation with Mr. Average. Is it possible she's forgotten him so soon? He smiles, picturing her hands securely tied behind her back and her lovely neck in a noose.

His attention is diverted by a couple of older women laughing under a Coors Light neon sign, and he mulls going over and introducing himself, giving the old biddies a thrill.

Normally he doesn't waste time with older women, but what the hell, it might provide an interesting diversion. He's heard they make great lovers, that their experience more than makes up for their wrinkles. Older women are just so grateful for the unexpected attention, especially the ones over sixty, the ones old enough to be his mother.

Maybe one night it might be fun to give one a try. But not tonight. Tonight he has research to do. He intends to find out everything he can about Paige Hamilton. This is one wildflower ripe for the picking.

He stares toward the hallway that leads to the washrooms at the back. He's been in

Boston three months, and he never stays in any city more than six. Maybe it's time to consider leaving. Women here are a little more sophisticated than they were in Denver. And they're understandably cautious, given that two women have been reported missing already. That silly little Tiffany Sleight's picture has been all over the news for days. Probably what spooked Lulu.

He orders her another white wine spritzer and settles with the bartender. "Wish the fat lady goodbye and good luck," he instructs the bemused young man behind the long bar. Then he walks purposefully toward the entrance without so much as a glance in Wildflower's direction, opens the door, and disappears into the night.

CHAPTER NINE

Chloe heard the giggling from behind the closed bathroom door.

"What are you guys doing in there?" she asked, pausing before opening it. She prayed they weren't playing another one of those "you show me yours, I'll show you mine" games she'd caught them at the week before. Then she'd been the model of parental calm, careful not to shame or embarrass them, assuring them that while it was natural to be curious about the physical differences between boys and girls, their bodies were private and it was important to respect them.

"What's 'respect'?" had come four-year-old Sasha's immediate response.

Chloe couldn't remember her answer. Her mind was a roiling mess of conflicting thoughts and emotions: her husband was an unrepentant womanizer; he was a liar and a cheat; she hated him; she would divorce him, take him for every cent he had. Yet how could she leave him? They had two beautiful children together. And despite everything, she still loved him. Love didn't just disappear overnight, not when you'd been together for virtually all your adult lives.

He hadn't really wanted to get married. She was the one who'd pressured him into a commitment by getting pregnant. They'd been dating since high school. It was time to shit or get off the pot, she'd told him, stopping just short of an ultimatum. But he wasn't ready. And she knew that. So his acting out this way wasn't altogether his fault. Didn't she share at least part of the blame?

"No, you do not," she heard Paige say. *"You are in no way responsible for Matt's bad behavior. Your husband's the guilty one here, not you."*

But maybe if I'd been more attentive, Chloe thought, continuing her silent argument with her oldest and best friend. Maybe if I'd taken more of an interest in his work, paid less attention to the kids and more to him, maybe if I'd been more adventurous in bed . . .

"No!" Chloe said loudly, pushing open the bathroom door with such vehemence that it slammed against the wall. "Oh, God," she said, her eyes widening in alarm at the sight that greeted her.

"Sorry, Mommy," Sasha whimpered, backing toward the white enamel tub.

"What have you done?" Chloe's eyes darted between Sasha and her brother, her voice teetering dangerously close to a shriek.

"We were just playing," Josh said.

Chloe noted the total absence of an apology in his voice. Were males incapable of taking ownership of their misdeeds? Did it start this young? Or was it something in their DNA? "Look at this mess," she cried, feeling all semblance of control slipping away. "There's toothpaste all over everything."

"We were just brushing their teeth," Sasha said, offering up the stuffed pink bunny in her hands for her mother's inspection.

Chloe stared at the dozen dolls and stuffed animals littering the white tile floor, their plush exteriors covered in thick blue toothpaste. "They're ruined."

"You can wash them," Josh said matter-of-factly.

"The hell I will," Chloe shot back.

Sasha gasped. "Mommy said a bad word," she whispered, her big brown eyes widening in a combination of surprise and fright.

Chloe felt her body recoil in horror as she acknowledged the fear on her daughter's

87

face. It was a look she understood all too well. Hadn't she stared at her own mother with that same look? Of course, her mother had had alcohol as an excuse for her outbursts, outbursts that were predictable only in their frequency. What excuse did she have?

Stop this, Chloe told herself. *Stop this now. There are worse things in life than toothpaste covering a bunch of plush toys. Things like an unfaithful husband, things like a man who has so little respect for his wife that he advertises his infidelity on dozens of dating websites, that he uses his real picture.*

"What's respect?" she heard Sasha ask.

What answer had she given? What did she know of respect?

"These things are going in the garbage," Chloe said.

"No!" Josh cried, bursting into tears as Chloe began gathering up the toys.

They glommed onto her Rolling Stones T-shirt, the toothpaste coating the giant teeth and protruding tongue. Could anything be more fitting?

And suddenly she was laughing at the absurdity of it all. She sank to her knees, falling back against the cabinet beneath the sink and letting the toys drop to the floor beside her. Sasha was instantly in her lap, her little arms surrounding Chloe's neck, pulling her mother's face into her delicate blond curls, while Josh went about the business of removing the stuffed toys from the danger of his mother's wrath.

"I'm sorry, Mommy," Sasha said again.

Chloe kissed her daughter's forehead, sudden exhaustion replacing her anger. "I'm sorry, too, sweetie." She looked up at Josh. "It's okay, Joshy. I won't throw them out."

"You can put them in the washing machine," he said, erasing his tears with the back of his hand. "It says right here that they're machine washable." He pointed to the paste-covered tag protruding from a powder-blue teddy bear's seams.

Chloe felt a burst of pride at her son's growing ability to read. "I know. I'm sorry I yelled." She beckoned him toward her.

It took a few seconds for him to be coaxed into his mother's outstretched arms, and even then, he refused to let go of the stuffies in case this was some sort of trick.

"What you did wasn't good," Chloe told her children, careful to keep her voice soft and steady. "You made a big mess, you wasted all that toothpaste, you created a lot of work for Mommy . . ."

"You were screaming," her son said, not ready to forgive her.

"I know. I was very angry."

"Are you still angry?" Sasha asked.

"No."

"Are you happy?"

"That's pushing it," Chloe said, tears falling down her cheeks.

"Don't cry, Mommy," Sasha said, using her hair as a tissue to wipe the tears away. "Be happy. We'll clean everything up."

"No. That's okay. I'll do it," Chloe said. "Just please . . . don't do it again. You have to take care of your things, you have to respect them . . ." *That word again,* she thought.

"Like we have to respect our penises," Sasha agreed solemnly.

Dear God, Chloe thought.

"You don't have a penis," Josh told his sister, rolling his hazel eyes toward the ceiling. "You have a regina."

Help me, Chloe prayed. "It's a *va*gina," she said, gently extricating herself from her children and struggling to her feet. "Now, while I go throw these stuffies into the washing machine, I need you to get out of your dirty clothes and into your pajamas. And I need you to brush your teeth. Assuming there's any toothpaste left. Can you do that for me?"

"You promise you're not going to throw

the stuffies out?" Josh asked, still not convinced.

"You promise you're not going to do this ever again?" Chloe asked in return, unconsciously lifting her hand to her cheek.

"I promise it'll never happen again," she heard Matt say.

Both children nodded.

"Okay," Chloe said, banishing Matt's voice from her brain. "I promise, too. Now get moving. I'll be back in five minutes."

The children disappeared into their respective rooms as Chloe finished picking up the toys. She carried them to the combination washer-dryer in the small, rectangular laundry room beside the master bedroom, and tossed as many as would fit into the bin. The rest would have to wait, she thought, dropping the remainder to the floor, along with her T-shirt, then walking into her bedroom and pulling a lightweight gray sweatshirt over her head.

She caught sight of her reflection in the mirror over the chest of drawers opposite the queen-size bed. "You look awful," she said to the woman in the glass. Her hair was a mess, dozens of stray hairs having come loose from her ponytail, and her face was devoid of makeup and streaked with tears, her eyes threatening more. "And this stupid sweatshirt," she said, pulling at its sides. "No wonder your husband cheats on you. Maybe if you wore makeup and dressed up once in a while . . ."

"Stop this," she heard Paige admonish, as she had admonished herself earlier. *"Stop this right now."*

"I need a drink," she said, marching down the stairs into the kitchen, and reaching into the fridge for the bottle of wine she and Matt had shared at dinner the night before.

No, a drink is the last thing I need, she decided, returning the bottle of white wine to the shelf and closing the fridge door. Alcohol was her mother's way of dealing with unpleasantness, not realizing that it succeeded only in making her equally unpleasant. Or maybe she just didn't care.

Chloe shook thoughts of her mother out of her head. She had no time for unnecessary distractions. Her mother wasn't the problem right now. Her husband was. And it was important that she be sober when Matt came home. She needed to be calm and coolheaded, not give him a reason to lash out.

Not that he needed a reason.

She looked at her watch. Almost seven o'clock. Matt would be home soon, tired from showing houses all day, complaining about the capriciousness of buyers, the stubbornness of sellers. He'd gobble down the dinner she'd made earlier — meat loaf, his favorite — then retreat to his laptop, ostensibly to go over his paperwork, to prepare for the next day.

At least that's what he'd tell her, but who knew for sure? It was just as likely he'd be checking his various dating sites to see which women had responded favorably to his picture and expressed interest in getting to know him personally. How many times had he sat there swiping to the right, right there in front of her nose?

Was that part of the thrill?

The phone rang.

Chloe answered the landline on the counter in the middle of its second ring.

"Hi, babe," Matt said.

"What's up?" Chloe asked, already knowing what his response would be.

"Looks like I'm going to be stuck at the office for a while," he told her. "My clients have some last-minute changes in the offer they want to present, and I can't risk passing it off to my assistant. You know how incompetent she is."

"I understand." Chloe reached for her laptop with her free hand and clicked onto Perfect Strangers, scrolling past her husband's profile to check out the seemingly endless display of male pulchritude. It would serve Matt bloody well right if she swiped right on one of them. How she'd love to give her husband a taste of his own medicine!

"I might be pretty late," Matt said.

"Okay."

"Is everything all right? You sound kind of funny."

"I'm fine."

"The kids giving you a hard time?"

"Nothing I can't handle." She almost laughed.

"Okay. Well, I should be home by ten."

Chloe closed her laptop and took a deep breath. "I'll be waiting."

CHAPTER TEN

They'd met during her first year of high school and almost immediately became a couple.

She was fourteen and a virgin. He was seventeen and had already had multiple partners. A classic bad boy with a hair-trigger temper, as quick with his fists as he was with his charm, he was the captain of the football team, the captain of the swim team, the captain of the basketball team. "The captain of fucking everything," Chloe used to tease him, trying to sound less virginal. What better match for the captain of fucking everything than the prettiest girl in school? And not only pretty, but with the biggest breasts, the lushest lips, the bluest eyes. She was smart, too, although that seemed to matter less.

He started pressuring her to have sex almost immediately. "Men have needs," he'd told her with all the swagger a seventeen-year-old boy could muster. "Come on, Chloe. You're my girl. You can't expect me to wait forever."

She'd tried talking to her mother about it, but Jennifer Powadiuk could rarely be counted on for parental advice of any kind. Her second husband had just left her and she was drinking even more than usual. Chloe would often come home from school to find her passed out on the couch. "It's called a power nap," her mother would snap when Chloe raised the issue. "And don't give me that look. You remind me of your father when you look at me like that. And you know what a prick he was."

Actually, Chloe had no idea what kind of man her father was, as he'd disappeared from her life when she was barely three months old. She wasn't even sure her mother's first husband had been her biological father. She looked nothing like the photographs of him she'd found stuffed into a box at the back of her mother's closet, and Chloe often suspected the reason he'd left was because he realized he'd been duped.

"What difference does it make?" her mother had demanded when questioned about it. "They're all the same." She'd poured herself another scotch. "They all leave eventually."

Chloe couldn't risk Matt leaving.

By the time Chloe's fifteenth birthday rolled around, she was no longer a virgin. And Matt, all smiles, was still captain of fucking everything.

Of course, there were rumors, even then. Chloe heard the whispers in the halls — "I saw Matt making out with Shannon Philips on the Common." "Krista says he has the biggest you-know-what she's ever seen." "Do you think Chloe knows about Eva? Should we tell her?" — but was determined to ignore them. The other girls were just jealous, she convinced herself. Matt loved her. He wasn't going anywhere.

They moved in together after graduation and Chloe got a job at an upscale women's clothing store on Newbury Street, courtesy of her mother's third husband, who knew the owner, and she helped put Matt through college, intending to complete her own degree at some point in the future. That point never came. Matt, as restless and unfocused as ever, kept switching majors, then dropped out altogether, two credits short of graduating, when he decided he'd rather sell real estate.

"The market's hot and so am I," he'd told her with a laugh.

A joke — but not.

"Kidding on the square," Paige's mother would have said.

Chloe smiled at the thought of Paige's mother. How often she'd wished she'd had a mother like Joan Hamilton — kind, warm, thoughtful. The kind of woman who put her daughter's happiness ahead of her own, the kind of mother who was there when her daughter needed her.

She'd always found it puzzling that Paige had been more of a daddy's girl. As much as Chloe had liked and admired Paige's father, she'd always found him a bit over-whelming, his alpha-dog energy tending to suck up all the oxygen in the room. The kind of man you assumed would live forever. And then suddenly he was gone.

They all leave eventually, she heard her mother say.

She'd met Paige ten years earlier when Paige moved into the studio apartment across the hall from the one-bedroom apartment Chloe shared with Matt. They'd become fast friends, which was unusual for Chloe, who'd never really had any female friends. But she'd liked Paige immediately. Paige looked you in the eye when she talked to you. She seemed genuinely interested in what you had to say. Her attention didn't automatically shift to Matt when he entered the room.

Maybe that was why Matt had never really taken to Paige. "I just don't get what you see in her," he'd say with a shrug, a refrain he'd returned to repeatedly over the past decade. "I mean, she's okay. I'm not saying there's anything wrong with her. I just find her cousin Heather much more interesting."

By "interesting," of course, he meant *interested* — in him.

Although she'd never confided her suspicions to Paige, Chloe had always suspected that something might have happened between Matt and Heather. Heather, it seemed, had a thing for other women's men.

Chloe hadn't planned on getting pregnant. She was on the pill. But then she forgot to take it for a few days, which threw her whole cycle out of whack. Or maybe she'd forgotten "accidentally on purpose," as Matt always claimed. And so, she and Matt got married — a small ceremony at City Hall, attended only by Paige and a handful of Matt's coworkers. His parents were long divorced and living on opposite sides of the country. He wasn't close with either of his brothers. Chloe's mother had developed a sudden and intense passion for ballroom dancing, and was too busy practicing for an upcoming event in Florida to attend the wedding of her only child.

And then Chloe had suffered a miscarriage, and Matt was understandably upset and resentful. He'd called her names and thrown things. When she'd tried to reason with him, he'd slapped her so hard her ears rang for hours afterward. Of course, he'd apologized profusely, sworn it would never happen again. There followed a lot of late nights at the office, several disturbing hang-ups on the phone. The whispers started up again. Chloe pretended not to hear them. This was her fault, after all.

It took her nearly two years to get pregnant again. Then Josh was born, and Chloe gave up her job — she was now the store manager — to be the kind of stay-at-home mom her own mother had never been. Matt had been right about Boston's hot real estate market and was doing very well. But Chloe was now totally dependent on her husband for money, and while he could be as generous as he was quick to anger, she'd always suspected that his generosity was tied directly to his infidelities. Still, suspicions weren't proof.

But while Chloe may have been a fool where Matt was concerned, she wasn't stupid. She opened her own bank account and began secretly socking money away. In the eight years of their marriage, she'd managed to save almost five thousand dollars. In case of an emergency, she told herself. If Matt ever ran into trouble, she'd be there to save the day.

After Sasha was born, Chloe and Matt moved to a house across the river in Cambridge, and a year later, Paige met Noah and moved into his downtown apartment. Chloe and Paige had remained best friends, although that friendship was sorely tested after Paige confided she'd seen Matt nibbling another woman's neck on a night he was supposedly at the office "up to his ears in paperwork."

"I just thought you should know," Paige had told her, tearfully. "I'd want *you* to tell *me*."

It turned out that nobody had to tell Paige anything. She'd come home to discover her cousin in bed with Noah, and packed her bags immediately. No dilly-dallying around for her. No second-guessing. No burying of her pride. No waiting around and hoping the affair would blow over. One strike and she was out.

And Heather was in.

Noah had replaced a diamond with a zircon.

Men! Chloe thought, wondering if Noah was sorry. Would Matt be sorry when she left *him*? *If* she left him, she corrected with her next breath. There could still be an explanation, something that would persuade her to ignore the evidence of her own eyes once again.

Her cellphone rang, interrupting her reveries. She was hunched over her kitchen table, drinking her third cup of coffee and scrolling through Perfect Strangers and Match Sticks on her laptop. The kids were asleep. The laundry was almost done, the stuffies returned to their near-normal fluffiness. It was almost ten thirty. Matt still wasn't home.

Chloe glanced at the caller ID before answering. "He's not home yet," she said instead of hello.

"How are you doing?" asked Paige.

"Not great. I'm sorry I didn't call you. I know I said I would."

"It's okay. I was out anyway. I was just worried."

"Don't be."

"Is there anything I can do?"

"Like what?" Chloe asked.

"I don't know. Slap Matt around a bit? Go all Solange in the elevator with Jay-Z."

Chloe laughed through her tears. "We

don't have an elevator." Besides, "going all Solange" was more Matt's style than hers.

Not that she could ever admit that to Paige. It was too humiliating.

"Look," Paige said. "It's late. Why don't you go to bed? You don't have to do anything tonight. You can sleep on it."

"You wouldn't sleep on it, and you know it."

"No, but . . . you have to do what's right for *you*. Not what *I* would do. Or what *I* think you should do. It's what *you* think that counts."

"What's to think about? My husband is a liar and a cheat," Chloe said, her voice gaining vehemence with each word. "He's on multiple dating sites, for God's sake. Who knows what kind of STDs he's exposing himself to, exposing *me* to. How can I stay with someone like that? Someone who shows so little respect for our marriage. For me. How can I have any respect for myself if I do?"

"Respect" — that word again.

There was a moment's silence. Chloe knew what Paige was thinking because she was thinking the same thing: Because you've stayed before. Because you always do.

This time was different, she realized. This time he'd gone too far.

Chloe heard the key turn in the front door lock. "He's home," she whispered into the phone.

"Call if you need me."

Chapter Eleven

Paige put down her phone, imagining the scene unfolding at Chloe's, trying to gauge Matt's response when confronted with proof of his indiscretions. Would he shrug and laugh it off, claiming it was all a giant misunderstanding? Or would he acknowledge the obvious and fall to his knees, begging Chloe's forgiveness? Or worse, would he react angrily, even violently? Despite Chloe's vehement denials, Paige felt certain that Matt had struck her on more than one occasion.

And how would *she* react if, despite everything, Chloe decided to stay with Matt? Yes, she'd told Chloe that she had to do what was right for her, not anyone else. But did she really mean it? Could she just stand by and continue to see her best friend humiliated and abused? Wouldn't that make her at least partly complicit?

Paige shook her head. She couldn't allow

her mind to dwell on such troubling questions. Her head was already swimming with thoughts of Sam and the stupid thing she'd done.

"What is the matter with you?" she asked her reflection in the mirror over the bathroom sink.

True, their date had gone much better than she'd expected. Sam was attractive, personable, soft-spoken, and surprisingly modest. He didn't monopolize the conversation; he didn't drone on about his accomplishments; he seemed genuinely interested in hers. And he was easy to talk to. Maybe even too easy. But why had she told him about her cousin? And what on earth had possessed her to invite him to her uncle's party? She barely knew the man. Yes, he seemed genuine, but everything he'd told her could be a lie. He could be a crazed serial killer, for all she knew.

She laughed. "Now you're just being silly." Sam Benjamin had been unfailingly polite. He hadn't even tried to kiss her good night. What kind of serial killer was that?

She heard her cellphone ping with an incoming text as she was brushing her teeth. Her first thought was that it was Chloe. But surely it was too soon for it to be Chloe, and besides, Chloe would phone, not text.

106

Noah? she wondered, returning to her bedroom, angry at herself for even considering the possibility.

She grabbed her phone from the nightstand and saw that the message was from Sam. No doubt texting to say he'd thought things through and had had a change of heart regarding her uncle's party.

Except he hadn't.

Just wanted to say how much I enjoyed our evening. Hope we can do it again soon.

Paige read the simple message several times, and then several times more. Was it possible the man was as nice as he seemed? *Tell him that you're sorry, that you were too hasty, that you've reconsidered, that you must rescind your invitation, and hope he understands.* Instead, she wrote, *Me, too.* Goddamn it! What was the matter with her?

Sleep well, came his instant reply.

Paige clicked off before she was tempted to respond again. She turned off the bedside lamp and climbed under the covers. But after ten minutes of flipping from one side to the other, her mind ricocheting between thoughts of Sam and worry about Chloe, she realized she wasn't going to sleep at all, let alone sleep well. She sat up in bed, turned on the light, and grabbed her phone, checking Match Sticks to see whether she

107

had any new hits to her online profile.

"Beats counting sheep," she muttered, swiping left on the first three responses, then staring at the fourth in disbelief. "You've got to be kidding."

Mr. Right Now smiled back at her, bedroom eyes beckoning.

"Holy shit," she whispered, noting that Mr. Right Now was on his computer and would be instantly aware if she swiped right on his picture. "No," she said. "You're way too good-looking. There's got to be a catch." Men who looked like models dated women who looked like models. And while Paige knew she was attractive, she also recognized that she wouldn't be gracing the cover of *Vogue* anytime soon. Still, he'd swiped right on *her* picture, so he must be interested.

Was she?

What about Sam?

"What about him?" Paige asked. Just because they'd gone on one date, just because she'd invited him to her uncle's party, just because he'd texted her to *sleep well* didn't mean she owed him anything. She'd just come out of one serious relationship. She wasn't about to risk another heartbreak by rushing into another. She could hardly be accused of cheating on a man she'd just met.

She held her breath and swiped right. "Oh, God. What have I done now?"

There was a knock on her bedroom door. "Paige?" her mother said.

Paige reached for her robe, securing it around her as the door opened. "Mom? What's the matter? Are you all right?"

"I'm fine, darling. I was just going to grab a snack from the kitchen, and I thought I heard voices."

"Just me," Paige acknowledged. "Talking to myself again."

"Is there a problem?"

"Having trouble sleeping."

"Me, too. Must be something in the air. How was your date?"

Paige saw the hope in her mother's eyes. "Nice. Really nice," she added for good measure.

"Oh. That's so . . . nice." Joan stared at her daughter, as if waiting for her to say more. "Well, I guess I'll see you in the morning," she said after a silence of several seconds. "Can I get you something from the kitchen?"

"No, thanks. I'm good."

"Good night, darling. Sleep well."

Sleep well.

"You, too," Paige called to the closing door. She heard the familiar ping of her

phone and saw a message from Mr. Right
Now.

Hey, Wildflower, the text said.

That was it.

Hey, she texted back.

No response.

That's strange, she thought, staring at her
phone for two more minutes before lying
back down, about to turn off the light when
another text arrived.

Sorry about that, came the message. *Wasn't
sure what to say next. I'm pretty new to all
this. Obviously.*

Sweet, Paige thought. *Me, too,* she replied.

So, what happens next?

Why don't you tell me about yourself, Paige
responded, intrigued.

*Well, I'm thirty-six, from San Francisco
originally, an only child, parents married fifty-
plus years, have an MBA from Berkeley.*
Another lengthy pause, then, *I probably
should tell you that I've been married before.
For three years. My wife died two years ago,*
he continued without prompting. *Cancer.*

How awful, Paige wrote back, thinking of
her father. *I'm so sorry.*

*Yeah, it was tough. It took me a long time to
get over it. I quit my job, traveled for a while.
Moved to Boston a few months ago, so don't
know a lot of people. Just starting to put*

myself out there. Joined a bunch of dating sites, hoping to meet someone. What else can I tell you? I like jazz.

I like jazz, Paige told him.

Another seemingly interminable pause.

Then, *Look. I'm clearly not very good at this. Are you game for meeting up in person?*

Was she? What about Sam? *Sure. When did you have in mind?*

How about Wednesday? Six o'clock? The Bleacher Bar inside Fenway Park?

Sounds interesting. I've never been there.

Good. I like introducing people to new things.

So okay, then, I'll see you Wednesday.

See you then. Good night, Wildflower.

Paige returned her phone to the nightstand and lay back down, excitement over Mr. Right Now overwhelming the lingering guilt about Sam. Within seconds, she was sound asleep.

CHAPTER TWELVE

Chloe was sitting at the kitchen table, her laptop open in front of her, her husband's handsome face smiling seductively up at her, when he walked into the room.

"Hi, babe," he said, his voice soft and sweet. "You didn't have to wait up."

Chloe took note of the thick hair falling carelessly into Matt's dark eyes and the hint of stubble framing his cheeks and chin, emphasizing the natural pout of his lips. She tried to imagine never kissing those lips again, never feeling those eyes staring lovingly into hers. Damn it. Did he have to look so good? And was there no depth to which he could sink that would make him less desirable to her? Was she really that shallow? "I thought you might be hungry," she said, closing the computer. Was she ready to throw it all away? "I made meat loaf." She motioned toward the plate of food sitting on the counter by the micro-wave.

"Ah, babe. I'm sorry. I grabbed a sandwich at the office. You should have told me you were making meat loaf."

"My fault," Chloe said, accepting the blame.

"Well, it's nobody's fault," he corrected with a smile. "These things happen. I'm sorry. You're the best." He walked around the table to kiss the top of her head.

She caught a whiff of unfamiliar perfume. "What kind of sandwich?" she heard herself ask.

"What?"

"You said you grabbed a sandwich at the office. What kind?"

"Seriously?"

She twisted her head to look up at him. "Seriously."

"Ham and cheese." He laughed. "You want to know what kind of cheese? It was cheddar," he said before she could respond.

"Did you close the deal?"

He looked confused by the sudden shift in the conversation. "Well, we submitted an offer. They have twenty-four hours to sign something back. Is everything okay?"

"Why wouldn't it be?"

"I don't know. You just seem kind of . . . I

don't know . . . off. Kids give you a hard time tonight?"

"Nothing I couldn't handle," she said, a virtual repeat of their earlier exchange.

His hands were suddenly on her shoulders, his fingers expertly working their way into the tense muscles at the base of her neck. He knew just where to touch her, exactly how much pressure to apply. Could she really give that up? Could she bear never to feel those hands on her body again?

She was being too hasty, she decided in that instant, judging him before all the facts were in. There had to be a logical explanation, something that would justify his behavior, a reason for his presence online that she hadn't considered. Maybe someone was setting him up, perhaps a colleague at work, jealous of Matt's good looks and ongoing success. That person could easily have joined all these dating sites in Matt's name, hoping to discredit him. Just a few weeks ago, they'd had several of Matt's coworkers over for a barbecue. One of them could have found that picture of Matt and submitted it, then figured out a way to return it without anyone being the wiser. It was possible.

It wasn't possible.

No matter how she tried to spin it, no

matter how convoluted and irrational her efforts became to exonerate her husband, she knew the truth. And the truth was that Matt was guilty. Of lying, of cheating, of everything. He'd been doing the same thing for years. The only uncertainty was what she was prepared to do about it.

"I'm going to bed," Matt said, his hands sliding off her shoulders.

No. Don't leave me, she thought, feeling his hands hovering just out of reach, like a phantom limb. She fought the urge to grab those hands, to pull them around her, to glue him to her side.

"You coming?" he asked, already in the doorway.

"Soon. I have to put a few things away." She nodded toward the plate of food on the counter.

"Well, try not to be long. I've got to get some sleep. I'm exhausted."

Chloe felt her own exhaustion wrapping around her like a blanket. *You don't have to do anything tonight,* Paige had told her. *You can sleep on it.* Which was exactly what she needed to do, Chloe decided. She needed time to digest what had happened, to figure out a plan. She couldn't go running off half-cocked. After all, she wasn't the only one who would be affected by the decisions she

115

made. She had two small children to consider, two children who loved their father, whose lives she couldn't just turn upside down without serious deliberation. She owed those children a clear head. Whatever she was going to say could wait till morning.

Except it couldn't.

"Wait," she said.

Matt stopped, leaning into the doorway in a way that emphasized his lithe but muscular physique. As if he was taunting her, showing her what she would be throwing away. As if he knew what was on her mind. As if he was daring her to put it out there.

Chloe took a deep breath and opened her laptop. "You want to explain this?" she said.

He didn't move. "Explain what?"

Chloe twisted the computer toward him. "This."

"What is it?" He remained stubbornly where he was, glancing only briefly at the screen.

"You really going to make me spell it out?"

"Apparently so," he said. Then, "What is it you think you see, Chloe?"

"I don't *think* I see anything," she said, fighting to stay calm, to keep her growing anger in check, even as she felt her voice rising. "I *know* what I'm seeing. I'm seeing your picture on a fucking dating site. On a whole bunch of them."

"Please watch your language and lower your voice."

"Don't tell me to lower my fucking voice."

"Do you want to wake up the kids? Do you want them to hear their mother swearing like a truck driver?"

"Do you want to explain this?"

"No, I don't. I've been working my ass off all day and night. I don't appreciate coming home to a bunch of crazy accusations."

"Crazy accusations?" Chloe lifted the laptop off the kitchen table, waving the screen toward him. "Are you seriously going to deny this is a picture of you?" *Please deny it! I'm begging you to deny it. I'll find a way to believe it. Just say it's all a big misunderstanding, that you can explain everything.*

"What are you doing on a dating site?" he asked instead.

"What?"

"You heard me. Are you checking out guys behind my back?"

"Are you kidding me? You're actually trying to turn this around?"

"You can't troll these sites without being a member," he said, moving quickly to the table, commandeering her laptop, and quickly tapping on the keys. Seconds later,

117

Chloe found herself staring at the selfie she'd taken this morning and submitted along with a brief profile. *Outgoing and curious. Loves kids and traveling.* "Well, what do you know?" he said. "Look who we have here — looks like the pot calling the kettle black."

Chloe fought to retain control, even as she felt the ground giving way beneath her. "I'm not the one who needs to explain anything."

"I think you do."

"Fine. I'll explain. At least I *can* explain. I joined these sites this morning after some woman called to tell me you were on them . . ."

"Some woman being Paige Hamilton? You know how that bitch is always trying to stir up trouble . . ."

"Paige isn't a bitch, and it wasn't her. I don't know who it was. It doesn't *matter* who it was. What matters is that you're on these sites, pretending to be single . . ."

"What matters is that you joined these sites to spy on me."

"You can't be serious."

"You don't trust me, Chloe. You never have."

"Don't you dare make this about me."

"You've always been insecure and needy,

no matter what I do, no matter how hard I work or try to please you, to reassure you . . ."

"This is your way of reassuring me?" Chloe brought her hands to her head, as if to keep it from exploding. The conversation was becoming increasingly surreal. "By looking for women online?"

"I can't do this right now," Matt said, turning away. "I'm tired. I'm going to bed."

"Don't you dare walk away from me."

"There's no point in continuing this discussion now," he said. "You're upset, you're irrational, you're way overreacting."

"I'm overreacting?" she repeated, her voice at least an octave higher than just seconds ago.

"I don't appreciate being yelled at."

"I don't appreciate being lied to," she countered.

"I haven't lied to you."

Chloe slammed the back of her fingers against the computer screen. "This *isn't* you?" *Please tell me it isn't you. Find a way to make me believe this isn't you.*

The silence that followed was almost unbearable. "It's me," Matt said finally.

"Oh, God." Chloe felt the tears she'd somehow managed to keep at bay now in free fall down her cheeks.

"Oh, babe. Please don't cry," he said, walking quickly to the table and sinking into the chair beside her. "You know I can't bear it when you cry."

"Why?" she asked when she could find her voice. "I don't understand why."

"I don't know why," he said, his own eyes clouding over with tears. "I swear to God, I don't know. It started as a lark, a joke. This guy at work — Tony Marshall, you remember him, I think you met him at that cocktail party last year, he's not the best-looking guy — anyway, it's not important. But he's on these sites, and he's always bragging about the hordes of women he's been meeting — all the 'pussy he's been getting,' I believe was his delicate way of putting it — and I thought, shit, if he's making out like such a bandit, how would I do?"

Chloe fought the urge to gag.

"So, I joined a bunch of sites, and right away I got all these responses from women saying they wanted to hook up."

"How many?" Chloe asked. "How many have there been?"

"None," he told her. "I swear. I never followed through with any of them."

"You didn't?"

"No. That wasn't the point. Honestly, babe. I just liked the attention. I admit that

I was tempted. Hell, I'm human. Who doesn't want to feel desired? But then I thought of you and how sweet you are, and how much I love you. I thought of the kids and everything I stood to lose. And I couldn't do it."

Yes, Chloe thought. *It makes sense. What he's saying makes sense.*

"I know it was a crazy thing to do. It was juvenile and risky and downright stupid. But I love you, Chloe. I would never purposely do anything to hurt you. You have to believe me." He fell to his knees in front of her, his head burrowing into her lap, his shoulders heaving with the force of his sigh.

Chloe lowered her face to the top of his head, burying her lips in his thick brown hair, inhaling his masculine smell.

Combined with the unmistakable scent of another woman's perfume.

There was no point in asking for an explanation. She knew he'd have one. One of the women at the office, he'd say, maybe even giving her a name, rounding out his fabrication with an amusing anecdote designed to make Chloe smile. Or maybe he'd say that it was the agent acting for the seller, the one he'd told her about months ago, they'd worked together before, the one who always stood too close and wore too much perfume. "You don't remember?" he'd ask, looking wounded by her continuing suspicions.

"I think you should leave," Chloe said, her voice so quiet it was barely audible. Had she said anything at all?

"What?" His head jerked up.

"I want you to leave," she said, more adamantly than before. She stood up so abruptly that Matt almost fell over. "Now."

"Chloe, this is crazy. You're being . . ."

"Irrational?"

"I don't get it. I thought . . ."

"You thought you got away with it," she said simply. "Again." She took a deep breath. "I love you, Matt. Despite everything. Some part of me probably always will. But you were right. I *don't* trust you. And I don't believe you, no matter how hard I try or how much I want to. You're a liar and a cheat, and as much as I'll probably hate living without you, I'll hate myself even more if I let you stay."

Chloe watched Matt's hands ball into fists at his sides and braced herself for the full force of his fury. But there was only silence. Was he going to hold firm, refuse to leave? she wondered as he turned on his heels and disappeared up the stairs. Would she find him in their bed, already asleep, when she grew tired of waiting and joined him? Would she create a scene or just crawl in beside him?

She felt his heavy footsteps pacing the floor above her head, heard him rummaging through the closet in their bedroom. Less than five minutes later, she heard those footsteps hurrying down the stairs, and watched her husband stride purposely past her, overnight bag in hand. She heard him mutter something under his breath as he pulled open the front door and vanished into the night.

It was only after the door slammed shut behind him that his words reverberated back to her: "You'll be sorry."

CHAPTER THIRTEEN

The lawyer's office was located on the ground floor of an old two-story redbrick house on Portland Street, normally a five-minute drive from Chloe's Binney Street address, but taking almost twice that time because of continuing roadwork in the area. It seemed that all of Cambridge was under construction, the ubiquitous orange-and-black pylons that lined the streets and interrupted the flow of traffic starting to feel more like a permanent installation than a temporary inconvenience.

The bus for day camp had picked up Josh and Sasha just before nine, and Chloe had spent the rest of the morning, as she had the previous morning, combing through the list of divorce lawyers online. She finally settled on Pamela Lang, partly because she liked her photograph, partly because her office was in the area, and mostly because, of the half dozen family law practitioners she'd already tried, Pamela Lang was the only one who could see her before the end of the month. Matt hadn't so much as phoned since he left, and already Chloe was second-guessing her decision, wondering if she'd done the right thing. It was important that she see someone soon, before she had a chance to change her mind.

Not that she *couldn't* change her mind, she reminded herself as she left the white Hyundai that Matt had bought her for their last anniversary at the end of the street and pushed her way through a stubborn curtain of late-July heat toward the lawyer's office. Even now she was hoping that Matt could come up with an explanation that would somehow redeem him, convince her that he would never stray again. Maybe he would agree to marital counseling, something he'd rejected in no uncertain terms in the past. "We don't need some stranger meddling in our lives," he'd told her the first time she'd suggested they might benefit from counseling. "There's no problem we can't solve ourselves. We just have to be honest with each other."

Which was exactly the problem. He wasn't honest.

"He's a liar and a cheat," Chloe whispered as she pushed open the heavy oak front door and stepped inside the dark wood, air-conditioned foyer. She wiped the perspiration from her neck and pulled at the waist of her red-striped sundress, standing for another minute outside a second door, this one made of translucent glass. *Pamela Lang and Richard Fogler, Attorneys-at-Law* was painted across the rippled glass surface in swirling black cursive.

Fighting the urge to flee, Chloe opened the door and stepped inside a small waiting area, where a middle-aged receptionist with bright orange hair and huge, round, black-rimmed glasses sat behind a large oak desk, leafing through the latest issue of *InStyle* magazine.

"You must be Chloe Dixon," she said with a smile so wide that it exposed both rows of teeth. "We spoke earlier. I'm Trudy. Come in. Have a seat." She motioned toward four navy-blue chairs propped against the ecru-colored wall, her smile so persistent that Chloe felt obliged to return it. "Pamela's running a little late, but she should be back any minute."

Chloe automatically checked her watch. Her meeting with the lawyer was scheduled for one o'clock and it was past that already. The camp bus would drop the kids off at three and she couldn't be late getting home.

Josh was already suspicious that something was wrong.

"Where's Daddy?" he'd asked at breakfast, the same question he'd asked yesterday.

She'd lied and said that Daddy was very busy at work, but there was only so long she could keep using that as an excuse.

"Can I get you a cup of coffee?" Trudy asked.

"No, thank you." Chloe checked her watch again, more for show than necessity. Several minutes later, she checked it again. She glanced back at Trudy, who was still smiling as she flipped through the pages of her magazine. "I'm sorry," Chloe began, not sure what she was apologizing for. "But my kids get home at three o'clock and, obviously, I have to be there." She held up her left wrist and pointed at her watch, an oversized Michael Kors that Matt had bought her for Christmas.

"I don't know what to tell you," Trudy said, her smile as big as ever. "Pamela's meeting ran longer than she expected. And the traffic . . . you know . . . with all this construction . . . I'm sure she'll be here any minute."

"Maybe I should come back tomorrow," Chloe said after another ten minutes had passed.

"I'm afraid she's fully booked for the rest of this week, and she's away all next week at a conference," Trudy said, checking her boss's schedule on her computer. "I could give you something the week after that."

"No, that's too late."

For the first time, Trudy's smile threatened to disappear. "She really should be back any second. Is there someone you can call . . . for your kids?"

Well, I can't very well call my husband, Chloe thought. *"Hi, hon. It's me. I'm stuck at the divorce lawyer's and I was wondering if you could go back to the house I kicked you out of and look after the kids till I get back."*

And she couldn't call Paige and impose on her again. Besides, with the traffic, it was unlikely Paige could get there in time anyway.

Which left only one option. "Dear God," Chloe moaned, punching in her mother's digits on her cellphone.

Jennifer Powadiuk lived in a small apartment off Harvard Square, just minutes away, although her heavy schedule of dance competitions across the country meant she was rarely there. Chloe had no idea if she was even in the city, not having heard from her in six weeks. (*Came in second in the tango competition in Tampa,* read her last email. *Should have won.*)

"Please answer," Chloe whispered as the phone began ringing. She pictured her mother staring at her caller ID, trying to decide whether to pick up. After six rings, her mother's breathy whisper came on the line: *"Out tap-dancing my little head off. But do leave a message. Preferably one that's X-rated."*

Chloe sighed, about to click off when her mother came on the line. "Chloe? Is that you?"

"Where are you?" Chloe asked, hearing chatter in the background and the clinking of glasses, which meant her mother was likely at a bar, regardless of what city she was in.

"What can I do for you, Chloe?" her mother asked, ignoring the question.

"Are you in town?"

"Yes. I don't leave till Friday."

"Where are you going?"

"Toronto. There's an international polka competition —"

"Look, Mom," Chloe interrupted, once again glancing at her watch. She didn't have time to listen to her mother's upcoming agenda. "I have a favor to ask you."

"Yes, of course. Why else would you be calling?"

Really? Chloe thought. *You have the nerve to sound indignant? You're trying to make* me *feel guilty? You, who were never there, who never . . .* She stopped. Now was not the time to start recounting her mother's failings. "I was wondering if . . . Look, I'm stuck somewhere and I might not be able to make it home by three o'clock when the kids get back from camp. I was hoping you might be able to come over . . ."

"Of course," her mother said. "I'll leave now."

"Really?"

"You needn't sound so shocked, Chloe. I love those children, and I don't see near enough of them."

Whose fault is that? Chloe asked silently, deciding not to voice that thought out loud. "Thank you," she muttered instead, opting to leave well enough alone. "I'll try to get home as fast as I can."

"No need to rush. I assume my key still works?"

"It still works." Something else she'd have to do before the end of the week, Chloe realized: change the locks.

"Good. Then I'll see you later."

"Thanks again," Chloe said, but her mother had already clicked off. "Well, well. Will wonders never cease," she said, shaking her head.

"You found someone?" Trudy asked.

"My mother," she said, amazement clinging to her voice.

"Mothers are the best."

Chloe nodded, although she didn't buy it. Maybe mothers like Joan Hamilton. Not mothers like Jennifer Powadiuk. Still, maybe age was mellowing her. Maybe she really did love her grandchildren, despite not seeing them very often. Would Josh and Sasha even recognize the woman who'd be there to greet them when they got off the bus?

Yes, her mother could be charming. Yes, she could be funny and even sweet on occasion. When the occasion suited her. When she could use it to her advantage.

Remind you of anyone? Chloe thought.

"Dear God, I married my mother," she whispered, the realization forcing the words from her mouth with such force, she started choking.

"Oh, dear," Trudy said. "Can I get you some water?"

"No, it's okay. I'll be fine." Chloe cleared her throat. Clearing her mind of such unwelcome thoughts wouldn't be nearly as easy.

She heard the door open behind her.

"I'm so sorry I'm late," a woman said, appearing in front of Chloe, hand extended. "I'm Pamela Lang. Thank you so much for waiting."

Chloe stared into the kind face of a woman perhaps a decade her senior, her brown hair streaked with gray and pulled into a tightly secured bun at the nape of her neck. She was wearing a navy jacket over a matching skirt and white blouse, seemingly impervious to the summer heat. Chloe felt immediately safe.

Pamela Lang indicated her inner office with a sweep of her hands. "Shall we get this show on the road?"

Chloe rose to her feet. *By all means,* she thought. *Let's get this show on the road.*

CHAPTER FOURTEEN

He was waiting for her when she returned home almost two hours later.

Chloe closed the front door, hearing the television blasting upstairs. "Mom?" she called, walking toward the living room. "Joshy? Sasha?"

It was then that she saw him. He was sitting on the plum-colored sectional, his feet stretched toward the navy leather ottoman between him and the large-screen TV on the opposite wall. The look on his beautiful face was one of barely concealed contempt. "Nice of you to finally put in an appearance," he said.

"What are you doing here?" she asked her husband. "Where's my mother?"

"Last I saw her she was passed out in Josh's room."

"Oh, God."

"And in answer to your first question, I'm here because my son called me at work, hysterical because you weren't home; his grandmother was sprawled across his bed, he thought she might be dead, and he didn't know what to do. I rushed right over, found the old drunk asleep in his room, got the kids settled down, made them some peanut butter and jelly sandwiches, and assured them that your mother was, regrettably, very much alive. Then I told them they could watch TV in our room until you got home."

"Thank you," Chloe said quietly, collapsing onto the right wing of the sectional, tears of anger filling her eyes. "I guess I should have known better."

"Yes, you should have," Matt agreed. "Where the hell were you anyway?"

She fought the urge to tell him it was none of his business. "What difference does it make?"

He shook his head. "You know, I always thought that, however scattered and irresponsible you can be sometimes . . ." He paused half a second to let his words sink in. ". . . that you were a great mother, that you would never put our kids at risk . . ."

"I didn't put our kids at risk," she began, then stopped. He was right. She should have known better than to rely on her mother, no matter what the circumstances.

There was a moment's silence. "So, what

did she say?" Matt asked. "This lawyer you went to see. Pamela Lang, was it? Not a bad-looking woman for a professional ball-buster."

Chloe's eyes shot toward her husband. Her mouth opened to speak, but no words emerged.

"Your laptop was open," he offered by way of explanation.

"No. I closed it before I went out."

"My mistake. Guess I opened it."

"You had no right."

"Just trying to find out where you were," he said. "To figure out what was so damn important that you left our children alone."

"I didn't leave them alone."

"Sorry. Called your mother. Don't think the courts will find there's much of a distinction."

Chloe felt a sliver of panic snaking its way through her chest to her throat, making speech both difficult and painful. "Are you threatening me?"

Matt leaned toward her, resting his elbows on his knees. "I'll do whatever I think is necessary to protect my children, Chloe. You should know that."

"Does that include pretending to be single and trolling for women online? I don't think that exactly qualifies you for father of the year. Do you?"

"I made mistakes, Chloe," Matt said. "I admit it. But my mistakes never put our children in harm's way."

Chloe nodded, trying to make sense of his words, to understand what he was getting at. She couldn't. "So, what are you saying?"

"What are you *doing*?" he countered.

"I don't understand."

"You're the one who went to a lawyer, Chloe. Not me. Do you want a divorce? Is that what this is all about?"

Chloe hesitated. After almost two hours with Pamela Lang, she still wasn't sure what she wanted or what she was going to do. "I just wanted to know my options."

"You wanted to know what's in it for you," he corrected. "How you can suck me dry."

"No," she insisted. "But I *do* have rights."

"As do I. Especially where my children are concerned."

"So, are you saying that if we get a divorce, you're going to fight me for custody?"

"Are we getting divorced, Chloe? Is that what you really want? Because it's not what I want," he said before she could answer. "God knows it's the last thing in the world that *I* want."

"What *do* you want?"

"I want this silly misunderstanding to be

over. I've been trying to give you some space, give you time to calm down, but I want to come home. I want to be a father to our kids. I want my life back. I want *you.* I want *us.*" He pushed his hair away from his forehead in a gesture that Chloe had always found unbearably sexy.

She swallowed the renewed threat of tears. Could she do it? Could she pretend this was all some *silly misunderstanding*? "You asked me before what I really want . . ."

"Tell me."

"I want the truth," Chloe said. Did she? Or did she just want her husband to be more convincing in his lies?

Matt said nothing for several long seconds. "These women," he finally conceded. "I swear. They meant *nothing* to me."

Chloe no longer fought to keep her tears at bay. "Well, they mean something to *me,*" she cried, making no attempt to wipe those tears away.

He was on his feet, moving toward her. "I see that now. And I'm so sorry I hurt you. I promise to do better . . ."

"How many women have there been, Matt?"

He froze. "Oh, God. Do we really have to?"

"How many?"

He sank back down. "What good will talking about this do?"

"How many?" she repeated.

"I don't know." He threw his hands up in the air. "Half a dozen, maybe."

"Half a dozen," she repeated, silently doubling that number. Matt had always manipulated figures, exaggerating or underplaying them to his advantage, even when there was no need. A four-hour plane ride became five; he'd paid two hundred dollars for a sweater, not three; he'd won fifty dollars on a bet, not five or ten, depending on whom he was talking to.

He'd cheated on her with half a dozen women, not twelve. Or fifteen. Or twenty.

She'd been turning a blind eye to his infidelities — to his casual cruelty — for as long as she'd known him. He wasn't going to change. This is who he was, who he'd always been. The only question now was, who was she?

"I think you should go now," she said, surprised by the calmness in her voice when her heart was beating so fast it felt as if it was about to burst from her chest. "Thanks for coming over this afternoon. I appreciate it. I really do." She stood up, glancing toward the front door.

He looked confused. "What? I'm being

dismissed?"

"I'll call you."

"*You'll* call *me*? Like this is all up to you?" He rose slowly, even menacingly, to his feet.

"I think we've said everything . . ."

"So, I tell you the truth and you punish me for it? That's how this works?"

"I need time to think."

"No. You don't need time. *This* is what you need." And suddenly his arms were around her, his hands everywhere on her body, on her breasts, on her buttocks, between her legs; his mouth in her hair, on her neck, on her lips.

She tried pushing his hands aside, twisting out of his reach.

"*This* is what you need. You know it is."

"No!" she said, louder this time, pushing him away with all the force she could muster. "Stop! Please . . ."

"*Please, please, please,*" he mimicked, stumbling back against the ottoman. "That's the whole problem in a nutshell. Isn't it, Chloe? You don't know *how* to please a man. If you did, do you think these other women would be necessary?"

"Oh. God."

"You're pathetic, Chloe."

"Get out of here."

"I remind you that this is my house, too."

139

"Get out before I call the police."

"You bitch . . ." He raised his right arm into the air, his hand a fist.

"Daddy!" Sasha called from upstairs. "Josh is being mean to me."

"Josh," Matt called back, his arm returning slowly, even reluctantly, to his side, his eyes never leaving Chloe's. "Stop being mean to your sister."

"Mommy!" Sasha said seconds later, appearing in the entrance to the living room. "Josh!" she yelled toward the stairs. "Mommy's home." She ran to her mother, throwing her arms around Chloe's hips. "Grandma's sleeping," she announced.

"I know, sweetheart," Chloe told her. "I'm so sorry about that."

"I thought she was dead," Josh said, entering the room. "I didn't know where you were, so I called Daddy."

"You did great, sweetie."

"Daddy said we could watch TV till you got home."

"And now I'm afraid that Daddy has to leave," Matt told him.

"Where are you going?" Josh asked.

"I have work to finish up, slugger," Matt said, tousling his son's hair. "But don't you worry." He smiled at Chloe. The smile sent shivers down her spine. "I'll be back."

CHAPTER FIFTEEN

"Maybe you should call the police," Paige suggested.

They were sitting at the kitchen table, Chloe across from Paige and Joan Hamilton, their dinner plates barely touched in front of them, the smell of leftover KFC lingering in the air like a malodorous gas.

"And say what?" Chloe asked, her fingers playing with the skin of an uneaten drumstick.

"That your husband threatened you . . ."

"Except he didn't," Chloe said, letting go of the drumstick and wiping her hand on her jeans. "Not really. I mean, all he said was that he'd be back."

"He assaulted you," Joan reminded her.

"He'll say that I'm exaggerating," Chloe argued, "that he was just trying to kiss and make up. He'll make it sound like this whole thing is my fault, that I'm the one who entrusted our kids to an irresponsible drunk, and he's the put-upon husband who had to leave work in the middle of his busy afternoon to rush home and protect them. I know Matt," she continued before either woman could object. "I know how convincing he can be."

"So, what are you going to do?" Paige pushed her plate to the center of the table.

Chloe stared at Paige and her mother. She'd called Paige in a panic after Matt left, and Paige and her mother had arrived at her door, complete with a bucket of Kentucky Fried Chicken, within the hour. "I don't know *what* to do."

"You need to keep a record," Joan said, taking charge. "That's the first thing. You need to keep track . . . of Matt's visits . . . the things he says . . . how they make you feel . . . everything. Write it all down . . . dates, times, everything that happens. Don't leave anything out, no matter how trivial it seems. Be as specific as you can."

Chloe nodded. Paige's mother could always be relied on for sound, practical advice. She was everything a mother was supposed to be — loving, thoughtful, wise. Unlike her own mother, who was none of those things. Chloe pictured Jennifer, still sprawled across Josh's bed, so drunk that Chloe hadn't been able to rouse her. Still, she'd have to figure out a way to wake her up soon so the kids could get to sleep. They'd already watched more television in one day than she normally allowed in a week. Chloe glanced at her watch. It was almost seven thirty, their usual bedtime. She pushed herself away from the table and left the room. "Kids," she called from the foot of the stairs. "Time to get ready for bed."

"Awww," came the expected response.

She returned to the kitchen to find Joan Hamilton clearing the dishes from the table and Paige putting the bucket of leftover chicken in the fridge. "No — you don't have to do that. Please . . ."

"Please, please, please," she heard Matt mimic.

"You've already done so much," Chloe told them. "I can't thank you enough for dinner, for being here . . ." She burst into tears before she could complete either the sentence or the thought.

"Any time," Paige said, immediately at Chloe's side.

"No thanks required," Joan said, joining them.

"I feel terrible," Chloe told Paige, "making you break your date . . ."

"You didn't make me do anything," Paige said. "It was just some guy I met online. I texted him that something unexpected came up and hopefully we could reschedule."

"And what did he say?"

"Nothing," Paige acknowledged.

"I'm sorry."

"Don't be. If he's interested, he'll try again."

The three women formed a tight circle, their arms gripping each other's waists, their foreheads touching.

"What's going on?" a small male voice asked from the doorway.

"Hi, sweetheart," Chloe said, whisking away her tears.

"What are you doing?"

"Having a group hug," Joan said.

"Can I have one?" Sasha asked, her round little face peeking out from behind her brother's wiry frame.

"You certainly can," Paige said. She held out her right arm, beckoning the children forward.

Sasha was instantly at the women's sides, but Josh hung back, waiting to be coaxed.

"Come on, you," Joan said, obliging. "Group hug's not complete without you."

"Josh doesn't like *Paw Patrol* anymore," Sasha said as her brother pushed his way into the group.

"What's *Paw Patrol*?" asked Paige.

"It's a kids' TV show," Chloe explained.

"It's stupid," Josh said.

"I thought you liked *Paw Patrol.*"

"It's for babies."

"I'm not a baby," Sasha protested. "I'm a big girl."

"Yes, you are," Chloe said.

"I know how babies are made," Josh announced as the circle split apart.

"You do?"

"Jennifer told me."

Chloe felt the color drain from her cheeks. "My mother told you how babies are made?"

"Right before she fell asleep."

"We thought she died," Sasha said solemnly. "But Daddy said she was just very tired."

Not nearly tired enough, Chloe thought.

"Do you want me to tell you?" Josh asked them.

Chloe nodded, holding her breath.

"The man puts his penis into the woman's regina," her son began.

"Ew!" said Sasha, looking horrified.

"And the penis has these millions of sperm. But the regina has only one egg. So, all the sperm have to go racing to the egg to see who can get there first." He paused dramatically before finishing with a flourish.

"And Sasha and I won the race!"

"Hooray!" said Sasha, jumping up and down, clapping her hands above her head.

Chloe bit down on her lip to keep from laughing. Beside her, she saw Joan beaming from ear to ear and Paige turning to face the wall, her shoulders shaking.

I'm the real winner, she thought, grabbing her children and hugging them close. "You certainly did," she told them. "God, I love you."

"I love you, too," Sasha responded immediately.

"Yeah," said Josh, wriggling out of her embrace.

"Now go get into your pajamas," Chloe said.

"Where am I going to sleep?" Josh asked. "Jennifer's still in my bed."

"Don't worry, sweetheart. She'll be gone by the time you're ready."

"She's funny," said Sasha.

"Yeah, a real laugh riot." Chloe listened as her children bounded up the stairs. "Oh, well. I suppose it could have been worse. She could have showed them illustrations from the *Kama Sutra.*"

"Her story about the sperm and the egg was actually kind of sweet," Joan said.

" 'Sweet' is the last word I would use to

describe my mother."

"Well, she *is* creative. You have to give her that," Paige said.

"I don't have to give her anything."

"Are you talking about me?" a voice asked. "God, what's that horrible smell?"

Chloe turned to see her mother standing in the doorway. She was wearing bright pink skinny jeans and a turquoise T-shirt with the words DANCING QUEEN written in rhinestone capital letters across its front. Her blond hair was cut very short, and her hazel eyes were having trouble focusing, giving her the look of a deranged pixie.

"Paige and I picked up some Kentucky Fried Chicken on our way over," Joan told her, explaining the source of the odor. "I can heat you up a piece, if you'd like."

"God, no. That stuff'll kill you."

"Unlike booze," Chloe said.

"Oh, dear. Are you going to get all pissy on me because I took a little nap?" She turned toward Paige. "I'm sorry . . . you are . . . ?"

"Paige Hamilton. We met a few years back. This is my mother, Joan."

"You called in the troops, did you?" Jennifer asked her daughter.

"The kids thought you were dead," Chloe said, choosing not to mention Matt.

Jennifer whooped with laughter. "Nonsense. I was just showing them this new dance step I've been working on — I'm a dancer," she explained to Paige and Joan, her grandchildren momentarily forgotten. "I've won many competitions across the country. I don't suppose Chloe has told you anything about that. No, she wouldn't," she said without pause. "Anyway, I was showing them this little twirl and I got a bit dizzy, so I thought I'd better lie down. I guess I must have dozed off for a few minutes."

"A few hours," Chloe corrected.

"Yes, well. It's not easy looking after two rambunctious children at my age." She straightened her shoulders. "My daughter called me this afternoon and I dropped everything to come over, and this is the appreciation I get. Is that the way you treat *your* mother?" she asked Paige.

"You told them how babies are made," Chloe reminded her.

"Did I?" Jennifer shrugged. "Well, it's time they knew."

"And it's time you said goodbye," Chloe said.

Jennifer glanced at her watch. "Oh, my, yes. That it is. Dance practice in an hour. Can't keep Tyrone waiting. He's so handsome. All the girls wanted him for a partner.

148

But, well . . ." She patted her hair, offering the three women her most coquettish smile. "Say good night to the kids for me. Nice meeting you, Janet."

Joan didn't bother correcting her.

"And always lovely to see you . . ."

"Paige," Paige offered.

"Of course." Jennifer smiled. "Don't bother walking me to the door," she told Chloe. "And feel free to call me anytime."

The women waited until they heard the front door close.

"Well, I don't know about you," Joan said, "but I could use a drink."

CHAPTER SIXTEEN

"How about some weed instead?" Chloe suggested.

"Seriously?" Paige asked. "I remind you that this woman standing next to me is my mother."

"Your mother who smoked more than a few joints in her youth," Joan told them. "Oh, darling. Don't look so shocked. I'm a child of the sixties after all. Or seventies. Whatever. We were too stoned back then to keep track." She giggled, eyes sparkling.

"Seriously?" Paige said again.

"Although I haven't touched the stuff in forever," Joan admitted. "Your father wouldn't allow it in the house. He was a bit of a square in that regard."

Chloe couldn't help laughing at the expression on her friend's face.

"Who *are* you?" Paige asked Joan as they walked toward the living room. "And what have you done with my mother?"

They waited until the kids were asleep before lighting up. "This might be a bit stronger than what you're used to," Chloe warned Joan, watching the older woman take a deep inhale.

"Lovely," Joan said, holding the smoke in her lungs as long as she could before releasing it, then passing the joint to her daughter.

"I don't know," Paige said. "This doesn't seem right."

"Nonsense, darling. We're bonding. Now take a drag and pass it along."

"How come I didn't know this about you?"

"You never asked," Joan said.

"Is there anything else I should know?" Paige took a drag, as directed, before passing the hand-rolled cigarette back to Chloe. "Like what?"

"Like . . . I don't know . . . did you do any other drugs?"

"A little hash," Joan said as the joint was returned to her waiting fingers. "Oh, and I tried LSD once, but I didn't like the way it made me feel."

"I don't believe this," Paige said.

"Oh, and maybe some cocaine and a wee bit of heroin," Joan continued before dissolving into raucous laughter. "Sorry, girls. Just teasing about the cocaine and the heroin. Ah, this is delightful," she said, taking another drag before passing the joint back to her daughter.

The women sat for several long minutes in silence, passing the joint around until it had all but disappeared. Chloe felt the tensions of the day gradually lifting from her shoulders. So what if Matt was making vague threats to take her to court for custody of their children? He'd never go through with it. So what if the five-thousand-dollar retainer required to hire Pamela Lang would render her effectively broke? She could take out a loan. Or ask her mother.

The thought sent Chloe into more spasms of laughter.

"What's so funny?" Paige asked.

"My mother told my children how babies are made," Chloe wailed, laughing even harder as Paige and Joan joined in.

"Speaking of sex," Paige said.

Had they been? Chloe wondered.

"Did I ever tell you about Marie and her daughter?"

"Who's Marie?" Chloe and Joan asked together, causing another round of giggles.

"A woman from my work. From where I *used* to work," Paige qualified, pushing the unpleasant reality aside and sliding down the sofa to sit on the floor. "Marie's daughter is twelve, and she came home from school one day and told her mother that in health class that afternoon they'd learned to put condoms on bananas."

"They teach that in school?" Joan asked.

"It's part of the new sex ed curriculum."

"Wish we'd had that when I was in school," Joan said.

"Yes, well," Paige said, her eyes widening, then blinking closed. "What was I talking about?"

"Putting condoms on bananas," Chloe told her.

"Right. Well, Marie was trying to be this cool mom, you know, trying not to look too shocked, when her daughter explains that they use condoms to keep the C-word inside."

"The C-word?" Joan and Chloe asked in unison, causing another fit of laughter.

"Marie doesn't know what her daughter's talking about. Then she realizes the kid means semen. And Marie's still trying to play it cool, so she says, 'That's really interesting, honey. But you know, it's spelled with an *S*.' And the kid says, ' "Cock" is spelled with an *S*?!' "

All three women were now doubled over, laughing. "Oh, God. Oh, God," Joan said, holding her stomach. "I think I just wet my pants."

A cellphone rang from somewhere beside them.

"What's that?" Paige asked.

"I believe it's your phone," her mother told her.

"Nobody knows I'm here," Paige said.

"Your *cell*phone," Chloe reminded her.

"I think she's stoned," Joan confided, as Paige stretched for her purse on the floor next to the ottoman.

"It's Sam," Paige whispered, staring at the caller ID.

"Who's Sam?" Chloe asked.

"This man she met online," Joan answered.

"The one you were supposed to see tonight?"

"No," Paige said. "Another one."

"She's very popular," Joan said.

"Apparently," Chloe acknowledged, feeling even more guilty. She'd been so wrapped up in her own life, she'd barely given a thought to anyone else's.

"He's a dentist," Joan said. "Answer it before he hangs up."

Paige struggled to her feet. "Hello? Yes, hi, Sam. Just a sec while I go into another room."

"Aw, you're no fun," her mother called after her.

"So," Chloe said after Paige was gone, "a dentist, huh?"

"They went out the other night."

"The evening obviously went well."

"I think so. She's invited him to my brother-in-law's birthday party."

"Wow. Won't Heather be surprised," Chloe said, the name lodging in her throat like a piece of hard candy. "Oh," she added.

"What is it?"

"I just realized who called to tell me about Matt," Chloe said, seeing Heather's smug face through the lingering haze of the marijuana they'd just smoked.

"What's wrong?" Paige asked, reentering the living room. "You look like you've seen a ghost."

"It was Heather who called Chloe to tell her about Matt," Joan said.

Paige sank to the floor. "Why am I not surprised?" She shook her head. "What can I say? She's a cunt."

Chloe gasped, glancing warily toward Paige's mother.

"It's okay, dear," Joan told her. "Paige is right. Heather *is* a cunt. Or should I say, a *regina*?"

Once again, the room filled with laughter.

"So what did the dentist have to say for himself?" Chloe asked.

"He asked if I wanted to go to a movie Saturday night."

"And do you?"

"Apparently."

"Good for you," Chloe told her. "Maybe something good will actually result from one of these dating sites."

"Did Paige tell you I'm on one, too?" Joan asked.

"What?" Chloe asked.

"Meet Sunflower," Paige said.

"Apparently, nobody uses their real name," Joan explained. "And since Paige goes by Wildflower, I thought I'd stick with the floral theme. Paige enrolled me this afternoon. Show her," Joan said as her daughter clicked onto Autumn Romance. "It's a dating site for seniors. There's my picture. What do you think?"

"I think you look lovely."

"No. I have no chin anymore. It's just kind of disappeared into the wrinkles on my neck." Joan brought her hand to her jaw-line, pushing at her flesh.

"Your chin is fine," Paige told her.

"Age seventy, widowed, loves reading and good wine," Chloe read. "No mention here about good weed."

"It *was* good, wasn't it? Have I had any . . . what do you call them . . . likes?"

"No responses so far," Paige said, and Chloe could hear the relief in her friend's voice even though she tried to hide it. Paige clicked off the site and returned the phone to her purse.

"Mommy," a voice called from the hallway. In the next second, Sasha materialized, rubbing her eyes with one hand, clutching a small pink blanket in the other. Chloe ran to the child, scooping her into her arms.

"Baby, what are you doing up?"

"I had a bad dream."

"Oh, sweetie. I'm sorry."

"I dreamed you died."

"Well, it was just a dream, sweet pea," Chloe told her, kissing her cheek. "As you can see, Mommy's very much alive."

"I don't want you to die."

"I'm not going to for a long, long time."

"Most people don't die until they're very old," Joan added for good measure.

Sasha looked over at Joan, her eyes growing wide. "Uh-oh," she said.

"Well, that sobered me up fast," Joan said with a laugh. "I think that's our cue to leave."

"You smell funny," Sasha told her mother.

"Definitely our cue to leave," Paige said.

"Will you be okay?" she asked Chloe.

"I'll be fine." She walked them to the front door, Sasha already asleep in her arms. "Call me tomorrow? I want to hear all about this dentist."

"You got it."

Chloe watched them climb into Paige's car and back out of the driveway. "Good night, flowers!" she called after them.

CHAPTER SEVENTEEN

He's doing a walking tour of the city.

And why not? He's still something of a tourist after all. He hasn't been here that long. And he'll be leaving soon. Another few weeks, maybe a month, and it will be time to head elsewhere. Wouldn't do to outstay his welcome.

Too bad, because Boston is a great city. So much to see and do. Art, culture, fine restaurants. Not that he's interested in any of these things. But Boston also has lots of small, dark bars. And lots of eager women. He'll be sad to go. What was it his mother used to say? *"All good things must come to an end"?* Well, she was right about that anyway, if little else.

Originally, he was considering Atlanta as his next stop, but he's thinking it'll still be too hot there even a month from now, and he's not a huge fan of the heat, having grown up in Gainesville, Florida. So maybe

Cincinnati or Cleveland. Cleveland is home to the Rock & Roll Hall of Fame, so that place might be worth a visit. Not much else there, though, as far as he can tell, so come fall, he might just cross over into Canada. He's heard autumn is beautiful in Northern Ontario, the ordinary green leaves of summer turning a brilliant variety of red, yellow, and orange. People come from all over the world to see nature's spectacular display of fall colors, he remembers reading. He finds this fact amusing, as what the changing colors really signify is that the leaves are dying.

Of course, there is beauty in death. He knows this better than anyone.

He pictures the girl now lying lifeless on the floor of his apartment, the graceful way her body went limp as he squeezed the final breath from her lungs at the stroke of midnight, the delicate way the light faded from her soft brown eyes, the horror of what was happening to her evaporating like dew in the early morning sun. A soft, milky film has since covered those eyes, and rigor has caused her limbs to stiffen and her flesh to turn an alabaster shade of white, so that she looks more like a statue than a human being. She has become, truly, a work of art.

Which would make him an artist, he

thinks, feeling a surge of pride.

He was almost tempted to stay with her. Still, he couldn't very well waste a whole day admiring last night's handiwork. *What's done is done.* Something else his mother was fond of saying, no cliché too insignificant for her to espouse. And it's a beautiful Saturday morning, the sky an iridescent shade of blue, the temperature hovering in the mid-seventies. All in all, a great day to be alive, he acknowledges, a slow smile tugging at the corners of his lips. Too bad Nadia had to miss it.

Nadia, he repeats silently. Twenty-seven years old. Originally from Romania. Named after some once-famous gymnast. Recently quit her job as a nanny when the children's father got a little too hands-on for her liking. No family. No friends. No ties to the community. Looking for work. Looking for love. *In all the wrong places,* he sings silently, recalling the old song his mother used to hum.

Looking for Mr. Right.

Finding Mr. Right Now.

He laughs out loud, attracting the attention of an elderly woman walking toward him along Hull Street. He tips an imaginary hat in her direction. "Beautiful day," he says in passing.

"That it is," she says.

He considers complimenting her on her hair — older women are so grateful for even the smallest of compliments, and you don't see many of them with gray hair these days — but by the time he forms the sentence she is crossing onto Salem Street, and the moment is gone. Once more he ponders choosing an older woman as his next target. It would make for an interesting change of pace, at the very least, a break from all these self-absorbed millennials.

And he knows exactly whom he would pick: Joan Hamilton.

Mother of Wildflower.

He laughs into the palm of his hand, proud of his amateur sleuthing. Not that it was difficult to ferret out the information he sought, what with Facebook, LinkedIn, and Instagram to aid in his search. All those heartwarming pictures Paige has posted on @paigehamilton of her and her mother, #JoanHamilton, #BestMotherInTheWorld, as well as several with a beautiful blonde named Chloe, #BestFriendForever. He's never been much into blondes, but still, best friend Chloe might make for another interesting change of pace.

Thank you, social media, he thinks. *How did the world manage without you?*

He could start with Paige's mother. Follow up with her closest friend.

That would teach Paige to treat him so cavalierly, canceling their date at the last minute, after the expensive steaks were already marinating and the salad chilling in the fridge. The apartment was immaculate. Everything was set to go. He'd had such plans.

Luckily, he had Nadia waiting in the wings, primed through weeks of subtle online seduction to take Paige's place. Of course, he'd had to postpone his plans from Wednesday to Friday to accommodate Nadia's schedule, and the poor girl had borne the brunt of his frustration over the delay, but some things were unavoidable.

I'm so sorry. Something unexpected has come up and I have to cancel. Can we reschedule?

He still bristles when he thinks of it.

After all his careful plotting and meticulous research, the pride he'd taken in determining which approach would work best on her. She'd already demonstrated that mere good looks wouldn't be enough to win her over, that he'd have to come at her from a different angle. The key, he'd decided, was to appeal to her emotions, to tug at her heartstrings. Hence, the parents married fifty years and the young wife dead of cancer. That, along with the offhand mention of an MBA to appeal to her intellect, as well as the lie that he liked jazz, tossed in at the last second because of a picture she'd posted of herself in a Herbie Hancock T-shirt. Combine those elements with the seeming awkwardness of his approach and he was on his way. Up until the very last minute.

I'm so sorry. Something unexpected has come up and I have to cancel. Can we reschedule?

Count on it, he thinks.

He laughs again, this time drawing unwelcome stares from the long line of noisy tourists clogging the narrow sidewalk in front of the Paul Revere House. He turns down Hanover Street on his way to Union and the marketplace at Faneuil Hall. But Faneuil Hall is even more crowded with weekend visitors than he expected, the café that is his destination already filled to overflowing.

He sees them almost immediately. They are sitting at a table against the far wall, sipping their coffee, Paige digging into her brunch of bagels and smoked salmon, her mother eagerly attacking her plate of straw-berries-and-whipped-cream-smothered waffles. It is no accident he's here. *Thanks again, Instagram,* he thinks. *Saturday brunch at Faneuil Hall. #BestBrunchInTown. #Best MomInTheWorld.*

He watches them for a while, thinking it might be fun to do the two women together, make one watch while he tortures and defiles the other. *Defile,* he repeats silently, rolling the word over on his tongue, feeling an immediate lift to his spirits. He loves that they have no idea he is watching them, of the hours he has spent online — *thank you, white pages, Boston, Mass., for providing me with Joan Hamilton's address* — that they're blissfully unaware of the danger they are in, of the cruel fate that awaits them. Still, he can't very well stand here forever, hoping a table will free up.

He debates leaving, maybe heading over to the Public Garden across from Boston Common and taking a ride in one of those silly swan boats, the kind you pedal yourself, when he spots an empty seat at a tiny, round table in the back, a table that will allow him a view of Paige and her mother, albeit one that's partially obstructed. He makes a beeline for it, squeezing between several tables and deliberately stepping on the foot of a young woman whose bare legs are stretched across his path. She cries out, a

165

combination of surprise and pain, and reaches down to grab the injured toes peeking out from the sandal of her right foot. He sees that her toenails are painted bright coral and he notes with satisfaction that he has chipped the polish on her big toe, ruining what was, no doubt, an expensive pedicure. "I'm so sorry," he says, temporarily abandoning his smile for a look of well-practiced concern.

"That's okay," she tells him, small, dark eyes lingering on his. *You can step on my toes anytime,* those eyes say.

It would be so easy to get her to abandon her companion — another stupid girl whose smile indicates she likes what she sees.

Too easy, he thinks, glancing back toward Paige and her mother.

He's set his sights on bigger game.

"I guess I'll live," the girl says.

I guess you will, he thinks, continuing to the table at the back.

He orders a double espresso and relaxes in his chair, his cock tingling with the lingering feel of the girl's bare toes crushed beneath his heavy shoe. Psychiatrists would no doubt label him a sexual sadist, the most dangerous of psychopaths, and they'd be right. Sex and pain have always gone hand in hand for him. Although the sex act itself is incidental, merely one of the weapons in his arsenal. It's the pain he inflicts that he gets off on more than anything else. Add a dollop of fear and you have the recipe for pure bliss.

He doesn't know where this came from — what made him the way he is — and in truth, he doesn't care. Was he, as Lady Gaga so eloquently put it, *born this way*? Or did his childhood somehow shape him into the man — some might say *monster* — he has become? Nature or nurture, the eternal question. Perhaps a combination of the two. But what difference does it make, really? Especially to his victims. He doubts this will be the question on Paige's lips when he silences them forever.

He can recall lying in bed as a child, listening to the strange and muffled noises emanating from his parents' bedroom. He remembers tiptoeing down the hall and peering into the darkness of that small room, seeing his father on top of his mother, his mother struggling beneath him, pleading with him to stop, his father ignoring her cries as he pounded relentlessly into her. And he remembers that he enjoyed watching his mother suffer, this weak, stupid woman who thought begging would save her. He remembers being excited by her pain, eager to see and hear more.

That was the moment he knew for sure that he wasn't normal.

He'd suspected it for some time, having always felt a curious detachment from the world around him. While the other kids at school could often be found laughing uproariously at some dumb joke, or crying because a beloved pet had died, he'd felt nothing except maybe contempt for their weakness. He took to mimicking the looks he saw on their faces and echoing the joy or sadness he heard in their voices, so as not to appear different or strange. He gave them what he understood instinctively they needed. His burgeoning good looks made fooling them easy, especially the girls. Girls believed what they wanted to believe, despite all evidence to the contrary.

And the more indifferent he appeared, the more sought-after he became. The worse he behaved toward them, the more they gravitated to him. *Treat 'em mean to keep 'em keen.* Now *that* was a saying he could believe in.

It seemed that girls, like the women they would grow into, liked to suffer for love. And he was more than happy to give them what they wanted. Which is why he has yet to respond to Paige's text.

But he will. When the time is right.

Let her twist in the wind for a while.

He leans back in his chair, remembering the first time he touched a girl's breast, and can actually feel that small lump of flesh in his hand even now. The girl's name was Sara — he can't be bothered trying to remember her last name — and she was fifteen, the same age as he was. Outgoing. Pretty. Not too smart. They went to a party and before long, they were in someone's bedroom, making out. He reached for her breast and waited for the thrill he'd heard the other boys boast of. But he felt nothing. Until he squeezed, hard, and Sara let out a startled cry, and suddenly every inch of his body was on fire.

He quickly developed a reputation for liking things rough, and as he got older, his tastes grew ever more extreme. When the local girls no longer wanted to play along, he sought out professionals, women who'd do almost anything if the price was right. They'd let him tie them up and whip them till they cried for mercy; they'd let him choke them almost to the point of unconsciousness; they'd let him bite them, violating them with whatever objects he had at hand. His fantasies grew more perverse, more violent. It soon wasn't enough to pay women to pretend. He wanted the thrill of the real thing.

His fantasies consumed him. His favorite one involved meeting a girl and dazzling her with his wit and charm, hanging on her every word, making her feel as if she was the only woman in the world, and then, when she'd been sufficiently dazzled, when she was lost in a fantasy of her own, one that involved a diamond ring and a long, white gown, he'd awaken her from that ridiculous dream with the cold shower of reality, and the feel of cold steel around her wrists.

He orders another espresso from the waitress, a girl with rainbow stripes in her naturally brown hair, who bends over to allow him a peek down her ruffled white blouse as she places the tiny cup in front of him, probably thinking this little display will get her a bigger tip. *Women are so obvious,* he thinks, trying to pinpoint the exact moment murder became an integral part of his fantasies.

Probably around the time his mother died, he decides, seeing his mother's gaunt face in the dark brown surface of his coffee. She'd gotten sick. Some form of cancer. His father had promptly deserted her — "Pretty Boy here can take care of you" being his parting words.

He was twenty-one and still living at home, having decided to forgo college to apprentice as a mechanic at a local gas station. He knew the job was beneath him, but he liked it because it allowed him plenty of time to cultivate his fantasies. He also enjoyed working alongside the handful of newly released convicts from one of the five prisons in the area, soaking up their expertise in criminal activities like online hacking, and reveling in the stories involving rape and violence. For most of these men, their only regret was having been caught.

He would have no such regrets, he'd decided, because he would never be stupid enough to get caught.

He pictures himself at his mother's bedside, watching her suffer with a pain so intense that even a veritable pharmacy of drugs couldn't reach it. How easy it would have been to simply reach out and cover her nose and mouth with the palm of his hand, to end that suffering once and for all.

Except the truth was that he enjoyed watching her suffer. He loved monitoring her fight for each labored breath, the unwillingness of her body to let go even as her eyes begged for release. He studied her as dispassionately as he'd once studied frogs in biology class, and when she died, he felt . . . nothing. Maybe a touch of regret that the show was over.

Her death left him surprisingly well-off, the result of an insurance policy naming him her sole beneficiary. He sold the house, quit his job at the gas station, and took off across the country, working when the mood struck him — a good mechanic was always appreciated — honing his fantasies, indulging them whenever he could, never staying anywhere for very long.

Three years ago, he made his ultimate fantasy a reality. Penny Grover of Bowling Green, Kentucky — his first kill, messier than he would have liked, but then, it was early days. He was still perfecting his craft. *How many have there been since?* he wonders, although he knows the answer full well: sixteen women so far.

The explosion of dating sites online has played right into his murderous hands, becoming his unwitting accomplices. He pulls out his phone, checking his latest list of volunteers. *So many women,* he muses. *So little time.*

The air stirs beside him and he looks up to see the smiling face of the young woman whose toes he mangled earlier. She is chewing on her lower lip as she drops a neatly folded napkin onto the table in front of him, then hurries away. He reaches over and unfolds the napkin, knowing what he'll see even before he spots her name — "Carrie" with a heart instead of a dot over the *i* — along with her phone number. He pockets it with a laugh, realizing only after doing so that the table where Paige and her mother were sitting is now empty.

"Shit," he mutters, furious at his momentary lapse of attention. Then he remembers Nadia, sprawled across the hardwood floor of his living room, patiently awaiting his return.

And as his mother used to say, you should never keep a lady waiting.

CHAPTER EIGHTEEN

Joan Hamilton tapped her foot impatiently as she waited to capture someone's attention. She'd been standing in the middle of half a dozen converging cosmetics counters on the main floor of Nordstrom's for the better part of five minutes and so far, not one salesperson had offered to help her. Admittedly, the staff all seemed to be busy, but where had all these customers come from? Had every woman in Boston suddenly run out of moisturizer? "Excuse me," she said to a young woman dressed head to toe in black (including leggings, despite the outside heat), but the girl chose to ignore her as she hurried past to service someone else.

Or maybe she just didn't notice me, Joan thought, recognizing that women became increasingly invisible to much of the outside world as they aged, even to other women. The older you got, the more you tended to blend into your surroundings, to become part of the wallpaper, your voice swallowed up by the noise around you, no longer heard or appreciated. Such a shame, really, because experience had given older women if not wisdom, then at least many more interesting things to say.

She did a slow spin around, trying to ignore the overpowering smell of conflicting perfumes, and catching sight of her reflection in a nearby mirror. The woman looking back at her was only vaguely familiar, being at least two decades older, ten pounds heavier, and an inch shorter than Joan remembered. "Who *are* you?" she asked. "And what have you done with Joan Hamilton?"

"I'm sorry," a voice chirped from somewhere beside her. "Did you say something?"

Joan spun toward the sound. A skinny young woman with braided black hair wrapped around her head like a towel was smiling in her direction, her eyes seemingly focused on something just beyond Joan's left ear. The name tag on her black sweater identified her as *Gray*. "Your name is Gray?" Joan asked.

"Like the color," the girl said.

"How unusual."

"Not really. There was another girl named

Gray in my class all through high school, and a boy named Grayson. And a friend of mine is dating a guy named Grayden. Not to mention, I know two Haydens, a Kayden, and a Tayden."

"Tayden?"

"I know, right?" She shrugged. "Can I help you with something?"

Joan was still trying to come to terms with all the Haydens, Kaydens, and Taydens. There were such interesting names now. Not like when she was a kid, when all the girls were named Sue or Carole or Mary. Or Joan, she realized, her lips curling into a frown.

"Something wrong?" Gray asked.

"Just trying to remember what I came in for."

"You're so cute," Gray said with a giggle.

I'm cute? Joan wondered. *When did I get cute?* She'd never been cute in her life. She decided it must be code for "old." "I need some moisturizer. And maybe some new lipstick. Usually I just go to the drugstore and buy whatever's on sale, but I don't know. I feel like treating myself. My skin's been feeling a little dry lately, and I have this big party to go to next week . . ." She broke off mid-sentence, realizing she was nattering on about something this young woman obviously couldn't give two figs about. And what century had *that* expression come from?

"Yeah? What kind of party?" Gray surprised her by asking. She pulled a nearby high-top chair toward them and motioned for Joan to sit down.

"My brother-in-law's eightieth birthday," Joan said, stepping up into the seat.

"Yeah? Wow. Eighty. Good for him. Do you mind my asking how old you are?"

"Seventy," Joan said, the word emerging as a sigh. Just the sound of it hit Joan right between the eyes.

"Well, you look fantastic. I never would have guessed. You have great skin for someone your age."

"Thank you." *I think.* "I still feel thirty." *Maybe forty.*

"Well, you look great. My grandmother is seventy and she looks way older than you do." Gray reached under the counter and pulled out a jar of something creamy and white. Then she gently pushed Joan's wispy blond hair away from her face and dabbed some of the thick cream onto her cheeks, massaging it in with delicate, but firm, fingers. "How do you like it?"

"Feels wonderful."

"It's the best. Use this every morning and

night and you'll see a difference in no time. Let me show you the proper way to apply it." She held a small mirror to Joan's face so she could watch her demonstrate the proper circular motion.

Joan cringed at the close-up view of the enlarged pores and lines that had laid siege to her face sometime during the last decade. The one good thing about the decline in your eyesight as you aged, she decided, was that you didn't notice the ravages of time unless you were wearing your glasses. Or someone was shoving a mirror up under your nose. "Do you have any eye creams?"

"We certainly do." A small, green bottle materialized between Gray's fingers, as if by magic. "This serum is a real miracle worker, and the good news is that you only need to use a tiny bit." She deposited a few drops under Joan's eyes, patting them gently with her fingertips until the thick liquid was completely absorbed. "And I'd really recommend this cream as well. It firms and lifts. Do you use masks?"

"Sorry. What?"

Another round, white jar miraculously appeared in the palm of the girl's hand. "Brush this on every other night, let it sit ten minutes, then apply the two eye treatments — first the serum, then the cream —

and finish up with the moisturizer. I swear, you'll be glowing. Plus, I think I have just the perfect lipstick for your coloring. Here," she said, rubbing something peachy-pink on the back of her hand and holding it out for Joan to examine. "Strong but subtle. What do you think?"

"I think you have a deal." Joan slid off the chair and reached into her purse for her credit card. "How much do I owe you?"

"Let's see," Gray said, toting up the charges. "That'll be fourteen hundred and twenty-three dollars and ninety-five cents. Plus tax."

Joan paused to let the figure sink in. Surely she'd heard the girl incorrectly. "Excuse me?"

"I know. Expensive, right? But you did say you wanted to treat yourself. And these products are top-of-the-line. Trust me. Come your husband's birthday party next week —"

"My brother-in-law," Joan corrected, sharper and louder than she'd intended.

"What?"

"It's my brother-in-law's birthday," Joan said, lowering her voice to a more appropriate level. "My husband is dead."

"Oh," Gray said, her smile disappearing. "I'm so sorry." She looked around the large, brightly lit space, as if searching for someone to come to her rescue. "So, are we doing this?" she asked when it became obvious that no one would.

That'll teach me to be nice to old ladies, Joan could almost hear her thinking. "Sure," she said. "Why not?" She handed Gray her credit card. What the hell? she thought. She could be dead by next week.

"When did I get cute?" she asked, throwing open the door to her condo and dropping her shopping bags at her feet.

"Mom?" Paige asked, walking down the hall toward her. "You were gone so long, I was starting to get worried. Are you okay?"

"The salesgirl said I was cute," Joan told her daughter. "When did I get cute?"

"I think it was around four o'clock yesterday afternoon." Paige glanced toward the bags on the floor. "I thought you were just going out for some moisturizer. What'd you do? Buy a lifetime supply?"

"I bought a few dresses."

"A few?"

"All right. Five."

"You bought five dresses?"

"I wanted something for your uncle's party and I couldn't make up my mind. You'll help me decide, then I'll take the others back."

A look of concern flooded Paige's face. "Are you sure you're okay?"

"Yes, darling. I'm fine," Joan assured her daughter. "Just feeling a little . . . I don't know . . . old."

"You aren't old."

"I'm not young. And don't you dare tell me you're as young as you feel, because right now I feel about a hundred." She retrieved her shopping bags from the floor.

"Here. Let me help you with those."

"Don't you dare," Joan warned, walking toward the living room and plopping down on the sofa, letting her purchases spread out at her feet.

Paige sank down beside her. "What's wrong, Mom?"

"Do you know anyone named Gray?"

"I don't think so. Why?"

"Apparently it's a very popular name these days, that and Grayden and Hayden and Tayden. Tayden, for God's sake. Who names a child Tayden?"

"I'm going to assume that's a rhetorical question."

"I guess every age has its more popular names," Joan mused. "When you were born, every other little girl was named Chloe or Heather."

181

"Good thing you named me Paige. Not too many of those."

Joan nodded. Paige had been her second choice for a name. Heather had been her first. But her sister-in-law had given birth first and beaten her to it, a fact Joan had never shared with her daughter.

It seemed that Heather had started stealing from Paige even before she was born.

"What's wrong, Mom?" Paige asked again.

"Have you ever looked at yourself in a three-way mirror?" Joan asked, changing the subject.

"Mom, for God's sake. Is that what's bothering you? Nobody looks good in those."

"My bum has completely flattened out and is now circling my knees," Joan continued, ignoring her daughter's interruption. "And where's my waist? I distinctly remember having a waist. Not to mention, my skin's all wrinkly and covered with these stupid little brown spots. And my legs . . . I used to have such great legs . . ."

"You still have great legs."

"Look at all these little purple veins," Joan said, standing up and pulling her black slacks down past her hips, letting them drop to her ankles.

"Did you just pull down your pants?"

Paige asked.

Joan promptly pulled them back up and flopped back on the sofa. "Sorry, darling. I'm obviously having a moment."

"It's quite a moment. Maybe I should call Sam and cancel."

"Don't be silly. You're not canceling any more dates." Joan gave her daughter's thigh a reassuring pat. "Did you ever hear from that other guy again?"

Paige shook her head.

"You could text *him,*" Joan suggested.

"No. I've already apologized. If he's interested, he'll get in touch. What are you going to do tonight?"

"Well, it'll probably take me half the night to put on my new moisturizers," Joan said, only half-joking. "And I was thinking I might go downstairs to the gym, try out those expensive new machines they put in." She sighed. She hadn't used the gym since she'd moved in, wasn't even sure what floor it was on.

"That's not such a bad idea," Paige said, pushing herself to her feet and crossing to the doorway. "Nice panties, by the way."

Joan laughed. "Thank you, darling."

Paige looked at her mother with worried eyes. "I love you, Mom. You know that, don't you?"

"I know, Wildflower," Joan said with a wink. "I love you, too."

CHAPTER NINETEEN

It turned out that the gym was located on the second floor.

Joan exited the elevator and followed the winding hallway past the closed doors of the men's and women's locker rooms, the pool, and the massage room, where according to the small sign hanging from the doorknob, a massage was currently in progress. "Didn't even know we had a massage room," Joan muttered as she proceeded around a curved corner, past the two guest suites, toward the recently renovated gym. Even before she reached it, she could hear the hum of the equipment radiating down the hall. *What am I doing?* she wondered as she raised her fob to unlock the door. She was seventy years old and hadn't exercised in years. Nothing she put herself through now was going to make a whit of difference. Her rear end wasn't going to get any higher or plumper no matter how many squats she did. Her stomach wasn't getting any flatter no matter how many sit-ups she performed. Her waist wasn't getting any smaller no matter how many weights she managed to hoist above her head. She should just go back upstairs and moisturize.

Not that almost fifteen hundred dollars' worth of expensive creams was going to make a difference either. Whatever had possessed her? She'd never been someone to throw money around carelessly. Unlike her late husband, who'd been as profligate as he was generous. Her eyes teared up with the memory of his handsome face. Even days away from death, he was handsome. At least in her eyes. *How dare you go and die on me,* she thought, hearing the click that unlocked the gym door and pulling it open. She might as well go in and have a look around.

The combination of smells hit her first — the newly installed gray carpet, the machines, the sweat, the Lysol. A white-haired man was doing a gentle jog on the second of four treadmills. He was dressed in blue gym shorts and his white T-shirt was spotted with perspiration. Thin wires connected his earphones to the TV attached to his machine, and he was watching one of the all-news channels. Joan recognized the picture filling the screen as the young woman who'd gone missing the previous week, although she couldn't remember her name. From what she could gather from the information scrolling across the bottom of the small screen, the girl's mutilated body had been discovered just hours ago in a landfill on the outskirts of town. There was speculation of a possible serial killer.

Poor girl, Joan thought, her eyes skipping down the row of machines — in addition to the treadmills, there were several elliptical and rowing machines, as well as two medieval-looking contraptions connected to an assortment of weights and pulleys — along the mirrored wall. She caught the reflection of an attractive older woman — *still at least a decade younger than me,* Joan thought, wistfully — doing a side plank at the far end of the rectangular room, under the supervision of a good-looking young man who was probably her trainer. The man was tall, tanned, and appropriately muscular, with closely cropped dark hair and an engaging smile. The black T-shirt stretching across his expansive chest read INSPIRATION, PERSPIRATION, VALIDATION. *Really?* Joan wondered. *It's as simple as that?*

"Well, hello, Joan," the woman called, scrambling to her feet and wiping the sweat from her forehead. "Haven't seen you in a while. How've you been?"

Joan fought to remember the woman's name, but it wouldn't come. Just another one of the great things about aging — the loss of easy recall. Names, dates, places, all once readily available, now gone. To be replaced by what? Chatter. Noise. Insignificant nonsense. And so arbitrary. Why could she remember the name of Kim Kardashian's second husband — Kris Humphries, for God's sake! — and not the name of people she saw regularly? Why did she even know who Kim Kardashian was? "I'm so sorry," she said, approaching the woman. "I've forgotten your name."

"Give me a minute," the woman said with a laugh. Then, "It's Linda."

Joan smiled, noting that Linda was wearing the latest in workout attire — navy leggings and a tight, hot-pink T-shirt that matched her equally hot-pink sneakers. She felt instantly self-conscious about her own pair of loose-fitting yoga pants, old white T, and dirty white running shoes. "I'm sorry," she said again.

"Please," Linda said. "It happens to me all the time." She checked her watch, then turned to her trainer. "We done here?"

"We are."

"Good. I'm running a little late. Do you

mind if I take off?"

"Pretty sure I can find my way out," her trainer said.

"Well, nice seeing you again," Linda said to Joan, wrapping a towel around her neck. "This is Rick, by the way. If you're ever in the market for a good trainer, he's your guy." A second later, she was gone.

Joan noticed that the man on the treadmill had also left the gym during the last few minutes. "I am, actually," she heard herself say.

Rick was checking his cellphone. "Excuse me?"

"In the market for a good trainer," Joan explained, although she hadn't been. "That is, if you're free . . ."

"You mean right now?"

"If you're free," she said again. What was she thinking? It was Saturday night. He was a good-looking man. Of course he wouldn't be free.

Rick shrugged, tucking his phone into the back pocket of his black sweatpants. "Well, my girlfriend just canceled on me, so, yes, as a matter of fact, I am free."

"Oh. Well. Good."

Neither moved.

"I charge a hundred dollars an hour," he said.

"Sounds reasonable." She had no idea if it was reasonable or not, but if she could spend almost fifteen hundred dollars on moisturizers, she could spend another hundred on a trainer.

"Okay. Well, then. Great. Should we get started?" He smiled, an expansive grin that drew his mouth up toward his eyes. "What are your goals?"

"Goals?"

"What you'd like to achieve," he explained.

"Let's see," Joan said, mulling through a variety of options. "I guess I'd like a flatter stomach, a plumper backside, and a smaller waist."

Rick paused a moment, his smile wavering. "Would you settle for better shoulders and arms?"

Afterward, they went out for a bite to eat.

"Probably not the healthiest choice," Joan said, finishing off her third slice of thin-crust margarita pizza, the muscles of her thighs and arms still twitching from the hour-long workout.

"Not the worst choice either," Rick said, taking a bite of his second. "Pizza's actually pretty nutritious when you don't cover it with junk. Although it wouldn't hurt for you

190

to eat a little slower," he advised, "take time to digest your food properly."

"I can't help it," Joan said. "I've always been a fast eater."

"Bet you hate red lights," Rick observed, carefully chewing his food.

Joan laughed. "They make me crazy. How'd you know?"

He just smiled. "You're pretty intense."

"I am?"

"That was no easy workout I put you through."

Joan smiled, feeling quite proud of herself for successfully mastering the series of squats, lifts, and other tortures he'd thrown her way. Pizza had been her reward to herself for not tossing in the towel after the first twenty minutes. "Thanks for joining me tonight," she said.

"Thanks for inviting me."

In truth, Joan had been surprised when he'd taken her up on her casual offer. She'd been expecting him to beg off, then disappear as quickly as possible. Did he have a thing for older women? she wondered now. Was he expecting more from the night than a few slices of margarita pizza?

What would she say — what would she *do* — if he were to suggest going back to her apartment for a little "dessert"?

Her husband had been her only lover for the almost forty years they were married, and they'd gradually developed a form of erotic shorthand. He knew exactly where to touch her, how much pressure to apply, what she liked, and just as important, what she didn't like. Could she adjust to another pair of hands — a much *younger* pair of hands — caressing her body?

"You said your girlfriend canceled your date?" she said, trying to stop the sudden flood of images — naked flesh and disparate body parts — somersaulting through her brain.

"Yeah. She has this big test on Monday, so she has to study."

"Really? What's she studying?"

He hesitated, as if he wasn't sure.

"You don't know what she's studying?"

"To be honest," he said, then hesitated again, as if deciding whether honest was what he really wanted to be, "she's in summer school. Finishing off her high school diploma." He produced a smile that could only be described as sheepish.

"High school? How old is she?" Joan bit down on her tongue. She hadn't meant to sound so shocked, so judgmental.

Rick took another measured bite of his pizza, chewing it even more deliberately than before. "Nineteen."

Joan almost burst into tears. *I'm pathetic,* she thought, her heart starting to race. A foolish old woman who'd let her ego-fueled fantasies trump her common sense. Just because a handsome young man was impressed that she'd managed a few deep knee bends without fainting didn't mean he wanted to have sex with her. No — the only thing Rick had been interested in tonight was a free meal. She took a deep breath, weighing her next question carefully. "Can I ask you something?"

"I'm thirty-four," he said.

"That wasn't my question."

Rick looked her in the eye. "Sorry. Guess I'm a little defensive on the subject. Some of the guys at the gym razz me about having a girlfriend fifteen years younger than I am."

"My husband was ten years older than me," Joan offered. "It was never an issue." It never was when it was the man who was older, she thought.

Rick smiled. "So, what's your question?"

It was Joan's turn to hesitate. "I was just wondering . . . Do men your age . . . I mean . . . this is going to sound silly . . ."

He waited, cocking his head to one side like an inquisitive puppy.

"Do men *your* age ever look at women *my* age . . . like, you know . . ."

"You mean sexually?"

"Yes."

He took a few seconds to consider his answer. "You want me to be honest?"

"Please."

"No," he said simply, dropping what was left of the pizza in his hand to his plate.

Joan laughed, wincing with the pain of a sudden, sharp stab to her chest.

"Sorry," he said, misinterpreting the wince. "I didn't mean to insult you. It's not that I don't find you attractive. You're a beautiful woman. God knows you're in great shape," he rattled on. "But, like I said, I have a girlfriend . . ."

"Oh, no! Please. I wasn't trying to come on to you, I swear," Joan said, feeling beyond mortified. There was another pointed jab to her chest. He was right, she thought. She'd wolfed down her pizza much too fast. "I was just curious, that's all. And I appreciate your honesty. I really do." She grimaced with the jolt of yet another sharp pain, a pain that was now spreading to her back and reaching into her jaw.

"Are you okay?" Rick asked, the discomfort in his eyes changing to worry.

Joan reached inside her purse and removed her cellphone, pushing it across the table toward him. "Could you call nine-one-one?" she asked, trying to keep calm. "And then could you call my daughter? Her name's Paige. She's in my contacts. Tell her to meet me at Mass General . . ."

The name of the hospital was the last thing Joan remembered speaking before she lost consciousness.

CHAPTER TWENTY

She was dreaming about her mother.

In her dream, she was a child of five, and her mother was chasing her around the kitchen table with the large wooden spoon she used for baking. The cake batter she'd been preparing to put in the oven was spreading across much of the linoleum floor, the result of Joan having snuck up behind her seconds earlier, shouting "boo!"

Joan felt her lips curve into a smile, recognizing this as a memory rather than a dream, although it was actually her mother's memory. Still, her mother had told that story so many times, Joan had usurped it as her own. It was the only time her mother had ever struck her, and even though it was more of a tap than an actual slap, and Joan had forgotten about it by nightfall, her mother had felt bad about it for the rest of her life, repeating that story to anyone who'd listen, as if it were a penance.

Mothers are like that, Joan thought. *They feel responsible — they feel* guilty *— about everything.*

Joan's smile was swallowed by a frown. Her mother hadn't had an easy life. She'd suffered three miscarriages before Joan was born, then two in the years following. Her marriage had been strained, money was always tight, she had a weak heart, and she'd died of a stroke a week before her sixty-fifth birthday. Two years later, Joan's father had succumbed to a massive heart attack at the age of sixty-eight.

Heart disease obviously ran in the family, which was why Joan had never expected to make it to seventy.

And yet here I am, she thought, sensing movement beside her but refusing to open her eyes, not ready to abandon her mother just yet. She marveled that, at her age, she still thought about her mother almost every day.

Would Paige think about her as often when she was gone? Joan wondered. Or would it be thoughts of her father that constituted the bulk of her reveries?

Not that she begrudged Paige the love she felt for her dad. Not that she could have competed, even if she'd tried. Robert Hamilton had been such an extraordinary man in every respect. As a businessman, a husband, a father, a lover. In all their years together, she'd never been tempted to stray, knowing she already had the best. After he died, she'd assumed her romantic life was a thing of the past. She certainly had no desire to marry again. She'd tucked away her libido and carried on.

She hadn't counted on the loneliness.

Was that what was responsible for her recent behavior? Joining a dating site and, even more bizarre, imagining that a man thirty-six years her junior could be attracted to her? She hadn't had even one response to her online profile, for heaven's sake. That should have told her something. And that something was that she was no longer considered desirable. By men of any age.

Who settles for a wrinkly old lady when even the most grizzled, balding, flat-bottomed old man could wrangle a date with an attractive woman half his age? Assuming his wallet was as fat as his belly, she thought, considering, only half-facetiously, whether she should add the word "wealthy" to her profile.

"Mom, are you all right?" Paige asked from somewhere above her head.

Joan pushed herself up in bed, hating the concern she heard in her daughter's voice.

When had their roles reversed? she wondered. When had Paige become the anxious parent, watching her with nervous eyes, arms outstretched to grab her should she stumble and fall? "I'm fine, darling." She opened her eyes and took a quick glance around her bedroom, trying to decide whether it was day or night. "What time is it?"

"Almost two o'clock. Monday," Paige added.

"I know it's Monday. Oh, my goodness." She'd only meant to take a short nap after lunch, as the doctor had suggested after signing her release from the hospital the previous afternoon.

"You were making faces," Paige told her.

"I was?"

"What were you thinking about?"

Joan shrugged, pretending not to remember.

"I have to leave in a few minutes," Paige said. "I have that job interview at three thirty. Do I look all right?"

"You look beautiful. I've always loved that suit. And blue is such a nice color on you."

"Thanks. I shouldn't be too long."

"You'll do great. I have a good feeling about this one."

"You say that about every interview,"

Paige reminded her. "Are you going to be okay alone?"

"Of course I am." Joan swung her legs out of bed, as if to underline her assertion. "You have to stop worrying about me, darling." She felt immediately guilty. It was her fault that Paige was so worried. It wasn't every day you got a phone call from a total stranger telling you your mother had suffered a possible heart attack and been rushed to the hospital. Her second such visit in less than a week.

Of course, it turned out that she hadn't had a heart attack at all, even though the emergency room doctor had decided to keep her in the hospital overnight for observation. "Looks like it was a combination of indigestion, muscle strain, and anxiety," he'd pronounced the next morning.

"I'm so embarrassed," Joan had said.

"Better safe than sorry," had come his automatic response.

"I'm sorry," Joan said now.

"For what?" Paige asked.

"For causing a scene. For ruining your date."

"We've been over this. You didn't ruin my date. As a matter of fact, if it'll make you feel better, you probably saved me."

"Saved you? From what? I thought you liked Sam."

"I do. That's part of the problem."

"Liking him is a problem?"

Paige shrugged.

"I'm sorry, darling. It's none of my business."

"Stop saying you're sorry. You have nothing to apologize for."

"I made you worry for nothing."

"I'm just happy there was nothing to be worried about."

"Bev calls it the age of hypochondria," Joan mused aloud, thinking of her sister-in-law.

Is it a headache or is it a brain tumor? Is it a muscle spasm or the first sign of ALS? Is it a heart attack or is it gas?" she heard Bev say in her breathy whisper. *"I mean, this should be the best time of our lives. The kids are grown. We have money. We have freedom. And yet, there's this constant specter of death sitting on our shoulders, just watching and waiting . . ."*

"Which reminds me," Paige said, interrupting the soliloquy in Joan's head and sending Bev's words scattering in all directions. "She phoned while you were sleeping, said to give her a call."

"Okay."

Bev was probably the last person Joan wanted to talk to. While their relationship had always been cordial, they'd never really been close, and since Heather had absconded with Paige's live-in boyfriend, they'd been even less so. Bev alternated between apologizing for her daughter's behavior and trying to excuse it. Joan wasn't interested in either apologies or justifications.

"What are you going to do for the rest of the afternoon?" Paige asked.

"I don't know. Maybe go for a walk."

"Nothing too strenuous."

"Nothing too strenuous," Joan repeated. "Now go to your interview. Knock their socks off."

"I'll try." Paige leaned over to kiss Joan's forehead. "Love you."

"Love you, too." She watched her daughter walk from the room, not moving till she heard the door to the apartment close behind her. Then she reached for the phone on the night table beside the bed, punching in her sister-in-law's number, then hanging up before it could connect.

Was there somebody else — *anybody* else — she could call? A friend, maybe? Except she really didn't have any friends. Not anymore. The bulk of her friends had been

Robert's friends, and those friendships had pretty much disappeared in the months after Robert died. The truth was that her daughter was her best friend, and that wasn't fair to Paige. It put too much responsibility on her slender shoulders. And the last thing Joan wanted was to be a burden.

She pushed herself off the bed and retrieved her purse from the mint-colored, overstuffed chair by the window, fishing inside it for her cellphone. She pulled it out and clicked on Autumn Romance, scrolling through the long list of available seniors for her profile. "Oh, my goodness," she said, noting that she had two recent responses.

The first was from a man calling himself Lonesome Dove. The accompanying photo was of an elderly gentleman with gray hair and a shy smile. He gave his age as eighty-two, and said he was a widower who liked opera, traveling, and detective fiction. Joan also liked the opera and traveling, and while she'd never been into detective fiction, she loved novels, so it would seem they had a few things in common.

Still, he was eighty-two.

Not that the twelve-year difference in their ages was insurmountable or even particularly relevant at this point. They were both adults. But he was *eighty-two*! Two years older than her brother-in-law, and four years older than her husband had been when he died. How many years — how many *good* years — did he have left?

She wasn't young anymore. Selfishly, she didn't want to spend whatever time she had left playing nursemaid. She'd already seen one man through the last year of a fatal illness, watched helplessly as his once-strong body and formidable will succumbed to the merciless assault of his disease. She'd watched as pain replaced hope in his eyes. She couldn't do it again.

She swiped left, watched Lonesome Dove disappear.

The second man called himself Simply Pete. Simply Pete said he was sixty-five and very fit, and his photograph — a tanned, nice-looking man in a T-shirt that showed off his sculpted biceps — seemed to bear that out. He was divorced and interested in women who were adventurous and outgoing.

"I'm adventurous and outgoing," Joan told his picture, swiping right before she could chicken out.

The phone on her nightstand rang.

Joan tossed her cellphone into her purse and answered the landline before it could ring again. "Hello?" she said, expecting to hear her sister-in-law's voice, reprimanding her for not returning her earlier call.

"Is Paige there?" she heard instead. A voice clogged with tears and filled with terror.

"Chloe?" Joan asked. "What's wrong?"

"It's Matt," Chloe cried. "He took the kids! I don't know what to do."

"Call the police," Joan said. "I'll be there as fast as I can."

CHAPTER TWENTY-ONE

Joan arrived at Chloe's house within forty minutes, despite the rush hour traffic, never having driven so fast, or so recklessly, in her entire life. Chloe was waiting for her at the front door, her cellphone in the palm of her hand, her beautiful face swollen from the nonstop parade of tears falling from her eyes.

"Where are the police?" Joan asked, ushering Chloe inside but leaving the front door open. "Did you call them?"

"They said there's nothing they can do, that we're not divorced or even legally separated, and that Matt's their father, which means no crime has been committed . . ."

"Okay. Okay. Tell me exactly what happened. Start from the beginning." Joan led Chloe into the living room and sat down beside her on the plum-colored velvet sectional, stepping on a stray piece of Lego and hearing it crack beneath the heel of her shoe. "Do you want some water?"

Chloe shook her head, spraying tears in both directions. "The kids were in day camp. The bus picks them up every morning and brings them home a little after three. Except this afternoon, there was no bus. I waited and waited. I was starting to get scared, thinking maybe there'd been an accident or something. So I called the camp and they told me that my husband had picked the kids up around two o'clock. And I started yelling, 'What do you mean, he picked them up?' and they said that they didn't have any instructions not to let him, that the kids seemed delighted to see him, and were quite excited to go with him, that I should have phoned them if there were problems. And it's true. I never called them. But it never occurred to me that he would do something like this . . ."

"Okay, okay. Slow down. Take a deep breath," Joan advised, lifting Chloe's hands inside her own and noting they were ice cold. "Have you spoken to Matt?"

"I've called his cell a million times. He's not picking up. I called his office. They said he left early and could they take a message? I didn't know what to do, so I called Paige."

"She's at a job interview."

"I'm so sorry to bother you. I didn't mean for you to have to come over . . ."

Joan brushed away Chloe's concerns with a shake of her head and a wave of her hand. "You said you spoke to the police and they told you there's nothing they can do?"

"They said that no crime has been committed," Chloe repeated. "That under the circumstances, it's too early to put out an Amber Alert, and that all we can do for the time being is wait. If Matt doesn't bring the kids home by suppertime, then I should call them again and they'll send someone over to talk to me." Panic pushed its way through Chloe's tears. "You don't think he'd hurt them, do you?"

"Do you?" Joan asked, alarmed at the prospect.

Chloe shook her head. "I don't think so, no. I mean, he has a temper, but he's never . . . but I don't know. He's so angry. Oh, God. Oh, God. If he hurts them, I'll die."

"Okay, okay. Try to calm down," Joan urged. "We're getting way ahead of ourselves here."

"Where are they? Where has he taken them?"

"Is it possible there was anything that was arranged before you kicked him out? A birthday party or a dentist appointment?"

"No. I'm the one who always takes them to things like that. Oh, God. Why is he doing this?"

"I don't know," Joan said, feeling increasingly useless.

"What if he just takes off with them and disappears? What if I never see them again?"

"That's not going to happen," Joan told her forcefully. "Matt has a job and a life here in Boston. He's not just going to abandon that." She heard her phone ping in her purse. "Maybe you should call the bank."

"The bank? Why?"

"Do you have a joint account?"

"Yes. Why? You think he's closed it?"

"I think you should call the bank."

"I have to find their number." Chloe ran into the kitchen.

Minutes later, Joan heard her talking on her landline. She released a deep sigh, pushing her fine hair away from her forehead and extricating her cellphone from her purse, expecting to see a message from Paige. Instead she saw another response from Simply Pete. She opened it, then fell back against the sofa's pillows in horror. Simply Pete had sent her a message — *Just how adventurous are you?* — accompanied

209

by another photo — this one a close-up of him from the waist down, a significant bulge protruding from his skimpy, leopard-print thong. "Oh, my good God."

"What?" Chloe asked, reentering the room.

Joan passed her the cellphone. "A romantic gesture from a would-be suitor."

Chloe's face filled with disgust. "What the hell is the matter with these guys? Do they honestly believe women are turned on by this sort of thing?"

"Beats me," Joan said, clicking off the site. "This is a whole new world for me. Were you able to find anything out with the bank?"

"The good news is that the money's still in the account," Chloe said, plopping down next to Joan. "The bad news is that it's only a few hundred dollars. I asked them if Matt had any other accounts, but they said they couldn't give out that kind of information." She glanced aimlessly around the room. "What am I going to do now?"

"You're going to sit here beside me," Joan told her, "and we're going to wait until Matt brings the children home."

"Really?" Chloe asked, her eyes once again flooding with tears. "You're not going to leave me?"

Joan took the younger woman in her arms and held her tight. "I'm not going to leave you."

It was closing in on six o'clock when Matt brought the children home.

"Oh, my God! Oh, my God!" Chloe cried, racing to the front door and pulling Josh and Sasha into her arms, smothering the surprised looks on their faces with kisses.

Thank heavens, Joan thought, watching from the living room.

"You're squeezing too tight," Josh protested, wriggling free of his mother's embrace as Matt stepped inside the foyer and closed the door behind him.

"Daddy took us to the movies and then McDonald's," Sasha said. "I had French fries *and* Chicken McNuggets."

"She didn't finish all her fries," Josh said.

"Did, too," Sasha protested.

"No, you didn't," her brother insisted.

"Okay, okay, you guys," Matt interrupted. "No fighting. Remember what I told you. Mommy's going through a bit of a hard time, and she needs you to be extra good."

"Excuse me — what?" Chloe said.

"Is your tummy hurting?" Sasha asked her mother.

"No, sweetheart. I'm fine. I was just worried, that's all."

"Why were you worried?" Josh asked, looking at her with his father's eyes, a hint of accusation in his voice. "We were with Daddy."

"I didn't know that. Daddy forgot to tell me."

"Sorry about that. Guess Daddy has a lot on his mind these days," Matt said, catching sight of Joan for the first time. "Who the hell are you?"

Sasha gasped. "Daddy said a bad word."

"I know you," Josh said to Joan. "You were here last week."

"Yes, I was," Joan said. "And I had such a good time that I had to come back and see you again."

"Would you mind taking the kids upstairs while I talk to my husband?" Chloe asked her. "Just for a few minutes."

"It's too early to go to bed," Josh said.

"Well, maybe we could watch some TV," Joan said.

"*SpongeBob?*" Sasha asked, slipping her hand through Joan's as Josh raced ahead up the stairs.

Chloe nodded. "Thank you," she whispered to Joan.

"Nice meeting you, whoever you are," Matt called after them.

"What the hell do you think you're doing?" Joan heard Chloe demand as she neared the top of the stairs.

"If you're going to yell, I'm going to leave," Matt said with the kind of passive-aggressive calm that made Joan want to go back downstairs and punch him in his handsome face, put a dent in his perfect nose.

She stopped on the landing, straining to hear more of the conversation above the newly turned-on TV in the master bedroom.

"You had no right to take them without telling me," Joan heard Chloe say.

"I had every right. I'm their father."

"Is this the way it's going to be?" Chloe asked.

"That's up to you. You're the one who's being unreasonable."

"*I'm* being unreasonable?"

There was a long pause.

"Look, Chloe," Joan heard Matt continue. "You asked for this fight. All I want is to come home and for us to be a family again."

"And you think that pulling stunts like this is going to help your cause?"

"Just trying to show you how complicated things can get."

"Meaning what?"

"Meaning you need to think long and

213

hard about what you're doing to this family."

"What *I'm* doing," Chloe repeated. "What about what you've already done?"

Joan could almost see Matt shrug. "I can't change what's happened. You're responsible for what happens next."

"I think you'd better leave."

Another pause. "Next move is up to you, Chloe. But I wouldn't wait too long, if I were you."

"Are you threatening me?"

Joan heard the incredulousness in Chloe's voice, followed by the snicker in Matt's. The next thing she heard was the sound of the front door slamming shut.

CHAPTER TWENTY-TWO

She was back in Nordstrom's, returning all five of the dresses she'd purchased on the weekend, when she heard the familiar, breathy voice behind her. "Joan? Is that you?"

Run, Joan thought, knowing that she couldn't, that she was trapped among the rows of expensive designer dresses as securely as if she were locked inside a metal cage. She forced her lips into a smile and swiveled toward her sister-in-law.

In stark contrast to Joan's black T-shirt and jeans, Bev was wearing white pants and a stylish navy blazer over a crisp white blouse. Her dark hair was pulled into a neat chignon at the nape of her neck, and long, heart-shaped rhinestone earrings dangled from her ears. The earrings slapped against Joan's cheeks as Bev stepped forward to embrace her, kissing the air on both sides of Joan's head, then standing back to take a good look at her. "Well, you're looking well. That's a relief. I was starting to worry. You don't return my calls, you don't answer your cell . . ."

"I'm sorry. I've been a little preoccupied lately."

"Something wrong?"

Joan did a silent tally of recent events: she'd spent the better part of last night trying to comfort her daughter's distraught and panic-stricken best friend; her recent attempts to rejoin the dating world had resulted in a hospital stay and a picture of a man in a leopard-print thong; and her presence was expected at a party for her brother-in-law's eightieth birthday, while her own husband, the man's identical twin, lay dead in the ground.

She sighed, knowing she was being unfair. Bev had every right to celebrate her husband's birthday. Such occasions *should* be celebrated. "Everything's good," Joan said. She had no desire to discuss her recent travails with Bev, whose expressions of sympathy tended to be so over-the-top, they had the strange effect of making you feel worse.

"Everything all right with Paige?"

"Fine," Joan said. "She's great."

"*Is* she? That's so good to hear. Has she

found a new job?"

There followed the questions Bev didn't ask, but Joan heard anyway: *Is she still pining over Noah? Is she finally ready to forgive Heather for stealing him away?*

"Not yet," Joan said, answering the question Bev *had* asked. "But she had a very promising interview yesterday. So we're keeping our fingers crossed."

Bev promptly crossed the manicured fingers of both her hands and held them up. "Oh, she'll get it. I'm sure," she said with a vehemence that suggested the opposite. "She's so bright. How could someone not want her?" Her face turned almost as red as her nail polish. "I meant . . ."

"I know what you meant."

"I'm sure she'll find a new beau in no time, too," Bev added, only making matters worse.

Joan wasn't sure if she was more surprised that her sister-in-law had raised the subject of Noah, however obliquely, or that she'd used the word "beau."

"Actually, there's someone already," Joan said.

"Really?"

"Well, it's still pretty new," Joan backtracked, already regretting having spoken. "You'll meet him on Saturday."

"She's bringing him to the party?"

"I've been meaning to call and ask if that's all right."

"Are you kidding? That's wonderful. Heather will be so pleased. She's hated the chill that's been between them ever since, well, you know . . ."

Joan nodded.

"It's not really Heather's fault, you know," Bev surprised her by continuing.

"No? Whose is it?"

"Noah had been pursuing her for months, texting, sending flowers. He finally wore her down."

"I know. Poor thing. What choice did she have? Oh, wait," Joan continued without pause. "She *did* have a choice. She could have told the creep to bugger off."

"I had no idea you were still so angry," Bev said.

Joan shrugged. Truthfully, neither had she. She'd never been that fond of Noah, always thought Paige could do better. But she could never forgive anyone who hurt her child.

"Heather said she ran into the two of you last week and that you barely acknowledged her. I told her she must be exaggerating, that her aunt would never be that rude . . ."

"No," Joan said. "She wasn't exaggerating."

Bev looked as if she were about to burst into tears.

"Look," Joan said. "I'm sorry if I've upset you. None of this is your fault, and neither one of us likes to see our daughters hurting. So, can we just leave it at that and agree not to discuss it further?"

Bev nodded, a weak smile playing with her bright red lips. "I see someone's been shopping," she said after several seconds, her voice tentative, her eyes wary.

"Thought I'd buy a new dress for the party. That is, if you still want us there. Believe me, I'd understand if you . . ." *Please say you don't want us there.*

"Of course we want you there," Bev said immediately. "Ted would be devastated if you weren't at his party. You know how fond he is of both you and Paige."

It was true. Her brother-in-law had always adored his niece, often proclaiming that he was sure there'd been a mix-up at the hospital and that Paige, not Heather, was really his offspring. And Michael and his wife would be flying in from New Jersey for the festivities, so how could Joan and Paige not be there?

219

"Can I see?" Bev pointed at the shopping bags.

"Actually, I'm returning these. I may be a while . . ." Joan glanced around the brightly lit space for a salesperson, spotting an exceptionally handsome young man lingering in the next aisle. "Please don't let me keep you."

"Oh, you're not keeping me. Looks like we had the same idea. Heather wants a new dress for the party, too, and I offered to treat her."

Joan tried not to blanch at the renewed mention of her niece. "She's meeting you?" She raised her hand in the air and snapped her fingers in the direction of the handsome young man. "Excuse me. Could you help me here, please?"

"With pleasure," he said, approaching. "Except I don't work here."

"Oh. I'm so sorry. I saw you standing there and I thought . . ."

"No problem," he said, touching her arm before leaving her side.

That was odd, Joan thought, his touch lingering. She wondered how long he'd been hovering, if he'd been eavesdropping on her conversation with Bev. *Don't be silly,* she admonished herself with her next breath. Why on earth would a gorgeous young man

220

be interested in the conversation of two old ladies?

A salesman approached. He was wearing a black jacket that was at least two sizes too small for his already shockingly slender frame, and his skinny black pants ended at mid-calf, highlighting clean-shaven legs and bare feet inside pointed, black suede loafers. His blue-black hair was long on one side and shaved on the other. Clearly a fashion statement of some sort, Joan thought, forgetting about the gorgeous young man and trying to picture what the salesman's haircut would look like on her. "Can I help you?" he asked, his voice pinched, his accent unrecognizable.

"I'd like to return these dresses." Joan began pulling them out of the bags.

"All of them?"

"Yes. All five. I bought them on Saturday."

"Was there something wrong with them?"

"They just didn't look right."

"Pity," he said, taking the bags from her hands and heading toward the nearest counter, Joan and Bev following.

"This is a nice one," Bev said as the salesman started removing the dresses from the bags. She held up a teal-blue cocktail dress with a jeweled collar. "I would have thought it suited you."

"Too high-waisted," Joan said.

"And this one?" Bev ran her hand across a black sheath with a scooped neck.

"Too low-cut."

"But what on earth were you thinking with this one?" Bev's long, thin nose crinkled in disapproval as she examined a blush-pink dress with rows of ruffles crisscrossing the bodice.

"I don't know. I guess I thought the ruffles would be flattering."

"On a twelve-year-old, maybe. Oh, God. This one's even worse." She held up, then quickly dropped, a floral print A-line midi to the counter. "Looks like something we wore back in the sixties."

"I think that's why I liked it."

"Well, those days are dead and gone, thank goodness. I, for one, don't miss them a bit." Bev looked over the last of the five dresses — a beautiful beige silk dress with pearl buttons and long, loose-flowing sleeves that Joan could barely remember purchasing. "What was the matter with this one?"

Joan stared at the dress. "I don't know." In truth, she hadn't bothered trying that one on, so discouraged had she been with the others.

"It's perfect for you. I insist you try it on and let me have a look."

"I thought you were meeting Heather."

Bev checked her watch. "I still have twenty minutes. Besides, she'll be late. She always is. Now go on. I insist."

"She's right," the salesman said. "I think the dress will look divine."

Joan decided there was no point in arguing. The faster she tried on the damn dress, the faster she'd be out of here. She had no desire to risk another run-in with her niece. "Okay. Fine. Give it to me."

"There's a little sitting area just outside the fitting rooms where your friend can wait," the salesman said, leading the way.

Joan emerged from the fitting room minutes later, wearing the dress. She did a little twirl in front of her sister-in-law. "What do you think?"

"I think it's perfect. What do *you* think?"

"I think you're right."

Bev clapped her hands. "Wonderful. Then it's settled. She'll keep this one," she told the salesman, who'd returned to check on them.

"Excellent," he said. "So we'll only be returning four. I'll see you back at the counter whenever you're ready."

"Thank you," Joan told Bev minutes later, as they waited for the salesman to rewrap the dress.

"What for?"

"If it weren't for you, I wouldn't have my beautiful new dress."

Bev's hands fluttered girlishly around her face. "No thanks necessary. I'm just glad I was able to help." She stared at Joan, as if waiting for her to speak.

"Well," Joan obliged. "Till Saturday night."

"Till Saturday," Bev said. "You know that I just want everybody to get along and be happy."

Would that it were so easy, Joan thought, catching a streak of panic flash through Bev's eyes. "What?" she asked, turning around, although she already knew what — *who* — she would see.

"Hi, Mom," Heather said. "Auntie Joan. Always a pleasure."

"Heather," Joan acknowledged, all but wresting the bag from the salesman's hands. "Well, if you'll excuse me, I should get going."

"See what I mean?" Joan heard Heather say to her mother as she was walking to the escalator. "Could she be any more rude?"

Joan didn't hear Bev's answer. She was too busy trying to breathe.

CHAPTER TWENTY-THREE

She decided to walk home, partly for the exercise and partly because she wanted to clear her head of all things Heather before seeing Paige. She wondered how many minutes — make that seconds — had elapsed before Bev told her daughter about the new man in Paige's life. No doubt the news that Paige would be bringing him to the party would influence Heather's choice of what dress to buy. No way would she chance being outshone by her cousin. Knowing Heather, who no longer had Paige's taste to rely on, and whose own imagination had always been limited at best, that meant she'd probably select something tight, low-cut, and ultra-sparkly.

Joan did a mental run-through of Paige's closet, trying to select something from the predominantly low-key options, not finding anything with enough "wow" factor. Paige had already nixed the idea of purchasing anything new for a party she was loath to attend in the first place, insisting that she wasn't going to compete with Heather on any level.

Of course, that didn't mean Joan couldn't compete on her behalf.

Maybe she'd buy something for Paige. If Bev could treat Heather to a new dress, well, then, she could certainly do the same for *her* daughter.

Except she couldn't.

Paige had made her feelings crystal clear, and Joan had to respect her wishes. Her daughter was an adult, and her mind was made up. There would be no new dress, and that was that.

Damn that Heather anyway.

Not doing a very good job of clearing my head, Joan thought. "Time to move on," she announced to a photograph of a comely young model, whose picture took up half the large front window of a hairdressing salon sandwiched between two upscale designer boutiques. The model was sporting a similar haircut to the one worn by the oddly accented salesperson at Nordstrom's — chin-length on one side and closely cropped on the other.

Joan studied her own reflection in the glass, trying to superimpose her face onto the model's, to fit her forehead under the girl's straight bangs, to picture what it would be like with only half a head of hair.

It was then that she spotted another reflection, this one of a young man — the same man who'd touched her arm in Nordstrom's earlier? — leaning against the door of a shop across the street, watching her. She spun around.

But if anyone had been standing there, he wasn't there now.

So now she was seeing things. And it wasn't just a bunch of squiggles and bright lights. Joan shook her head, wondering if hallucinations of handsome young men could qualify as an ocular migraine.

In the next second, she was pushing open the hairdressing salon's heavy glass door and approaching the buxom brunette behind the reception counter.

"Can I help you?" the receptionist asked.

Joan glanced back at the window, then took a deep breath. "I was wondering if anyone was available to do my hair."

"Mrs. Hamilton?" the concierge asked, as if he wasn't sure, as she entered the beige marble lobby of her condominium.

"Yes, Eddy. It's me," she told the clearly startled young man, stopping briefly to pat the newly shorn side of her hair. "What do you think?"

"Oh, my God, look at you!" a voice exclaimed before he could respond. "It's Linda," the woman reminded Joan, leaving the bank of elevators where she'd been standing. She was wearing the same hot-pink top and navy leggings as when Joan had last seen her at the gym, and the slight flush to her cheeks told Joan she'd probably been out jogging. "Are you all right?" she asked, approaching cautiously. "Rick told me about having to call an ambulance for you the other night. What happened?" Her eyes circled Joan's hair. "Did the doctors have to shave your head?"

"God, no. Nothing like that. It was just indigestion. I'm fine." Joan's fingers fluttered around her head without landing. "I've just been to the hairdresser's."

"You did that on purpose?"

"Oh, God. Is it that bad?"

Linda quickly backpedaled. "No. Of course not." She coughed into her hand. "You just caught me by surprise, that's all."

"I felt like a change."

"You got it."

"Oh, dear." Tears filled Joan's eyes. What had she done?

"No, no," Linda said. "It's just *so* differ-

228

ent, that's all. Once you get used to it, it's actually quite . . . cute."

"Cute?" There was no mistaking the horror in Joan's voice.

"Flattering," Linda amended.

"Really?"

"Absolutely."

"I don't know what possessed me," Joan said as the elevator doors opened and a man exited, glancing quickly at Joan before averting his eyes. "I think I scared him."

"Nonsense," Linda said, leading Joan into the now empty elevator. "Really, the more I look at you, the more I like it." She coughed into her hand a second time, a sure tell she was lying. "I wish I had the guts to do something like that. But Jason likes my hair long, so what can I do?" She waved both hands toward her straight, shoulder-length auburn hair. "Gotta keep your man happy." The elevator doors opened onto the sixth floor. "You have time for a cup of tea?"

Joan was about to refuse, then decided she wasn't quite ready to face Paige's reaction. "Tea sounds great." She followed Linda down the beige-and-brown-carpeted corridor to her apartment.

Linda unlocked her door and pushed it open, stepping inside the gold-flecked marble foyer. "Hello? Anybody home? Ja-

229

son, honey?" She walked toward the kitchen on her right. "Guess he's not here. Thank God," she added, not quite under her breath, motioning for Joan to have a seat at the newspaper-strewn, marble-topped island in the middle of the black-and-stainless-steel kitchen. "Not that I don't adore the man," Linda continued as she filled a kettle with water, "but ever since he retired, he's always . . . underfoot. Breakfast, lunch, dinner. I don't get two minutes to myself. I turn around, there he is. If I'm going out, it's 'Where are you going? What are you doing? When will you be back? What's for lunch?' He's making me crazy. Well, you know how it is."

"No, actually, I don't." For the second time since running into Linda, Joan's eyes filled with tears. Even after her husband had retired from running the construction company he'd cofounded with his brother, Robert Hamilton had continued to be active, taking Life-long Learning courses at Boston University, reading everything he could get his hands on, playing tennis twice a week. Even a terminal diagnosis had barely slowed him down.

What she wouldn't have given to have him always underfoot!

The pink lingering on Linda's cheeks immediately disappeared. "I'm so sorry. I forgot. What a stupid thing to say! I'm really so sorry."

"It's okay."

"How long has it been?"

"Two years."

"You must miss him terribly."

"I do."

"He had a twin brother, didn't he?"

Joan nodded.

Linda smiled. "I remember riding up in the elevator with the two of them one day, and I swear I couldn't tell them apart. Did you ever get them confused?"

"God, no. To me, they didn't look alike at all." It was true. While Joan had always found her husband to be an incredibly sexy man, she'd never been remotely attracted to his brother.

The kettle whistled that the water had come to a boil, and a minute later, Joan was sitting in Linda's art-filled, gold-and-white living room, holding an oversized blue mug filled with steaming hot tea that smelled of mint and strawberries. Linda was perched at the end of a white overstuffed chair to her left. Between them stood a six-foot-high bronze sculpture that resembled a giant Oscar.

"So, what did you think of my trainer?"

Linda asked.

"He was great," Joan told her.

"Yeah, he's the best. I'm sorry I had to run out on you like that."

"Oh, that's —"

"We had this dinner party to go to," Linda continued before Joan could finish her thought, "and I still had to shower and wash my hair. You know the drill." She stole a glance at Joan's head. "Well, I guess that won't be much of a problem for you now."

"Is it really that bad?" Joan asked.

"No," Linda assured her. "Besides, it's just hair, right? It'll grow back in no time."

Joan took a sip of her tea, felt it burn the tip of her tongue, and cried out in pain.

"Are you okay?" Linda asked, leaning so far forward in her chair that she seemed in danger of falling off.

"Yes. Fine," Joan said, calculating how fast she could gulp down her tea without scalding her throat, and get the hell out of here without appearing even more unhinged than she already did. "So, how was the party?"

"It was okay. The hostess isn't the best cook, but she has some interesting friends." She gasped.

This time it was Joan leaning forward in her chair. "What's wrong?"

Linda lowered her mug to the white slate

coffee table in front of them. "There was this man. Harold . . . Harry . . . yes, Harry. Harry Gatlin. That's it. Tall, nice-looking, a retired professor, his wife died maybe three years ago . . . a lovely man. What do you think?"

"What do I think about what?"

"Would you like to meet him?"

"What?" What was happening?

"Well, it just occurred to me . . . You're both around the same age, you lost your husband, he lost his wife. You're both very . . . interesting." Another furtive glance at Joan's hair.

"I don't think so," Joan said.

"Are you seeing someone?"

"No, but —"

"Then, come on. He's a doll. Trust me. He's well traveled, cultured, funny." She laughed. "He was telling me about his attempts at online dating. Real horror stories. Can you imagine doing something like that?" she asked, as Joan squirmed in her seat.

"Still, I give him credit. It's not easy putting yourself out there. Tricky enough when you're young, but at our age . . . So, what do you say? Can I make a few subtle inquiries?"

Joan doubted there was anything that the

woman sitting across from her could say or do that might be considered remotely subtle. Still, anything would be an improvement over the likes of Simply Pete and his leopard-print thong. She rose decisively to her feet. "Sure, why not?"

"That's the spirit."

Joan carried her mug back into the kitchen, depositing it in the stainless-steel sink. "Thanks for the tea." She turned around to find Linda gathering up the newspapers strewn across the island countertop.

"Isn't it awful about that poor girl?" Linda was saying, pointing to the picture of Tiffany Sleight on the front page. "They're saying she was raped and tortured." She shuddered, accompanying Joan to the front door. "So, I'll call you after I speak to Harry."

"I'm curious," Joan said, stopping in the doorway. "What are you going to tell him about me?"

"That there's this lovely woman in my building I think he should meet."

"What about my hair?"

Linda paused. "Why don't we let that be a surprise?"

CHAPTER TWENTY-FOUR

He hates surprises, always has. They have a way of turning into disasters.

Like the time his mother decided to throw a surprise party for his father's fortieth birthday, and she invited all his friends, and made all his favorite foods, and even bought a stupid birthday cake, one of those gooey, sugary concoctions like the kind you had when you were a kid, with lots of icing and rainbow-colored flowers running amok across the top.

Well, her husband surprised her, all right — by not coming home until well after all the guests had gone home, the smell of alcohol on his breath, the scent of another woman on his fingers. And when she'd dared to get angry, he'd responded by scooping up a fistful of that gooey white icing and forcing it down her throat, then grinding what was left of it into her face and hair.

The next morning, the remnants of last night's surprise lay smeared across the kitchen floor, like a coat of sticky varnish, and his mother sat nursing a swollen eye. He could have told her this would happen, had she been smart enough to ask for his opinion. Of course, brains weren't exactly her strong suit.

Truth to tell, she got what she deserved.

So much for surprises.

Which is why he's always taken such pains with his preparations, and why he feels so blindsided, so betrayed, by the events of the last several days. He'd calculated everything so carefully, down to the most insignificant detail, only to see his meticulous planning backfire when circumstances beyond his control threatened to ruin everything.

Take Tiffany Sleight.

Yes, please, as the old joke goes, *somebody take her.*

He'd spent weeks wooing that bitch online, going slow, teasing her with compliments, giving her his best bad-boy-in-need-of-a-good-woman persona, advancing only to withdraw, answering some of her texts within minutes, waiting days to respond to others, whetting her appetite while keeping her off balance, setting up two separate assignations and then not showing up to either, pleading last-minute cold feet and a fear of rejection, then begging for a chance to redeem himself, "treating her mean to keep her keen."

And it had worked, as he knew it would, as it always did.

He'd been confident that after having been stood up twice, sweet Tiffany would be loath to confide in her friends that she was setting herself up for a possible strike number three. And even if she did tell someone, so what? The name he'd given her was as fake as his excuses. The minute he showed his handsome face, she'd be putty in his hands.

And everything had unfolded exactly as scripted. Any trepidations she might have had dissolved the minute they locked eyes. All it took was thirty minutes of pretending to be interested in every stupid word she uttered, and she'd followed him willingly into the night, into his apartment, into his trap.

"Why are you doing this?" sweet Tiffany had asked, her hands shackled behind her, the tears streaming down her cheeks disappearing into the rope around her neck. A silly question.

What could he say, after all? Because he could? Because he enjoyed it? Because he hated the lemon scent of her cheap perfume? Because she was too dumb to live? How about . . . all of the above?

He'd finished her off relatively quickly — that lemon scent was making him nauseous — then disposed of her in a landfill outside of town, reasoning that by the time anyone discovered her body — *if* anyone discovered her body — she would be nothing but a pile of foul-smelling bones. He hadn't figured on someone's dog escaping his yard and rummaging through the mountain of garbage in a desperate search for food, unearthing the poor girl's rotting remains while there was still enough of her left to identify.

That was the first surprise.

The resulting front-page news had put the city on edge. There was talk of a possible serial killer. And while part of him was pleased to have his work acknowledged, however obliquely, he feared that the women of Boston might not be as quick as they'd been to risk their lives for a handsome stranger.

He needn't have worried. There was no shortage of stupid women.

Take Nadia.

Yes, please. Somebody take her.

Nadia had been both pretty and not too bright. She'd told him stories of growing up poor in Romania, and of the overly handsy boss in the nearby suburb of Newton whose employ she'd been forced to flee. She even gave a pretty good blow job, not always the easiest thing to accomplish with a knife pressed to your throat. Best of all, she'd made such a considerate corpse, leaving only a minimum of mess for him to clean up.

By the time he'd returned from his little surveillance mission at Faneuil Hall, Nadia's muscles had started losing their rigidity, making her arms and legs easier to manipulate. He'd stuffed her into two overlapping heavy-duty garbage bags, thrown her clothes, a bunch of rags, and the remains of their dinner on top of her, and waited till the early morning hours to carry her out to the trunk of his car.

Which was when he ran into surprise number two.

Mrs. Imogene Lebowski.

The stupid old bat owned the three-story rooming house that he was temporarily calling home. She lived on the ground floor and rented out the top two. He'd found her through Airbnb, and quickly snapped up the third-floor furnished apartment, which had proved ideal for his purposes. Imogene, in turn, was thrilled to have such a reliable, good-looking young man for a tenant, especially since he would be around for a few months. Unlike most guests, who were usually gone within weeks, if not days.

He loved the transients and tourists who filed through the second-floor unit. They moved in; they moved out. In between, they kept to themselves and minded their own business. They had no interest in making friends or sniffing around where they didn't belong. If he passed them on the stairs, he kept his head down and kept moving. They did the same.

It was perfect.

As was Mrs. Imogene Lebowski, who was eighty-eight years old and generally sound asleep before ten.

Except, of course, for the night he went to dispose of Nadia's body.

He shuddered at the memory, watching himself struggling down the two flights of stairs with the garbage bags containing her body. He made it to the bottom and was reaching for the door reserved for renters when it suddenly opened and there stood Imogene.

She was wearing a long, blue nightgown and a look of total confusion. Her feet were bare.

"Mrs. Lebowski?" he asked, as shocked to

see the octogenarian as she was to see him. "What are you doing here? Are you all right?"

Truthfully, he didn't give a rat's ass how she was. He cared only that she was there, her watery gray eyes fixed on the garbage bag on the floor behind him. Had he made more noise than he'd realized when stuffing Nadia's body inside it? Had he woken up the old bat, arousing her suspicions?

"Who are you?" she asked.

"Who *am* I?" he repeated, wondering what game she was playing.

"What are you doing in my house?"

"I'm your tenant, Mrs. Lebowski. Don't you know me?"

"Of course I know you," she said, although her eyes said otherwise. "What are you doing?"

"Just throwing out a bunch of old crap. What are *you* doing?"

Imogene Lebowski sighed. The sigh said she had no idea.

Either she was sleepwalking or she was having some sort of seizure. Or maybe it was the onset of dementia. He didn't know and he didn't care. All he cared about was getting away from her as fast as he could. "Mrs. Lebowski," he began. "I don't think you should be out now. It's two o'clock in the morning. You should go back to bed."

If she found it odd that he was throwing things out at two in the morning, she gave no such indication. She just stood there. Staring at the large green garbage bags containing Nadia's body.

"Mrs. Lebowski," he repeated. Then, laying a gentle hand on her arm, as he'd done with Joan Hamilton in Nordstrom's that afternoon, "Imogene."

A coquettish smile appeared at the corners of her lips. When she spoke, her voice fluttered girlishly between octaves. "You're a very handsome young man," she said. "Has anyone ever told you that?"

He lowered his chin modestly. *You've got to be kidding me,* he thought. "Thank you. Now, I really think you should be getting back to bed."

"Could you help me?"

For an instant, he thought she might be propositioning him. Then he saw the look of fear in her eyes and realized she wasn't sure where her bed *was. Shit,* he thought. Escorting her back to her room meant leaving Nadia's body at the foot of the stairs, unattended, for at least five minutes. He didn't know if the tenant in the second-floor unit was home or not. What if he was out and came back to discover the bag lying

242

there? What if he peeked inside? What if he called the police? Shit. *Shit.*

Still, what choice did he have? If he refused, he and Imogene could be standing here till morning. "Okay," he said, taking her elbow and leading her into the warm night air.

Luckily, she'd left the front door unlocked, and he guided her inside the foyer, leaving the door open as he escorted her to the master bedroom at the back of the house. The place had that "old people" smell, he was thinking as he maneuvered her gently toward her bed. "My daughter wants to put me in a home," she confided as he was tucking her inside the wrinkled, stale-smelling sheets.

"Get some sleep," he said, wondering if he should do everyone a favor and simply finish her off now, save her daughter the trouble and expense of putting her in a home. It would be so easy, he thought, to press a pillow over her nose and mouth until she stopped breathing.

Although it would probably be more fun to strangle her, to watch those watery gray eyes turn milky white.

"You're a very sweet man," she whispered, interrupting his thoughts. "You won't let my daughter put me in a home, will you?"

"Wouldn't dream of it." He pulled her blanket up around her shoulders. "Now get some sleep." *Then die,* he added silently.

"Good night," she whispered as he was tiptoeing from the room.

"Good night," he said firmly, as a car door slammed outside. *Shit,* he thought, racing to the front door. *What now?*

But if there'd been a car, it had vanished into the night.

Just his imagination getting the better of him. Another unpleasant surprise.

He wasn't used to anything getting the better of him.

Everything else went pretty much according to plan. He carried the garbage bags with Nadia's remains to his car, which he'd parked at the side of the road just prior to bringing her body downstairs, then tossed it in the trunk and drove to the suburb of Newton, where he threw it into a large garbage bin behind a McDonald's not far from the home of Nadia's former employer. If anyone were to check its contents, which was highly unlikely, "Mr. Handsy" would be the first one the police would suspect. And wouldn't that be fun!

But that all happened a few days ago, and there's been no mention in the media of another body turning up, so it seems he's

244

safe for now.

Which brings him to Paige Hamilton, the biggest surprise of all. Not only did she cancel their date at the last minute, she's made no attempt since to contact him. At the very least, he expected her to reach out with another apology and a plea to try again. But no, she obviously considers herself too good for that, and is waiting for him to make the next move.

And he will. In his own sweet time.

He's decided to lie low for a week or two. Paige Hamilton has thrown him off his game, and Mr. Right Now needs time to rest and recharge his batteries.

But don't worry, Wildflower, he thinks with a smile. *I'll be back, meaner and wilier than ever.*

And there will be no more surprises.

CHAPTER TWENTY-FIVE

"Well, isn't this a pleasant surprise," Kendall Bates greeted Heather upon her return to work. "Nice of you to finally show up."

Heather quickly tucked the bags from Nordstrom's beneath her desk and began shuffling papers around in an effort to appear busy, in case one of the other dozen or more account people on the floor happened to be watching.

"Marsha's been asking for you."

"Shit." Marsha was her supervisor, and it was just Heather's unfortunate luck that she'd come looking for her on the one afternoon — all right, maybe more than one — she took an extra hour for lunch. Heather checked her watch. More like two extra hours, she realized. "What'd you tell her?"

"That you'd been complaining of an upset stomach, so you might have gone upstairs to lie down."

"That's the best you could come up with?"

"What'd you want me to tell her — that you took off half the afternoon to go shopping for a party dress?"

Heather rolled her eyes, glancing around the large, open space that housed the third-floor offices of McCann Advertising, while reaching into the largest of the bags and ignoring the not-so-subtle rebuke. "You want to see what I got?"

Kendall slid her chair from her cubicle across the aisle to Heather's desk as Heather removed the skimpy, red-beaded cocktail dress from the layers of tissue paper surrounding it. "Wow," Kendall exclaimed. "That's some dress. Where's the front of it?"

"You think it's too low-cut?"

Kendall shrugged. "You know what they say — if you've got it, flaunt it."

"I have it, and I intend to." Heather laughed as she stuffed the dress back inside the bag. "Wait till you see the shoes." She withdrew a box from the second bag.

"You got Louboutins?"

"Feast your eyes." She opened the box and removed one rhinestone-covered pump, balancing its five-inch heel in the palm of her hand.

"Wow. How much did those set you back?"

"Not a dime. My mother paid for them."

"Nice mom. Think she'd consider adopting me?"

Heather was returning the shoe box to the bag when she felt a large shadow looming over her. She didn't have to look up to know the shadow belonged to her supervisor, Marsha Buchanan. She should have smoked a joint before returning to work, she was thinking, something to take the edge off a possible confrontation. She made a mental note to call Brandon later. McCann Advertising's former courier was dismissed a few months back over his more lucrative sideline of supplying weed to employees. Heather had been one of his best customers.

"You're not throwing up, are you?" Marsha asked, her distinctive gravelly voice dripping sarcasm. The voice hinted at too many late nights spent drinking and smoking, but the hints were misleading, as Marsha neither drank nor smoked. As far as Heather could tell, the woman, only a few years her senior, had no vices at all. If not for her simple gold wedding band and the myriad pictures of three chubby little children that littered her desk, Heather would have suspected Marsha was still a virgin. There was just something sexless about people who were overweight, she'd always thought. In fact, it was hard for her to imagine women as plain as Marsha Buchanan, with her unfashionable brown bob and flat, no-nonsense shoes, having sex at all. Heather couldn't help wondering what Marsha's husband saw in her. He was a good-looking man. She'd flirted with him at last year's office party, which hadn't exactly endeared her to her superior.

Oh, well, she thought, pushing her purchases farther under her desk with her left foot.

"I hear your stomach has been giving you problems," Marsha said.

"I'm feeling much better now, thank you."

"Yes, I understand the medical staff at Nordstrom's is top-notch."

Heather sighed, hearing giggles from across the aisle. "I'm sorry I was a little late getting back from lunch," she began. "I must have eaten something that disagreed with me . . ."

"Save it. I'm just checking to make sure you got that presentation off to the client."

What presentation? Heather thought. "What client?" she asked, the words out of her mouth before she could stop them.

The look of mild irritation on Marsha's face morphed into outright anger. "Seriously?"

"You mean Johnson and Johnson?"

"No, I mean *Johnson and Applebaum.* Of course I mean Johnson and Johnson. You were at the meeting yesterday. Dick West-lake asked us to send over the presentation electronically, which I assured him would be taken care of immediately."

"I'm sorry," Heather said. "I'll get right to it."

"You were supposed to get right to it yesterday."

"I know, but my computer was acting up. I couldn't get it to do anything."

"Really? Did you report the problem to IT?"

"I was going to, but —"

"Save it," Marsha said again. "Just do it. Now."

Damn it. She'd forgotten all about that stupid presentation the minute she'd left the meeting. Truth be told, she hadn't been paying that much attention to anything that was going on in that boardroom. All that endless, essentially meaningless chatter about consumer package goods. They should call it "the bored room," she thought, smiling at her own cleverness.

"Something funny?" Marsha asked.

Heather jumped at the sound of her voice. Why was Marsha still here? Was she going to stand there watching her until she was certain the job was done? Was that really the responsibility of a supervisor? Did she have nothing better to do? "Was there something else you needed?"

"Just get it done." Marsha Buchanan swiveled around on her flat heels and marched down the corridor.

"Jealous bitch," Heather whispered, bringing up the appropriate file on her computer.

"Have you ever considered another line of work?" Kendall asked. Heather tossed the question aside with a wave of her hand, although she was thinking that maybe Kendall was right. She'd never really enjoyed advertising, having gone into it only because her cousin, Paige, had made it look so easy. She would have much preferred working in retail, perhaps managing a high-end boutique, like Paige's friend Chloe used to do. But her father had made his displeasure with this idea clear, so she'd followed her cousin into advertising instead, toiling for several years as an account coordinator before finally being promoted to her current position.

("Congratulations!" her mother said. "It's about time," said her father.)

He was right, of course. Over the years, Heather had watched a succession of young women move on and up, including Marsha

Buchanan, who'd started working for Mc-Cann Advertising at roughly the same time she had. And now Marsha, who'd had it in for her from day one — probably because she was dumpy and frumpy while Heather was beautiful and slender — was her boss.

People always talked about fairness in advertising. But how fair was that?

The only thing that gave Heather any satisfaction was that Paige had lost her job around the same time that Heather received her promotion.

She looked across the large, open-concept space, with its wall of windows overlooking the Charles River, bleached hardwood floors, and exposed ceiling pipes. McCann Advertising was made up of three distinct divisions, each occupying its own floor: strategy, the creative department, and the account people. Account people consisted of account coordinators, managers, supervisors, directors, and finally, group account directors, all of whom worked in cubicles, side by side. This lack of individual offices suggested an equality that didn't exist. In practice, there was a definite hierarchy.

The job of account manager was considered a relatively junior position. As the name suggested, account managers were responsible for the day-to-day managing of an account. Among other responsibilities, these included getting estimates to the client of work to be done and getting the client to sign off, getting production "workback" schedules ready and delivered to the client, and arranging for and managing the day-to-day meetings.

It sounded simple enough, but Heather was always screwing up. One time, she forgot to respond to an email from a client who had a question requiring an immediate answer. Another time she neglected to include a small but essential item in an estimate, which resulted in extra costs, for which there'd been no contingency. Yet another time, she'd set up a meeting but failed to include some key people and prepare everything that was needed for it. Each incident had resulted in a reprimand. Still, Heather remained convinced that it was the jealousy of others, and not her own laziness and incompetence, that was the source of her problems.

They were envious of her looks, her wardrobe, her family's wealth and stature, as well as her handsome and successful lawyer boyfriend, the boyfriend she'd stolen from her cousin. Humble, perfect Paige, who always made a point of playing down her constant string of promotions when everyone — everyone but Heather's father — could see how full of herself she really was. Paige, who "sure knows her stuff," as her father was fond of saying. Paige, who would never forget to respond to a client's email or be caught unprepared.

Except, of course, she had been. Caught very unprepared indeed.

How Heather loved to relive the night her cousin had come home early to discover her in bed with Noah! The look on her face had been priceless. Whenever Heather was bored during one of those endless meetings with clients, she conjured up the expression of shock and betrayal on Paige's face. It never failed to make her smile.

And now Paige had a new boyfriend. At least, according to her mother, who'd spilled the news as soon as her aunt Joan was out of earshot.

"She has a new boyfriend?" Heather had repeated.

"She's bringing him to the party."

"She's bringing him to the party?"

"Apparently."

"Who is he?"

"I don't know."

"What do you mean, you don't know?"

"What do you mean, what do I mean, I don't know?"

"What?"

Heather squirmed in her seat, recalling the futility of that conversation. The only thing that was clear was that her mother didn't know anything: not the mystery man's name or occupation, not how long he and Paige had been seeing each other, not how serious their relationship was, not even if he was as good-looking as Noah. "Shit," she said aloud.

"Problems?" Kendall asked.

"Nothing I can't deal with."

There was one person who could give her the information she craved. Heather reached for the phone, punched in the number, and waited while it rang twice before being picked up.

"Hello," the voice said.

"Chloe. It's Heather. How are you?"

"Heather," Chloe repeated, surprise infiltrating the coolness in her voice. "This is a shock. What can I do for you?"

"I have to be in Cambridge for a meeting tomorrow," Heather lied. "And I was thinking that it's been way too long since we've seen each other. I thought maybe we could have lunch."

"You want to have lunch?"

"My treat," Heather said, hoping to sweeten the pot. While she and Chloe had never been close — they were more "friends-in-law," as oh-so-clever Paige had once quipped — that relationship had pretty much ended when Paige moved out of Noah's apartment.

"I don't think that's a very good idea," Chloe said.

"Please," Heather said, understanding such groveling was necessary for her to obtain the information she craved. God, she could use a joint. "It's important. Really."

"Really?" Chloe repeated, turning the statement into a question. A second's silence. Then, "Okay, you have my curiosity."

That's what I was counting on, Heather thought with relief. "Great. I'll pick you up at one. You still on Binney Street?"

"Still here."

"See you tomorrow." Sensing the other woman's continued ambivalence, Heather hung up the phone before Chloe could change her mind. She wondered if Chloe suspected she'd been the anonymous caller informing her of Matt's extracurricular activities.

"What meeting do you have tomorrow in Cambridge?" Kendall asked.

"Do you always listen in on other people's conversations?"

Kendall shrugged, then brought her hand to her mouth, pointing with both her index finger and her eyes toward the approaching figure of Marsha Buchanan. "Have you emailed that presentation to the client yet?" Kendall asked under her breath.

"Shit," said Heather, as Marsha sidled up beside her. "Shit."

CHAPTER TWENTY-SIX

"So, what do you think?" Heather asked Noah, holding her new dress up against the gray tube dress she'd been wearing all day.

"Nice," Noah said, barely glancing in her direction.

Heather immediately positioned herself between Noah and the large-screen TV he was watching.

"Hey," he said. "You make a better door than a window."

Heather rolled her eyes toward the low ceiling. Had he always spoken in such tired clichés? "You didn't even look."

"I looked," he said. "I said it's nice. Now could you please move? The bases are loaded."

"I'm not moving until you take a good look."

Noah's exasperated sigh all but shook the room. He swiveled toward her, his hands dropping into his lap, his thick, dark hair falling across his forehead, his pale blue eyes opening wide. "Okay. I'm looking."

"And?"

"It's lovely. Now could you move?"

"You don't like it," Heather said.

"I *do* like it."

"It looks better on. With the right shoes." She glanced toward her bare feet.

"I'm sure it does."

"What does that mean?"

"What does *what* mean?"

God, Heather thought, refusing to budge. He was as bad as her mother.

A great roar suddenly shot from the TV.

"Shit!" Noah said, almost as loud.

"What happened?"

"Martinez hit a homer. They just hit a grand slam. And I missed it."

"And that's my fault?"

"You're the one standing in front of the TV."

"Only because you won't take two minutes to give me your honest opinion."

"You want my honest opinion?" Noah said angrily. "Fine. I'll give you my honest opinion. You're right — I'm not crazy about it."

"What do you mean, you're not crazy about it?" Heather's voice veered dangerously close to a wail. "What don't you like?"

"I don't know. It's kind of gaudy, isn't it?"

"*Is* it?"

He shrugged, leaning on his left elbow, straining to see around her. "It just looks a little . . . cheap."

"Cheap? It cost over a thousand dollars!"

"That's not what I . . . You spent over a thousand dollars for *that*?"

"My mother bought it for me," Heather said. "What do you mean, it looks cheap?"

"It's a little short, that's all. And skimpy-looking," he added.

"It's not skimpy-looking, and it's supposed to be short."

"Well, good, then. It is what it's supposed to be. Can I watch the game now?"

"It fits perfectly."

"Okay. Then, clearly, I'm wrong. It's perfect."

"You think it's too low-cut?" Heather asked, watching Noah's hands grip the sides of the sofa.

"I think it's perfect," he repeated, his eyes darting back toward the TV, the edges of his voice radiating fury.

"You're not just saying that?" Heather pressed.

Which was when Noah snapped. "Of course I'm just saying that! I'll say anything to get you to move your ass out of the way so I can watch the game. I've had a long, shitty day and I've been looking forward to this game all afternoon. So, if you would kindly shut up about that stupid dress and get the hell out of my way, it would be greatly appreciated. In fact, it would be fucking *perfect!*"

Heather burst into tears and fled the room.

"Thank you," Noah called as she slammed the bedroom door behind her.

She threw the dress onto the bed, then plopped down on top of it, feeling its heavy layer of beads digging into her backside. "Damn you, Noah Sherman!" She stood up, sat back down, then stood up again, fighting the urge to throw a full-scale, *Real Housewives*–like tantrum. Instead she pulled her tube dress up over her head and tossed it to the dark blue broadloom at her feet, stomping on it until it resembled a big, gray puddle.

She grabbed the new dress off the bed and slithered into it, then studied herself in the full-length mirror on the back of the bedroom door. "You look fantastic," she said to her reflection. Admittedly, the dress was a little short and more than a little tight. And yes, it was scooped perhaps an inch or two too low. But wasn't that the point? She

261

looked great. She pushed her shoulder-length hair away from her pale face and wiped the remaining tears from her eyes. "You look great."

What was the matter with Noah, anyway? Just because he'd had a shitty day at work didn't give him the right to take it out on her. It didn't give him the right to be sarcastic and rude.

Heather knew he didn't mean the things he'd said. What bothered her more were the things he *hadn't* said. And what he hadn't said was that her cousin would never be caught dead in a dress like that. No, not precious, *perfect* Paige.

She knew he still thought about her. Sometimes he'd be expounding on some issue — Noah rarely talked when he could expound — and she'd dare to offer an opinion, and he'd give her that look, the look that said she was way out of her depth, that she didn't have a clue what she was talking about. And maybe she didn't. She'd never been very interested in politics or issues that didn't directly concern her. Talk about history bored her every bit as much as talk about movie stars bored him. In truth, she and Noah had very little in common except sex. And even that wasn't as intense as when Paige had been the unwitting third side of the triangle. Every so often, Heather would catch Noah staring off into space, and she knew he was thinking about Paige, wondering if he'd made a mistake.

Just like her father, she thought. The way he used to joke that the hospital had made a mistake, sent him and his wife home with the wrong infant, that Paige, born two days later and released the same day as Heather, who'd been jaundiced as an infant and kept in the hospital an extra couple of days, was really his child.

Heather was the youngest of her parents' three children, and the only girl. Her brothers, Vic and Jordan, were both brilliant students and held master's degrees in business. Heather had been a mediocre student at best — "my dumb one," her father used to tease — and she'd quickly learned to take refuge in her brothers' shadows, afraid of her own opinions, adopting and repeating theirs instead, latching onto the end of their sentences as if to make them hers, ultimately relying on her burgeoning beauty to speak for her.

And it worked — for a while. She had her father's eye, if not his ear. Or his respect. And then Paige, her virtual twin, had started speaking up at family gatherings, challenging the assertions of the others, putting forth reasoned arguments of her own, effortlessly stealing the spotlight. "That girl sure knows her stuff," became Ted Hamilton's all-too-familiar, go-to refrain. Followed by a wink and the inevitable corollary, "I think the hospital must have made a mistake."

Heather hadn't set out to hate her cousin, just as she hadn't purposely set out to steal her boyfriend. Both things had just kind of happened, and one didn't have to have a master's degree in psychology to understand why. She might be "the dumb one," but she wasn't stupid.

She'd spent years in silent competition with Paige, only to come up short. And she'd finally won. She had her cousin's apartment, her career, and her man. She was pretty much living her cousin's life. And yet she was unhappier than she'd ever been. She was no good at her job, she wasn't sure she even *liked* the man she was supposed to love, and the really strange thing was that she probably missed Paige more than Noah did.

Heather stared at her reflection in the mirror, watching a new set of tears fill her eyes and fall down her cheeks. Noah was right — the dress *was* skimpy. It was too short, too tight, and way too low-cut.

And damn it — she liked it!

Of course, Paige would never be caught dead in anything so obvious. She would show up to her uncle's birthday party wearing something both understated and sophisticated. "And boring," Heather said aloud.

Just as Noah was boring.

"You're boring!" she shouted at the closed door. "Do you hear me? *Bor-r-ing!* You have bored me to actual tears." She approached the mirror, laying her forehead against the glass and swiping the tears away with the back of her hand.

The bedroom door suddenly opened, almost knocking her over. "Shit!" she cried, stumbling backward.

"Sorry," Noah said. "I didn't know you were standing there."

"You could have knocked."

"I heard yelling. I thought something might be wrong."

"Yeah, right. What is it — the fourth-inning stretch?"

Noah smiled. "Rain delay. And it's the seventh-inning stretch, actually."

"Great." Heather turned away and scooped her gray dress off the floor. "You'd better get back before it stops raining and you miss another exciting, grand-slam thingamajig."

"I don't know," he said. "Looks like all the exciting thingamajigs are happening in here."

Heather sniffed up the last of her tears. "What does that mean?"

"It means that I was wrong about the dress. It looks terrific."

"Really?"

"Really."

Heather looked toward her bare feet. "You want to see my new shoes?"

"Do they have high heels?"

"Five inches."

Noah's smile widened. "Then I would love to see your new shoes."

Heather quickly slipped them on. The extra five inches made them roughly the same height. "They're like the ones that Kim Kardashian was wearing in *US Weekly.*" She bit down on her tongue. Noah hated when she talked about celebrities.

But Noah was already reaching for her, and the obvious lust in his eyes told her that she finally had his full attention.

CHAPTER TWENTY-SEVEN

It was raining when Heather pulled up in front of Chloe's house in Cambridge at five minutes to one the next afternoon.

She sat in the new, sporty white Lexus her parents had given her for her recent promotion, repeatedly glancing at her image in the rearview mirror and praying the rain would stop. The rain, combined with the heat, would spell disaster for her hair, hair she'd spent nearly an hour blow-drying and straightening this morning, which had made her late for work. "Nice of you to honor us with your presence," Kendall had said in greeting.

"Fuck off," Heather had mumbled underneath her breath, wondering when Kendall had turned into such a cunt.

"Your hair looks very nice, by the way," Kendall said.

So maybe not such a cunt after all, Heather thought, checking her reflection in the small, round mirror she kept in the top right-hand drawer of her desk. Pleased with what she saw.

Luckily, Marsha Buchanan was out of the office in meetings all day, so there was no one else around to complain about the lateness of her arrival or question her commitment to her job. It had been mercifully easy to slip away early to meet Chloe for lunch. With any luck, she'd be back at work before anyone could take note of how long she'd been gone.

Of course, she hadn't counted on the sudden downpour that had resulted in a multitude of traffic delays. Did no one in Boston know how to drive in the rain? It wasn't as if it was a rare event, Heather thought, hoping the downpour would stop as suddenly as it had started and she could just sit tight and wait it out. But after almost ten minutes spent checking her hair and touching up her makeup, the rain seemed to be getting worse, and she couldn't very well sit here all afternoon. You'd think Chloe would glance out her front window and understand her predicament, spare her the inconvenience of having to get out of the car to ring the doorbell. It wasn't like this was a *date.*

Heather debated honking her horn, then decided that would be rude. It might not be a date, but it had been her idea. Not only her idea, but her treat. *What the hell,* she decided, blasting her horn three times in rapid succession. If she was going to pay for the damn meal, then Chloe could damn well make her way to the car, unescorted.

The front door opened almost immediately and Chloe appeared. She was wearing sneakers, baggy jeans, and a sloppy blue T-shirt, her blond hair pulled into a loose ponytail. She didn't exactly get dolled up for the occasion, Heather thought, feeling vaguely insulted and definitely overdressed in her ruffled orange cotton blouse and black leather skirt, just like the skirt Gwyneth Paltrow had worn to a recent event.

Chloe hurried down the front steps, shaking the rain from her shoulders as she opened the car door and slid into the beige leather seat beside Heather. She wasn't wearing a stitch of makeup. Not a hint of blush, not a stroke of mascara, not a dab of lipstick. And yet, there was no denying how beautiful she was. Heather felt instantly dowdy.

"Well," Chloe said in lieu of hello. "You going to tell me what this is all about?"

"Hello to you, too," Heather said.

"I think we can forgo the pleasantries, don't you?" Chloe said. "What are you up

269

to, Heather?"

"What am I up to?" Heather repeated, trying to figure out what was happening. "I thought I was buying you lunch."

"Yeah, well, *I'm* not buying the innocent act. So, suppose I spare you the expense and you spare me the aggravation, and you just tell me what you're after."

For a moment, Heather was speechless. While she'd been anticipating a certain amount of resistance from Chloe, she hadn't counted on outright hostility. "Wow. I didn't realize you had such a poor opinion of me."

"Really? You're surprised?"

"Frankly, yes."

"You slept with my best friend's fiancé."

"Well, technically, they weren't engaged."

"They were living together," Chloe reminded her.

"And now he's living with me." Heather brought her hands together in her lap and tried not to squirm. This was not going according to plan. "I didn't exactly twist his arm, you know."

"Yes, I'm sure you were quite blameless."

Heather turned slowly toward the other woman. "I'm not sure what you want me to say."

"I want you to tell me why you called this little meeting."

"I honestly just wanted to touch base."

"You wanted to touch base," Chloe repeated.

"Yes. This might surprise you, but I don't have a lot of friends . . ."

"It doesn't surprise me."

"Okay." Heather felt tears hovering. *Definitely* not going the way she'd planned. "You're really not going to make this easy for me, are you?"

"Not everyone's as easy as Noah," Chloe said.

"Wow. Okay. Listen, I know you and Paige are best friends and everything, but . . . I always considered you my friend, too. And I honestly just wanted to reconnect, find out how you are, hear about the kids. Find out what Matt's been up to."

Chloe nodded knowingly. "You know exactly what Matt's been up to."

"Excuse me?"

"You didn't think you were actually fooling anybody with that little stunt you pulled last week, did you?"

Heather felt the color drain from her cheeks and was glad she'd applied that second layer of blush while waiting for the rain to stop. "What little stunt?"

Chloe rolled her eyes. "Really? You're going to play dumb?"

"My dumb one," Heather heard her father say.

"I honestly have no clue what you're talking about."

Chloe reached for the door handle. "Then I don't think we have anything else to discuss."

"Wait," Heather said, grabbing Chloe's arm, and feeling the other woman instantly recoil. "Okay, yes. I assume you're talking about the phone call."

"Not so dumb after all," Chloe said. "Just . . . mean."

"I wasn't trying to be mean."

"No? What *were* you going for?"

Heather took a few seconds to regain her composure and gather her thoughts. Truthfully, she wasn't sure why she'd phoned Chloe with the news that Matt was on multiple dating sites, except as possible payback for Chloe choosing Paige over her. Plus, she'd been high, and it had been kind of fun. "I just thought you deserved to know, that's all."

"And you thought that an anonymous phone call was the best way to tell me."

"I didn't think you'd appreciate the news coming from me."

Chloe shrugged. The shrug told Heather she was probably right.

"I just know that I would want to know if Noah were cheating on me."

"Oh, I think you can pretty much count on that happening."

"Now who's being mean?" Heather asked.

Neither woman said anything for several seconds, the only sound coming from the rain beating against the car's windshield.

"So, what *did* happen with you and Matt?" Heather heard herself ask.

Chloe's laughter filled the small space. "You're unbelievable." She shook her head. "You know, you might actually be considered charming, if you weren't such a bitch. What the hell? There's no big secret," she continued before Heather could react. "I confronted Matt; we had a big fight; I kicked him out; I'm talking to a lawyer and probably filing for divorce. Satisfied?"

Heather wasn't sure what she felt. "I just thought you should know," she said, her voice a whisper.

"Look. The truth is, whether I like it or not, you probably did me a favor. So . . . did you get what you came for? Are we done?" Once again, Chloe moved to open the door.

"Wait," Heather said. "At least till the rain lets up a bit."

"So, we're not done," Chloe said. "There's

273

more going on inside that devious little mind. Let me guess: your mother told you that Paige would be bringing a date to your father's party . . ."

"Paige is bringing a date to my father's party?" Heather interrupted, opening her eyes as wide as three layers of mascara would allow.

"You're playing dumb again."

God, how she hated that word. "Okay, so she told me," Heather admitted. "And I'm curious. Last I checked, that wasn't a crime. How do you know what my mother told me, anyway?"

"Paige told me that her mother confessed she'd let that information slip."

"You've been speaking to Paige."

"Pretty much every day."

"And she knows I invited you to lunch."

"I called her the second I hung up with you."

"And the two of you thought it would be fun to have me drive all the way out here in the rain . . ."

"Well, we didn't know it would be raining. That was kind of the icing on the cake."

"Okay. You can get out of the car now," Heather said, angry tears taking the place of her curiosity.

"What were you doing on those dating

sites, anyway?" Chloe asked, her hand on the door handle. "Things not going so well with Noah these days?" She didn't wait for an answer, bolting from her seat, the heavy car door slamming behind her as she darted through the rain toward her front door.

"Things are great," Heather called after her. "You think you're so damn smart, don't you?" she continued as Chloe disappeared inside her house. "You just wait. We'll see how smart you are." She lowered her head to the steering wheel and cried.

She might not know much, but she knew all about getting even.

Chapter Twenty-Eight

"For God's sake, Heather," Noah said, his voice burrowing underneath the bathroom door. "What are you doing in there?"

"I'm almost done." Heather checked, then rechecked, her makeup in the round magnifying mirror on the wall beside the large, rectangular mirror over the sink. Was that a blemish forming underneath her skin, right smack in the middle of her right cheek? *Damn it.* She hadn't had a pimple in years. It had to be stress. Her father's upcoming party, her escalating brushes with her supervisor, the humiliating encounter with Chloe, the rain. She reached for her concealer, dabbing at the offending imperfection until it almost disappeared, then applying an extra coat of the concealer under her eyes for good measure. She'd already had to redo her makeup after today's fiasco with Chloe, her supposedly waterproof mascara having left a trail of telltale black tears down her cheeks. The stains had been removed, but the sting remained, and was now translating into a giant pimple below the surface of her skin. "Damn you, Chloe," Heather said, applying yet another stroke of concealer.

She fluffed out her hair, tamped it down again, and promptly fluffed it back up, but it still didn't look right. The rain had indeed done a number on it. "Damn frizz," she mumbled, wetting the sides of her hair, then removing her hair dryer from its cramped quarters inside the cupboard beneath the sink. This was all Paige's fault. She'd obviously convinced Chloe to go along with her little scheme to embarrass her cousin. "Sore loser," Heather muttered, lifting the hair dryer to her head and turning it to maximum strength.

"What are you doing now?" Noah wailed from outside the door.

"Hold your horses. I'll just be a minute."

"You said that ten minutes ago."

"You're slowing me down," Heather warned.

"We're already twenty minutes late."

"So, another few minutes won't make any difference. Who shows up right on the dot for dinner, anyway?"

"I guarantee you that everybody else will

be on time."

Heather rolled her eyes at her reflection and continued blow-drying her wet ends, trying to corral them into some sort of style. Since when had Noah turned into such a whiner? Although he was probably right. The lawyers of Whitman, Loughlin were a very conservative bunch. They'd undoubtedly arrived en masse at the restaurant in Little Italy at precisely seven o'clock. So reliable. So predictable. So boring. *"Bor-r-ing,"* Heather said over the continuing blast of hot air from the dryer.

"What did you say?"

"I said that if you wanted me to be on time," she shouted, "you should have gotten an apartment with more than one bathroom! I can hardly move in here."

"The bathroom is not the problem."

He was right. The bathroom was not the problem. Heather hated *everything* about Noah's apartment. Traces of Paige could be discovered in virtually every room: the carpet she'd chosen for the bedroom, the floral throw pillows on the living room sofa, the pewter salt and pepper shakers in the center of the glass dining room table, even the goddamn mirror over the goddamn sink in the tiny, cramped, goddamn bathroom. Not to mention, could the lighting be any less flattering? How could Noah expect her to be ready on time?

"Two more minutes," she said, shutting off the dryer and shoving it back into the cupboard, spying the remainder of a joint hidden behind a bottle of nail polish remover. She tucked her hair behind her ears, wondering if she had time to smoke it. *Better not,* she thought. Noah had made it very clear he didn't approve of her propensity for weed, despite the fact that it was legal now in Massachusetts. *Damn it,* she thought, closing the cupboard door. Why did everything in her life have to be so damn difficult?

She'd returned from Cambridge only to find Marsha Buchanan waiting at her desk, her meetings having wrapped up earlier than expected. "I've scheduled a performance review for you this coming Monday at ten o'clock," she'd told Heather. "Be on time."

Heather knew that a performance review was merely a formality, the first step toward being dismissed. She'd be given a stern warning and the chance to shape up. If her superiors didn't see a significant improvement in the coming weeks, she'd be out of a job. And she wouldn't have the excuse of a New York takeover to make her firing more palatable, thus handing her father yet another reason to compare her unfavorably with her cousin.

Heather had returned home, exchanged her orange blouse and leather skirt for sweats, and wolfed down a cold piece of pizza from the fridge, looking forward to sex with Noah to make her forget her shitty day. Except she'd forgotten about the scheduled dinner with Noah's colleagues.

Damn that Chloe anyway. She might be Paige's mouthpiece, but would it have killed her to be nice? Or at the very least, more forthcoming? But no, Heather had been forced to waste half the afternoon driving to Cambridge and back, risking both her job and her life — Boston drivers were the worst — and what had she learned? Nothing! Paige's mystery man had remained a stubborn blank. The news that Chloe and Matt were likely headed for divorce had made the afternoon only slightly more palatable.

"What's going on in there?" Noah asked.

"Can you back off? You're making me crazy."

"I'm making *you* crazy?"

Heather gave her hair one final toss and took a deep breath, tucking her tight red jersey inside her dark blue designer jeans. Considering everything she'd had to deal with, she didn't look bad at all. She pulled open the bathroom door. "Okay. Ready to go."

Noah's hand reached toward her cheek. "Is that a pimple?" he said.

"So, then, Shiloh says, 'Stop singing, Lance. You're *distracting* me from my sleep!' " Brianne Palmer brought both hands to her chest in a gesture that combined both shock and delight. "Can you imagine? She's only three! What three-year-old uses words like 'distracting'?"

"Unbelievable," Nicole Barry said, dropping her fork to what little remained of her chocolate lava cake dessert. "She's so smart." Nicole pushed herself away from the table, patting her eight-months-pregnant belly.

"Shiloh is definitely gifted," Kaitlin Seymour agreed. "I've always said that. You could tell from the minute she was born — eyes wide open — that she was special."

"Girls definitely develop faster than boys," Brianne said. "I mean, Lance is a great kid, but he's no Einstein."

"Oh, but little boys are so cute," Nicole said, her hand tracing wide circles on her stomach.

Kaitlin smiled at Heather across the long

table for eight. "We should stop. All this talk about children is probably boring poor Heather to tears."

"Yes," Heather agreed, looking up from the tiny mirror secreted in the palm of her hand in time to see the other woman's smile freeze on her face.

"Oh," said Kaitlin.

"Did she just say we're boring her?" Nicole asked Brianne.

"What?" said Heather, quickly returning the mirror to her purse. "I'm sorry. I must have misunderstood."

"I was just saying that all this talk about children must be boring you to tears."

"Oh," Heather said. "*Oh, no.* Not at all. I'm sorry. I thought you said . . . It doesn't matter," she said, when she couldn't think of anything. The truth was that she'd tuned the other women out somewhere between the salad and the entrees, numbed by the unrelenting onslaught of adorable anecdotes regarding their respective offspring. What was the matter with these women? Did they have nothing else to talk about?

She'd perked up momentarily when the name Tiffany was mentioned because she thought they were referring to the famed jewelry store, but it turned out they were talking about some girl whose body had turned up in a landfill recently, and mulling over the prospect of a serial killer in their midst.

"Please," one of the women — she couldn't remember which one — had interjected. "My mother says that if you've raised teenage daughters, serial killers are a walk in the park!"

They'd all laughed, and the conversation had quickly segued back to their children.

So boring.

Not that their husbands, who'd grouped around the other end of the table after ordering dessert, were any better, their conversation a mind-numbing combination of work, wine, and sports. She'd tried to feign interest in what they were saying, but they'd lost her somewhere between tort law and Tom Brady, although she'd perked up momentarily when the handsome quarterback's name was mentioned.

In the end, she'd allowed her mind to drift, first imagining what the cute waiter pouring drinks at a nearby table would be like in bed, then on to her encounter with Chloe, which led to thoughts of Chloe's husband, Matt, and what *he* had been like in bed — which, truth to tell, hadn't been all that great. Not that they'd actually made it to the bed.

Still.

How she'd love to have waved that little flag in front of Chloe's smug little face! *"Remember that housewarming party you threw when you moved to Binney Street?"* Okay, so Matt had been drinking, and he and Chloe had obviously been fighting and were barely speaking to each other. Heather had gone upstairs to use the bathroom, and when she'd opened the door, Matt was standing there, and he'd shoved her back against the sink, kicked the door closed behind him, pushed her clothes aside, and pushed his way inside her.

The whole thing had taken less than two minutes. He'd barely looked at her, choosing instead to concentrate on his own reflection in the mirror above the sink. When he was done, he'd smiled — more at his image than at her — zipped up his fly, and returned to his other guests. Heather had pulled up her panties and lowered her dress, her thighs quivering, her back sore from being repeatedly slammed up against the hard enamel. She hadn't heard Paige approach.

"What's going on?" Paige asked.

Heather spun around. "What do you mean?" Had Paige seen Matt leave? Did she suspect what had happened?

"Are you all right?"

"I'm fine. Why?"

"I don't know. You were just standing there, looking kind of . . ."

"I'm fine," Heather repeated. She went back downstairs, hung around a while, then left the party early. Matt had waved a casual goodbye.

"What's going on?" Noah asked now, suddenly at her side.

"What?"

"You were a million miles away. What were you thinking about?"

Heather shrugged, the surrounding restaurant coming back into focus. She heard the clatter of dishes, the hum of conversation, the sound of women laughing.

"I think we bored poor Heather to tears," Kaitlin said, as she'd said earlier.

How long ago was that? Heather wondered, as Noah was explaining that he had an important meeting first thing in the morning and wanted to do some additional research before going to bed.

Which meant no sex. The end to a perfect day.

As soon as they got home, Noah sat down at the dining room table and buried his nose in his work. Heather washed her face, applied Clearasil to her offending blemish, climbed into bed, and watched back-to-back repeat episodes of *The Millionaire Match-maker,* while scrolling through various dating sites on her phone. She wasn't surprised to find Matt still on them. God, he was a handsome devil. "You've got some nerve," she told his photograph, not without admiration. Noah, on the other hand, had turned into a crushing bore.

Had he always been so dull?

What had Paige seen in him, anyway?

She was tired of being bored — with Noah, with her job, with her life.

She glanced back at the phone in her hand. What she needed was a little excitement.

CHAPTER TWENTY-NINE

The house on Peach Drive was typical of the homes in the affluent suburb of Newton — two-story, white clapboard, well maintained. It sat back from the street in the middle of a sprawling, manicured lawn ringed by tall, leafy trees and blossom-laden shrubbery. Heather had no idea what kind of trees or shrubs they were, nor did she care. Nature had never been her thing. Pink flowers, red flowers — what difference did it make? What interested her far more was the prominent FOR SALE sign at the side of the road. And the name of the listing agent writ large across its bottom: Matthew Dixon.

She pulled into the driveway and put her car in park, although she left the engine running. It was hotter today than yesterday, even at almost six o'clock in the evening. Mercifully, it had stopped raining. Still, she couldn't risk the lingering humidity doing weird things to her freshly coiffed hair, so staying in reach of the car's air-conditioning was a must. She checked her image in the rearview mirror, grateful to see that the Clearasil had done its job. Yesterday's budding blemish was now little more than an unpleasant memory, although if you looked closely, a vague outline of it remained.

Heather doubted Matt would look that closely. Just in case, she undid the top two buttons of her white blouse, adjusting her breasts to peek out from the top of her white-lace, push-up bra.

She hadn't bothered with panties.

He should be here any minute, she thought, checking her watch. And wouldn't he be surprised! She laughed, pleased at her own cleverness.

She'd spent most of the morning on her computer, investigating houses for sale in the surrounding suburbs, zeroing in on Matt's listings. "Aren't you the busy little bee?" Kendall had commented from across the aisle, erroneously assuming Heather was actually doing her job.

Heather had selected the house on Peach Drive because of its proximity to the city proper. While it was important she choose a property away from the Boston core in order to minimize the risk of running into anyone she knew, there was no point in casting her net too far afield. Besides, she'd always hated the suburbs. She often joked that she developed nosebleeds when she strayed too far from Beacon Hill.

Next, she'd called Matt's office and spoken to his assistant, giving the woman a phony name, and telling her she was interested in seeing the house on Peach Drive as soon as possible. "Mr. Dixon says he can meet you there at six o'clock this evening," the assistant told her after checking with Matt, who was out of the office on another showing. "Would that work for you?"

It would indeed, Heather thought now, a slow smile spreading across her face. She stole another glance at the rearview mirror, her eyes smiling mischievously back. At exactly six o'clock, a car pulled to a stop on the street in front of the house. Heather watched Matt step out of his car, adjusting his beige linen suit jacket and smoothing back his hair before striding confidently up the driveway, every arrogant step proclaiming dominance over his domain.

Heather took a deep breath and pushed open her car door.

Matt's smile was firmly in place and his hand already extended in greeting as the high heels of Heather's pink, open-toed shoes made contact with the intersecting gray bricks of the driveway. "Mrs. Turner?" he asked, approaching.

Heather paled. Was it possible he didn't recognize her? *Oh, God. How embarrassing!*

Matt's smile dissolved as he drew nearer, his eyes narrowing. "Heather?"

Thank God, Heather thought. "Fancy meeting you here," she said with a laugh.

"I don't understand. What are you doing here?"

"Waiting for you."

"I think there must be some mistake." He glanced at his watch. "I'm meeting a client here at six o'clock."

"Mrs. Turner," Heather said.

"Yes. Do you know her?"

"I *am* her."

He seemed startled. "You got married?"

Heather laughed. "No. God, no."

"I don't understand," he said again. "You told my assistant your name was Mrs. Turner? That you were interested in buying this property?"

"And that part is true," Heather improvised, hearing a hint of anger mingling with the confusion in Matt's voice. "About wanting to see the property. Noah and I have been talking about maybe buying a house in the area." *Damn it,* she thought. Of course

Matt would be confused and angry. He'd driven to Newton expecting to find an eager buyer, pocket an easy commission, and instead he'd found . . . her.

What had she been thinking? What if Matt were to speak to Noah?

Although that was highly unlikely, she assured herself. The two men had never been friends and there was no reason for them to get chummy now. Noah had always considered Matt something of a jerk, and had only tolerated him because of Paige's friendship with Chloe. Now both Paige and Chloe were out of the picture, and Noah was . . . well, teetering at the edge of the frame. "I didn't think you'd agree to see me if I used my real name," Heather explained, anticipating Matt's next question. "Because of Chloe and Paige and Noah and everything."

"Never really understood that friendship, to be honest," Matt said, his earlier swagger returning to his eyes. "Always thought Noah could do better." He grinned. "Nice to see he has."

Heather felt a flush at her cheeks and a tingle between her legs.

"Besides, I never let my personal life interfere with business. You really think you might want to buy this house?"

"Well, I'd like to see it first." She laughed.

291

"Of course." Matt motioned with his hand toward the front door. "Right this way."

"So, Mrs. Turner," he said, a confident smile in his voice, "what are your thoughts so far?" They were standing in the all-white master bedroom on the second floor, having completed their tour of the main floor and finished basement.

"It's beautiful," Heather said. *The bed certainly looks comfortable,* she thought, picturing Matt and her rolling around on top of it.

"Well, like I said, the owners renovated a year ago, and spared no expense. New kitchen, new bathrooms, new furnace, new roof. Everything top-of-the-line. And wait till you see what they've done in here." He crossed the bedroom into the black-and-white en-suite marble bathroom.

Heather followed. "Very impressive."

"Marble countertops, two ceramic sinks, one claw-foot tub, heated marble floor and towel racks. And the pièce de résistance," he said with a wink, pointing toward the shower at the far end of the room.

Heather put an extra wiggle in her walk and pushed out her backside as she peeked inside the cavernous space, the marble walls outfitted with the latest in hardware.

"There's certainly enough . . . stuff."

"Oversized rain showerhead, plus a variety of sprays coming at you from all directions. Plenty of room for two. Or three," he added, coming up close behind her. "So, what do you think?"

"Well, it's stunning, of course."

"I'm sensing a 'but.' "

"But . . . maybe it's a little grand . . ."

"Grand?"

"For Noah."

"For Noah," Matt said, his breath on the back of her neck.

"I mean, it's just the two of us," she said, her voice wobbling as he pressed himself against her.

"Just the two of us," he repeated, his fingers brushing her hair to one side as his lips grazed the side of her neck.

Her breath caught in her lungs.

"You didn't really come to see the house, did you?"

She felt him pull away. *Come back,* she thought. *Come back.* "Why would you say that?"

He placed both hands on her shoulders and slowly spun her around.

Was he going to kiss her again?

"Because you raced through the downstairs rooms," he said instead. "You showed zero interest in anything, including the truly spectacular walk-in closet that women all but swoon over, and you haven't asked a single question."

"Maybe because you explained everything so well."

"Maybe. But I doubt it. Why the charade, Heather? Did Chloe put you up to this?"

"What? No."

"Is this some sort of test? Is that why you're here?"

"No!"

"Then what's this all about?" He pushed her back against the countertop, cupping her chin in his hand and squeezing hard.

"I just wanted to see you."

"Why?"

"I heard about you and Chloe."

"How?"

"I don't understand."

"How could you know about me and Chloe? Paige isn't speaking to you, and Chloe sure as hell wouldn't confide in you. Unless . . ." His hand dropped to his side, a look of admiration creeping into his eyes. "Unless you're the one who tipped off Chloe."

"Tipped her off about what?"

He laughed. "You've been a very bad girl," he said, his voice a low growl she found almost unbearably sexy. "Haven't you . . . Mrs. Turner?" His hand reached between her legs. "Well, well," he said. "I think we may have just discovered why we're here."

Heather groaned. *What the hell,* she thought. This was what she came for, after all. Her chance to screw both Matt and Chloe, payback for the little stunt Chloe had pulled the other day. *And let's not forget Noah,* she thought, mindful of his growing lack of interest. "Disappointed?" she asked, feeling on surer ground.

"Pretty sure of yourself, weren't you?"

"Pretty sure of *you,*" she said.

Without another word, Matt unzipped his pants and pulled up her skirt.

Really? Heather thought, as he entered her, slamming her roughly and repeatedly against the marble counter. *We're doing it here, in the bathroom, against the sink? Again? When there's a perfectly good bedroom with a nice, comfortable bed only feet away?*

Was this the way he was with Chloe? Heather almost felt sorry for the woman. *Her back must be a mass of bruises,* she thought, as Matt continued pounding his way inside her. She was wondering how much more she could take when he pulled out of her, spinning her around and slapping her, hard, on her bare buttocks.

"What the . . . ?"

But he was already moving away, zipping up his fly and straightening his jacket.

"I don't suppose we could take a shower," she said, only half in jest. She could use a spray of something soothing on her back and between her legs.

"We need to get out of here before the Stewarts come home," Matt said matter-of-factly. "I told them we'd be out by seven. Come on. You can fix your hair in the car."

"What's wrong with my hair?" She glanced at the long mirror over the counter. "Oh, God." Her hair was a mess, the roots already curling with perspiration.

"Come on," he said, hurrying her down the stairs and out the front door.

"We have to stop meeting like this," she joked as they approached her car.

"Probably a good idea," he said, taking her at her word. "Call me if you're ever serious about buying a house."

"Absolutely." Heather watched through her rearview mirror as Matt got behind the wheel of his black Audi and drove off without so much as a backward glance. "Well, what did you expect?" she asked her reflection, angry at the tears she saw forming. "Why are you crying? Surely you weren't expecting hearts and flowers."

No, her reflection said silently. *But a little foreplay might have been nice.*

"You got exactly what you came for," Heather admonished her image. She wiped the tears from her eyes, threw the car into gear, and backed out of the driveway.

Why was getting what you wanted always such a damn letdown?

CHAPTER THIRTY

"Heather?" Noah called from the living room as she walked through the apartment door.

Heather winced. She'd been hoping Noah would be working late, as he often did, and that she'd have time for a hot bath before he got home. "Yup, it's me." Disappointed? she wondered. Maybe hoping it was someone else?

"Where've you been?" Noah poked his head into the hallway. "It's late."

"Is it?" She made a show of checking her watch. He was right. It was almost seven thirty.

"Where've you been?" he asked again.

"It's just been one of those days," she said, silently berating herself for not having prepared an alibi on the tedious drive home.

"Tell me," he said, approaching and taking her hand, guiding her into the living room.

What's going on? she wondered, as he sank down beside her on the sofa, still holding tight to her hand. Had Matt phoned him and boasted of their tryst? Was this sudden interest in her day part of some elaborate ruse, a prelude to his tossing her out on her sore back? "Well, I told you that Marsha Buchanan has been giving me a hard time lately . . ."

He nodded, waited for her to continue.

Which was *definitely* not the Noah she'd come to expect. That Noah was always interrupting her, correcting her, telling her to speed things up, that he didn't need to hear every trivial little detail.

"Well," she continued, "she's called for a performance review on Monday, which means if I don't shape up, I'll probably lose my job."

A look of genuine concern settled on Noah's handsome face.

Not that he was anywhere near as good-looking as Matt, Heather thought. But then, few men were. Few men were as arrogant either.

"I didn't realize things were that bad."

"She picks on me for every little thing," Heather elaborated, warming to her subject. "Honestly, I don't know what her problem is. I think she's just jealous or something."

"So, what'd she pick on today?"

"Same old crap. We have another presentation tomorrow, so I thought I'd better stay late, make sure everything was ready. I even had to cancel my hair appointment." She motioned vaguely in the direction of her head, hoping this little ad lib would be enough to keep him from questioning what had happened to her hair.

Noah's hand reached up to tuck some stray strands behind one ear. "Looks nice," he said.

"No, it doesn't."

"Yes, it does," he insisted. "It's sexy."

Why was he being so nice to her? Heather wondered. Was he setting her up?

"What else?" he asked.

"Else?"

"You look like you've been crying."

Shit, Heather thought. When had he become so observant? Or she, so transparent? "I'm just feeling a little overwhelmed, I guess."

He drew her back against the pillows, began planting soft kisses along the side of her neck.

You've got to be kidding me, Heather thought. *Tonight? Of all nights?*

"You smell so good," he said.

Seriously? She felt his hand on her breast.

300

Good God! She jumped to her feet.

"What's the matter?" he asked.

"I just feel kind of . . . I don't know . . . grubby."

He smiled. "I like grubby."

Shit. What was she supposed to do now?

"It's okay," he said, as if he could read her mind. "I know just the thing."

"You do?"

"Don't move." He pushed off the sofa and left the room.

Seconds later, she heard the bathwater running, and a few minutes after that, he was back in the living room. "Your bath awaits, milady."

"You poured me a bath? That's so sweet."

"Yeah, well. I realized I haven't been the greatest boyfriend in the world these last few weeks."

"You don't have to be the greatest . . ." She felt an unfamiliar, and decidedly unpleasant, stab of guilt.

"Sure I do. Anyway, go have your bath, and I'll see you after."

"What about dinner? I'm starving."

"We can worry about that later. Go have your bath before the water gets cold."

She nodded, wobbling toward the hallway.

"Love the shoes," Noah called after her.

She stayed in the bath for more than half an hour, topping it up with hot water regularly to soothe her sore back and wondering what to do about Noah. Clearly he was in an amorous mood. But what about her? Could she have sex with more than one man on the same night, within hours of each other?

Not that she hadn't done it before. She'd had sex with both Johnny Valente and his brother Vince at a frat party, but that was almost fifteen years ago and she'd been pretty wasted. Then there was that six-month period a couple of years back when she was dating three different guys and sleeping with all of them.

Good times, she thought with a smile.

Of course, none of those had been exclusive relationships, and she was pretty sure the men had been doing the same thing, so technically she hadn't been cheating. Tonight was different. She'd definitely crossed a line. She felt another twinge of guilt. *Damn it.* Why had Noah picked tonight of all nights to turn into a knight in shining armor?

Except he wasn't exactly wearing armor, she thought as he walked into the room, carrying a tray, with nothing but a towel around his waist. The tray contained a selection of cheese and crackers and two glasses of champagne.

"What's this?"

He perched on the side of the tub. "You said you were starving."

"So I did."

"There's Brie, cheddar, and Cambozola, which, if memory serves, is your favorite."

"Wow." She helped herself to a cracker with a thick slab of Cambozola.

"Have some champagne." He lowered the tray to the tile floor and handed her one of the glasses.

"What's the occasion?"

"Does there have to be an occasion?"

"No. It's just that . . ." Dear God, was he going to propose?

He bent toward her, covering her mouth with his. She felt his tongue slide between her teeth.

"Careful," she mumbled. "I have a mouthful of cheese and crackers."

"Move over." He stood up, discarded his towel, and climbed into the tub. He raised his glass, clinked it against hers. "To you."

"Right back at you," she said, taking a slow, careful sip of the bubbly liquid, wondering if she was going to find an engagement ring at the bottom of her glass. She'd have to be careful not to choke on it.

Would she say yes?

And was she seriously considering marrying a man she'd cheated on less than two hours ago? A man she'd been considering dumping?

Why not? Heather thought, imagining the look of shock and dismay on Paige's face at the sight of her new engagement ring. She hoped the ring would be at least four carats, big enough to make an impression. She hoped Noah wouldn't demand it back in the event she called off the wedding somewhere down the road. Of course, if she were to marry him, then it would be hers to keep, even if she decided against keeping the groom. Heather took another sip of champagne, looking for the telltale sparkle at the bottom of the glass.

But Noah was already removing the glass from her hand and depositing both slender flutes on the floor beside the tub. "Turn around," he instructed.

What now? she thought, scooting into position, waiting for him to surround her with his arms, hold a diamond ring up to her eyes.

"Where's the soap?" he said instead.

"What?"

"The soap," he repeated. "What'd you do with it?"

She fished through the water, finding the soap between her legs and passing it over her shoulder.

"I'll do your back," he said.

"No," she began. But he was already running his soapy hands across her shoulders and down her spine.

"What's this?" he asked, stopping.

Heather held her breath. "What's what?"

"There's this big red mark."

"There is?"

"Looks really sore. Can't you feel it?" He pressed down on it with his thumb.

Heather bit her tongue to keep from crying out. "I guess I must have banged into something at work."

"Looks pretty nasty. Poor baby," he said, his hands leaving her back to massage her breasts. "How's this feel?"

"Not bad," she said.

"Just not bad?" he teased, pressing his erection against her.

"Why don't we go into the bedroom?" she suggested, swiveling back around.

His response was to grab her legs and position them around his waist. "Why don't we stay right here?"

"No, I'd really rather —"

"You're always complaining I'm not spontaneous enough," he said, his hands lifting her into position.

Really? she thought as he entered her. What was it tonight with men and bathrooms? Was there a full moon?

"You didn't like that?" he asked when they were out of the tub and drying off.

"It was okay," she said.

"Just okay?"

"Except for the part where I almost drowned."

He laughed. "Sorry about that. Guess we should stick to dry land."

"Sounds like a good idea." *A better idea would have been for you to propose, so that I could show off my new engagement ring at the party on Saturday night. Guess that's not happening.*

"You all right?" he said.

"Sure. Why do you ask?"

"I don't know. You seem a little distracted. What are you thinking about?"

"Did you know that Paige is bringing a date to my father's party?" Heather asked in reply.

Noah stopped drying his legs and stood up straight. "No. How would I know that? Who is it?"

"Does it matter?"

He shrugged. "Just curious." He grabbed his bathrobe from a hook on the door. "I'm gonna go watch the game," he said.

"What about dinner?"

"I think there's some leftovers in the fridge."

Not to mention, the one standing right here, Heather thought as he walked from the room. She could tell by the slump of his shoulders that he was more than just curious about the man Paige would be bringing to the party.

He was upset.

CHAPTER THIRTY-ONE

He's lying on top of his bed, his hand down the front of his pants, scrolling through his phone for pictures of his most recent dates. This is how he prefers to think of the women he kills. As dates, not victims. After all, he isn't some cowardly stalker lurking in a dark alley, waiting to ambush whatever unsuspecting female stumbles into his path. He takes great pains to woo his women; he pours his heart out in texts and phone calls, suggests meeting up only when they feel comfortable, buys them drinks, seduces them with his charm and good looks, makes them feel special. He never resorts to threats or violence to get them to go with him. They follow him willingly, enter his apartment eagerly, their heads already spinning with thoughts of wedding bells and forever.

They get forever, all right, although not quite the forever they had in mind.

Forever dead, he thinks with a smile,

308

stroking himself with greater urgency.

He watches the women parade before his eyes, like contestants in a perverse Miss Universe pageant: Chelsea, with her long neck in a noose; Tiffany, tear-filled eyes wide with terror; Nadia, seconds after she drew her final breath.

And then there she is, the woman who will be his crowning glory, his parting gift to the great city of Boston: Paige Hamilton, aka Wildflower. He's snapped at least a dozen pictures of her in the last few days. In one, she is standing outside the building where she lives with her mother; in another, she is emerging from the towering John Hancock Building, brown hair blowing in the breeze; in yet another, she is climbing into a taxi on Commonwealth Avenue.

He groans as his climax approaches, his body shuddering with the welcome release. He sits up quickly, wipes himself off, tucks himself in. It's time to get this ball rolling. He's been patient long enough. What was it his mother used to say? *"If the mountain won't come to Mohammed . . ."*

Time to go to the mountain, he decides, switching from photos to messaging on his phone, no longer annoyed that Paige has yet to contact him. She's cagey, that one. He admires that. Hasn't he known from the first night he saw her that she wouldn't be as easy as the others, that she would be a true test of his skills?

Hey, Wildflower, he types. *Sorry for the delay in getting back to you. Really hoping we can try again.*

He is waiting for a response when he thinks he hears someone at the door.

He clicks off the phone, listens as the knock becomes louder and more insistent. "Who is it?" he calls out.

"It's Jenna Lebowski," a woman calls back.

Jenna? She must be his landlady's daughter, the one who wants to put Imogene in a home. What the hell does she want?

"The police are downstairs," she says, answering his silent question. "They want to ask you a few questions."

His heartbeat quickens. *The police are here? What does that mean?* That someone saw him dragging Nadia's body to his car? That someone identified him as the man they saw with Tiffany Sleight on the night she disappeared? That there will be no more "dates"? That he will never get the chance to turn his fantasies about Paige into a reality?

He checks his demeanor in the mirror on the wall by the front door, making sure he looks calm and presentable. *Well, obviously way more than presentable,* he thinks, noting the look of pleasant surprise on Jenna Lebowski's face when he opens the door.

She's at least fifty, and round in the manner of sturdy Polish stock. Her hair is a touch too platinum for her black roots, but is otherwise nicely styled, and she's neatly dressed in navy pants and a red blouse. She wears a crucifix around her neck. He wonders what it would be like to strangle her with it, to watch the tiny gold Jesus slice deep into her flesh.

Blood of Christ, he thinks, careful not to crack a smile.

Not quite what the church had in mind.

"I'm so sorry to bother you," Jenna Lebowski says, her cheeks blushing almost as red as her blouse.

"Did you say the police are here?"

"They're downstairs talking to my mother now."

What the fuck? he wonders. Has the old bat lodged some sort of complaint against him? He should have finished her off when he had the chance. "Is this about last week? She was very confused and I was just trying to help . . ."

"What are you talking about?" Jenna asks.

"Your mother. I found her wandering around outside at about two in the morning. I managed to get her back into bed . . ."

"Oh, God. No. I'm so sorry. I had no idea. No, this isn't about that. I don't know what this is about."

Apprehension mingles with relief. If the police weren't here about Mrs. Lebowski, why *were* they here? He retrieves his key from the small plastic dish he keeps on the counter of the tiny galley kitchen, locking the door behind him and pocketing his phone as he follows Jenna down the stairs and around to the front of the house. A police car is parked on the street.

Two officers, one male, one female, stand on opposite sides of Imogene Lebowski in the front foyer. They're both young, late twenties or early thirties. The man is white, with reddish hair and a wide swath of freckles smeared like peanut butter across the bridge of his nose. The woman is black, her natural dark curls squeezed into a tight bun and sitting high on her head. *She's quite beautiful,* he thinks, realizing that he's never "dated" a black woman. Judging by the way she's lowering her eyes, refusing to meet his gaze head-on, he knows she'd be open to it. And her being a police officer would definitely give their encounter some added spice.

Providing, of course, that she isn't here to

arrest him.

"Officers?" he says, acknowledging Mrs. Lebowski's girlish wave with a nod. "Is there something I can help you with?"

"I'm Officer Petroff," the male officer says. "This is my partner, Officer Martell. You are?"

"Steve Winniker," he says, the name he gave Mrs. Lebowski, the name on the fake driver's license in the wallet in his back pocket.

"We're investigating a shooting in the area that occurred last Saturday night," Officer Petroff says.

"A shooting?" He vaguely recalls reading something about a shooting near the harbor. *What is the neighborhood coming to?*

Officer Petroff checks his notes, although he suspects this is all for show. "Victim's name was Richard Ashenbrand. You know him, by any chance?"

He shakes his head. "No."

"Happened around two A.M., a few blocks from here. It appears that Mr. Ashenbrand may have been targeted."

"I don't understand." He looks directly at Officer Martell. "How can I help?"

"We're canvassing the area," Officer Martell tells him, still avoiding contact with his eyes. "Trying to find anyone who might have seen or heard anything."

He smiles at Mrs. Lebowski, wondering what she's already told them. While it's doubtful she recalls anything of what happened that night, he doesn't want to be caught in a lie. And he's just told her daughter that the two of them were together at precisely that time. He glances in Jenna's direction, but her round Polish face reveals nothing.

"I *was* awake," he tells the police officers, "and I *did* hear something, now that I think about it."

Officer Martell's large brown eyes instantly shoot to his.

"I thought it was a car door slamming," he continues without prompting, "but it could have been a gunshot, I guess. I looked down the street, but there was nothing, so I forgot about it."

"Your windows face the street?" Officer Petroff looks toward the ceiling, as if trying to get a feel for the layout of the house.

"Uh, no. They don't." *Damn it,* he thinks. What's the matter with him? He knows better than to volunteer information. All he had to say was, "Sorry, officers. Didn't see or hear a thing," and that would have been the end of it. "Actually, I wasn't in my apartment. I was helping Mrs. Lebowski."

"You were?" asks Imogene.

"At two in the morning?" The question comes from Officer Martell.

He quickly explains the events of last Saturday night. "I got her back into bed," he concludes, "and I was returning to my apartment when I heard what I assumed was a car door slamming. I looked, but, like I said, I didn't see anything."

"And then what?" asks Officer Petroff, clearly the more suspicious of the two officers.

"What do you mean?"

"Did you go anywhere?"

"Just to bed."

"Do you mind my asking what kind of car you drive, Mr. Winniker?" The question comes out of nowhere.

"A Subaru."

"Color?"

"Black. Why?"

"A neighbor reported seeing a black sedan speeding off at about that time."

"Well, there's no shortage of black sedans," he says, then stops. He's volunteered as much information as he's going to. He shrugs and shakes his head, as if to say, *"If there was a black car speeding off at two in the morning last Saturday, it wasn't mine."*

Although it probably was, he realizes.

Speeding off to dispose of Nadia's body.

He almost laughs. How ironic it would be, after everything he's done, to be arrested and hauled off to jail for something he *didn't* do, to be tripped up by a random neighborhood shooting while transporting his latest "date" to a dumpster in Newton!

"Do you own a gun, Mr. Winniker?" Another question out of left field.

"God, no," he says. "Guns scare the crap out of me. Pardon the language," he says to Officer Martell. And it's true. He hates guns. Although not because they scare him. More because they're so impersonal. If you're going to take someone's life, you should be prepared to get your hands dirty. You owe your victims that much, at least. A knife, a rope, a strong pair of hands. So many options from which to choose. Only cowards choose a gun.

He pictures his hands around Officer Martell's lovely throat. He wonders if they're going to ask to search his apartment, then relaxes with the knowledge that they lack sufficient grounds. He's watched enough crime shows to know that a few vague suspicions aren't going to be enough to get them a search warrant. He proffers a sympathetic smile, a smile that says, *I wish I could be more help.*

"Well, thank you." Officer Petroff hands him his card. "If you should remember anything else, don't hesitate to give us a call."

"Will do."

He watches as they climb into their patrol car and drive off.

"Scary stuff," Jenna Lebowski says after they've gone.

He extricates the phone from his side pocket and notes that Paige has yet to text him back. *You don't know the half of it,* he thinks.

CHAPTER THIRTY-TWO

Paige sat, wrapped in a towel, at the edge of her bed, her clothes spread out around her like an ornate Japanese fan: the black-and-white, silk-and-chiffon, sleeveless cocktail dress with its discreetly plunging, ruffled neckline, the lacy peach-colored bra and panties for underneath, the delicate white cashmere shawl for overtop. A pair of black, thin-strapped, open-toed high-heeled pumps sat on the floor by her feet. A black-and-white alligator clutch rested on the side table. Everything waiting for her to stop sitting and get moving.

Except she couldn't.

She'd been trying for the better part of twenty minutes — ever since she got out of the shower — to get dressed, to do her hair, to put on her party face for her uncle's eightieth birthday bash. And yet here she sat, as if paralyzed from the neck down, unable to rouse her various body parts into action.

A failure.

This wasn't how her life was supposed to have turned out.

She was thirty-three years old. She was smart. She was attractive. She'd always imagined she'd have a loving husband, two bright, well-adjusted children, and a successful career by now. Instead she was single, unemployed, childless, and living with her mother, a woman who was obviously experiencing some late-life crisis of her own. How had that happened?

Not that she was without prospects, she reminded herself, trying to coax her limbs into action. Her recent job interview had gone well and a follow-up meeting was scheduled for next week. Her relationship with Sam was progressing nicely, if cautiously, both afraid to push too far, too fast.

And, to her great surprise, Mr. Right Now was back in the picture. When he hadn't contacted her again after she'd canceled their previous date, she'd assumed she wouldn't be hearing from him again.

And now, suddenly, here he was.

Hey, Wildflower. Sorry for the delay in getting back to you. Really hoping we can try again.

319

You're a little late, she berated him silently, knowing he would have been the more suitable choice for tonight's party, the kind of gorgeous that would have made Heather's jaw drop and Noah definitely sit up and take notice.

Noah, she thought, watching his face materialize in the mirror across from her bed. *Damn him anyway.*

She should have been over him by now. Not only had he been unfaithful, he'd been unfaithful with her cousin! The two were living together. He'd replaced her as easily as a roll of toilet paper! So why was she wasting even a moment of her time pining over the miserable son of a bitch?

She was a modern woman. She didn't put up with this kind of shit. She wasn't about to forgive and forget, or wait patiently for him to come to his senses and come crawling back to her. She wasn't Chloe. She could never forgive a betrayal of such magnitude.

She hated him.

So why did the thought of him with her cousin still bring tears to her eyes? Why did the prospect of being in the same room with him again send her heart racing and make her go weak in the knees?

How was it possible to love someone you hated?

And how could she go to this stupid party and watch her father's surviving twin laugh and dance and, damn it, *breathe,* while her former lover cavorted with her own virtual twin? She knew Heather would be draped all over Noah, hanging on to his every syllable, making a great show of her conquest. "I can't go," she muttered. "I can't."

"Please, darling," she heard her mother say. *"For me. I don't think I can do this alone."*

"You'll have Michael," she'd reminded her. Her brother and sister-in-law had arrived that afternoon and were staying at the Ritz, where the party was being held.

"It's not the same."

"Fine," Paige acquiesced, although it wasn't. But she'd been too preoccupied trying not to blanch at her mother's shocking new hairdo to argue further.

The last couple of weeks had seen a series of unsettling events where Joan Hamilton was concerned: the ocular migraine and severe indigestion, both of which had resulted in visits to the ER; the uncharacteristic shopping sprees; the hiring of a personal trainer; the sudden desire to start dating; the shaving of half her head. Was her mother in the midst of a nervous breakdown? Or was it possible there was something even more sinister at play? A brain tumor, perhaps?

Please, no, Paige thought.

There was muffled ringing from somewhere beside her.

Paige twisted her head from side to side, trying to determine the source of the sound. Her cellphone, she realized, her hand rummaging through her clothing, ultimately locating the phone beneath the thin cashmere shawl and bringing it to her ear without checking the caller ID.

She let it ring three more times without answering, hoping it was Sam, calling to cancel. Which would free her up to contact Mr. Right Now, invite him to the party instead. Although it was unlikely he'd be free on such short notice, or that he'd agree to go even if he was. What man in his right mind willingly subjects himself to the kind of scrutiny he was sure to receive at tonight's affair?

And what was the matter with her, considering dumping a man as nice — as *real* — as Sam for a man she hadn't even met, a postage-size illusion on a dating app?

Was she just using Sam? Was that the sort of person she'd become?

Was she more like Heather than she liked

to think?

"Shit." Paige answered the phone before she could ask herself any more troubling questions. "Hello?"

"Hi."

"Chloe," Paige acknowledged, not sure if she was disappointed or relieved by the sound of her friend's voice. "Everything okay?"

"Everything's fine," Chloe said, although she didn't sound fine. "Does there have to be a problem for me to call?"

"No, of course not. Just that you sound kind of . . ."

"Kind of what?"

"Kind of like there's a problem."

"You got that from 'hi'?"

Paige smiled. Chloe was right. She was transferring her own anxiety onto her friend. "Guess I'm just nervous about this stupid party. I can't seem to get my ass in gear."

"Oh, shit. The party's tonight? I forgot all about it."

Now Paige knew there was something wrong. "Has something happened?"

"Nothing's happened," Chloe insisted. "We'll talk tomorrow."

Paige glanced toward the clock beside her bed. Sam would be arriving any minute. She couldn't afford to waste any more time. "You're sure you're okay?"

"I'm sure."

"Okay."

"Okay," Chloe repeated. "Now get that gorgeous ass in gear, get out there, and knock 'em dead."

Paige nodded as she disconnected the line and pushed herself to her feet. She debated responding to Mr. Right Now's text, then decided he'd still be there in the morning and she didn't have time for more distractions, however tempting they might be.

Ten minutes later, she was fully dressed and made up, her hair pulled into a loose chignon at the nape of her neck. "Not bad," she said, dropping her lipstick and cellphone inside her clutch, then immediately retrieving her phone and rereading the message from Mr. Right Now. "What the hell," she decided. What was she so conflicted about? She and Sam had only been on a few dates. They were hardly exclusive. They weren't even lovers. She was free to date whomever she pleased. There was no way you could call it cheating.

Hey, there, yourself, she typed. *Wasn't sure I'd hear from you again. Sorry again about last week.*

As long as it doesn't happen twice, came

the quick response.

The phone in the kitchen rang — the concierge informing her of Sam's arrival.

Damn it, she thought. Could Sam's timing be any worse? *I have to go now,* she wrote. *Can we continue this later?*

She waited, but there was no reply.

Oh, well, she thought, dropping her phone back into her clutch and leaving the apartment. She was halfway to the elevator when she heard the familiar ping.

She quickly checked the message from Mr. Right Now.

It was short and sweet: *I'll be here.*

CHAPTER THIRTY-THREE

Chloe had no sooner disconnected her call with Paige than her landline rang. "Hello?" she said, exchanging one phone for the other.

Silence.

"Hello? Paige? Is that you?"

Still nothing.

"Hello? Is someone there? Anybody?"

Chloe stared into the receiver, waiting for whoever was on the other end to respond, then hung up when it became clear that no one would. Probably a wrong number, she decided. Or her mother, drunk dialing.

People rarely called her landline anymore, aside from the usual assortment of scam artists looking for suckers and charities looking for donations. She should probably consider getting rid of it altogether. It was an unnecessary expense, and money would undoubtedly be an issue now. She poured herself a glass of iced tea, then sat down at the kitchen table, tea in one hand, cellphone in the other, fighting the urge to call Matt.

But she was still too upset and angry, and it was important that she have a cool head when she confronted him.

Of course, Paige had sensed something was wrong immediately. She'd have to watch that. She didn't want to become the kind of friend who called only when there was a problem. Especially when that problem was always the same problem, when that problem had a name: Matt.

Chloe glanced at her watch, deciding to give the kids an extra few minutes of "tech time" before going upstairs and getting them ready for bed. They needed more time to calm down, and so did she. She didn't have the stamina for another scene like the one they'd had earlier.

Josh and Sasha had spent the day with their father and had come home full of — what was the expression Paige's father used to use? — *pee and vinegar?* Yes, that was it. Pee and vinegar. Funny expression, she thought, although somehow exactly right.

They'd burst through the front door at just after six, eyes wild with a combination of too much sugar and not enough rest, cheeks stained with dried chocolate and cotton candy. "What's all this?" she'd asked, wetting her fingers and trying to wipe away the sticky pastel residue from her son's chin.

"Daddy took us to a street fair in Somerville," Josh explained, wriggling out of reach and waving to his father, who was watching them from behind the wheel of his car.

"It was so fun," Sasha said, throwing both hands up, as if she was releasing fistfuls of confetti into the air.

"Why can't Daddy come in?" Josh asked as Chloe was closing the front door.

"Daddy has stuff to do," Chloe told him.

"Why can't he do it here? Why won't you let him come home?" Part questions, part accusations.

"It's complicated, sweetie." Chloe had hoped this would be enough to satisfy her son. She wasn't ready to have this conversation. She was still hoping that she and Matt would be able to sit down together and decide the best way to explain the situation to the children.

"What's 'complicated'?" asked Sasha.

"Daddy says you won't *let* him come home, that you're mad at him and you're getting a divorce," Josh said.

"What's a divorce?" Sasha asked.

"It means Daddy can't live here anymore," Josh told his sister, whose eyes were already filling with tears.

"I don't want a divorce," Sasha cried. "I want Daddy!"

"Okay, we're getting way ahead of ourselves," Chloe had said, trying to keep her anger at Matt from exploding in her children's faces. How dare he put her in this position! What was the matter with him? Yes, he'd been furious when informed she was filing for legal separation. But he'd calmed down when assured he'd have generous access to the kids. The last few days had passed without incident. There'd been no further outbursts, no more heavy-handed attempts to convince her of the error of her ways, no more threats about custody. He'd even managed to be civil, almost cordial, when he picked the children up this morning. Chloe was beginning to feel hopeful that, while a reconciliation remained highly doubtful, they might be able to successfully co-parent.

She took another sip of her tea, shaking her head at her capacity for self-delusion. Did she still honestly think there was any chance for her and Matt to get back together? What was it going to take to convince her that the man she'd married was an unrepentant womanizer, that her marriage was over, that he would never — *could* never — be the man she wanted him to be?

"I hate you!" Josh had shouted at her as he ran up the stairs, Matt's voice weaving through his to bounce off the walls and echo throughout the small house. "Daddy's right!" he yelled from the upstairs hallway. "You're a bitch!"

"What did you say?" Chloe yelled back, thinking that she must have misheard.

"He said you're a bitch," Sasha repeated, trying to be helpful.

Chloe burst into a combination of laughter and tears.

"What's a bitch?" Sasha asked.

Help me. "It's not a very nice word, sweetie."

"Like 'shit' and 'fuck,' " her four-year-old said knowingly.

"Yes," Chloe agreed, too stunned to say anything else.

"You said a bad word!" Sasha shouted up the stairs at her brother, then burst into tears of her own.

"Oh, please don't cry, baby." Chloe wrapped her daughter in a tight embrace. "Everything's going to be okay."

Was it? she wondered now. How could everything be okay when her husband was calling her a bitch in front of her children?

The phone on the kitchen counter rang again.

Chloe pushed herself away from the table and answered it. "Hello? Hello?" she repeated when there was no response. "Shit," she said, hanging up, listening as it rang again seconds later. "Okay, listen," she said into the receiver. "You obviously have the wrong number . . ."

"Is this Chloe?" an unfamiliar male voice asked.

"Yes. Who's this?"

"You don't know?"

"Should I?" Chloe raced through her memory to place the voice.

"Come on, Chloe. Don't play dumb. I hate women who play dumb."

A sliver of fear wormed its way beneath her skin. "Who *is* this?"

"You know what I like to do to women who play dumb?" the voice continued, as if she hadn't spoken. "I like to fuck them in the ass until they bleed and beg for mercy . . ."

Chloe slammed the receiver down with such force, it jumped back into the air, like a serpent poised to strike, then fell toward the floor, dangling from the end of its coiled black cord. "Shit." What the hell was that about?

She retrieved the receiver and quickly pressed *69, knowing even before she heard the recorded voice that the caller had blocked his number.

"Shit," she said again. "What the hell is going on?" Then, "Okay, calm down." It was just an obscene call. A pathetic, old-fashioned obscene call. People got them all the time. They were entirely random. There was no reason to be concerned. She could have been anyone.

Except the caller knew her name.

"Come on, Chloe. Don't play dumb. I hate women who play dumb."

Chloe tried again to place the voice, but it remained a mystery.

"You know what I like to do to women who play dumb?"

Chloe sank back into her chair at the kitchen table, burying her head inside her hands, trying to conjure up a face to match the angry voice, but nothing materialized.

Her first thought, of course, was that it was Matt. But Matt's voice had an entirely different timbre to it. And after all their years together, she knew its every nuance and inflection. There was no way he could have disguised it so totally that she wouldn't recognize it.

Her cellphone rang.

She glanced at it warily, letting it ring a second time before answering. "Hello?"

"You remember what happened to poor little Tiffany Sleight, don't you?" the voice said menacingly. "First, I fucked her till she bled and begged for mercy . . ."

The cellphone dropped from Chloe's hands, its face shattering upon contact with the tile floor. Seconds later, both children came running down the stairs into the kitchen.

"Mommy!" yelled Sasha, rushing to her side. "Mommy!"

Josh lingered in the doorway. "Why are you screaming?" he asked, again more accusation than question, his eyes darting between his mother and the phone at her feet.

Chloe hadn't realized she'd been screaming. "I'm sorry. I didn't mean to scare you."

"I'm not scared," Josh said. "Who said I was scared?"

"*I'm* scared," Sasha whispered.

"It's okay, sweetie," Chloe told her. "There's nothing to be afraid of." She reached down to retrieve her phone, bringing it warily to her ear, hearing nothing.

"Is it broken?" Sasha asked.

"Yes."

"Can you fix it?"

"No. I'll have to get a new one." *And a new number,* Chloe added silently. She

understood that while the call to her landline might have been random, a call to her
cellphone was most definitely not.

But if the caller wasn't Matt, who else
could it be?

"Who called?" Josh asked, as if reading
her mind.

"No one," Chloe said, tossing her injured
cell onto the counter and leading the children out of the room. "Wrong number."

CHAPTER THIRTY-FOUR

She saw them as soon as she walked into the room.

They were standing in front of the ballroom's north wall of floor-to-ceiling windows overlooking the Boston Common. Heather was dressed — barely and predictably — in something tight and red. Noah was tastefully attired in the stylish modern tuxedo Paige had helped him select for his sister's wedding last November. Just as Paige had suspected, her cousin was draped all over him, one arm circling his back, the other touching his arm, her head repeatedly grazing his shoulder, her eyes reaching adoringly for his as they chatted with their guests.

Was it her imagination or did he look as uncomfortable as Paige felt, maybe even a little embarrassed? She decided it was probably just wishful thinking on her part and forced herself to turn away before Noah could catch her staring.

There were easily 150 people in the large, beautifully appointed room whose palette was a soft mingling of beige, white, and silver. At least a dozen round tables with white tablecloths and magnificent mauve-and-white floral centerpieces occupied the far half of the room. Smiling waiters with silver trays of hors d'oeuvres floated across the subtly patterned beige carpet, weaving expertly among the guests.

Paige shook her head as one approached with an array of tiny grilled cheese sand-wiches. Just one glance at Noah with Heather had sent her stomach into free fall and caused her to lose her appetite.

"I'll try one," Sam said, lifting a miniature sandwich off the tray and popping it into his mouth. "Sure you don't want one? They're delicious."

"Not hungry." Paige felt all eyes in the room shift toward her, as if she'd screamed the words at the top of her lungs.

"You okay?" Sam asked.

She glanced at him, although only briefly. The truth was that she'd barely looked at him since he'd arrived to pick her up. Not that he wasn't presentable — even hand-some — with his newly trimmed hair, dark blue suit, pink shirt, and paisley tie. But he was no Mr. Right Now. No one — certainly not Heather — would look at him and think she'd traded up. And wasn't that the whole point of bringing a date to the party? *I'm the worst person in the world,* she thought. "I'm fine," she told him.

"Have I told you how lovely you look?" he whispered.

"You have. Thank you."

"You are definitely the most beautiful woman here."

"Thank you," she said again, wondering what was the matter with her. Sam was a good man. He looked good, he smelled good, he said all the right things. So why was she so irritated by him? What was her problem?

"Ready to rumble?" he asked, taking another step into the room.

"Do I have a choice?"

"You always have a choice."

"Paige, darling," a voice said, making the choice for her.

Paige watched her mother make a beeline for her, long rhinestone earrings bouncing toward the shoulders of her beige silk dress. "Mom! You look gorgeous," she said, realizing she meant it. Joan Hamilton's features had been energized by her new haircut, which had knocked at least ten years off her age, emphasizing the cut of her cheekbones and bringing a mischievous sparkle to her deep blue eyes.

"Thank you, sweetheart." Joan looked toward the man at her daughter's side. "You must be Sam."

"A pleasure to meet you, Mrs. Hamilton."

"Please call me Joan."

"Where are Michael and Deborah?" Paige pretended to search the room for her brother and his wife when she was really checking to see whether Noah was looking.

Joan peered through the roomful of guests. "They were beside me a second ago. Oh, dear. So many people. I had no idea your uncle was so popular."

Paige felt a renewed surge of annoyance, this time at her uncle. If Ted Hamilton was popular, it was only because of his more outgoing brother. It wasn't fair that the two men weren't sharing this evening.

The wrong twin had survived. The wrong twin was celebrating.

"Don't forget to wish him a happy birthday," her mother said, as if aware of Paige's thoughts.

"Of course," Paige said, absently watching her uncle as he stood with his wife by the far wall, accepting the congratulations of friends and colleagues. She bent forward, as if to kiss her mother's cheek. "Did Noah say anything to you?" she whispered.

"Just hello," her mother whispered, pretend-kissing back. "I ignored him. As should you," she added pointedly.

Paige nodded, leaving her mother and wending her way through the crowd toward her uncle, Sam at her side.

"Deep breaths," he cautioned as they approached.

"Well, look who's here," Ted Hamilton exclaimed, opening his arms wide. "One of my very favorite people in the whole world."

"Happy birthday, Uncle Ted."

"Thank you for coming," he said, lowering his voice. "I know this can't be easy for you. You can't know how sorry I am."

Paige nodded, not sure if he was referring to the fact that her father wasn't here or that Heather and Noah were. Possibly both.

"Paige, darling," his wife said, breaking into the conversation. "So glad you decided to come. And who's this handsome fellow?"

"This is my friend, Sam Benjamin."

"So nice to meet you, Sam," Bev said, giving him a not-too-subtle once-over. She smiled. *Not as handsome as Noah,* the smile said. *Score one for Heather.*

"Very nice to meet you both," Sam said. "Happy birthday, sir. Many happy returns of the day."

"Thank you. My wife throws one hell of a party, doesn't she?"

"Well, the ballroom was Heather's idea," Bev demurred, glancing toward the floor-to-ceiling windows. "Such a beautiful view."

"Did you know that the Boston Common is the country's oldest public park?" Sam asked.

"Well, I knew it was old," Bev said with a laugh. The laugh was bigger and more robust than it needed to be.

"Established in 1634."

"Which makes it almost as old as me," Ted Hamilton joked.

Really? Paige thought. *We're talking about the Boston Common? Next, we'll be talking about the weather.*

"Lovely day today, wasn't it?" Bev said obligingly.

"At my age, every day aboveground is a lovely day," Ted Hamilton said.

"Oh, Ted," his wife giggled. "Eighty's hardly old anymore. You have lots of years left."

"Excuse me," Paige said, feeling her blood begin to boil and turning away before she started screaming.

"Breathe," Sam said again, following her.

"I'm not sure how much of this I can take."

"Then you'd better brace yourself," Sam said, peering over her shoulder. "There's a woman headed this way . . ."

Paige swiveled in the direction of his gaze. "Oh, shit."

"Hello, Paige." Her cousin was standing in front of her, a slow smile stretching toward her ears.

"Heather," Paige acknowledged, feeling all eyes in the room swivel toward them. There was a moment of silence as Paige tried to choose between grabbing her cousin by the throat or fleeing the premises.

"Aren't you going to introduce me to your friend?"

"Why?" Paige heard herself ask. "Do you want to fuck him?"

Heather's cheeks blushed the same color as her dress. "Excuse me!"

"Whoa," Sam said softly, his hand reaching for Paige's elbow.

Paige brushed his hand aside. "Of course, you don't always need to know their names, do you? If I'm remembering correctly . . ."

"Maybe dial it down a notch," Sam whispered to the back of Paige's head.

Paige ignored him. *This* is *dialed down*, she thought.

341

"Okay, look," Heather said, regaining her composure along with the upper hand, "I can see you're upset."

"Can you? Can you really see that?"

"But this is hardly the time or place. It's my father's birthday. This is a celebration . . ."

"A celebration," Paige repeated.

"Breathe," Sam said again.

". . . and I was really hoping you'd be able to rise above whatever issues you may have with me . . ." Heather continued.

"The issue being that you fucked my boyfriend," Paige interrupted. "I assume that's the issue you're referring to?"

". . . and that you could put your feelings for me aside," Heather persisted stubbornly. "For my father's sake, if not your own."

Paige felt her hands forming fists at her sides.

"For *your* sake," Sam said to Heather, "I think I'd walk away while I still had all my teeth."

Paige almost laughed. Leave it to a dentist to reference teeth.

Heather sighed and shook her head. "Poor you," she told Sam. "You obviously have no clue what you're getting yourself into."

"I wouldn't waste too much time worrying about me."

"Suit yourself. Just don't say I didn't warn you." Heather smiled over her shoulder at Paige as she walked away. "I'll tell Noah you said hello."

CHAPTER THIRTY-FIVE

It was after eight o'clock when dinner was finally served and almost ten when Ted Hamilton, responding to intermittent, halfhearted cries of "Speech, speech!," finally pushed his chair away from his table in the center of the room and stood up to speak.

Joan breathed a sigh of relief. It meant the party was almost over and she could go home. She was exhausted. From smiling. From making small talk. From worrying about her daughter. From pretending to be having a good time.

The evening had proved more of an endurance test than a celebration. Joan had never enjoyed large parties, especially ones where she knew only a fraction of the guests. She suspected that at least half the room consisted of aging former employees of the company the two brothers had founded, and not actual friends. She wondered how many people Ted Hamilton would be able to identify by name. Her husband would have known every single one.

She glanced across the table at Paige, who'd barely touched her food all night. She'd been too busy refilling her wineglass and pretending to be oblivious to Noah, who sat three tables away, Heather at his side. Paige had spent most of the evening in conversation with her brother and his wife, laughing a touch too loudly at Michael's jokes and pretty much ignoring Sam. This was a shame, Joan thought, because Sam seemed like a very nice man.

Which was exactly the problem, she understood. Paige wasn't ready for nice. It was too early for nice.

Maybe in a few months. Maybe not for another year. What her daughter needed now was time. Time to get over Noah's betrayal, to get him out of her system, to figure out what she wanted, to be receptive to a man like Sam.

This simply wasn't his time. Like a premature baby, Sam had arrived too soon.

What her daughter needed right now was a man she could fuck and forget.

Joan blushed at her silent use of the crude phrase, almost as if she'd spoken it out loud.

Robert had never approved of such language, let alone the thought behind it. She could barely believe she approved of it herself.

Not that she was a prude, by any stretch of the imagination. She'd had her share of lovers before she met Robert, her share of forgettable men. She was, as she'd recently reminded Paige and Chloe, a child of the sixties. She sighed, understanding that that decade was part of another era.

Indeed, another century.

Where had all that time gone?

"Mom?" a voice asked from beside her. Joan turned toward her son, who was staring at her through worried hazel eyes.

"Yes, sweetheart?"

"Are you all right?"

"Yes, sweetheart. Why do you ask?"

"You had this very strange look on your face," he told her. "And you went all pink. Are you having a hot flash?" He grabbed her wrist, feeling for her pulse.

"I'm fine," she told him, trying to shake free of his grasp. "And I'm a little old to be having hot flashes, don't you think?"

"You're a little old to be shaving half your head," he said. "Besides, some women have hot flashes all their lives. Stop fidgeting and let me get a read. Your heart rate is slightly elevated."

"What's happening?" Paige asked from across the table.

"Your brother is playing doctor."

"I *am* a doctor," Michael reminded her.

My son, the cardiologist, Joan thought, half-expecting him to pull a stethoscope out of the breast pocket of his gray suit and hold it against her chest.

"What's the matter with her?" Paige was already half out of her seat.

"Sit down," Joan told her. "I'm fine." She brought both hands to her lap, registering the worried faces around her: Michael and Deborah, Paige and Sam, a rather boring couple named Walt and Lisa Something-or-other, and two recent widows, both named Anne, all of whom were staring at her as if she were about to explode. "Honestly, everybody. Stop worrying. I'm fine. We're missing the speech."

"Everything all right over there?" Ted Hamilton asked, pausing in his opening remarks and causing the entire room to glance in their direction.

Joan caught Noah's eyes drift toward Paige, then turn away when he saw her looking.

"Everything's fine," Joan said, forcing a laugh. "I'm so sorry. Please continue."

"Well, as I was saying," Ted Hamilton began again, referring to the notes in his hand, "I want to thank you all for coming tonight. I'm sure you have better things to do with your Saturday nights than attend an old man's birthday party."

There followed the appropriate protests — "You're not old!" "Who are you kidding?" "We should all look so good at your age!" — before he was allowed to proceed.

"I especially want to thank my wife, Bev, for arranging this wonderful event, for sending out the invitations, for choosing the menu and selecting the wine . . ."

"Noah selected the wine," Heather interjected loudly, causing a wave of chuckles to sweep through the room.

"Apparently, Noah selected the wine," Ted said to another such wave.

Joan watched Paige's shoulders stiffen and her jaw tense.

"Thank you, Noah. And thank you, Heather, for . . ." He paused, once again checking his notes, as if he weren't sure exactly what Heather's contribution had been. ". . . for assisting your mother. I'm sure you were a great help with everything."

Now it was Heather's shoulders that stiffened and jaw that tensed. Joan almost felt sorry for the girl.

She paid little attention to the rest of her brother-in-law's speech, choosing to concentrate on the sound of his voice rather than his words. She found that if she closed her eyes and just listened, it was almost possible to hear her late husband. Of course, Robert wouldn't have needed notes. His speech would have been funny and smart and effortless.

And brief, Joan thought, as Ted droned on.

"Mom," her son said, gently squeezing her arm. "Are you okay?"

"Is she all right?" Paige asked immediately.

So much for closing my eyes, Joan thought, opening them wide. "Would you please stop?" she whispered. "I'm *fine.*"

"And lastly," Ted Hamilton said, "I want to say a few words about my late brother, Robert, who wasn't as fortunate as I am and didn't live to see this wonderful day. As I'm sure that all of you know, twins share a special bond, and it's hard to imagine one more special than the one I shared with Robert. We grew up together, we played sports together, we even dated the same girls."

"Oh, Ted," Bev said, giggling like a schoolgirl.

"Eventually we formed a business together," he continued, "and the success of our company was due, in no small measure, to my brother's input and tireless work ethic . . ."

In no small measure, Joan repeated silently, understanding by the renewed stiffening of Paige's shoulders that her daughter was thinking the same thing. The success of the brothers' company had been due almost *entirely* to Robert's input and tireless work ethic, his brother having largely tagged along for the ride.

"Robert was the yin to my yang. He was the practical one, I was the dreamer," Ted continued. "He was the calm, I was the storm; his was the voice of reason when my voice was off on multiple flights of fancy; I had big ideas, he knew how to make those ideas a reality. Together, we built a great company."

Wow, Joan thought. *Talk about revisionist history.* She'd underestimated her brother-in-law. It took talent to give with one hand and take with the other, to praise and demean at the same time. In a few broad strokes, Ted had painted himself as a man of imagination and vision while relegating his dead brother to the more boring realms of reason and common sense.

"Here's to you, Bobby," Ted concluded,

using the diminutive Robert had always hated. He lifted his wineglass into the air, the rest of the room quickly following suit. "I miss you, brother. How I wish you were here."

Tears filled Joan's eyes. She'd been wishing the same thing every day for the past two years.

"I'd also like to extend my gratitude to Robert's wife, Joan, for being the best wife my brother could have hoped for, and to their children, Michael and Paige, who made him proud every single day. Michael, a big thank-you to you and Deborah for flying in from New Jersey to celebrate with us tonight, and Paige, what can I say? You know that I've always considered you more a daughter than a niece."

Joan watched the already stiff smile freeze on Heather's face.

"Thank you for being here tonight, and know that Bev and I are always here for you." He returned his notes to his tuxedo's inside jacket pocket. "And that's it, everyone. Enjoy the rest of the evening. Coffee and birthday cake are on the way."

"Excuse me," Joan whispered, rising from her seat as a waiter approached with plates of something chocolate and gooey. She couldn't sit there another minute. She couldn't breathe. She needed air.

"Where are you going?" Michael asked. "Are you okay?"

"Is she okay?" Paige echoed.

"I have to pee, if that's all right with the two of you."

"I'll come with you," Paige said.

"Stay right where you are. I'm perfectly capable of peeing on my own." Joan marched purposefully from the room, locating the women's washroom off the main lobby and locking herself in a stall, lowering the lid of the toilet seat, and sitting down. She took a series of long, deep breaths, the last one emerging as more of a strangled cry.

"Are you all right in there?" a voice asked from one of the other stalls.

Damn it. She hadn't realized anyone else was in the room. "Yes, thank you. Quite all right."

There followed the sound of a toilet flushing and water running. Seconds later, a door whooshed shut and Joan was finally alone. "Goddamn it," she whispered. She had to get a grip, give her brother-in-law the benefit of the doubt. It was possible he'd meant well. He couldn't help that he was such a self-centered bonehead. She had to pull herself together, especially for Paige.

She had to set an example, be gracious and resilient, show her daughter that there was life after loss.

Joan took another deep breath, then exited the stall and left the washroom. It was time to go home. Maybe she could get a ride with Paige and Sam. But when she returned to the ballroom, she saw that her daughter's chair was empty. "Where's Paige?" she asked Sam.

He looked uncertain. "I assumed she was with you."

Joan glanced around the room. People were finishing their dessert and starting to take their leave. Some were approaching Ted's table to say their goodbyes. She watched her brother-in-law rise from his seat to shake their hands and kiss their cheeks, reveling in the attention. She saw his two sons graciously thanking everyone for coming. She saw Bev basking in the ongoing compliments. She saw Heather twisting from side to side, her eyes conducting a subtle scan of the premises.

And she saw something else: Just like Paige, Noah was nowhere in sight.

CHAPTER THIRTY-SIX

"You remember what happened to poor little Tiffany Sleight, don't you?"

Chloe sat cross-legged on her bed in her pink-striped cotton pajamas, her laptop balanced on her knees. It was nine o'clock; the kids had finally settled down and given in to sleep; there'd been no more disturbing calls to her landline. All was quiet.

Except for the threatening voice that continued whispering in her ear.

"You remember what happened to poor little Tiffany Sleight, don't you?"

In fact, Chloe was only vaguely aware of what had happened to the young woman, other than that her body had recently been discovered in a landfill outside the city. She'd avoided delving into the gory details, knowing they would only upset her. There was only so much unpleasantness she could deal with at a time, and she'd decided to concentrate on those things over which she had at least a semblance of control.

"Don't do it," she whispered now, her hands hovering over the keyboard. Yet, even as she was saying the words, her fingers were already zeroing in on the letters, pressing T-I-F-F-A-N-Y S-L-E-I-G-H-T into the search box, and watching as the screen filled with photographs and articles about the slain woman.

She was a pretty girl, Chloe thought, studying a close-up of the young woman's face, her shy smile presaging no hint of the horrifying fate awaiting her. Long brown hair, a pleasant if narrow face, almond-shaped eyes, a slight overbite. Twenty-eight years old and a graduate of Boston University, she'd worked as an executive assistant at Google, whose head office was located mere blocks away, in Kendall Square. Had they ever crossed paths? Chloe wondered, bringing the screen closer to her eyes, staring at the young woman's face until it degenerated into a series of black-and-white pixels.

Tiffany had recently broken up with her boyfriend, the various articles confirmed, and had a reputation as a loner. "She was really quiet," one coworker confided, declining to give her name. "She kept to herself most of the time." Her coworkers had reported her missing when she'd failed to show up for work. "She was meeting some guy for drinks," another colleague offered, which seemed to be all anyone knew. Tiffany had volunteered nothing about the man she was meeting and no one had asked. Police had questioned her former boyfriend, but he had an airtight alibi for the night she disappeared and was not considered a suspect. No one had reported seeing her the night she vanished. Her body had been discovered purely by accident when a hungry dog went foraging through a landfill for food.

Chloe closed her laptop, not wanting to read the details of how Tiffany died, then opening it again when curiosity got the better of her.

She read that despite the decomposition, there was still enough left of Tiffany Sleight to determine she'd been raped and tortured before being strangled and repeatedly stabbed. Both her neck and wrists bore telltale ligature marks, and signs of petechial hemorrhaging behind her eyes revealed she'd been rendered unconscious, then revived, several times before being mercifully finished off.

How awful those final hours, Chloe thought. How terrified that poor girl must have been!

What kind of man was capable of such monstrous behavior?

There were rumors of a possible serial killer, but so far, police were playing down such conjecture. Should she call them? she wondered, glancing toward the phone beside her bed.

And say what exactly?

That she'd been the victim of an obscene phone call, that the caller had known her name, that he'd alluded to Tiffany Sleight, that he could well be the monster they were looking for?

She pictured them trying to keep a straight face. *Do you have any idea how many women get calls like that every day?* she heard them ask. Then, *Didn't you phone the station just last week to erroneously report your husband had kidnapped your children?* No, she couldn't call them, she decided, knowing they would likely dismiss her as a hysteric, the female equivalent of "the boy who cried wolf."

She closed her laptop and grabbed her remote from the night table, flipping on the TV. After an hour of the mind-numbing antics of assorted Kardashians, she felt her anxiety start to lessen. What she needed now was a large bowl of strawberry ice cream.

She turned off the TV and climbed out of bed, tiptoeing down the stairs and into the kitchen. Flipping on the light, she grabbed a large spoon from the cutlery drawer and opened the freezer, eating the ice cream directly from the carton.

The phone rang.

Chloe's body went as cold as the ice cream slithering down her throat. *Don't answer it,* she told herself, her hand already reaching for the receiver. *Please let it be Paige calling to report on her evening,* she pleaded silently. "Hello?"

"Enjoying your ice cream?" the voice asked.

Chloe's head spun toward the window at the back of the house as her hand shot toward the light switch on the wall, throwing the room into darkness. She fell to her knees, her hand over her mouth to keep from screaming.

"Oh, Chloe. Why'd you go and do that?" the voice said in her ear.

"I'm calling the police," she said, her heart beating wildly.

"The police can't help you, Chloe."

The line went dead.

Chloe immediately called nine-one-one. To hell with whether they dismissed her as hysterical. Someone was watching the house. She was in danger.

Two officers arrived ten minutes later, Chloe opening the door before they could knock, the details of every call pouring from her mouth before they'd stepped inside. They did a quick search of the grounds, but found nothing. They asked if she was married and she told them that she and her husband had recently separated, and no, they weren't on the best of terms. They asked if she thought he could be behind the calls, and she said she honestly didn't know. They asked if she thought he was dangerous and she said she didn't know that either. "Did your husband know Tiffany Sleight?" they asked.

My God. Did he?

"I don't know," she told them. Was there no end to the things she didn't know?

The officers jotted everything down and said they'd pay Matt a visit. They brought up the possibility of her taking out a restraining order against him.

"Can I do that?" she asked.

"I'd certainly look into it," the older of the two officers advised, promising to drive by the house at intervals throughout the night.

Chloe watched as the men returned to their patrol car, then locked the door, fighting the urge to call Paige, beg her to come over and spend the night. "Sure," Chloe admonished herself, doing a quick check of the downstairs rooms before returning to the second floor. "Put your best friend's life in danger, why don't you?"

She checked on the kids and was gratified to find them sleeping soundly. "Thank you, God," she whispered, turning off the lights in her bedroom and peeking through the closed curtains onto the empty street below.

She'd been against the move to Cambridge when Matt first suggested it, wanting to remain in Boston proper. But Matt had been adamant that such a move would be great for their marriage, as well as for their children. He'd argued that Cambridge, home to both Harvard and MIT, was one of the most sought-after housing markets in the northeast US and that due to decreasing land space and escalating prices, they'd make a killing, financially, when they did decide to sell. He'd promised that if she was unhappy, they'd move back to the city.

Just another one of the promises he'd broken over the years.

Chloe lay down on top of her bed and closed her eyes, doubting she'd sleep. But seconds later, she found herself wandering through a crowded street fair, trying to keep a wad of pink cotton candy from sticking to her hair. "Look, Mommy," Sasha squealed from somewhere beside her. "A clown!" Chloe looked up to see a faceless man running toward her. "Out of the way, bitch," he shouted, knocking her to the ground.

The phone rang.

Chloe bolted up in bed. She grabbed the phone, bringing it to her ear without speaking.

"Chloe?" a man shouted. "Chloe, are you there?"

"Matt?"

"What the hell are you trying to pull now?"

"What? What are you talking about?"

"The police were just here. You told them I've been harassing you, that you think I'm some sort of serial killer . . . ?"

"I never said that." Chloe tried to explain the events of the evening, but Matt wouldn't listen.

"For your information, I've been with clients the whole goddamn night," he interrupted, "going back and forth with offers, busting my ass trying to make a living to support my children and my crazy-ass wife. I've got half a dozen people willing to vouch for me, happy to swear I never left their side, and that the only phone calls I made tonight were business-related. I come home, exhausted, to find the police at my door, asking me questions about some girl named Tiffany Sleight!"

"Someone's been calling me, threatening me," she explained again.

"And you automatically assumed it was me?"

"I didn't know what to think."

"Well, if you think you have trouble now, just wait till I —"

Chloe reached down and pulled the phone plug out of the wall before Matt could say another word. Then she burst into tears.

"Mommy?" Sasha said from the doorway, Josh appearing behind her.

"Oh, sweeties. I'm sorry. Did I wake you up?"

"Was that another wrong number?"

"I'm afraid so."

Sasha ran toward the bed, climbing in beside Chloe. "I'm scared. Can I sleep with you?"

In response, Chloe pulled down the bedspread and beckoned Sasha underneath the covers. "You, too," she told her son, who was hovering in the doorway. She watched him push one reluctant foot in front of the other, allowing himself to be coaxed into her bed.

"You should call Daddy," he told her.

"No. I don't think that's a good idea."

"He could protect us," Josh said.

"He has a gun," Sasha announced.

"What?"

"Daddy has a gun," she repeated.

"No, of course he doesn't have a gun," Chloe said.

"Yes, he does," Josh said. "He showed us."

"Daddy showed you a gun?"

"It's very heavy," Sasha said, snuggling into Chloe's side.

"He let you hold it?" Chloe could barely contain her horror.

"It wasn't loaded," Josh said.

"I don't care. You shouldn't be anywhere near guns."

"It's for protection," Josh insisted.

"We don't need protecting," Chloe said, managing to sound much surer of herself than she felt.

Someone was threatening her.

Matt had a gun.

Seconds later, both children were asleep, their warm little bodies pressed against hers. Chloe lay between them, afraid to close her eyes, the clock beside her bed ticking off the seconds till morning.

CHAPTER THIRTY-SEVEN

Paige hadn't meant to look at him, to acknowledge his presence in any way. And she hadn't. Not until about five minutes before, when she'd swiveled around in her chair at the same moment he'd swiveled around in his. And their eyes had connected, and his lips had creased into a tentative smile, and she'd turned away before hers could do the same.

"You okay?" Sam asked.

"Will you excuse me?" she asked in return. "I want to check on my mother."

And maybe that had been her intention when she fled the ballroom. But instead of checking on her mother, she found herself cutting through the lobby, imagining Noah chasing after her, his hand reaching for her shoulder as she stepped outside to gulp at the warm night air. "Paige," she heard him say, his voice floating through the soft breeze of her fantasy to graze the back of her neck.

"Paige," the voice said again.

She spun around.

And there he was.

"Noah," she said, her voice almost inaudible over the pounding of her heart.

"I've been hoping for the chance to speak to you," he said. "How are you?"

"Fine," she said, not capable of words more than one syllable. "You?"

"I'm good. You look beautiful."

"Thanks."

"I've always liked that dress."

Had she known that? Paige wondered. Was that why she'd picked it? "You look nice, too," she managed to spit out, choosing not to think about it.

Noah patted the black leather lapels of his tuxedo jacket. "This was your choice. As I recall, I thought it was way too radical. You had to work hard to persuade me."

"Oh, I can't take too much of the credit," she heard herself say. "As I recall, you're pretty easy to persuade." She watched him wince and glanced quickly away, biting down on her bottom lip and noting that several of the party guests had come outside and were now waiting by the valet stand for their cars.

"Okay. I guess I deserved that."

"Guess you did," she said, warming to the sound of her own voice. "Should you be out here? I don't think Heather will be too happy if she sees us together."

"Probably not," he admitted.

"And yet, here you stand."

"I was hoping we could talk."

"About what?"

"I thought maybe we could clear the air."

She almost laughed. "Air's pretty thick. Not sure it can be done."

"We could try."

"Why?"

He seemed surprised by the question. "Why?"

"What's the point?"

"I don't know. Maybe there isn't one. I just know that I really hate the way we left things . . ."

"You mean with my cousin on top of you in bed?"

This time it was Noah who looked away. When he looked back, a small smile was playing with the corners of his lips. "Heather told me you were in a rather feisty mood tonight."

"She used the word 'feisty,' did she?"

His smile spread to his eyes. "I miss that feistiness," he said. Then, "I miss *you.*"

Paige felt her body sway toward him. She

fought to hold her position. "Maybe you should have thought of that before you started fucking my cousin."

Noah released a slow, deep breath. "So . . . back to that."

"Back to that."

"Look. I understand you're angry . . ."

"How generous of you."

"Give me a break, Paige. I'm trying to apologize here."

"I'm not interested in your apology. I thought I made that pretty clear when I moved out."

"That's just it. Everything happened so fast. You ran off, you wouldn't answer my calls, you carted your stuff out the next day —"

"And Heather carted her stuff right in."

"It's more complicated than that."

"Heather is many things," Paige shot back. "Complicated is not one of them." She noticed a friend of Bev's watching them from the valet stand. The woman put her hand in front of her mouth to whisper something to her companion. "We should go in. People are starting to talk . . ."

"Walk with me," Noah said.

"I don't think that's a good idea."

"Walk with me," he said again, taking her by the elbow and leading her down Avery

Street toward Washington.

"What's happening?" Paige asked him when they reached the corner. "What are we doing?"

"I don't know, damn it." Noah threw his hands up in the air. "Believe me, this is not the way I envisioned this evening going."

"And how did you envision it going?"

"Not like this." He stared in the direction of the old Paramount Theatre. "Look. I'll be honest. I was kind of hoping you wouldn't show . . ."

"Heather didn't tell you I was coming?"

"Oh, no. She told me. She even said you were bringing a date. I tried to tell myself it didn't matter, and then in you walked . . ."

"And?"

"It matters," he said.

Paige found herself holding her breath. Wasn't this exactly what she'd been wanting to hear?

"So, what's the story with this guy?" Noah asked.

"I don't think that's any of your business."

"I'm asking anyway."

"You have a hell of a nerve."

He shrugged.

Paige turned away. She'd always found Noah's shrugs unbearably sexy. Was this what it had been like for Chloe all these years? The constant push-pull, the loving and the loathing, the longing for the fairy-tale ending, for the kiss before the final credits, for that pivotal moment when the frog turns into the handsome prince.

"Is it serious?"

"Are you?" she asked, incredulous. "What exactly is going on here, Noah? What are you trying to say?" Had seeing her with another man been all the push Noah needed to realize the terrible mistake he'd made?

"That I miss you," he said again. "That I miss *us.*"

The words swirled around her head, making her dizzy. "I miss you, too," she admitted.

And then she was in his arms, and he was kissing her neck, her cheek, her eyes. And it was almost enough to block out the stubborn image of Heather straddling his naked body.

Almost.

And then his lips found hers, and it was almost enough to blot out the lingering, bitter taste of his betrayal.

Almost.

"I'm so sorry, Paige. I was an idiot."

"Yes, you were."

"It's just that we were going through a rough patch," he said. "I was in the middle of a very complicated case. You'd lost your job and were crying all the time, wandering around the apartment in those god-awful gray sweats, no makeup, dirty hair, moaning about how unhappy you were."

Whoa. Wait a minute. What?

"And I admit, it kind of got to me after a while," he continued, seemingly oblivious to the sudden stiffening of her shoulders. "I had my hands full at the office. I was worried about money. I mean, your being fired made things more than a little tight. We were fighting constantly. Nothing I said or did was right. You had no patience for me at all. You probably don't remember, but you were short with me all the time. And then Heather started coming over. And she's got her hair just so, and she's always laughing and happy and —"

"You're saying what happened was my fault?" Paige interrupted.

"No, of course not. I'm just trying to explain why I was so susceptible."

"You slept with my cousin because I was wearing sweatpants?"

"That's not what I'm saying."

"My hair was dirty and Heather's was *just so*?"

"Stop twisting my words."

"Then stop talking, you fucking idiot!"

370

Paige shouted. "No, I'm wrong," she corrected, marching back toward the hotel. "*You* aren't the idiot. *I'm* the idiot! What the hell was I thinking? Once a frog, always a frog!"

"Please lower your voice," he cautioned, following her. "People are staring."

She came to an abrupt stop. "Well, then, I think it's time we gave them something to stare at, don't you?" And with that, Paige hauled back and slapped him, hard, across the face.

Behind her, she heard a collective gasp, then saw her cousin pushing herself to the front of the small crowd.

"What's all the commotion out here?" Heather asked, the smile sliding from her face as soon as she saw Paige and Noah. "What's going on?" she asked, as Noah brushed past her into the lobby, eyes down, cheek red. Heather glared at her cousin, then turned on her five-inch heels and hurried back inside the hotel.

"If you'll excuse me," Paige told the group of stunned onlookers, who parted as one to let her pass.

Sam jumped to his feet as soon as she entered the ballroom.

"Let's get out of here," she said.

CHAPTER THIRTY-EIGHT

She was all over him even before they were through the door of his North End apartment, tugging at his tie and pulling at his belt buckle. "Paige, hold on," Sam said, kicking the door closed with his foot.

"What's the problem?" she asked, covering his mouth with her own.

"Can we just slow down for half a sec?"

"What for?" Paige asked. She didn't want to slow down. Slowing down meant time to think, and thinking was the last thing she wanted to do. She didn't want to think about what had happened. She didn't want to think about what she was doing now. She didn't want to think about anything. "Help me out here," she said, pulling Sam's jacket away from his shoulders and trying to push it down his arms. "That's better," she said, as it fell to the floor. Her fingers went immediately to the buttons of his shirt. "I've always liked a man in a pink shirt," she muttered between kisses to his neck, trying to generate some sort of a response.

"Paige," he said, stilling her fingers with his own. Not exactly the response she'd been hoping for.

"What's the matter? Why are we stopping?"

"I'm just not sure . . ."

"Not sure about what?" Paige asked. "Don't you want me?"

"Of course I want you."

"Then what are we waiting for?" She reached down and grabbed the hem of her dress, pulling it over her head and letting it drop to her feet. She kicked it aside, standing before him in her lacy, peach-colored underwear. "Your turn," she said.

"Can we at least go into the bedroom?"

"Sure. Whatever," Paige said, confused by his seeming reticence. "Lead the way," she said, although she was the one taking his hand and navigating her way in the dark between the sofa and a wing chair into the hallway.

"That's my boys' room," he said, stopping her when she tried entering the first of the two bedrooms.

"They're not in there, are they?" she asked playfully.

"No, of course not. They're with their

mother this week."

"So, are we okay now?" she asked, trying to laugh as they reached his room. What was the matter with him? Why was he acting so weird? She reached behind her to unhook her bra, tossing it aside as they stumbled toward his bed. She grabbed his hand, placing it firmly on her now bare right breast. God, was she going to have to do everything? "Kiss me," she instructed, starting to lose patience.

He kissed her, but it was more a kiss of desperation than passion. On their previous dates, she'd loved the way he kissed — soft, tender, just the right amount of tongue. Now there was no tongue at all, just an unsatisfying mashing of his lips against hers, his mouth parting just enough for their front teeth to grind together.

She dropped to her knees, discarding his belt and pulling down both his pants and his underwear in one fell swoop, surrounding him with her mouth, trying to coax his limp penis into action. *Come on,* she thought. *Come on.* And then she felt his hand on the top of her head, his fingers taking hold of her hair, pulling her away.

"Paige, stop," he said.

"What? Why?"

"It's not going to work."

She stared up at him through the darkness. "Why the hell not?" Anger mixed with humiliation. "What's your problem?"

"What's *yours*?" he countered.

"Mine?" *Really?* "I'm not the one with the problem here."

"I think you are."

"Then I think you'd better tell me what it is, because I don't have a clue."

"Okay, listen," he said, pulling up his pants and turning on the bedside lamp, bathing the small room in a soothing amber glow. He sank down on the bed's beige comforter, causing it to billow out around him.

"I'm listening." Paige looked around for her dress before realizing she'd left it on the living room floor. She settled for her bra, snapping it back into place and pacing back and forth in front of him.

"Why don't you sit down." He patted the space beside him.

"Why don't you just tell me what problem you think I'm having."

"Okay, look." He hesitated, as if searching for just the right words. "When we first connected, I thought you were beautiful, smart, fun. I even thought, strange as this might sound, that there could be a future. I knew there were unresolved issues with regards to your family and your ex. I knew you were still hurting. And I'm not an idiot. I knew tonight was all about making a point, and I was cool with that. I've never been the instrument of anyone's revenge before, and to be honest, I was flattered."

"Still not sure what you're getting at."

"I was actually looking forward to the party."

"You certainly seemed to be enjoying yourself."

"How the hell would you know?" he snapped, his sudden anger catching Paige by surprise. "You barely looked at me all night. I don't think you said more than a dozen words to me the whole evening. It was like once you'd introduced me to your cousin, I'd served my purpose. From then on, I was just in your way."

"That's not true," Paige said, although she knew it was.

"And then you excused yourself to go to the bathroom, ostensibly to check on your mother, and I saw your ex take off after you, and the two of you were gone for the better part of fifteen minutes. It didn't take a genius to put two and two together. Even Heather figured that one out pretty quick. She was racing around the room like a chicken with her head cut off."

Paige bit down on her lip to keep from smiling.

"And then you come running back in, all flushed, and say 'let's get out of here.' We take off without a word to anyone, you say let's go to my place, and suddenly you're all over me. You can't get my clothes off fast enough, and damn it, Paige, I'd like nothing more than to return the favor. I've been wanting to make love to you from the moment I first laid eyes on you."

"So what's the problem?"

"The problem is I'm not stupid. I know tonight isn't about me. I know that what's happening is a reaction to whatever happened between you and Noah. That you've got all this excess energy you're desperate to get rid of. That I could be anybody. And much as I'd like to take advantage of the situation, I can't do it."

"Even if I want you to?"

"It's not just about you," he said. "I'm protecting myself here, Paige. Your cousin was wrong when she said I had no idea what I was getting myself into. I know *exactly* where this is headed, and it's down a one-way street. I've been down that road once already. I don't want to go there again. I deserve better."

Paige's eyes filled with tears. "Yes, you

do," she acknowledged, sitting down beside him and taking his hand. "You're a good man, Sam Benjamin."

"I know," he said. "Good man. Bad timing."

She smiled. "Maybe I could have a rain check someday?"

He smiled back. "You know how to find me."

"Paige?" her mother called from her bedroom as Paige entered the condo. "Darling, are you all right?"

"I'm fine." Paige walked into the family room and plopped down on the sofa, her clutch in her lap. *Horny, but fine,* she thought, as her mother entered the room, wearing a long blue nightgown and a worried look on her shiny face. "Did I wake you?" Paige asked her.

"No, I only got home about half an hour ago. I've been busy with my moisturizers . . ."

"Did you hear about . . . ?"

". . . what happened? Oh, yes. I believe that was the slap heard 'round the world. I have to admit, you made me very proud." Joan sat down beside her daughter, taking her in her arms and kissing her forehead. "How was it for you?"

Paige laughed. "I cannot begin to describe how good it felt."

"Oh, I'm so glad. It couldn't have happened to a more deserving fellow." She patted her daughter's hand. "And speaking of fellows, I wasn't sure you'd be coming home tonight."

"Believe me, it wasn't my idea."

"Oh, dear. Do you want to talk about it?"

"Not especially. Do you mind?"

"Of course not." Her mother pushed herself to her feet, looking almost relieved. "Think I'll go to bed, then, if you're okay with that."

"See you in the morning."

What a night, Paige thought when she was alone. It wasn't often that you rid yourself of one man only to be dumped by another.

Of course, there was still one man on the horizon, she thought, reaching inside her clutch for her phone. She checked her watch. It was after eleven o'clock. Was it too late to send a text?

I'll be here, Mr. Right Now had written earlier.

Still, she didn't want to appear too anxious. She clicked onto Match Sticks, scrolling through the sea of tiny faces for his photograph. "Looking for love . . ." she hummed absently, ". . . in all the wrong places."

And then, there he was.

Mr. Right Now.

"What's your real story?" she asked out loud, clicking off the site and collapsing on her bed, exhaustion covering her like a blanket. It was too late for anything but sleep. Mr. Right Now would have to wait until morning.

CHAPTER THIRTY-NINE

The fight started as the taxi was pulling away from the Ritz-Carlton Hotel.

"So, are you going to tell me what happened?"

"I already told you, *nothing* happened," Noah insisted.

"I don't believe you," Heather said for what felt like the hundredth time, and probably wasn't that far off.

"Well, that's your problem, then."

"No, it's *your* problem. Or it's going to be."

"Can you please lower your voice?" Noah said, lowering his own, as if to show her how it was done. "I don't think the driver is too interested in listening to your paranoia."

"On the contrary," Heather stated, "I think he's *very* interested. Aren't you . . ." She checked the name on his registration hanging over the back of the front passenger seat. ". . . Ricardo?"

"Sorry," Noah told him. "Please ignore her. The lady's had a few too many."

"The lady hasn't had nearly enough," Heather contradicted. "You married, Ricardo?"

"Yes, ma'am," Ricardo replied, dark eyes meeting hers in his rearview mirror.

"You ever cheat on your wife?"

"Okay, that's enough," Noah interjected. "Sorry about this, Ricardo. Bet you wish we'd taken an Uber."

"No, sir," came the quick reply. "I hate those guys. Personally, I'd like to shoot them all. In the head," he added, unprompted.

"I know just how you feel," Heather said, glaring at Noah, who sighed, closed his eyes, folded his arms across his chest, and refused further comment.

The fight resumed in the wood-paneled lobby of their apartment building. "This is not over," Heather said as they stepped into the ancient elevator.

"Oh, yes, it is."

"Don't count on it," Heather was saying as they were joined by a middle-aged couple whose frosty demeanor told Heather they were having problems of their own. The man gave a cursory nod in their direction while the woman stared straight ahead. Neither said a word until they reached the fourth floor.

"Have a pleasant evening," the man said as he and his wife exited the elevator.

"Don't think there's much chance of that," Noah said as the doors were closing.

Heather was already speaking. "I want to know what happened, Noah. And don't tell me nothing, because I'm not . . ." *Dumb?* ". . . naive."

Noah said nothing as he marched down the gray-carpeted hall toward their apartment, key in hand.

"Noah . . ."

He spun toward her. The move was so sudden and unexpected that Heather was forced to take an involuntary step back. Was he going to strike her? "Okay," he said instead, the simple word catching her equally off guard.

"Okay?" she repeated.

"I'll tell you everything. But can we at least wait till we get inside?"

"Of course."

He resumed his march down the hall, Heather at his heels, afraid to allow too much space between them in case he was planning to sneak inside and lock her out. *Maybe he's right,* she thought as they entered their apartment without incident. *Maybe I am paranoid.*

"So?" She followed him into the living room, watching as he removed his jacket and tie before tossing them carelessly over the back of the sofa.

"What do you want to know?"

Seriously? "I want to know what happened between you and Paige. And don't tell me nothing happened, because everyone was talking about it."

"And what were they saying?"

"I want to hear what *you* say."

"Fine," he said. "On one condition."

"You're hardly in a position to —"

"Do you want to know what happened or not?"

"What's the condition?" Heather asked.

"That that's the end of it. I'll tell you what went down, I'll answer any reasonable questions you might have, and then we don't talk about it ever again. Do we have a deal?"

Heather plopped down on the sofa, letting her evening bag fall to the cushion beside her, then kicking off her shoes and leaning back against Noah's discarded tuxedo jacket, detecting a hint of Paige's perfume clinging to the leather lapels. Which meant that they'd been standing awfully close to each other, close enough to touch. *Damn you, Paige,* she thought. *You'll pay for this.* "Deal," she said.

"Okay," Noah said. "I just don't want you to overreact. Paige is your cousin, she's family, and I've already caused enough problems between the two of you . . ."

"What are you trying to say, Noah?"

"That what happened wasn't entirely her fault," he said. "I'm as much to blame . . ."

"For God's sake, Noah. Just spit it out."

"The party was breaking up," he began. "Everyone was crowding around your uncle to say goodbye and I thought I'd sneak out for a minute to get some air. I guess Paige had the same idea, or maybe she saw me heading for the door and decided to follow me; I don't know. I just know that suddenly there she was, and she said something like 'walk with me,' and I thought I owed her that much. And we walked about a block or so, not very far, and she started talking about how much she missed me, and she got all teary, said she was sorry and wanted . . ." He hesitated.

"Said she was sorry and wanted . . . ?" Heather prompted.

"That she was sorry and wanted me back." Noah took a deep breath before continuing. "And this is where I screwed up, because I said that I was sorry, too. But

I just meant that I was sorry about the *way* it ended, that she'd deserved better than that. But she clearly misunderstood because suddenly she started kissing me. And I tried gently to get her to stop, but she wouldn't, until I finally had to push her away. She was furious, calling me names, screaming at me to shut the fuck up. And then just as we got near the hotel, she hauls off and slaps me. And everybody's there, everybody's watching. And then there you were, and I didn't know what to do or say because I knew how upset you'd be . . ."

"Why didn't you just tell me what happened when I first asked?"

"I don't know. I guess I felt responsible. If I hadn't agreed to go for that walk . . ."

"You had no way of knowing . . ."

"I should have been more careful. I'm a lawyer, for God's sake. I know better than to put myself in that kind of position."

"She was the one who came on to you."

"Yes, but in her mind, I'm sure she thinks I led her on."

Heather shook her head. "That bitch . . ."

"And that's exactly why I didn't want to say anything," he interrupted. "The last thing I want to do is cause more friction between the two of you. Not to mention, your families. I feel guilty enough . . ."

"You have nothing to feel guilty about," Heather told him. "This is my fault as much as yours. I should have known she'd pull something like this." Damn her cousin anyway.

There was a moment's silence.

"Okay?" Noah asked. "Can we put this behind us?"

"Not sure I can do that."

"We had a deal," he reminded her.

Heather nodded. The deal was never to talk about it again. It said nothing about getting even.

"Can we go to bed now?" He grabbed his jacket and tie and walked toward the hallway.

Heather didn't move.

"Are you coming?"

"In a minute."

"Okay. Don't be long. I'm exhausted."

"I'll be right there."

Noah paused in the doorway, as if he had more to say.

Now would probably be a good time to tell me you love me, Heather thought. But he didn't. He never had.

Bet you told Paige you loved her plenty of times, she thought, her anger at her cousin instantly resurfacing. She wasn't sure how she'd get back at Paige.

Only that she would.

Just like she got back at Chloe for that stupid stunt she'd pulled, making her drive all the way to Cambridge in the rain only to send her packing. She reached inside her evening bag and pulled out her cell, punching in the familiar number and waiting while it rang five times before being picked up. "Talk to me, Brandon," she said when McCann Advertising's former courier finally answered.

"I did exactly what you told me to," he said. "Pretended I was the guy who offed that Tiffany babe, told her she was next."

"And?"

"Scared the shit out of her."

"You're sure?"

"She called the cops."

Heather pressed the phone tighter against her ear, trying to contain her excitement. "How do you know?"

"I was there, wasn't I?"

Heather laughed, imagining the scene. "I owe you one."

"Hell, it was fun. Consider it my treat."

"We may have found you a new line of work."

"Speaking of which," he said, "is there anything else you need from me? I just got my hands on some excellent blow."

"Maybe another time."

"Heather?" Noah called from the bedroom. "What are you doing out there?"

"Gotta go," Heather said, closing the phone and jumping to her feet. "Hold your horses," she called back. "I'm on my way."

CHAPTER FORTY

He's tired. Tired and restless. Tired of being restless. Most of all, he's tired of waiting. It's almost midnight. Where the hell is she?

I have to go now. Can we continue this later?

What did she mean by "later"? Had he really expected her to contact him again tonight?

She's interested. He's sure of that. She's just taking a page from his playbook and *treating him mean to keep him keen.* Playing it cool, letting him dangle. He laughs. Before long, she'll be the one dangling.

From the end of a rope.

Still, he's frustrated. Frustrated and antsy. It's been too long since his last "date." The feel of Nadia's neck inside his hands, of her taut flesh between his fingers, is starting to fade. He can barely recall the sound of her muffled squeals or the smell of her blood as it flowed from her wounds. The palm of his hand no longer vibrates with each thrilling thrust of the knife.

He should write a book: *Serial Killing for Dummies: The Secret to Making a Woman Follow You Anywhere.* It's so simple, he's amazed that so few men have figured it out. You don't have to be rich; you don't have to be famous; you don't have to be funny; you don't even have to be all that good-looking. The key is making the bitch feel as if she's the only woman in the room, as if everything she says is interesting, her every opinion not only worth considering, but adopting. Women were desperate to be heard. So, all you had to do was make them think you were listening. If you could do that, you were home free.

He turns on the TV across from his bed, casually flipping through the channels. He settles on an old episode of *Dateline:* a conniving wife has paid some poor dope to off her husband for the insurance money. Of course the dumb bitch happened to take out a policy on her even dumber mate a scant two days before the murder, making her the obvious suspect and pretty much sealing her fate.

What is the matter with these people? Do they want to get caught? Do they not have the brains, the forethought, to realize such behavior might be considered, at the very least, suspicious? Can they not plan ahead, maybe take out the damn insurance policy a year or two in advance?

Of course, it takes both brains and patience to wait, to plan, to consider all the angles and consequences of one's actions.

Which is why he's decided against targeting Paige Hamilton's mother and best friend. The last thing he wants to do is spook this little Wildflower, a flower he intends to rip from its delicate stem, then grind beneath his feet. No, now that contact has been reestablished, he needs to focus his energy, keep his eye on the prize, which means sticking to the game plan and being patient for another week.

In the meantime, there's Audrey.

Probably not her real name, any more than Wildflower, which is fine with him. The more anonymous the better, at least to start out. He likes to save the good stuff for when they go on their real date, and he's forcing her to reveal the most intimate details of her life in the vain hope of postponing her death. Too much too soon takes away from the overall experience.

He and Audrey started texting a few weeks ago, feeling each other out, dropping hints about their likes and dislikes. Of course, his likes are all made up, crafted to suit the situation. Audrey likes working out, so so does he. In fact, he almost never works out, other than lifting weights, which are more-or-less a necessity when dealing with dead bodies. And she loves sad movies and romance novels, so he said he'd devoured *The Notebook,* although he's never read it and only caught a few minutes of the wretched thing on TV, just enough to make him want to puke.

Killing Audrey will be not only a pleasure, he decides, but a service to mankind. Such pathetic tastes should not be permitted to continue unchecked.

Sorry I've been out of touch for the last week, he texts Audrey now. He suspects that even though it's closing in on midnight, she'll still be up, and that even though she's all but given up on hearing from him again, she won't be able to resist answering his text. *I had a family emergency and had to go back to Madison. I wasn't sure when, or even if I'd be back, and I didn't think it fair to keep you hanging.*

God, I'm good, he thinks.

Reach out, withdraw. Flatter, then disappear. Abandon, then resurface. All part of his technique. He begins counting to ten, sensing Audrey's fingers already hovering over her keyboard.

Her response comes at the count of nine. *What happened?* she asks.

My father had a heart attack, he answers.

My God. Is he okay?

Hopefully, but not out of the woods yet. I may have to go back to Wisconsin.

I'll say a prayer for him.

Say one for yourself while you're at it, he thinks.

That means a lot, he texts in response, counting to ten before adding: *I was hoping we could maybe meet in person.*

I'd like that.

He hears footsteps on the stairs and leans forward on his bed, listening. *How about next Saturday night?*

Perfect. Where should we meet?

He climbs off the bed and walks toward the door. *Do you know Anthony's Bar over on Boylston?*

I'll find it. What time?

Seven o'clock?

Sounds great. You won't stand me up, will you?

He can hear the plaintiveness echo through her text. *No way.*

Good. See you at Anthony's next Saturday at seven.

Looking forward to it.

He disconnects, putting his ear to the

door, hearing nothing.

And then he hears the soft squeak that tells him someone is standing on the other side. "Mrs. Lebowski?" he says, throwing open the door, expecting to see his increasingly dotty landlady on the other side.

"I'm so sorry to disturb you," Imogene Lebowski's daughter says, hands fluttering nervously around her face. "I was just about to slip this under your door."

He takes the folded piece of paper from Jenna's hands without opening it. "Is something the matter? Your mother . . . ?"

"She's not good," Jenna says.

"Oh, I'm sorry."

"Yes, well, she's been going downhill for a while, and I've finally persuaded her to come home with me. We're just waiting for a spot in a long-term care facility to free up. She really can't function on her own anymore. The other day, she left the stove on all morning. And she wanders. Well, you know."

He nods, thinking how vulnerable Jenna looks, how easy it would be to get her out of her clothes and into his bed.

"I've been cleaning up all afternoon, getting her stuff together, trying to get organized." There is a moment's hesitation. "I'll be putting the house up for sale at the end of the month, which I'm afraid means —"

"— I have two weeks before I have to clear out," he says.

"I'm sorry. You've been the ideal tenant."

He smiles. "I was planning to leave soon anyway."

"Oh, well. Good. Then it all works out."

"My mother used to say that everything works out in the end." He recognizes that this conversation could have waited till morning, that the note was just a pretense. He knows she's hoping he'll invite her inside, but he has no desire to wrestle with those strong Polish thighs. No, Jenna Lebowski is a distraction, and he can't afford to be distracted. Time is suddenly of the essence, and there is still a lot of work to be done. "Well, good night," he tells her, holding up the note. "Thanks for the heads-up."

He closes the door on her confused expression. Two weeks doesn't give him a whole lot of time. There is much to accomplish.

He already has Audrey penciled in for next Saturday.

After that: Wildflower.

CHAPTER FORTY-ONE

As soon as the bus picked Josh and Sasha up for day camp on Monday morning, Chloe was in her car, on her way to the Cambridge District Court in Medford, hoping to convince a judge to issue a restraining order against Matt.

The police had suggested it, and Paige had been adamant she follow through. Once Chloe had informed her about the events of Saturday night — the threatening phone calls, the certainty that someone had been watching the house — "Well, who other than Matt could it have been?" Paige had argued — combined with the knowledge that Matt had a gun — good God, he'd showed it to their children, allowed them to hold it! — well, what choice had he left her?

The city of Medford was located a little over three miles northwest of downtown Boston on the Mystic River in Middlesex County. It had a population of close to sixty thousand people and was home to Tufts University. The courthouse itself, described as a "sad place" in a not-too-flattering online review, was a two-story, sprawling white building on Mystic Valley Parkway, with limited parking and a staff that, again according to multiple online reviews, was neither particularly friendly nor helpful. Still, it had one thing going for it that the Middlesex District Court — located a brisk five-minute walk from Chloe's house — did not, and that was distance. There was less chance of her running into anyone she knew in Medford.

The reviews were certainly right about the limited parking, Chloe found out quickly enough. It took her longer to find a parking spot than the drive to Medford itself. She ended up leaving her car several long blocks away and then running through the persistent morning drizzle in open-toed pumps that were neither comfortable nor waterproof. She'd left the house in such a hurry she'd forgotten her umbrella, so by the time she reached the building's front entrance, the floral-print silk dress she'd selected, hoping to make a good impression on the judge, was spotted with rain, her feet were soaking wet, and her hair clung tightly to her head like layers of damp feathers. *So much for making a good impression,* she thought, entering the main lobby and shaking the rain from her shoulders like a wet dog. *More like a drowned rat,* she thought, catching her woeful reflection in a nearby pane of glass.

"My God," she whispered, her eyes taking in the unexpectedly high number of people in the crowded waiting area, lining up to have their belongings go through the X-ray machines. What had she expected? That she would be the only person in need of the court's services? But this many? At barely nine o'clock? What were all these people doing here?

Please don't let there be anyone here I know, she prayed, getting in line behind an elderly black woman and a pink-haired teenage girl with a small silver hoop between the nostrils of her upturned nose.

"What's the holdup?" the pink-haired girl whined to no one in particular. "How long can it take to put your things through an X-ray machine?"

The elderly black woman smiled. "You might as well get used to it, hon. Nobody moves too fast around here."

"Great." The girl tugged at the side of her spiky pink hair and twisted her skinny torso toward Chloe. She was wearing a cropped white T-shirt that exposed her belly button, her belly button sporting a bigger variation of the hoop that pierced her nose. "This is such bullshit," she said, extricating a piece of paper from the back pocket of her low-rise jeans and using it to scratch the side of her cheek. "I shouldn't even be here. I got a ticket because this Nazi cop claims I went through a stop sign, which is total bullshit."

"You didn't go through the stop sign?" Chloe asked, relieved for the distraction the girl provided.

"I didn't even *see* the stupid thing. There was this big tree right in front of it. It's not my fault the city's too cheap to trim its stupid branches. Anyway," she said, continuing her indignant rant, "that's not even the problem."

"It isn't?"

"No. I tried explaining all this to the cop, that it was the city's responsibility to trim the stupid tree so people could see the stupid stop sign, and there was no way I could afford a two-hundred-and-fifty-dollar ticket, and he said he sympathized but the ticket was already written and there was nothing he could do. He said that people were being caught by that stop sign all the time and I could fight it if I wanted. I asked him, how do I do that? And he said to wait for a second summons. But I swear I never got one. And then I get a notice telling me I've been fined an additional hundred dollars, and I'm gonna lose my license if I don't pay up. So that's why I'm here. To talk to somebody who can help me. Because it's not fair. None of this is my fault."

Chloe smiled. A girl with spiky pink hair and piercings through her nose and navel expected life to be fair. Somehow she found that both sweet and reassuring. "Well, I wish you luck."

"Thanks," the girl said. "Why are *you* here?"

The smile faded from Chloe's face as she tried to think of a suitable response.

"We're moving," the woman in front of the pink-haired girl informed them.

"Thank God." The girl turned away from Chloe, getting her large, fringed handbag ready for the X-ray machine. "Have fun," she called as she waved from the other side, disappearing down the long hall.

"Excuse me," Chloe said to a security guard, "but where do I go for —"

"File clerk. Upstairs," the guard told her with a jerk of his thumb.

Chloe pushed her body toward the stairs, thinking it wasn't too late to turn around and forget the whole thing. Except it *was* too late. Matt had a gun.

She had to wait another ten minutes in line at the file clerk's desk. The file clerk was a middle-aged woman with short brown hair and deep bags under watery gray eyes that said she was already exhausted and the day had barely begun. "Yes?" she said as Chloe approached.

"I need a restraining order," Chloe whispered.

"Sorry. Can't hear you. You'll have to speak up."

Chloe lowered her head and glanced surreptitiously from side to side, leaning against the high desk and hoping no one in line behind her could hear. "I need a restraining order."

"Family Court," the file clerk announced loudly. "Down the hall to your left."

Chloe stepped away from the counter, not lifting her gaze from the floor, sure that all eyes were following her down the hall. *Still not too late to turn around and go home,* she was thinking.

"Can I help you?" another middle-aged woman asked when she reached the appropriate room. The woman had dark skin, dark eyes, and dark, curly hair, all of which emphasized the white of her teeth when she smiled. Chloe was grateful for the smile. It almost made up for the stale smell of cheap perfume and perspiration pulsating from the beige walls.

"I need to take out a restraining order."

The clerk bent toward a drawer and pulled out a bunch of forms, handing them across the reception desk to Chloe. "You need to fill these out in as much detail as you can, but don't sign them before you're in front of a notary public or a clerk of the court."

Chloe took a cursory glance through the multitude of pages. "It's so much," she mumbled, the beginnings of panic stirring in her chest. *Damn it,* she thought. Paige's mother was right. She should have written everything down.

The clerk's muted smile signaled her compassion. "You can take them home, if that would be easier for you. Unless, of course, it's an emergency. Is it?"

"No," Chloe told her. "I don't think so."

"Are you in immediate physical danger?"

"My husband has a gun. Does that count?"

"Has he threatened you with it?"

"No."

"Lots of people have guns," the clerk said with a sigh. "How exactly has he been harassing you?"

"Well, we're separated, and I've been getting these horrible, obscene phone calls. My husband swears it wasn't him, but he's made vague threats before . . ."

"Sorry, honey, but you're going to need more than vague threats to prove to a judge that you need a restraining order. He'll be looking for specific facts, details of actual threats and abuse. The defendant, in this case your estranged husband, has to have either caused you physical harm, attempted to cause you physical harm, placed you in fear of physical harm, or forced you to have sex," she recited, as if by rote. "The judge can deny issuing an order if he finds there's no basis."

"So, what do I do? I'm not sure . . ."

"My advice would be to get a lawyer involved."

"Lawyers are expensive," Chloe said. It was important she keep her legal fees to a minimum. "So, say I go ahead and fill this out . . . What happens next?"

"You'll receive a court hearing where you can present your case, and then you'll wait for the judge's decision. I assume it's an ex parte order you're after."

"What's that?"

"An ex parte order means that your husband doesn't have to be notified of your intentions and that the hearing will be held right away, either in person or over the phone."

"Over the phone?"

"Only if no judge is available. But you're in luck. Judge Lewis is here today. You'll be asking him to issue a no-contact order that would limit or prevent your husband from contacting you and your children. This order can last up to ten business days, after which your husband will have the right to attend a hearing and present a defense."

"Oh, God. He'll be furious."

The clerk nodded, signaling she was well acquainted with Chloe's predicament. "What you do is up to you, of course," she said. "But again, you should probably consult a lawyer, see if there's a real basis for an order of this kind. It's going to cost you either way."

"What do you mean?"

"The fee is three hundred and fifty-five dollars to file a civil harassment restraining order unless physical harm or the threat of physical harm is present, which, in this case, you tell me isn't there. And there's no guarantee you'll be successful. So . . ."

"So, I should probably talk to my lawyer," Chloe said, conceding the inevitable.

"That would be my recommendation. But, as I said, it's entirely up to you."

Chloe stuffed the forms inside her purse. How could anything be up to her when her life was careening out of control? "Thank you," she told the clerk.

"Nice dress, by the way."

"Thank you," Chloe said again, fleeing the office before the woman could see her burst into tears.

CHAPTER FORTY-TWO

She was wearing pink, which was still her favorite color; it had been ever since she was a child. *I probably should have outgrown it by now,* Paige thought, swiveling around in the buttery beige leather tub chair, casually absorbing the spacious, modern reception area of JFI Advertising, located on the fifteenth floor of the John Hancock Tower in downtown Boston. Black-and-white photographs covered the few walls that weren't windows; the ultramodern furniture sat low to the dark hardwood floor. Paige noted that the young woman with geometrically cut white-blond hair sitting ramrod straight behind the emerald-green marble desk in the middle of the room was wearing all black. *I should have worn black,* she thought, tugging at the pearl buttons of her blush-pink cotton blouse and smoothing the nonexistent wrinkles from her gray A-line skirt. At the very least, she should have selected an outfit that was bolder, less conservative, more fashion-forward. This was a cutting-edge agency after all, and she was a grown woman, not a little girl.

Except she'd never felt more childlike, more vulnerable, in her entire life. Over six months of rejection had taken their toll, dug deep into the core of her self-esteem. Having been let go, through no fault of her own, from a job she loved was bad enough, but what followed had proved even worse. While she'd approached her first post-firing interviews full of confidence and optimism, by the third rejection that optimism had started to wane, and her confidence had fallen on decidedly shaky ground. It hadn't helped that Noah had picked that time to reject her as well.

Paige felt a smile tugging at the corners of her lips. That slap on Saturday night had gone a long way toward making her feel better. Not that she would normally condone such violence, she thought, picturing Chloe, and hearing the fear in her friend's voice as she'd recounted the events of her own Saturday night. Damn Matt anyway. What was the matter with him? Hadn't he caused Chloe enough pain? Did he have to terrorize her now as well?

She'd urged Chloe to take out a restraining order against him, but Chloe had texted an hour ago informing her that the clerk at the courthouse had advised first speaking to her lawyer, and her lawyer had confirmed that a judge was unlikely to issue such an order based on the scant evidence she had. *Looks like I'll have to wait till he shoots me,* had come Chloe's follow-up text.

A horrifying thought.

So, no, violence in any form should never be considered acceptable. Still, goddamn it, there was just no getting around it — slapping Noah had felt great.

Paige had spent a good part of Sunday morning imagining the scene that might have taken place later that night between Noah and Heather. How she'd love to have been a fly on the wall of the bedroom they'd once shared! Still, knowing Noah, he'd probably managed to come up with some plausible excuse for his behavior. He was a lawyer, after all, skilled at creating reasonable doubt. He and Heather had likely ended the evening having wild, crazy sex, which was the last thing Paige wanted to picture.

Then there was Sam.

Another scene she tried not to imagine. Except, of course, she didn't have to imagine it. She had only to remember all but dragging the poor man into his bedroom, shedding her clothes along the way, and virtually attacking him. What had gotten into her?

Not Sam, she thought, and almost laughed.

Another rejection. She sighed audibly.

"Ms. Lyons shouldn't be much longer," the receptionist said, misinterpreting Paige's sigh for one of impatience.

Paige nodded, hearing her cellphone ping in her purse. She quickly checked her messages. *Well, what do you know?* she thought, finding a text from Mr. Right Now. She'd texted him yesterday morning, apologizing for having had to cut short their contact the night before — how many apologies did that make? — and he'd been very gracious, telling her no apologies were necessary. *Just glad you're here now. Looking forward to getting to know you.*

Looking forward to getting to know you too, she'd texted back.

And then nothing. No suggestion that they should meet up. No trying to schedule another rendezvous. A case of once bitten, twice shy?

She'd checked her phone repeatedly throughout the day, but there were no further messages. She'd considered sending him another text, then decided against it. She was through throwing herself at men. If Mr. Right Now was really *looking forward to getting to know her,* he knew exactly what he had to do.

And now suddenly, he was doing it: *Hey, there, Wildflower,* his text read. *My turn to apologize. Unexpected visitors. What's going on?*

Waiting for a job interview, she messaged back.

What kind of job?

In advertising. Strategic planning.

Sounds impressive. Good luck.

Fingers crossed.

That was it. Their longest exchange so far. *Making progress,* she thought, returning the phone to her purse when it became obvious there'd be no more texts. She wondered if he'd check in later, inquire how her interview had gone. She shrugged, deciding that she wasn't going to waste time worrying about it. If he messaged her again, fine. If he didn't, also fine. She had more important things to worry about at the moment. Like her interview with Molly Lyons, senior vice president of JFI Advertising.

Not that there was anything to worry about, Paige told herself. Her previous interview with the head of HR had gone well, and she was well prepared for this one. She'd done her homework, going over the critical aspects of the job she was seeking, and what she could say about the skills and capabilities she possessed that made her the ideal candidate to fill that job. She'd visited the agency's website multiple times and checked out assorted industry publications to familiarize herself with key information about the company. She'd looked up Molly Lyons's profile on LinkedIn to get a sense of her background and any connections they might have in common.

She'd also brushed up on her own CV, recapping her career history and reminding herself of all she'd accomplished, her various wins and achievements. Details were important. In discussing her achievements, she had to take care to properly set up each situation, discuss how she'd handled it, and explain the results.

There were bound to be questions about past challenges she'd overcome or times in her previous position when she'd gone above and beyond. Perhaps there was a current advertising campaign she found particularly exciting or innovative.

Paige also had a few interesting questions of her own prepared. Employers liked that.

But ultimately, she knew that chemistry

was the key. It mattered less how good she'd been at her previous job, or how deeply she understood the business, than how well she connected with Molly Lyons. She had to banish negative thoughts of past rejections. She had to appear upbeat and positive. It was as important to listen as to talk. She had to be seen as both an individual stand-out and a team player.

In the end, of course, she could only be herself.

Would that be enough?

"Paige Hamilton?"

An attractive woman was walking toward her, hand extended in greeting. She looked exactly like her picture on the agency's website: younger than her forty years, with sleek, chin-length brown hair, a wide face, and an engaging smile. She was wearing cropped gray pants and a pink, short-sleeved sweater. "Wonderful to see that there's someone else who likes pink," Molly Lyons said, shaking Paige's hand. "Very nice to meet you."

Paige felt her body instantly relax. "Very nice to meet *you.*"

She called her mother from a bench in Copley Square within minutes of leaving Molly's office. The morning showers had given way to a beautiful, warm, sunny afternoon.

"So?" Joan Hamilton asked.

Paige heard the hope in her mother's voice. "It was fantastic. Great. Better than I could have dreamed."

"Oh, darling. I'm so glad."

Paige checked her watch. It was almost five o'clock. Her interview had lasted more than two hours. She and Molly had fit together like the proverbial hand and glove. Milk and cookies. Rod and reel. Pick a cliché. It fit. *They* fit.

"I mean, it's not a done deal," Paige qualified, not wanting to risk disappointment by getting too far ahead of herself. "I still have to meet with the head of the agency and a few other key people . . ."

"When will that be?"

"Probably next week. The president is out of town till next Monday, and the creative director is on holiday till Wednesday, so . . ."

"Next week," her mother said. "Well, we'll keep our fingers crossed."

Fingers crossed.

"So, I was thinking, maybe we could go out to dinner," Paige said. "My treat. A kind of mini-celebration for having had such a good interview and making it to the next level."

"Oh, darling. I'm sorry. I can't."

414

"You can't?"

"I'm so sorry."

"What's the matter? Don't you feel well?"

"No, sweetheart. I feel fine. It's just . . ."

"What?"

An uncomfortable pause. "I have a date."

"What?"

"I have a date."

"You have a date?" Paige repeated. "With whom? Someone you met online?"

"No. I don't think that's going to be my scene. It's with this man a woman in the building fixed me up with. Harry something."

"His name is Harry Something?"

"No, darling. It's . . . Gatlin, I think. He sounds very nice."

"You've talked to him?"

"He called earlier."

Paige swallowed, trying to digest the fact that her mother had a date. "Where is he taking you?"

"Antonio's."

Paige nodded. Antonio's was one of Boston's best Italian restaurants. "Wow. Okay. Wow," she said again.

"You're upset."

"No," Paige said, a touch too loudly. "No. Honestly. It just feels kind of weird, that's all. My mother has a date."

"It'll probably be just a one-night stand," Joan said.

"What?"

"Just kidding."

Paige tried to laugh, but the laugh stuck in her throat. Her mother was making jokes about one-night stands. "What time is he picking you up?"

"He isn't. I thought it was a better idea to meet him at the restaurant."

"Oh. Okay. Good idea." Her mother was obviously in full control.

"What will you do?" her mother asked.

"I don't know," Paige said with a shrug. Maybe she'd call Chloe, see if she felt like company. Or maybe Mr. Right Now would send her another message, suggest they meet up later for a drink.

"You'll call me if there are any problems," she told her mother before saying goodbye. "My mother has a date," she announced to the empty seat beside her. She stared at the small screen of her phone, willing it to ping with an incoming message, from Mr. Right Now. But the only notification she received was from the Gap, reminding her of their current sale.

Paige pushed herself to her feet and started walking toward Boylston. "The Gap it is."

CHAPTER FORTY-THREE

He'd probably gotten tired of waiting, assumed he'd been stood up, and left, Joan was thinking as she pushed open the front door of the small, outwardly unimpressive, redbrick restaurant at the corner of Cambridge and Blossom. Not that she would have blamed him. She was almost twenty minutes late, having changed both her outfit and her mind about going at least half a dozen times.

Why all the fuss about a man she wasn't at all sure she wanted to meet? Ultimately, she'd decided that it would be rude to cancel at the last minute, and settled on a pair of white slacks and a stylish turquoise blouse. It was just dinner, she told herself, securing a pair of long, dangling gold hoops in her ears. Harry Gatlin would hopefully prove to be an interesting diversion, but there was little chance she'd find him attractive and even less chance she'd want to see him again. And despite her joke to Paige about a one-night stand, she certainly wasn't going to have sex with the man.

Like that was ever going to happen again, she thought wistfully.

Joan's eyes searched the crowded restaurant's small, brightly lit interior — as unassuming and unpretentious as its exterior — for her date. *My date,* she repeated silently, holding her breath as she watched an elderly man struggle to his feet from a nearby table against the pale ecru wall. The man reached for the cane beside him as Joan braced herself for his approach, wondering if she had enough time to flee before he worked up sufficient speed to reach her. *Damn it.* This evening was going to be even worse than she'd imagined.

"Dad," she heard a woman say, a hand reaching out to grab the old man's jacket. "The bathroom's that way."

The man nodded and pivoted in the opposite direction.

"Thank you, God," Joan muttered under her breath, catching sight of movement in the far corner of the restaurant.

A man was waving. A tall, good-looking man, she realized as he stood up to maneuver his way around the white tablecloth–covered tables and wooden chairs to where she stood. A tall, good-looking, well-dressed man with slim hips and a twinkle in his clear blue eyes.

"Joan?"

"Harry?"

"Well, we know who we are," he said with a laugh. "That's a good thing."

Harry Gatlin had a full head of gray hair and was both taller and more muscular than Joan had expected. She wondered how it would feel to have those arms wrapped around her.

My God. What was she thinking? "I'm sorry I'm so late."

"That's quite all right."

"I'm usually very prompt."

"No problem. You're here now." He put his hand on her elbow to guide her toward their table at the back.

Joan felt her entire body tingle at the touch of his hand. *No. Put it back,* she thought, as they reached the table and his hand withdrew. What was happening to her?

"I took the liberty of ordering wine," he said as they settled into their seats. "I hope you like red."

"I do indeed." *I do indeed? Who talks like that? What's the matter with me?* She watched as the waiter poured two glasses of wine, then she quickly raised her glass.

"Cheers."

"Cheers," Harry repeated, clinking his glass against hers.

Joan took a sip of her wine. "Very nice."

"It is indeed," he said.

Was he making fun of her?

"So," he began. "Linda tells me you two live in the same building."

Joan nodded. "What else did she tell you?"

"Not much, actually. That you're a widow, attractive, bright, *interesting,*" he said, putting stress on the final word.

Joan laughed. "I think she was referring to my hair."

"I like your hair."

I like you, Joan thought. "Thank you," she said instead. "She said pretty much the same things about you."

"She thinks my hair is interesting?"

Joan laughed again. "She also said you're a retired professor."

"I am."

"What did you . . . *profess*?"

His turn to laugh. "Art history. Harvard," he added before she could ask.

"Impressive."

"Never hurts to name-drop Harvard," he said with a smile.

Joan felt her own smile pulling at the lines around her mouth. She quickly brought her lips together. "And what do you do now that you're retired?"

"The usual. Read, travel, play a little golf and a lot of bridge, spend time with my grandkids."

"How many do you have?"

"Four. Two girls with my older daughter, a boy and a girl with the younger one. I'm lucky. They all live relatively close by. You?"

"Not so lucky. My son lives in New Jersey. He has two boys I don't get to see as often as I'd like. And my daughter isn't married. Not that that matters anymore."

"Like the man sang, 'The times, they are a-changing,' " Harry said. "So, what do you do? Still working?"

"No. I never really did, to be honest. I mean, I had jobs after college — secretary, receptionist, bank teller, that sort of thing. But never anything you could generously call a career. A degree in English doesn't exactly qualify you for a whole lot of professions, unless you want to teach, which I didn't. No offense."

He smiled. "None taken."

"I probably shouldn't admit this, but I was never all that ambitious, and after I got married, I was quite happy to be a stay-at-home wife and mother. I toyed with the idea of going back to school and getting my master's degree once the kids were older, but something always seemed to come up."

"And now?"

"I don't know. I seem to be at some sort of crossroads. I have all this time, and I'm not sure what to do with it. I don't golf and I don't play bridge."

"You could take lessons."

"At my age? I'd never be any good."

"I've been playing both most of my life and I'm still not any good," Harry said with a shrug. "What about traveling?"

"I like traveling," Joan said. "But my husband was pretty much of a homebody. We'd go to Florida, Mexico, the Bahamas. He liked to go where the weather was warm and he didn't have to cross an ocean to get there. And now, well, I guess I'm not all that keen on traveling alone."

"It can be a little daunting at first, I admit."

"You travel a lot?"

"Whenever I can."

"What's your favorite place?"

Harry gave the question a moment's thought. "I guess I'd have to say India. The people, the sites. It's all so different, so *interesting*."

"Don't laugh, but when I was younger," Joan said, putting her elbows on the table and leaning toward him, "I had this fantasy about swimming in the pool in front of the Taj Mahal. Until I realized it was more of a wading pool, and the water was filthy, and the guards would probably shoot me if I set foot in it. You're laughing. I said, don't laugh."

"Sorry," he said, still chuckling. "That's really quite charming."

He thinks I'm charming, Joan thought.

The waiter approached with their menus.

"See anything that interests you?" Harry asked after a brief pause.

I certainly do, Joan thought, wondering what Harry Gatlin would look like without his clothes. *This is ridiculous,* she thought immediately. It had been years since she'd seen a man without his clothes. Unless, of course, you counted Simply Pete in his leopard-print thong. "I don't know. Everything looks wonderful."

"Yes, it does," Harry agreed, looking directly into her eyes.

Was he having the same thoughts she was?

"Their fish is delicious," he said. "As is their pasta. You really can't go wrong."

"You eat here a lot?"

"My late wife and I used to come here pretty frequently. But it's been a while."

Joan lowered her menu. "Linda told me

she died three years ago."

"Yes. Cancer."

"My husband, too. Two years last May."

"You never quite get used to it, do you?" he asked. "I mean, it gets a little easier with time, I suppose. But the idea that someone is . . ."

". . . just not there anymore," Joan said, finishing his sentence.

"Exactly."

"It's a hard one to wrap your head around."

He nodded. "And this whole dating business . . ."

The waiter approached. "Are you ready to order?"

"Think I'll try the *spigola*," Joan told him.

"I'll go with the spaghetti Bolognese," Harry said. "Feel like splitting a Caesar salad?"

"Sounds good. So," she said after the waiter had taken their orders and their menus and left the table, "Linda tells me you've tried online dating."

"Oh, God. Yes. The times, they have most *definitely* changed. It's not for me, I'm afraid. You?"

Again Joan thought of Simply Pete and his leopard-print thong. "Not for me either," she agreed. "You're actually the first date

I've had since my husband died."

He reached across the table to take her hand. "Well, I couldn't have asked for a nicer dinner companion."

"Thank you. You make it easy."

He smiled and withdrew his hand.

No, she thought, as she'd thought earlier. *Put it back.*

They talked all through the salad, the main course, and dessert. It was almost ten o'clock when they left the restaurant.

"My condo is just down the way," he said as they stepped into the warm night air. "If you feel like a nightcap . . ."

Joan put her hand through the crook of his arm. "Lead the way," she said.

CHAPTER FORTY-FOUR

"For God's sake," Paige said, vaulting toward the front door of their condo, "it's almost two o'clock in the morning. Where have you been?"

"My goodness," Joan said, closing the door behind her. "What are you still doing up?"

"What do you mean, what am I doing up? I got home from Chloe's at just after eleven and looked in your room, expecting you to be sound asleep. Instead, you weren't even here. I called your cell half a dozen times. You didn't answer. I've been worried sick."

"Oh, darling. You shouldn't have worried. I left the phone in my other purse. How *is* Chloe?"

"She's hanging in there," Paige replied, not quite ready to relinquish her anxiety. "I called Antonio's. They said you left there around ten."

"Yes. I had the *spigola* —"

"I called the hospital . . ." Paige interrupted.

"You called the hospital! Why, for heaven's
sake?"

"Why? Because that's where you ended
up the last time you went out with a man to
get something to eat."

"I can't believe you called the hospital."

"And the police," Paige went on, anger
replacing her earlier panic.

"You called the police? Oh, my God. What
did you say to them?"

"That I was worried. That you had a date
with some guy you didn't know, that you'd
left the restaurant with him hours ago but
you hadn't come home, and I was worried
because there was a possible serial killer on
the loose . . ."

"A serial killer. Oh, my God, Paige. You
don't think you overreacted just a tad? What
did the police say?"

"That I was overreacting," Paige admitted, feeling beyond stupid. "That you'd
probably just gone back to his place. I told
them that was ridiculous, that you weren't
like that, that you're seventy years old, for
God's sake . . . Oh, shit. That's what happened, isn't it? You went back to his place."

"Yes, darling," her mother said, walking
into the living room and collapsing on the

sofa. "He has this lovely apartment in Beacon Hill. Come sit, sweetheart. Try to calm down."

Paige gathered her silk robe around her and sank into the cushion beside her mother, tucking her bare legs underneath her.

"Do you need some tea?" her mother asked.

Paige shook her head, trying to decide exactly how much she wanted to know about her mother's evening. "You look beautiful."

"Thank you, darling."

"The turquoise suits you."

"Harry said it really makes my eyes pop."

Shit. "So, I take it the dinner went well."

"It did," her mother said. "He's a lovely man. Educated, attractive, a good conversationalist, a good listener . . ."

"You liked him."

"Very much."

"That's nice."

"Then we finished dinner," her mother continued, unprompted, "and there seemed to be so much more to talk about. Neither one of us was ready to call it a night, so we decided to continue the conversation back in his apartment."

"You talked till almost two o'clock in the

morning?"

Her mother paused perhaps a beat too long.

"Oh, God," Paige moaned. "You had sex with him?"

Her mother looked toward her lap.

"I'm sorry," Paige apologized immediately. "I wasn't trying to make you feel embarrassed or bad about yourself or anything. Honestly. I didn't mean to sound judgmental. I'm just a little surprised, that's all. Oh, my God," she said as her mother lifted her head. "You're not embarrassed. You're smiling."

"I can't help it," her mother said, her impish grin spreading toward her ears.

Paige wasn't sure whether to laugh or cry.

"To be honest," her mother continued, "I think Harry was just as surprised. I don't think he expected things to progress quite so quickly. But he kissed me, and it's been a very long time since anyone has kissed me like that — it was some kiss, let me tell you . . ."

Please don't, Paige thought.

"And so, when he suggested we go into the bedroom," her mother continued, oblivious to Paige's inner pleading, "I thought, well, what the hell? Why not? Go for it. I mean, who wants to play hard-to-get at my age? And to be honest," she said again, "I was quite turned on . . ."

Could you stop being so damn honest? Paige thought.

"Your father and I always had a very active sex life, and then he got sick, and well . . ."

"Okay, stop," Paige interrupted, no longer able to keep her thoughts to herself. "That's enough. Please stop."

"I'm sorry, darling. But you *did* ask . . ."

"Yes, and now I'm asking you to stop."

Tears sprang to her mother's eyes. "I'm sorry if I've disappointed you, darling."

"Oh, Mom, no. Please don't cry. You haven't disappointed me. That's not it. You could never disappoint me. It's just that, well, we're not girlfriends here. You're my *mother.*"

"And mothers don't have sex?"

"Well, they usually don't talk about it with their daughters. Unless it's to tell them not to."

Her mother laughed. "I'm sorry, darling. I'll stop." She patted Paige's bare knee. "Now go to bed. Get some sleep. It's been a long day."

Paige pushed herself off the sofa. She was almost at the hall when she stopped, her curiosity getting the better of her. *I'm going to regret this,* she thought. "Was it good?" she asked anyway.

"Oh, darling," came her mother's response. "It was wonderful."

Paige stared into the mirror over her dresser. "My mother's having sex," she told her tired reflection. *With a man she just met,* she continued silently. *A man who isn't my father.* Had she really expected her mother to remain celibate for the rest of her life? And was that what was really bothering her? Or was it that her mother was having more sex than she was?

Maybe it was less the fact that she was having sex than the threat that she could fall in love.

"I'm a horrible person," Paige whined, climbing into bed and pulling the covers up to her chin, trying to ferret out the source of her confusion. Had she expected her mother to bury her sexuality when she buried her husband? Had she assumed that while her mother might be interested in some form of companionship, it wouldn't include anything of a sexual nature? That Joan Hamilton was too grown up, too mature, too *old* for that?

Except that, in everything but years, Joan Hamilton was one of the youngest women

431

Paige knew. She had the energy, the curiosity, the *legs* of a woman decades younger. And wasn't the internet full of articles about the sex lives of senior citizens? Men and women in their seventies, eighties, and even — dear God! — their nineties, who were still not only interested in sex, but active participants.

She remembered reading about an outbreak of venereal disease in a retirement home somewhere in Florida. It appeared that the residents, free from responsibility and no longer concerned with either propriety or pregnancy, were making up for lost time and not only having sex, but having it often, and with multiple partners. Since most of them had come of age post-Pill and pre-AIDS, they'd never had much use for condoms and weren't about to start now. Safe sex was as foreign a concept as Facebook. As a result, venereal disease was rampant. And not just in that one home. Similar outbreaks were being reported in retirement communities throughout the country.

Had her mother taken the necessary precautions? Paige wondered.

"No, no, no. I am not going there," she admonished herself, trying to turn off all conscious thought. But the more she tried,

432

the worse things got. After half an hour of thinking about not thinking about anything, the result was a blinding headache. She sat up, turned on the light, and reached for her cellphone, opening her messages and re-reading the texts she'd received earlier from Mr. Right Now.

The first one had arrived when she was on her way to Chloe's.

So, Wildflower, how'd your interview go?

She'd texted back almost immediately. *Think it went great.*

A flurry of exchanges followed.

When will you find out if you got the job?

Don't know. Have another meeting next week.

Sounds promising. What exactly does a director of strategic planning do?

Too complicated to get into in a text.

And then nothing.

She'd waited for his reply, and when none came, concluded he'd assumed she was suggesting they talk in person, and he clearly wasn't ready to go that route again yet.

The next text had arrived two hours later. Chloe was upstairs getting the kids ready for bed, and Paige was sitting in the living room, staring at the two dozen pink and white roses Matt had sent his wife that afternoon, along with a note pleading for

433

another chance. Would Chloe give him one? Paige had wondered, hearing the familiar ping of her phone.

Sorry, Wildflower. Phone died. You were saying?

Paige had smiled, and was about to text him back when Chloe came back downstairs. She decided to wait till she got home.

But that was before she discovered that her mother hadn't returned from her date, and the frantic calls to the hospital and the police that followed. Now it was way too late to text a man who was, after all, a virtual stranger in every sense of the word. "Sorry, Mr. Right Now," she said, sleep tugging at her eyelids, wondering how many apologies the man would stand for before giving up on her once and for all. "We'll try again tomorrow. I promise. I'll be worth the wait."

CHAPTER FORTY-FIVE

It was Wednesday night and she was meeting him at Longfellows, an outrageously expensive steak house in the heart of Harvard Square. The Square had been pretty much the center of everything in Cambridge since the seventeenth century, and had been held in something approaching reverence ever since. Aside from being the site of Harvard University, it was chock-a-block full of historic buildings and landmarks, as well as home to a variety of upscale shops and places to eat.

Chloe had suggested going somewhere a little less punishing on the wallet, but Matt had been adamant. Nothing was too good for the woman he loved, he'd insisted, sending her two dozen long-stemmed, pink and white roses every day for the last three days to underline his point. Chloe had finally given in and agreed to meet him for dinner.

Not that she'd been persuaded by such

shallow theatrics. Matt was the unchallenged master of over-the-top gestures, the undisputed king at polishing dull surfaces until they shone, persuading you to overlook the rot underneath. His clients might be fooled, but Chloe was finally starting to realize that when things were so over-the-top, there was little chance they ran very deep.

Could she settle for a life of shiny surfaces? she wondered, cutting across the crowded square toward the restaurant. And was she seriously contemplating reconciling with a man she'd considered taking out a restraining order against only days ago?

Of course, Matt had been vehement, even convincing, in his denials, swearing up and down that he'd had nothing to do with the events of last weekend. He might be guilty of some admittedly stupid behavior, he'd told her, but making obscene, threatening phone calls and spying on her? No way was he capable of such things. No way would he stoop so low. He might be an idiot, he'd insisted, but he wasn't crazy.

I'm the crazy one, Chloe conceded, pulling open the restaurant's ornate wooden door and adjusting her eyes to the sudden darkness of the plush interior. Even though she'd never eaten here before, she knew exactly what to expect: the heavy wood

436

paneling, the oversized booths lining the blood-red walls, the scores of smaller tables in between, the dim lighting, the towering, glass-enclosed wine closet boasting hundreds of overpriced bottles, the decor suggesting a seriousness of purpose that didn't exist, unless that purpose was to sell as many expensive cuts of beef and bottles of wine as possible. Why did all steak houses look pretty much the same?

And speaking of sameness, wasn't the definition of insanity doing the same thing over and over and expecting a different result?

How many times did she have to be kicked in the head before she realized she was being slowly stomped to death? Why couldn't she be more like Paige? Chloe thought, as she'd thought often, recalling Paige's retelling of the slap she'd delivered to Noah's face on Saturday night.

Boston had been buzzing with the delicious gossip all week, people tweeting and sharing what they'd heard with their Facebook friends. Just this afternoon, someone had posted a grainy video of the incident on YouTube. A passerby had seen Paige and Noah embracing and, mistaking it for something sweet and romantic, impulsively recorded it, not anticipating the events that followed. Now the video was out there for everyone to see. Chloe smiled, trying to imagine Heather's reaction when she got wind of it.

Her smile lingered as the hostess led her toward the back room, where Matt was already waiting. It faded when she saw him chatting up a pretty, raven-haired waitress, then died completely as she watched the waitress lean forward to tap something into Matt's phone. Her phone number no doubt, Chloe understood, feeling another kick to the side of her head, and wondering if this would finally be the one to knock some sense into her.

"Chloe!" Matt exclaimed, jumping to his feet when he saw her. The waitress quickly disappeared. "You look beautiful."

"What was *that* about?" Chloe sat down across from him without acknowledging the compliment.

"What was what about?"

Chloe couldn't help admiring his composure. "How do you do that?"

"How do I do what?" Matt laughed. "Sorry. I'm confused."

She shook her head. "Nothing." What was the point in confronting him? He'd find a way to deny any impropriety. *"The waitress?"* she could hear him say, managing to sound as if he were the injured party. *"She was just writing down the name of a great bottle of wine."* He'd probably even name the bottle, maybe even offer to show her the message.

He can't help himself, she thought. *This is who he is, who he always will be.*

"Is that a new dress?" he asked.

Chloe looked down at the loose-fitting, white cotton dress she'd chosen because of its shapelessness. Matt had always preferred her in more formfitting attire. "No. It's old. I just don't wear it often."

"It's nice," he said, again managing to sound convincing. "This is a new suit," he volunteered, smoothing the lapel of his beige linen jacket. "I bought it especially for tonight. Hoping to impress you," he added, almost shyly.

"It's an impressive suit," Chloe said.

He smiled. "You're not going to make this easy for me, are you?"

"Should it be?"

"No, I guess not. That's okay. I don't mind a little hard work." He signaled for the wine steward and ordered a bottle of his favorite Zinfandel. "Who's babysitting the kids?"

"My mother."

"What?"

"I had no choice. The kid I'd lined up canceled at the last minute and I couldn't find anyone else, so I . . . I'm just kidding," Chloe said, enjoying the stunned look on Matt's face but unable to continue with the charade. Not everyone was as expert at lying as her husband. "It's Stephanie Koster from down the street."

"Shit. You really had me going there for a second."

"Sorry. Couldn't resist."

"You're in a strange mood," Matt commented after a pause.

"These are strange times."

"Yes, they are." Another pause. "It wasn't me, Chloe. I swear on my life, I'm not the one who made those calls on Saturday night. I was nowhere near the house. I would never hurt you. You have to know that."

"You have a gun."

"What?"

"The kids told me. For God's sake, it's bad enough you bought a gun, but what were you thinking, showing it to them, letting them hold it?"

"I was thinking that they might like to see a genuine antique from the Civil War that some clients gave me as a thank-you for finding them the house of their dreams," he explained, appearing genuinely flustered. "What? You honestly think I'd let them

440

anywhere near a real gun?"

"I'm sorry," Chloe apologized, equally flustered. What was the matter with her?

"Look," he began. "I don't blame you for thinking the worst of me. I know how disappointed you are. I know how angry you are. And you have every right to be. I've been a fool. I've done things that have hurt you deeply, caused you to lose faith in me, in us, in our marriage. But I love you, Chloe, and I swear, if you give me another chance — just one more chance, that's all I'm asking — if you give me one more chance, I'll do everything in my power to make it up to you. I'll be the best, most faithful husband any woman could ask for. You just have to trust me. I promise I won't let you down."

Chloe shook her head, her eyes filling with unwanted tears. How she wanted to believe him! "I really wish I could."

"You *can*."

"How? How can I trust you, when every time you leave the house for a showing at night or on the weekend, I'm going to be wondering if that's where you really are? When every time you call to say you're working late, I'm going to be asking myself what you're really doing? When every time you tell me you're with a client, I'm going to wonder who she really is?"

"Because I'll do whatever it takes, whatever you want, to prove it to you. I'll let you check my phone every night, I'll give you the password to my computer . . . Whatever I have to do to regain your trust, I'll do it."

"You'd do that?"

"I'll do anything."

"Okay." Chloe sank back in her chair, spotting the pretty, raven-haired waitress Matt had been talking to earlier at the far end of the room. "Let me see your phone."

"What?"

"You said you'd let me check your phone. I'd like to see it now."

"I don't see what this will prove," Matt said, removing his cellphone from his pocket.

"Open it to Contacts."

"This is silly, Chloe. It's mostly just business associates."

"Are you going to show it to me or not?"

Matt shrugged. "Fine. Have it your way." He pressed in his password and opened the phone to Contacts, then handed it across the table to Chloe. "I really don't see what this is going to prove."

She quickly scanned the long list of mostly female names. "Excuse me," she suddenly called out, lowering the phone and waving to the raven-haired waitress.

"Would you like to see your menus?" the waitress asked, approaching.

"In a minute," Chloe said. "First, I was just wondering . . . you look so familiar. Do you mind if I ask your name?"

"It's Avery."

And there it was, just like that — the final kick in the head.

"Avery Reid?"

"Yes." Avery cocked her head to one side, letting her long, straight hair fall across one shoulder. "Have we met?"

"No. But I believe you *have* met my husband."

"Nooo," the young woman demurred, glancing uneasily toward Matt. "Well, we talked for a minute while he was waiting for you."

"Chloe . . ." Matt began.

"And yet, here you are," Chloe said, holding up Matt's cellphone, and offering the clearly nonplussed woman her most indulgent smile. "I had a feeling I'd find you here. My husband is pretty transparent that way. Unfortunately, it may be a while before you hear from him. I'm afraid there are a lot of women ahead of you."

"Chloe . . ."

"Excuse me," Avery said, making a hasty retreat.

"Was that really necessary?" Matt asked, his face flush with anger, a vein throbbing noticeably at his temple.

"Yeah, it kinda was." She handed him back his phone.

"So, what now?" he asked, gradually recovering his composure.

Chloe picked up her wineglass and raised it to her lips. "I want a divorce."

CHAPTER FORTY-SIX

People were staring. Heather was sure of it.

All morning, she'd had the uncomfortable feeling that everyone was looking at her. Normally, she would have relished the attention, assumed her coworkers were secretly admiring her outfit or the fun way she'd styled her hair. But there was nothing new about either her hairdo or her lilac-colored dress, so it couldn't be that. Also, she thought she'd heard whispering, possibly even snickering, as she'd walked down the aisle toward her desk after an extended bathroom break. She quickly checked her shoes to make sure she wasn't trailing a stream of toilet paper behind her.

That was when she caught Kendall glancing at her from across the aisle.

"Hey," she said as Kendall turned away.

"Sorry?" Kendall asked. "Are you talking to me?"

"Do you see anyone else here?"

Kendall cleared her throat. "What's up?"

"I was just about to ask you the same thing."

Kendall shrugged.

"Has Marsha said anything to you?" Heather asked.

"About what?"

"About my job," Heather said, growing impatient. She'd had her performance review on Monday, and as expected, it hadn't gone particularly well. She had a month to start applying herself or start looking for another position.

Kendall shook her head. "No. Marsha hasn't said anything."

"But *somebody* has," Heather probed.

"Not about your job, no."

"What, then?"

Kendall glanced quickly up and down the aisle. "You really don't know?"

"For God's sake, Kendall. What the hell is going on?"

Kendall rolled her chair across the aisle until she was positioned beside Heather in front of her computer. "You haven't seen this?" She clicked onto YouTube.

"Seen what?" Heather watched as Kendall's fingers flew across her keyboard.

"At first I thought it was *you*," Kendall said, as the grainy image of two people embracing on a city street filled the screen. "But I knew that wasn't your new dress . . ."

Heather gasped. Despite the darkness of the night and the poor quality of the picture, there was no mistaking the identity of the people involved. Heather sank back in her chair, watching as Noah's lips moved from Paige's neck up to her eyes before landing passionately on her lips. The evidence was clear: Noah was hardly the victim of a sneak attack; that lip lock was nothing if not mutual.

If anything, Noah had been the aggressor.

And suddenly there were voices to go along with the humiliating video, although it was difficult to make out everything that was being said: *We were going through a rough patch . . . Heather started coming over . . . Hair just so . . . My fault? . . . Sweatpants.* And then louder, clearer: *Then stop talking, you fucking idiot!*

Followed seconds later by a loud, resounding slap.

"Turn it off," Heather directed.

Kendall immediately exited the site. "I'm sorry. I thought for sure you knew. Everybody's talking about it."

"Oh, God."

"I'm sorry," Kendall said again.

Despite her conciliatory tone, Heather

detected a slight glint in the other woman's eyes. She pushed herself away from her desk and to her feet. "Screw you," she said.

"I'm here to see Noah Sherman," Heather announced to the receptionist in the nondescript outer office of Whitman, Loughlin. She was still trying to catch her breath, having run the more than twenty blocks from her office in less than ten minutes.

The attractive young woman behind the towering mahogany desk checked her appointment calendar, then gave Heather a quick once-over. *Has she seen the video?* Heather wondered, tucking her hair behind her ears and straightening her shoulders, as if daring her to say anything.

"Do you have an appointment?"

"Just tell Mr. Sherman that Heather is here to see him."

"Heather . . . ?"

"Trust me. He'll know who it is."

"Is he expecting you?"

"No. It's a surprise."

The receptionist smiled indulgently. "I'm afraid that Mr. Sherman is in a meeting."

"Then get him out."

"Excuse me?"

"Get. Him. Out." Heather took a deep

breath, her final word escaping on a sigh. "Now."

The receptionist's face filled with worry. "Is something wrong? Is this an emergency?"

"Yes, to both questions."

"I'm so sorry. Your name again?"

"Heather," Heather all but shrieked, attracting the attention of a silver-haired, older man thumbing through a recent issue of *Vanity Fair* in a nearby grouping of leather chairs.

"Just a minute." The receptionist lowered her voice as she spoke into her phone. "Sorry to disturb you, Mr. Whitman, but there's a woman named Heather asking to see Mr. Sherman. She says it's an emergency." She hung up the phone. "Mr. Sherman will be right out. If you'd like to have a seat . . ."

Heather glanced toward the small seating area in the corner of the room. The silver-haired gentleman was staring at her with obvious concern. *Has he seen the video?* she wondered. "No, thank you. I'll stand."

"Can I get you anything?" the receptionist asked. "Some coffee or bottled water, perhaps?"

"Just Mr. Sherman."

"He should be out in a second."

And then there he was, entering the reception area from the hallway behind the bank of elevators, looking all business in his blue suit and navy-and-gold striped tie, concern causing his eyes to squint. "Heather . . . what's wrong? Has something happened? Your father . . . ?"

"My father's fine, you son of a bitch!" Heather said.

"Whoa. Hold on a sec—"

"Don't tell me to hold on a sec, you piece of shit —"

"Okay, hey. Calm down," he said, grabbing her roughly by the elbow, his fingers digging into her flesh. "You're making a scene."

"I thought you liked scenes," Heather snapped, yanking her arm away. "You piece of shit —"

"Okay. Stop. That's enough. I don't know what's going on here or why you're so riled up, but this is hardly the time or the place —"

"What? Not public enough for you?"

"Is there a problem?" someone asked, and Heather turned to see Colin Whitman, one of the firm's founding partners, watching from the hall.

"No problem, sir," Noah said, pale blue eyes radiating fury. "Just a slight misunder-

450

standing."

"Perhaps you could take that misunderstanding into your office," Colin Whitman said pointedly.

"Not necessary, sir. Miss Hamilton was just leaving."

"Miss Hamilton isn't going anywhere," Heather said.

"This is where I work," Noah reminded her, his voice flat, like the dull side of a knife. "You're embarrassing me."

"*I'm* embarrassing *you?*"

"Should I call security?" the receptionist asked.

"That won't be necessary," Noah said.

"By all means, call security," Heather instructed, spinning around. The waiting area was filling up with people, eager to see what the commotion was all about. "You want to know what's going on here?" Heather asked them. "Don't be shy. Come on in. I'll tell you what's happening. You should know about the kind of man you have working here."

"Heather, for God's sake —"

"He's a lying scumbag. That's what he is. I mean, you probably shouldn't be too surprised. You're lawyers, so you're pretty much all a bunch of lying scumbags, but Noah's special. He cheated on his live-in girlfriend with her cousin." She heard a gasp. "And how do I know that, you may ask? Because that would be me! I'm the cousin! Oh, hello, Bryce," she said, waving toward Bryce Palmer, whom she recognized from their recent dinner. "How are Brianne and the kids?"

Bryce Palmer looked toward his shoes and said nothing.

"Well, be sure to say hello," Heather said, spinning back toward the others. "Anyway, it was my father's eightieth birthday party on the weekend and my cousin, the one he cheated on, was at the party, and it seems that she and Noah reconnected in a rather big way."

"Heather —"

"But you don't have to take my word for it," Heather continued over Noah's objections. "Check out YouTube. The truth is there for all to see." She shook her head. "Isn't it awful? You can't do anything nowadays without someone recording it. There's just no such thing as privacy anymore. You'd think a cheating scumbag would know that."

The elevator door opened and a security guard appeared, his hand hovering over the gun in his holster, his eyes casting about nervously.

"Oh, hi, there. Just finishing up. I'll be right with you," Heather told the guard. "The reason I'm so upset is that Noah, my boyfriend and your esteemed colleague, told me that my cousin was the one who came on to him. But the video clearly shows that wasn't the case. And since all *my* colleagues have been laughing behind *my* back, I thought it only fair to return the favor. So, there you have it. The whole truth and nothing but." She smiled, walking toward the security guard and putting her arm through his, relishing the stunned looks on everyone's faces. "Enjoy the rest of your day."

Chapter Forty-Seven

They'd been texting for several days.

Hey, Wildflower, his texts invariably began.

Hey, yourself, Paige had taken to responding.

So, I've been doing some research.

On what?

On what a director of strategic planning actually does.

And?

I'm impressed.

So was Paige, although she hadn't let on.

What impressed you? she'd ventured.

The whole scope of what you do: the brand planning, the account planning, the media planning, etc. etc., the way you connect all the dots, figure out what the consumer wants and how best to reach them, what emotional buttons you need to push.

Sounds a little cynical.

On the contrary. Sounds like a good plan for how to be successful in life.

Except I'm currently unemployed.
But not for much longer.
I hope you're right.
You'll get the job. I have faith.

Nice to know somebody does, Paige thought. *What about you?* she'd asked. *What do you do?*

Stockbroker. Speaking of which, duty calls. Text later.

And then, the next day:

Hey, Wildflower.
Hey, yourself.
Sorry about yesterday. Things got a little hectic.
How so?
Client was getting panicky. Had to calm him down, convince him to hang in there.
How did you do that?
By reminding him that these are volatile times and the time to sell is not when the market goes down.
And were you successful?
I can be pretty persuasive.

I bet you can, Paige thought now, putting down the not-so-thrilling thriller she was reading and checking her phone for messages, finding none. Almost twenty-four hours had passed since Mr. Right Now's last text. Was he really that busy or was he just playing games? Why hadn't he made another suggestion to meet up in person? Maybe he was testing her interest, waiting to see if she would break established protocol and make the first move. Would she? she wondered, as the phone rang in her hand. "Chloe, hi," she said, answering immediately. "How are you?"

"I'm great," Chloe said, sounding as if she meant it. "I have big news."

Uh-oh, Paige thought, looking at the storm clouds gathering outside her living room window. Had Chloe done another about-face, agreed to forgive Matt, taken him back yet again? Would she never learn? How many times did she have to be betrayed?

"Matt's agreed to everything," Chloe said, interrupting Paige's silent litany.

"What?"

"He got served with divorce papers this morning, and I was bracing myself for this big explosion. But he just called and, believe it or not, he said he's not going to fight me. On anything. As far as the house goes, he says that when we sell, well, he naturally wants his half and, of course, he wants the listing." She laughed, babbling on before Paige could interrupt. "But he says there's no rush, that he's caused me enough grief, that the kids and I can stay here as long as we want. And he's not going to fight me on support. He says I'm being more than reasonable with what I'm asking for. And best of all, he's not going after custody. He's not even asking for joint custody, says he's given it a lot of thought, and because the kids are so young, they'll be better off with me, and that as long as he has generous access, he's happy, which, of course, I'm thrilled with. He says that just because he was a jerk when we were married doesn't mean he has to be one when we get divorced. Can you believe it?"

No, thought Paige. *I can't.* "That's so great," she said.

"Isn't it? I kept waiting for the other shoe to drop, for him to start laughing, tell me it was all a big joke, that he'd rot in hell before he paid me a dime, but he just kept apologizing for everything. He actually said that he hoped that when this is all over, we might be friends."

"Wow," Paige said. "That's quite a turnaround." Maybe Matt already had a replacement waiting in the wings, she thought. Or maybe he was hoping that such tactics would convince Chloe he wasn't such a bad guy after all, persuade her to withdraw her divorce petition and come back to him.

Would she?

"I'm not going to change my mind about

the divorce," Chloe said, as if Paige had spoken her thoughts out loud. "I know you're worried, but . . ."

"Hey," Paige said. "You have to do what's right for you. It doesn't matter what I think or what anybody else thinks. You have my support, no matter what you do."

"I know. Thank you. You're a great friend, and I love you."

"I love you, too."

"I have other news," Chloe announced.

Paige held her breath.

"I got a job."

"What?"

"Well, it's just part-time. Three days a week, from ten to two, so it doesn't interfere with the kids' schedule. At this little pastry shop in Harvard Square. I saw their sign in the window when I met Matt for dinner, and I called and asked if the job was still available and they said it was, so I went in to see them, and . . . well, I start Monday."

"That's wonderful."

"It's no big deal. Minimum wage and everything, but I'm kind of excited."

"You should be. Congratulations."

"Thanks. What about you? When's your next interview?"

"Not till the end of next week."

"What about that guy you've been texting?"

"Things seem to have stalled."

"They'll pick up again. I have faith."

That's what he said, Paige thought, as her phone pinged to indicate an incoming message. "Oh, my God. That's him," she said. "I can't believe it. He's texting right now."

"There you go. See what a little faith will do?"

"I'll call you later."

"Wait a few hours before you text him back," Chloe advised before hanging up.

Probably a good idea, Paige thought, opening the text.

Hey, Wildflower.

Hey, yourself, she texted back immediately. She'd kept him waiting long enough.

Sorry about taking so long to get back to you. Family emergency.

Is everything okay?

My mother hasn't been feeling well. Looks like I might have to head down to Florida for a few days.

I'm so sorry. Is it serious?

Hard to say. She's had a heart condition for years. Every so often it acts up. I'll know more once I talk to her doctors.

You're a good son.

No choice. I'm all she's got.

Your father?

Died last year. And I'm an only child. You?

I have a brother. He's a cardiologist in New Jersey. Maybe once you know what's happening with your mother, we could ask his opinion.

No response.

Damn it, Paige thought, as five minutes dragged into ten. She'd done it again. Gotten too personal. Appeared too eager. It was the "we" that had scared him off. She should never have said "we."

"Damn it," she said, closing her phone and tossing it next to her book on the cushion beside her.

"Problem?" her mother asked, coming into the living room, adjusting the diamond stud in her left ear.

"No. Just can't seem to get past chapter three of this damn book. You look nice. Is that a new blouse?"

"Yes. I bought it yesterday." She patted the ornate buttons at the front of her white silk shirt. "Do you like it?"

"It's lovely. Are you going somewhere?"

"I have a bridge lesson."

"Since when do you play bridge?"

"Since about an hour from now. It's my first lesson. I'm a little nervous. Harry says bridge players can be quite cutthroat. But

460

he loves the game, so I thought I'd give it a go."

Harry, Paige repeated silently. Of course. She should have known. Her mother had been spending almost every waking minute with the man since their date last weekend, and if she wasn't with him, she was talking about him. As much as Paige wanted to be happy for her, she couldn't help being a little resentful. Not that she begrudged her mother her happiness, but she'd gotten used to being the center of her mother's universe, to having her all to herself.

"Sweetheart? Are you okay?"

"What time will you be home? I was thinking maybe we could go to a movie . . ."

"Oh, darling. I'm so sorry. Harry is picking me up after my lesson and taking me somewhere nice for dinner. I might not be back until quite late. Are you all right with that?"

No, Paige thought. *I want you to stay here with me.* "Of course." She pushed herself off the sofa and walked toward her mother, folding her body into her mother's waiting arms and relishing the comfort of her embrace. *Don't leave me,* she thought. "Go," she said. "Enjoy your lesson."

"I will," her mother said, heading for the door. "Don't wait up," she called as the door closed behind her.

Which meant her mother would be having sex. Again. "Great," Paige said, returning to the sofa and picking up her book, hoping to lose herself in someone else's misery, but giving up when she realized she'd read almost another ten chapters and still had no idea what the damn novel was about. She closed the book and glanced at her watch. It had been more than two hours since Mr. Right Now's last text. She glared at her phone, trying to will another message into existence. But none appeared. "You're worse than Chloe," she told herself. At least Chloe was mourning the loss of something real, whereas she was pining for a relationship that hadn't even begun, with a man she hadn't even met. What was the matter with her? She was a strong, independent woman. The last thing she needed was a man who could be scared off by the word "we."

And then there it was, as if he'd sensed her growing impatience and was testing her newfound resolve: a message from Mr. Right Now.

Hey, Wildflower.

Paige debated whether to respond. *Two can play this game,* she thought, her fingers hovering over the phone's tiny keyboard, her mind ping-ponging between texting him back immediately or making him wait.

Sorry for yet another long delay in getting back to you, the text continued before she could make up her mind. *I'm not trying to be coy, I swear. I was able to book a flight to Florida last minute. I'm actually in a limo now, heading for the airport. Hoping to be away only a few days, and really hoping we've passed the texting phase and can give this another try, meet up in person one day next week. Anyway, here's my phone number. Feel free to call me anytime so we can get something definite in the books. Can't wait to finally meet you.*

Paige didn't hesitate. *Have a safe trip,* she texted back. *Hope all goes well with your mom.*

Then, throwing caution to the proverbial wind: *Can't wait to meet you, too.*

CHAPTER FORTY-EIGHT

"Bridge isn't like any other card game," the instructor was saying from the front of the small, windowless room, one of several meeting rooms on the second floor of the historic Lenox Hotel. The instructor, whose name, Joy Boothe, was scribbled across the white chalkboard beside her in elaborately swirling green cursive, was about fifty, tall and heavyset, with gold-streaked auburn hair that hung in loose ringlets to her broad shoulders, false eyelashes that were in constant flutter, and pink lipstick that was outlined in bright red.

Harry had warned her that most bridge teachers were somewhat eccentric, Joan recalled, trying to concentrate on the woman's introductory remarks. But whether it was Joy Boothe's disconcertingly girlish voice or the strange feeling that had been twisting through Joan's groin ever since she sat down, she was having trouble focusing.

She glanced around the room at the other five tables, each table consisting of four students, the women outnumbering the men by a ratio of four to one. Only two of the other students could kindly be described as middle-aged. The others had waved goodbye to sixty long ago.

"Most card games can be learned pretty quickly," Joy Boothe continued. "Bridge isn't one of them."

Not exactly reassuring, Joan thought, squirming in her seat and smiling at the nervous-looking woman opposite her, whose name was also Joan. A roomful of Joans, Susans, Gails, and Marilyns, she thought. Not a Tayden or Kayden in sight.

"To succeed at bridge," the instructor was saying, "you need three things: a fair degree of patience, a modicum of card sense, and lots of lessons. I'm afraid I can't help you with the first two, but I *can* give you enough tools in these first five sessions to enable you to play the game. To play the game *well* — well, that requires even more patience, better card sense, and many more lessons. It would also help to read my book, *The Joy of Bridge,*" she said, having the grace to look a little embarrassed, as a copy of the slim pamphlet magically materialized in her hands. "It's available for sale during the break for only twelve dollars, and I think you'll find it most beneficial. Okay, let's begin."

The pamphlet in her hands was replaced by a deck of cards. "Hopefully, I don't have to tell you what this is, or that playing cards consist of four suits: clubs, diamonds, hearts, and spades. If you don't already know that, this is going to be a very long three hours. In bridge, clubs and diamonds are the lower-ranked suits and are called minor suits; hearts and spades are higher-ranked and are the major suits. With me so far?"

Joan nodded, her stomach cramping.

"The dealer doles out thirteen cards to each player, who then arranges them in suits. And that's when things start to get interesting, because in order to play, you first have to bid. The purpose of bidding is to determine who plays the hand and who defends. You and your partner — that would be the person sitting across from you — have to win the bidding in order to play the hand. And to do that, you need to tell your partner what's *in* your hand. But of course, you can't just come right out and volunteer that information. You have to describe your holdings through an elaborate system called bidding. And bidding correctly is the hardest part of learning to play bridge. Which is why I devote the first four lessons in this series of five to covering the twenty possible opening bids." Joy paused to let these facts sink in.

I'm lost already, Joan thought, trying to recall what she'd had to eat earlier that day that might have upset her stomach. But she'd had nothing out of the ordinary, just her usual egg, toast, and coffee for breakfast and a tuna fish sandwich for lunch. She'd made the sandwich herself, so that couldn't be the source of her discomfort. Besides, it wasn't really her stomach that was giving her the problem. It was more a sinking sensation slightly lower down, as if her guts were about to fall out.

Now you're being silly, she told herself. *It's anxiety, pure and simple. You're just nervous about these lessons. It's not easy learning new things at your age and you've ventured a little far out of your comfort zone, that's all. It's been almost fifty years since you've been in a classroom. Of course you're going to be nervous. A few deep breaths and you'll feel better.*

She took a few deep breaths.

And felt worse.

"The first thing you have to do after looking at your hand and arranging it into suits,"

Joy Boothe continued, "is to count your points. An ace is worth four points, a king is worth three, a queen, two, and a jack, one. A singleton — that's having only one card of a particular suit — is worth two points, a doubleton — that's two of a suit — is worth one point, and a void in a suit is worth a whopping five points. Unless that's the suit your partner is bidding. But we'll get to that later. To open the bidding, you need at least twelve high-card points. Everybody still with me?"

Joan felt a line of perspiration break out across her forehead as a sharp twist to her groin caused her to grab her side. Was she having an appendix attack?

"Are you okay?" the Joan across from her whispered.

"Is there a question?" the instructor asked, looking in their direction, heavy black eyebrows disappearing into her hairline.

Joan pushed herself to her feet. "I'm sorry, but could I be excused for a minute?"

"Of course. The washroom is just down the hall to your left."

"Thank you."

"I'm going to hand out some sheets," Joy Boothe was saying as Joan left the room and hurried down the hall to the ladies' room.

Could she be passing a gallstone? Joan

wondered, finding an empty stall and relieving herself. Or maybe a kidney stone? she added, when she felt no relief. Except she'd heard that passing kidney stones felt much like giving birth. And while what she was experiencing was decidedly uncomfortable, there was no comparing it to the pain of childbirth.

Nor was it her appendix, she decided, pressing down on her right side. She remembered reading somewhere that if the appendix was about to burst, the pain would be greater upon letting go than pressing down, and that wasn't the case.

Besides, she'd been to the ER twice in the past few weeks and been given a clean bill of health each time. There was nothing wrong with her, other than an overactive imagination. *The age of hypochondria indeed!* she thought, standing up and adjusting her clothing, grateful that the pain seemed to be easing up, becoming more of an intermittent drill than a complete hollowing out of her inner organs.

She checked her reflection in the wall of mirrors over the line of sinks, touched up her lipstick, and pinched some needed color into her cheeks, then left the room. "An ace is worth four points; a king, three; a queen, two; and a jack, one," she recited as she walked down the hall. "You need a minimum of twelve high-card points to open the bidding." She took a deep breath before pushing open the door and reentering the class. "Piece of cake." She had absolutely nothing to worry about.

"So, how'd it go?" Harry asked, meeting her in the lobby of the hotel. "What'd you think?"

"Very interesting," Joan told him, trying to ignore the renewed cramping below her waist. "Very challenging." Especially when she'd missed half the class because she'd had to run to the bathroom every fifteen minutes. "We learned basic bridge terminology and about major and minor suits." She held out a bunch of sheets as well as the pamphlet she'd purchased from Joy Boothe during the halftime break, a gesture of atonement for spending so much of the lesson in the bathroom. "We're supposed to study this bidding chart outlining the progression of bids from the lowest to the highest, although today we just covered the first part, opening at the one level."

"And? Do you think you're going to like it?"

"I do," Joan said, a sudden spasm causing her to wince.

"You don't sound sure."

"No," Joan said, forcing a smile onto her lips. "I'm quite sure. I think it's a fascinating game, and what's more, I think I'm going to be very good at it."

Harry laughed. "Then I very much look forward to being your partner."

"I still have four weeks of classes before I'm ready for that."

"I'll be here," he said.

Joan felt a tingle of excitement at Harry's pronouncement. It meant he was planning to stick around, that he felt the same way about her that she felt about him.

That feeling was quickly overpowered by the sensation that something foreign had invaded her body and was squeezing her to death from the inside out. "Where should we go for dinner?" she asked, talking over the pain.

"I was thinking Legal Sea Foods. How does that sound to you?"

Another sharp stab twisted through Joan's groin.

"Or, if you don't feel like seafood," Harry said, misinterpreting the pained expression on her face, "we could do Asian. Or Italian. Or more traditional American. Whatever you prefer. Are you all right?"

"No," Joan said, clutching her stomach

and trying not to double over. "I think I need to go to the hospital."

"My God. What's happening?"

"I don't know. Something's very wrong."

"Okay," Harry said calmly, surrounding her with one arm while signaling the valet to bring his car around. "I'll call your daughter, tell her to meet us there."

Joan nodded. While the last thing she wanted to do was worry her daughter unnecessarily — again — she was in too much pain to argue. It felt as if every organ in her body was on fire.

It crossed her mind that she might be dying.

Now? she thought. Just when she was starting to feel more alive than she had in years? How fair was that?

"Hang in there," Harry said as he guided her into the front seat of his Audi and secured her seatbelt around her. "You're going to be all right."

She wanted to tell him not to worry. But the words wouldn't come. "You promise?" she said instead.

"I promise," he told her.

Chapter Forty-Nine

He's been preparing for tonight all day.

First thing this morning he went to the local butcher and purchased two top-grade sirloin steaks, the kind restaurants always classify as New York cut, although he has no idea why. He could look it up online, he supposes, find a way to toss such knowledge casually into tonight's conversation. It's the type of useless information that women always find both charming and impressive. ("How do you know such things?" they invariably ask.)

The steaks were very pricey. Even more expensive than they were the last time he made a similar purchase. He probably could have picked them up for half the price at the grocery store in the mall. But as his mother always used to say, you get what you pay for.

Not that she knew anything about quality. She, who considered flank steak a delicacy.

Which was just as well, he thinks, recalling her propensity for overcooking everything, for broiling a piece of meat until it resembled the leather insole of a shoe. *"I don't like seeing any blood,"* he recalls her saying. *"It reminds me that the piece of meat was once a living thing."*

He laughs. This is exactly what appeals to him.

Still, for his purposes, a cheaper cut of meat would have been more than sufficient. The women never eat very much. Not more than one or two bites, and always under protest. And they never think to compliment him on his efforts, his skill as a chef. But that's okay. The meat rarely goes to waste. He generally saves what they don't eat for his lunch the next day.

He overpaid for the vegetables as well. The small specialty shops where he prefers to buy his groceries — there are four such shops in a row along Summer Street that the locals affectionately refer to as "the four thieves" — take an almost perverse pride in gouging their customers, as if they are doing their clientele a favor by even allowing them inside the premises. *Soon they'll be charging an entry fee,* he thinks with a laugh.

He doesn't mind overpaying. He can't help that he likes nice things. After years of being fed bruised fruit and anemic-looking vegetables — he'll never understand the popularity of the adjective "wilted" that the better restaurants seem so fond of — he can't bring himself to buy anything but the ripest-looking watermelon for his water-melon and feta cheese salad, or the largest, healthiest-looking Idaho potatoes for the requisite side starch. He uses only the best ingredients and wine for his marinade, and only real butter and the richest of sour creams will do as toppings for his potatoes. He even buys the most expensive foil in which to wrap them.

Of course, all this is lost on the women he entertains.

Oh, they're impressed enough at first. That first glimpse of his immaculately clean apartment is always a turn-on, and the white linen tablecloth hiding the cheap glass table beneath, along with the delicate floral china, they love that. They admire his taste in art, wax ecstatic over the cheap prints on the wall. Nadia, poor thing, even asked if he'd painted the obvious reproduction of Van Gogh's *Starry Night*. It was a print, for God's sake. A photograph on a piece of paper. Not a real brushstroke in sight. He'd had to struggle to keep a straight face.

The so-called art isn't even his. The prints

— by Van Gogh, Renoir, Degas, Monet — came with the unit. He'd thought of replacing them at first, just as he'd replaced the cheap Melmac dishes and plastic placemats Imogene Lebowski had supplied, then thought better of it. Some things were best left the way they were, and he didn't want to chance insulting Mrs. Lebowski, who'd proved to be such an ideal landlady: old, partially deaf, more than half-senile. What more could he have asked for?

And now she's gone, off to her daughter's house to await being carted off to an institution. The second-floor tenant departed two days ago, which leaves him the home's sole remaining occupant.

Could things have worked out any better?

He was planning to leave soon anyway, and now he can take his time, relish his remaining conquests. He doesn't have to worry about making too much noise. The women can scream their fool heads off. No one will hear them. He can indulge his most lurid fantasies without the fear of disturbing his downstairs neighbor or waking poor Imogene. His last two kills will be his best.

First up is Audrey. Audrey, who likes sappy movies and working out.

He pokes at his marinating steaks with a fork, imagines doing the same thing to Audrey's pliant flesh. He'll give her a workout she won't soon forget.

Except, of course, she will. The dead don't remember anything. He laughs. That's all right. He's more than happy to keep the memories alive.

His phone signals the arrival of a text message, and he smiles. Wildflower, he thinks. Taking him up on his offer to call him anytime, to inquire after his mother, to make arrangements to meet him in person. Women are so predictable, he thinks, extricating his cell from the side pocket of his jeans. Even Wildflower has fallen into line.

But the message isn't from Wildflower, which both annoys and delights him.

Still on for tonight? comes Audrey's text.

Of course, he texts back, his shoulders stiffening. *Is there a problem?*

I was worried you might have had to go back to Wisconsin.

Wisconsin? What the hell is she talking about?

You said you might have to go back. To see your father.

His father? Shit. Of course. His sick father in Wisconsin. Not his sick mother in Florida. Shit.

How's he doing?

He's much better, thanks. Sorry. I forgot I

477

told you about my father.

Looks like my prayers worked.

Looks like they did.

So, I'll see you at Anthony's tonight at seven?

Wouldn't miss it. He disconnects, returning the phone to his pocket, feeling somewhat shaken. It's not like him to get his stories mixed up. He'll have to be more careful. The last thing he wants is to mess up now.

It's just that he's been so preoccupied with Wildflower.

The one who almost got away.

Almost.

"Almost only counts in horseshoes," he recalls his mother saying, yet another one of her more idiotic expressions. What does it mean, anyway?

He temporarily bristles when he recalls Wildflower's initial indifference, her casual disregard, the dismissive way she turned from him in the bar without so much as a backward glance. She thinks she's so good, so smart.

And she *is* smart. Smarter than he's used to, at any rate. A strategic planner. Which gives them something in common. What is he, after all, if not a strategic planner?

"And I have big plans for you, my little

Wildflower." Tonight would be a dress rehearsal of sorts, a chance to try out some new moves, test Audrey's reactions before springing them on Wildflower.

He gives the marinating steaks a final poke, then takes the juicy, ripe half-watermelon out of the fridge and starts cutting it into bite-sized squares. He'll use the same knife on Audrey later, he thinks with a smile. He arranges the pieces of watermelon on top of some lettuce, already artfully laid out on small plates, and then slices up some tomatoes to fill out the tableau, followed by a generous sprinkling of feta. The oil-and-vinegar dressing will be applied at the last minute. Balsamic vinegar of course. Extra-virgin olive oil.

He laughs. What the hell is an extra virgin, anyway?

The potatoes are already wrapped in foil, and he stabs at them with his fork, making a series of holes to allow the heat to penetrate. The oven is already preheating. He's learned from experience that it's best to have the potatoes prebaked. Big ones like these take at least an hour to heat through. Nothing worse than potatoes that are hard and undercooked. He'll pop them into the microwave at the last minute, letting them warm up while the steaks are being grilled.

That way he doesn't have to waste another hour making excruciating small talk. He'll have already put in his time at the bar. Having to listen to a woman natter on about her pathetic little life was interesting only when she knew she was on the verge of death.

He checks his watch. After five already. Just two more hours till Operation Audrey.

He's humming as he walks into the bedroom, although it takes him a minute to recognize the tune and put words to it. Something about Saturday night being the loneliest night of the week. Not for him, he thinks with a smile, recalling that his mother used to love that song. She'd sing it off and on for hours in her surprisingly pretty voice until his father would yell for her to "shut up already." And if she didn't shut up fast enough, well, a punch to the jaw would usually shut her up pretty damn quick.

He reaches into the top drawer of the nightstand beside his bed and retrieves the set of metal handcuffs that have served him so well during his stay in Boston. He'll get rid of them before he leaves town, as he prefers to start fresh with a new pair in each city he visits. A kind of good luck charm. He checks to make sure they lock properly, tosses the key to the nightstand, and throws the cuffs on the bed. They land beside the rope already laid out. He runs his hand along the rope's harsh fibers, expertly and effortlessly tying it into a noose, his erection stirring as he imagines twisting it around Audrey's throat.

He puts so much effort into this planning stage that it's almost anticlimactic how fast he knows it will all play out, how easy it will be to secure those clumsy handcuffs on Audrey's delicate wrists, to slip the deadly noose around her unsuspecting neck and tighten it until she is totally within his control. *"Have a seat,"* he'll whisper seductively in her ear, his lips grazing the side of her hair, as he pulls out her chair. Then, once she is comfortably seated, *"Close your eyes. I have a surprise for you."*

By the time she opens them, it will be too late.

He checks his watch again, amazed to discover that twenty minutes have passed since he last looked. He hurries back into the kitchen and pops the potatoes into the oven, so that they will be done by the time he's ready to leave. Then he walks back into the bedroom and selects the black silk shirt and pants he's decided on for his date with Audrey — he always wears black, not wanting to stand out more than he can help —

along with some fresh underwear and socks, laying them on the bed beside the rope and handcuffs.

He's humming as he strips naked and heads for the shower. Of course, he'll have to shower again later, when he's covered in Audrey's blood. But as his mother was so fond of saying, *"Cleanliness is next to Godliness."*

He laughs. Tonight he'll not only be clean. He'll be God himself.

CHAPTER FIFTY

"Mom?" Paige called toward the bedroom. "What are you doing? Are you all right?"

"I'm fine, darling," Joan said, adjusting her white silk shawl over her light-blue cotton dress as she walked into the living room where Paige was sitting, still struggling with the novel she'd been reading. "You have to stop worrying about me."

"You don't give me a chance! Three visits to the ER in as many weeks! That's probably some sort of record. Did you take your antibiotics?"

"I did, although I don't think they're really necessary anymore. I'm feeling much better now."

"You have to take them until they're all finished," Paige reminded her. "If you stop before you've taken the entire course, the infection will only come back, and the antibiotics will be less effective. Didn't you hear what the doctor said?"

"To be honest, it's a bit of a blur. I was in a lot of pain."

"Well, urinary tract infections are nothing to sneeze at. You're lucky it hadn't spread to your kidneys."

"Yes, dear." Joan twirled around in a small circle. "How do I look?"

"Beautiful. As always. Where are you off to tonight?"

"There's this dinner cruise down the Charles River. Believe it or not, I've never been on one, and Harry says they're quite magical." She paused, looking at Paige expectantly.

"What?" Paige asked.

"You've never said . . . what you think of Harry."

"Well, we didn't exactly meet under the best of circumstances."

"I know, but . . ."

"A crowded emergency room isn't the ideal place to get to know someone."

"You don't like him," Joan said.

"I didn't say that."

"You haven't said anything."

"He seems very nice," Paige told her. "It's just that . . ."

"What?"

An awkward pause. "He's the reason you were in emergency in the first place."

"What are you talking about?"

"I think you know."

Another awkward pause, this one longer than the first.

"You're talking about sex," her mother said finally.

"Well, you've obviously been having a lot of it lately . . . and as the doctor explained, things tend to . . . *thin out* as women age, and it's been a while since you were so . . . *busy.* You put two and two together and you get . . ."

"A urinary tract infection."

"Exactly."

"But you can't blame the thinness of my uterine wall on Harry," her mother offered in his defense.

Paige sighed. "I know."

"And it's not as if I wasn't an enthusiastic participant . . ."

"Okay. I get it, Mom. I don't need a —"

"Blow by blow?" her mother asked, deep blue eyes twinkling with mischief.

"Oh, God."

"You know, dear, you're a bit of a prude."

"Oh, God," Paige said again. Her mother was right. She *was* a prude. When had that happened? "I'm sorry. Harry seems like a very nice man. I actually liked him a lot."

"Really? You're not just saying that?"

"I'm not just saying that."

The phone rang.

"That'll be the concierge," Joan said, running into the kitchen to answer it. "Harry's here," she said, returning seconds later. "I said I'd be right down. Do you have plans for tonight?"

"Nothing definite." Actually, she had no plans at all. She and Chloe had talked of getting together, but then Josh had come down with an earache, so that finished that.

"You could call Sam," her mother suggested.

"I could," Paige agreed. She'd been thinking about him a lot lately. The truth was that she missed him. "But it's probably not a good idea."

"Maybe not." Her mother walked toward the door and opened it.

"Mom . . ." Paige called.

"Yes, dear?"

"No sex! At least till you're finished with the antibiotics. I don't want any more phone calls from the hospital."

"Yes, dear." The door closed behind her.

"God," Paige said, picking up her book, reading a few more boring paragraphs, then walking into the kitchen and tossing the novel into the garbage bin under the sink. "Enough of that."

Should she call Sam, confess that she missed him?

Or did she just miss having someone in her life?

It wouldn't be fair to call him before she knew for sure.

In the meantime, there was Mr. Right Now. Paige pulled her cellphone out of her pocket and checked for messages, finding none.

She wondered if he was back from Florida, and if his mother's condition had improved. What if she'd died? *Then I'll never get laid,* Paige thought, and laughed out loud. "You're a horrible person," she said, walking into the family room and putting on the television, aimlessly switching among the various channels for the next half hour, trying to find something — anything — of interest. There was *Nightmare Next Door,* followed by *Fear Thy Neighbor,* which was on opposite something called *Wives with Knives.* "Seriously? *Wives with Knives?*"

She settled on an ancient episode of *CSI: Miami,* then returned to the kitchen and made herself a cup of tea. She was finishing her tea and checking her phone for messages she knew weren't there when it rang.

"My mother got married," Chloe announced.

"What?"

"Yup. Just got a text from the blushing bride herself. Apparently, she met this guy at a dance competition last week and knew instantly he was Mr. Right. They eloped to Las Vegas yesterday."

"Wow. How many Mr. Rights does this make?"

"I believe this is Mr. Right number four. Or maybe five. Oh, and this Mr. Right is from Miami, so she'll be moving there at the end of the month, and can I please go over to her apartment this week and start packing up her stuff?"

"Wow," Paige said again. What else was there to say?

"Anyway, that's Josh crying again. I'll talk to you later."

Paige returned to the family room, about to settle into another episode of *CSI: Miami* when she decided, what the hell? If Chloe's mother could elope to Las Vegas with a man she'd just met, if her *own* mother was having such enthusiastic sex it had landed her in the ER, then what was *her* problem? What was she waiting for? So what if she looked pathetic because it was Saturday night and she didn't have a date? Hadn't he told her to call him anytime?

And wasn't *right now* the perfect time to

call the man calling himself Mr. Right Now?

She checked the number he'd left her, took a deep breath, then placed the call.

It rang twice before being picked up.

"Well, hello there," he said, his voice low.

Paige felt a sudden charge of electricity. He sounded almost as good as he looked. "Hi," she said. "Is this . . . Mr. Right Now?" A self-conscious chuckle escaped her mouth before she could stop it. She was grateful when he laughed along with her.

"It is. Is this . . . Wildflower?"

"It is."

"Well, Wildflower. I'm so glad you called."

"Are you still in Florida? Is this a bad time?"

"No. It's perfect. I just got back into town about an hour ago."

"How's your mother?"

"Much better. Thanks for asking. How are you?"

She could hear the smile in his voice. "Me? I'm fine." She hesitated briefly. "I was thinking maybe you were right, that it's time we give this another try."

"No maybes about it. At least on my end. How about Wednesday?"

"Wednesday is good."

"Great. Are you familiar with Anthony's Bar, over on Boylston? I know it's usually crowded and it can get pretty noisy, but —"

"Anthony's is great."

"Say six o'clock?"

"Six is good."

"No more last-minute cancellations?"

"I'll be there at six on the button."

"No!" Paige heard someone shout. "Don't . . ." There followed muffled sounds she couldn't quite make out, almost as if someone was fighting.

"What was that?" she asked.

"What was what?" His voice was light, untroubled. "Oh. Probably just the TV. Some guy getting the shit kicked out of him. Excuse the language."

She wondered if he was watching the same episode of *CSI: Miami* that she was, but didn't ask. "Are you going to tell me your real name?" she asked instead.

"I'll tell you mine if you tell me yours," came the sly reply. "Although I gotta say, I kind of like Wildflower."

"Then suppose we leave things the way they are for now."

"Till Wednesday, then," he said.

"Till Wednesday."

"Looking forward to it."

And then he was gone.

"Well, well," Paige said, exhaling a deep sigh of relief. "That wasn't so hard, was it?"

Maybe her luck was about to change. Her job prospects were sounding good. Mr. Right Now was sounding even better.

Maybe things were finally starting to look up.

CHAPTER FIFTY-ONE

Heather could hear her parents arguing in the next room. She didn't have to eavesdrop to know they were arguing about her.

I should never have come home, she thought, stretching out on the double bed in what had once been her bedroom, and covering her ears with her pillow. Still, what was she supposed to do? Where was she supposed to go?

After her outburst at Noah's office, she'd been too overwrought to return to work, so she'd called to say she was sick and wouldn't be back till morning. ("Food poisoning?" Kendall had asked with such obvious disbelief that Heather could almost see her eyebrows rise.) Then she'd gone to a movie, where she'd consumed an entire bucket of buttered popcorn along with a giant Coke, all the while rehearsing under her breath what she'd say to Noah when she returned to their apartment. ("Do you mind keeping your voice down?" a woman had turned around in her seat and muttered. To which Heather had replied, "Screw you.")

Heather knew that Noah would be angry, and that she needed to be prepared. Yes, she would tell him calmly, she understood she'd embarrassed him, and she was truly sorry about that. But he'd embarrassed her, too. Yes, she understood she might have gone too far, but so had he. And yes, maybe she was guilty of overreacting. But only because she loved him so much, and because he'd hurt her so badly. Surely he could see that he bore at least some of the responsibility for her lashing out the way she had. If he hadn't kissed her cousin, if he hadn't lied to her about it, if his indiscretion hadn't been captured on camera, if her coworkers hadn't taunted her with it . . .

She was well prepared for the mix of harsh words and stony silence that would un-doubtedly follow, suspecting it could be days, even weeks, before he understood her side of the story, or he got sufficiently horny, for things between them to return to nor-mal.

What she wasn't prepared for was to find all her belongings in three giant garbage bags outside their apartment door. What she hadn't expected was the note taped to the door telling her in no uncertain terms that their relationship was over and that if she dared to come inside or cause any kind of scene, he would call the police and have her arrested.

What she hadn't expected was to have to spend the night in a hotel, albeit the Four Seasons, while she figured out her next move, or to go into work the next morning only to be unceremoniously escorted out. "I'm being fired?" she'd asked, as the security guard waited in the aisle for her to clear out her desk. "I don't believe this!"

"I don't believe you're surprised," came Kendall's retort.

"You and Noah broke up?" her mother exclaimed when she showed up at her parents' home in Weston later that day, garbage bags in tow.

"You lost your job," her father said, as if he'd known all along this would happen.

"I'm thinking of suing," Heather told them.

To which they'd said nothing at all.

I should never have come home, she thought again. Except she couldn't stay at the Four Seasons forever. She couldn't afford even one more night. Her credit cards were already maxed out and she'd just lost her fucking job. The severance check they'd handed her on her way out the door wouldn't last long. Sure, she could apply for unemployment, but that could take months to come through. Meanwhile, the thought of looking for another job made both her head and her stomach ache. She needed time to relax, recoup, regroup, and decompress. Maybe take a little vacation. A beach or a spa would be ideal. She'd start job-hunting when summer was over.

Her father had proved less than sympathetic to her plans. He'd given her a week — a week! — to get her act together, and it was already Wednesday. Would he follow through on his threat to kick her out if she didn't at least make an effort to look for work?

"I'm working on my tan," she'd told him defiantly, tossing her pillow to the floor and climbing out of bed, deciding she should at least get out of her pajamas. It was almost noon, and the backyard awaited.

She checked her phone for messages, but there was still nothing from Noah, and her only emails were from a Calvin Klein outlet store and Walmart, both of which she sent directly to Trash. "Shit." She'd hoped that Noah would have come to his senses by now. Not that she would be so quick to take him back — she'd decided to let him squirm for a while — but still . . .

There was a knock on her bedroom door.

"Shit," she said again, her head collapsing toward her chest.

"Heather?" her mother called. "Are you up?"

"Yes, Mother. Just heading into the shower."

"Well, when you're done, your father would like to talk to you."

"Shit!" Heather said, louder this time.

"What's that?" her mother asked.

"I said 'sure thing.' Give me ten minutes."

"We'll be in the den."

"Can't wait."

"What?"

"I'll be there." She listened until her mother's footsteps had disappeared down the hall before entering her bathroom and turning on the shower. "Shit," she said again, sensing another lecture. She positioned her body directly under the torrent of hot water, repeating the word at the top of her lungs: "Shit, shit, shit, shit, *shit!*"

"I was talking to Walt Simon," her father was saying even before Heather entered the room. He was sitting, stiff-backed, feet crossed at the ankles, in one of two brown leather wing chairs in front of the large

496

stone fireplace that took up most of the east wall. Her mother was sitting in the other, her feet similarly crossed. Both were dressed as if to go out, although Heather doubted they had anywhere to go. She probably should have put on something more substantial than white shorts and an off-the-shoulder top.

"Who's Walt Simon?" she asked, eyes traveling across the built-in bookshelves lining the other walls. Had anybody actually read any of these books? she wondered.

"He's my bank manager."

Heather waited, wondering what this had to do with her.

"I told him about you, and asked if they were hiring. Apparently they are."

"What kind of job are we talking about?" Heather asked.

"They need tellers. Of course, you'd have to interview . . ."

"I don't understand," she said.

"What don't you understand?"

"Why you think I'd be interested in a job as a fucking teller."

"Heather, really!" her mother said. "Your language!"

"Bev, please," her father said, his face turning a dangerous shade of red. "I'll handle this."

"Handle what? Me?" Heather shifted from one bare foot to the other, wishing her father would have a heart attack and die. First, he'd given her all of one week to get her act together, and now he was telling her he'd found her a job. As a teller, for fuck's sake. "I can find my own job, thank you very much."

"Can you? I don't see you trying very hard."

"What do you think I've been doing all week?" Heather asked, managing to sound indignant.

"You mean other than sleeping till noon and lying around in the sun?"

"For your information, I've spent hours on my laptop, looking at what jobs are available in my field, trying to find something for someone with my qualifications," Heather lied, pretending not to notice the roll of her father's eyes. "It's going to take time. There's not a lot out there right now. Look at Paige. She's been unemployed for months. I don't hear you complaining about *her*."

"First of all, Paige isn't my daughter, much as I wish she were."

"Great," Heather muttered under her breath, hating her cousin more than ever.

"Secondly, she was a casualty of a New

498

York takeover, not her own irresponsibility."

"You saying I'm irresponsible?"

"You're the one who left work in the middle of the day."

"I had a very good reason for leaving the office that afternoon," Heather protested. "I'd just found out that Noah —"

"Noah," her father scoffed, his hands waving dismissively in front of his face, as if warding off a pesky fly. "Another one of your wise decisions. As if going after your cousin's boyfriend wasn't foolish enough. Did you really think that a man stupid enough to cheat on someone like Paige wasn't going to cheat on you, too?" He shook his head. "I can't believe a daughter of mine could be that dumb."

Heather's eyes filled with angry tears. "I am not dumb."

"Then prove it. Let me call Walt Simon and tell him you'll interview for that job."

Heather looked from her father to her mother, then back to her father. "There is no way I'm working as a fucking teller in a fucking bank. So you can take your fucking job and shove it up your fucking ass."

"Oh, Heather," her mother said as the color drained from Ted Hamilton's face.

"Okay, then," her father said, with infuriating calm. "I'm afraid you leave us no choice." He paused, whether to collect his thoughts or for dramatic effect, Heather couldn't be sure. "I'll arrange to have some money transferred into your account, enough for first and last month's rent on an apartment, plus enough to tide you over for a few months. Hopefully by the time your money runs out, you'll have found a job suitable for *someone with your qualifications.*"

Heather looked toward her mother. "I can't believe you're letting him do this."

"You have till the weekend," her father said. "If you haven't found a place by then, well, maybe you can persuade one of your brothers to take you in until you do."

"I don't need till the weekend," Heather said. "I'll be out of here this afternoon. In fact, you won't ever have to see me again. How's that?" She spun around on her heels, then fled the room, bounding up the stairs to her bedroom and slamming the door behind her. "Fuck you!" she cried, cursing her father, her mother, Noah, and Paige. Precious Paige. The daughter her father had always wanted.

"Heather, please," she heard her mother call. "Be sensible."

Heather sank down on the bed, her body shaking with rage. She had no idea where she was going to go or what she was going to do.

Only one thing was certain: she was way past sensible.

CHAPTER FIFTY-TWO

Chloe stood amid the chaos of her mother's small, furnished studio apartment, wondering where to start. There was stuff everywhere. Discarded underwear littered the scuffed hardwood floor. Glitzy dance costumes were flung across the open and unmade sofa bed like sequined pillowcases. Dozens of fashion magazines were stacked up against the walls like unpruned vines. Used tissues and scrap pieces of paper lay crumpled in every corner. A moldy, half-eaten sandwich sat on the counter of the tiny galley kitchen, beside a pile of unwashed plastic dishes. "Holy cow," the building supervisor exclaimed when he'd unlocked the apartment door to let Chloe inside. "Garbage chute's down the hall," he'd added without prompting. "Good luck."

Her first thought was that robbers had broken in and tossed the place, then vandalized it when they could find nothing of worth. Her second thought, which came to her when she stumbled over an empty vodka bottle, was that no robbers had been necessary. Her mother was more than capable of making a mess like this on her own.

And leaving it for someone else to clean up.

Still, Chloe couldn't remember any of the places she'd grown up in ever having been *this* bad. This was *like a tornado had swept through,* as she'd described it to Paige, texting her in horror as soon as the super left, adding, *I'll be here all night.*

I'd come help you, Paige had texted back immediately. *But I'm giving this online dating one more shot, and I'm on my way to the hairdresser at this very minute, followed by a mani-pedi and a bikini wax.*

You go, girl, Chloe had messaged back. She'd removed her own picture and profile from the dating sites she'd joined to check on Matt soon after posting them. Maybe one day, when her divorce was final, she'd work up the courage to actually try them. Right now, even the thought of dating terrified her. Matt had been the only man in her life since she was fourteen years old, the only lover she'd ever known. What would it be like to have another man's hands on her body, to feel another man inside her?

"Oh, God," Chloe said, banishing the thought and setting her mind to the task at hand. She started with the kitchen, emptying the fridge and the cupboards and drawers of their contents, and throwing everything that couldn't be recycled into one of the heavy-duty plastic bags she'd had the foresight to bring with her, garbage bags being one of the few items her mother didn't seem to have lying around. She dragged the bag to the door of the apartment and opened it.

The door across the hall opened almost simultaneously. Chloe found herself staring into the sleep-filled eyes of a skinny young man wearing precariously low-slung sweatpants and no shirt.

"Hey," he said with a smile, running a hand through his almost shoulder-length brown hair.

"Hey." Chloe estimated the boy's age as maybe nineteen or twenty.

"I thought I heard someone rattling around in there," he said.

"Sorry if I disturbed you."

"That's okay. You a friend of Jennifer's?"

"Not exactly. I'm her daughter."

"Mothers and daughters can't be friends?" he asked with a smile, as if no answer was required. "I can see a resemblance, now that you mention it. I'm Ethan."

"Chloe."

"Nice to meet you, Chloe. I really like your mom. She's cool."

Chloe nodded, unsure how to respond.

He rubbed his hairless chest. "Haven't seen her in a while."

"She's in Las Vegas."

"Yeah? Another one of those dance competitions?"

"Actually, she got married."

"No kidding! Wow. Does that mean she'll be moving out?"

Chloe nodded. "I'm here to pack up her things."

Ethan peered over her shoulder into Jennifer's apartment. "Looks like you've got your work cut out for you."

Chloe's phone rang. She pulled it from the side pocket of her jeans and checked the caller ID. "Excuse me," she said to Ethan. "Matt, hi." He was scheduled to pick the kids up from day camp this afternoon and keep them overnight. "Is there a problem?"

"No problem. Just checking to make sure Josh is good to go."

"Yeah, his earache seems to have cleared up." She smiled goodbye to Ethan, stepping

505

back inside her mother's apartment.

"Do you want some help in there?" he asked as she was closing the door.

"You mean it? That would be so great."

"Who's that?" Matt asked.

"I'll go put on a shirt."

"You're with some half-naked guy?"

Chloe laughed. "Not exactly."

"What exactly?"

Chloe decided to ignore the proprietary tone in Matt's voice. There was no point in disturbing the delicate truce they'd established by reminding him that such things were no longer his concern. Being Matt, his temper was bound to get the better of him occasionally, but he'd been making such an effort. Better to humor than upset him, she decided, especially when there was nothing to get upset about. "I'm at my mother's," she explained. "Believe it or not, she eloped to Las Vegas, and this kid who lives across the hall from her just offered to help me get her stuff together." She broke off when she realized Matt was no longer on the line. "Matt? Matt?"

"Something wrong?" Ethan asked, reappearing in a maroon T-shirt with a gold Harvard logo.

"Looks like we were disconnected." Chloe returned the phone to her pocket. "You go to Harvard?"

"I'm smarter than I look," he said.

Chloe laughed. "I'm not so sure. You really want to do this?"

Ethan shrugged. "Got nothing better to do."

"Well, then. Let's get to it."

They spent the next two hours packing things up and throwing things out.

"The place looks much bigger once you get rid of all the junk," Chloe marveled, plopping down on the now cleared-off sofa bed in the center of the room, and wondering what to do with the well-worn sheets. She could throw them out or offer them to Ethan. He'd already volunteered to take the dishes, the towels, and the old portable TV. What he didn't want, he said he'd take to Goodwill. "Looks like we're almost done," she told him, amazed by what they'd accomplished in a relatively short period of time. "You've been a godsend. I can't thank you enough."

A suitcase crammed with her mother's costumes and clothes stood at the door, holding it open, allowing some much-needed air into the apartment. She'd take it to FedEx in the morning, she decided. She was too tired to do it now. There wasn't a part of her that didn't ache.

"What do you want to do with these?" Ethan asked, pulling a large cardboard box out of the closet and withdrawing several small statuettes.

"What are they?"

"Dance trophies," he said, offering them up for her perusal. "About a dozen of them. First place in the tango; second place in the waltz; first place in the jitterbug. What's a jitterbug?"

Chloe laughed. "Believe it or not, that's before my time, too." She took one of the trophies from Ethan's hand and studied it. Thousands and thousands of dollars spent to win a trophy that was worth maybe five dollars at most. Still, when was the last time she'd come first in anything? "I didn't realize she was that good."

"She's great," Ethan said, joining her on the bed.

"How do you know?"

"I went to see her once."

"You did?"

"Yeah. A few months ago, a competition at the Park Plaza. One of those Spanish dances. She invited me and a couple of my friends. We thought it'd be good for a laugh, you know. But she was genuinely good. I was impressed. You've never seen her dance?"

"No," Chloe said, rotating her neck from side to side, hearing her joints creak. Her mother had never invited her.

"Your neck stiff?" he asked.

"My neck, my shoulders, my back."

"Turn around," he said. "They tell me that I'm very good at this."

Chloe swiveled around on the bed, as Ethan's hands moved to massage her shoulder blades. "Oh, my God. That feels sensational."

"It's a gift," he said with a laugh.

Chloe felt the muscles at the base of her neck responding instantly to his firm but gentle ministrations. "Oh, my God," she said again. "You have no idea how good that feels."

"Knock, knock," came a voice from the doorway.

Ethan jumped to his feet as Matt walked into the room.

"Matt," Chloe said, pushing herself off the bed, feeling guilty, though she wasn't sure why. "What are you doing here?" She glanced at her watch. "You have to pick up the kids . . ."

"I have time. Just thought I'd stop by and see if I could lend a hand." His eyes moved slowly from Chloe to Ethan. "But I can see no more hands are required." He smiled.

"I'm Matt, by the way. Chloe's husband."

"Ethan. Pleased to meet you." Ethan looked toward Chloe, as if he wasn't sure whether to sit back down or run. "So, I'll be in my apartment. Call me when you want me to come get the TV and stuff."

"Thank you so much, Ethan. For everything."

"Oh, and Ethan," Matt called as the boy stepped into the hall. "You can close the door after you."

CHAPTER FIFTY-THREE

It was after five o'clock when Paige finally returned home. Which meant she had less than an hour to change her clothes, apply fresh makeup, and make her way over to Anthony's Bar for her date with Mr. Right Now.

The afternoon had been a disaster. First, her hairdresser was running late, and Paige had been forced to cool her heels for almost half an hour till he was ready for her, which made her more than forty minutes late for her mani-pedi, which meant that the manicurist had already moved on to her next client, which meant Paige had to wait again, which made her really late for her bikini wax, which proved even more painful than usual. Then her phone died, so she couldn't even text Mr. Right Now to warn him she might be late, after promising to be there at "six on the button."

Could anything else possibly go wrong? she

was thinking as she hurried past the condo's concierge toward the elevators.

"Miss Hamilton," he called after her. "There's someone here to see you . . ."

"What? Who?" she asked, returning to the lobby.

"Hello, Paige," Heather said, rising from her seat behind a large marble pillar and walking toward her, the unmistakable scent of marijuana surrounding her like a stale but overpowering perfume.

Shit, thought Paige. *This afternoon just keeps getting better.*

"You two have got to be related," the concierge said with a smile, oblivious to the tension between them. "You look like twins. Guess you get that all the time."

"All the time," Heather said.

"Is something wrong?" Paige asked. "Your parents . . ."

"Alive and kicking. Unfortunately," she added, not quite under her breath.

Wow, Paige thought. Okay. "Are you high?"

"Don't be ridiculous," Heather said, although her unfocused eyes said otherwise.

"What are you doing here?"

"We need to talk."

Paige glanced at her watch. "I really don't have time right now."

"Make time," Heather said. "I'm sure you don't want an unpleasant scene in the lobby, which is freezing, by the way. Do they have to keep it so goddamn cold?"

Paige looked toward the concierge, who was watching them expectantly, his smile starting to waver. "Fine. Okay. Come on up." They walked toward the elevators. "You're sure this is necessary?" Paige asked, as they stepped inside a waiting elevator. "I mean, if it's about what happened with Noah . . ."

"What do you know?" Heather said, as the doors closed and the elevator started its ascent. "She's not just a pretty face."

Paige brought one hand to her nose to keep the sickeningly sweet smell emanating from Heather's hair and skin at bay. She hoped it wouldn't transfer to her own skin. She didn't have time to take a shower. "Look. I'm sure you've seen the video. It pretty much speaks for itself."

"It doesn't speak for *me*," Heather said.

"Okay, well, fine." Paige gulped at the fresh air as the doors opened onto the tenth floor and the two women stepped into the hall. "I can't believe you're going for the moral high ground here, but . . . whatever. Just try not to upset my mother."

"Your mother isn't home," Heather said.

"The concierge told me she took off about an hour ago."

That's odd, Paige thought. Her mother had told her that Harry was babysitting his grandchildren tonight, giving her a chance to stay home and study her bridge notes. Of course, plans change, and her mother might have tried to reach her after her phone died. "Fine. Okay. Come in." She unlocked the door. "But I really don't have much time."

"Big date?" Heather asked.

"As a matter of fact, yes." Paige walked directly into the kitchen and plugged her phone into the charger next to the landline.

"With Sam?" Heather asked from the doorway.

"No. Not with Sam."

"With Noah?"

"What? No, of course not with Noah!"

"You're trying to tell me you haven't seen him?"

"Not since your father's party, no."

"You haven't talked to him?"

"Why would I? I have no interest in the man anymore, Heather. I think the video made that very clear. He's all yours."

There was a long pause.

"We broke up," Heather said.

Paige sighed. The sigh said she wasn't surprised. "And you blame me?"

"Who else should I blame?"

"How about Noah?" Paige asked. *And yourself,* she added silently.

It was Heather's turn to sigh. "My father says that any man stupid enough to cheat on someone like *you* would, of course, do the same thing to someone like *me,* and I'm beyond dumb if I didn't see it coming."

"You're not dumb," Paige said, feeling almost sorry for her cousin. "And for a supposedly smart man, your father says an awful lot of stupid things."

Heather's eyes clouded over with tears.

"Look. For what it's worth," Paige said, "I'm sorry you're hurting . . ."

"I don't need you to feel sorry for me," came Heather's instant retort.

"I don't," Paige clarified. "Frankly, I think you're your own worst enemy. I said I'm sorry you're hurting. And I'm sorry your father's such an ass. And I'm sorry Noah's such a dick."

"He *is* a dick, isn't he?" Heather sniffed.

"Yes, he is."

"And my father really is an ass."

"Yes, he really is." Paige stole a peek at her watch. It was closing in on five thirty. "Look, Heather. I have to be somewhere at six o'clock . . ."

"I got fired," Heather said.

"What? Why?"

"Doesn't matter. I hated that stupid job anyway."

"Well, then, maybe that's a good thing. Now you can start looking for something you *do* like."

"And my father kicked me out of the house."

Shit. She was never going to get out of here. Paige grabbed her cellphone from the counter as it was charging. "Just a second," she told her cousin. She quickly texted Mr. Right Now that she likely wouldn't get to Anthony's Bar before six thirty, despite her prior assurances. *I'll explain everything later,* she wrote. "So, what are you going to do?" she asked Heather, returning the phone to the counter.

"I'm not sure. Travel, maybe."

"Travel?"

"I have enough money for a few months. I was thinking maybe I'd go to Europe."

"You don't think you should start looking for an apartment and another job?" Paige regretted her question the second it was out of her mouth.

"No, I don't think I should start looking for an apartment and another job," Heather snapped. "I know that's the responsible thing to do. I know it's what *you* would do.

But, news flash, I'm *not* you."

"Nobody said you were . . ."

"I am so sick of being judged and found wanting . . ."

"Nobody is judging you . . ."

"If you're so bloody perfect, why did Noah cheat on you in the first place?"

"Okay," Paige said, marveling at how quickly the conversation had shifted gears. "I think we've said everything that needs to be said."

"And, of course, *you* get to decide that."

"Yes," Paige said. "Yes, I do. Now, if you'll excuse me, I really have to start getting ready."

"For your big date."

"Yes, for my big date." She walked to the kitchen door, Heather on her heels. "Heather," Paige said, stopping abruptly and swiveling around. "You're high. You're upset. You need to go home and lie down."

"I don't have a home, remember?"

Paige glanced up at the ceiling, her head spinning. "So, what are you saying? You want to stay here?"

"No. Are you crazy? I definitely don't want to stay here."

"Then what *do* you want? Do you have any idea?"

The women stared at each other in silence

for several long seconds.

The landline rang.

Paige reached over and answered it, grateful for the interruption. Anything was better than this. "Hello?" she said.

"Oh, darling. Thank heavens I reached you," her mother said. "I've been trying your cell . . ."

"What's the matter, Mom?"

"I'm at the hospital . . ."

"What? No! Not again."

"No, darling. It's not me. I'm fine."

"I don't understand. Has something happened to Harry?"

"No, sweetheart. Just listen. I'm at Mount Auburn Hospital in Cambridge."

"In Cambridge? What are you doing there? Oh, God," Paige said, dread seeping into every pore. "It's Chloe, isn't it?"

"Yes, darling." Her mother audibly choked back tears.

"What? *What?*"

"She's been shot."

No, Paige thought. *This can't be happening.* "How is that possible? Who . . . ?" she asked, already knowing the answer.

"It was Matt. He shot her. The police are out searching for him now. And . . . and . . . he has the kids."

"Oh, God." To think that Matt could have

done something so awful, to think of her beautiful, sweet Chloe lying in some hospital bed. And then, an even worse thought. "Is she . . . Is she still alive?"

There was a long pause. "You need to get here as fast as you can," her mother said.

CHAPTER FIFTY-FOUR

Her mother was waiting for her just inside the door to the ER.

"How is she?" Paige asked, swiping at her tears with the back of her hand. She'd been crying for what felt like hours, although it had been only about thirty minutes since her mother's call.

"Are you okay?" the taxi driver had asked after ten minutes of listening to her sob in the backseat. "You need some water?"

"My friend's been shot," Paige had managed to blurt out.

Which had effectively ended the conversation.

"How is she?" Paige asked now.

"Still in surgery," her mother answered.

"How bad is it?"

"She was shot three times, once to the stomach, twice to the chest," her mother said, as if she couldn't quite believe the words coming out of her mouth. "It doesn't look good, darling."

"I don't understand. How did this happen?"

Joan led her daughter into the large waiting area, sitting down beside her on the blue plastic chairs. "From what I understand, Chloe was at her mother's apartment —"

"Yes," Paige interrupted. "Her mother asked her to go there and pack up her things."

"Yes, well, apparently the place was quite a mess, and the young man who lives across the hall offered to give Chloe a hand. They'd pretty much finished the job when Matt showed up. The neighbor — his name is Ethan, a very sweet boy — said Matt didn't look too happy to see him there, so he left. A short time later, he heard shouting, and then what sounded like shots. He opened his door to see Matt running down the hall. He went into the apartment and found Chloe on the floor, bleeding and unconscious. He called the police, then did CPR until the paramedics arrived."

"I don't understand. Who called *you*?" Paige asked.

"Ethan did. He checked Chloe's phone and found our number in her contact list. I tried to reach you, but something must be the matter with your cell . . ."

"Shit," Paige said, realizing she'd left her phone charging on the kitchen counter, and that she had no way of texting Mr. Right Now to cancel their date. After hearing the horrible news, she'd grabbed her purse and fled the apartment, forgetting all about him.

"What's happening?" she'd heard Heather call after her. "Where are you going?"

Hopefully her cousin wouldn't trash the place, Paige thought now. And hopefully Mr. Right Now wouldn't waste too much time waiting around for her to show up. She'd apologize in the morning, try to explain, although she doubted he'd believe her, or care, even if he did. That ship had most certainly sailed. She shrugged. Some things just weren't meant to be. "Any news about Matt?"

"Not yet."

"And for sure he has the kids?"

"Apparently, he picked them up at day camp, right on schedule. Big smile on his face. No hint anything was wrong, that he'd just come from shooting his wife."

Paige closed her eyes. "Oh, God. You don't think he'd hurt them, do you?"

The silence that followed was answer enough. "The police have issued an Amber Alert," her mother said, after the passing of several seconds. "Hopefully, they'll find them soon, safe and sound."

Paige felt a shift in the air and opened her eyes to see two men approaching. She knew instantly they were police detectives despite, or maybe because of, their drab attire. Brown suits, white shirts, striped ties that were too wide to be fashionable. *They don't call them "plainclothesmen" for nothing,* she thought, pushing herself to her feet.

"I'm Detective Gordon," the taller, thinner, and older of the two men said, introducing himself. "This is my partner, Detective McMillan. You are?"

"Paige Hamilton. Chloe's friend. How is she? Is she out of surgery? Have you found Matt?"

"She's still in surgery. And no, we haven't found Matt yet. Maybe you can help us. Do you have any idea where he might have gone?"

"No," Paige told them. "He and Chloe were separated. I don't even know where he's been living. You should check with his work." She gave them the name of the real estate company that employed him, and Detective McMillan turned away to relay the information into his cellphone.

"Does he have family in the area?" Detective Gordon asked.

"No. I think everyone's pretty spread out."

"What about a cottage?"

Paige shook her head.

"Close friends?"

"They didn't socialize much, other than for Matt's work. But Matt was a player . . ."

"A player?" Detective Gordon asked.

"You know. He had . . . women on the side," Paige explained. "Lots of them. He was on multiple dating sites. Chloe found out. That's why she was divorcing him."

"What dating sites?"

"Match Sticks, Tinder, Perfect Strangers — you name them, he's on them. At least, he *was*. He might have pulled his profile because he was trying to win Chloe back." She watched the detective jot this information down in his notepad.

"Hell of a way to go about it," the detective remarked. "Is there anything else you can think of that might help us find him?"

Paige tried to think of something — anything — that might be useful to the detectives. But her mind was a jungle of disparate thoughts, impossible to hack her way through. *While she was waiting to be manicured and waxed, her best friend in the world lay bleeding, possibly dying, on the floor of her lunatic mother's apartment, shot by her maniac of a husband, a man who would screw a keyhole if he felt the urge, a man who wasn't used to women saying no, a man who would rather murder the mother of his children than see her move on without him. If only she'd gone to help Chloe instead of getting her hair done, maybe this wouldn't have happened. Or maybe Matt would have shot her, too.* "Has anybody notified Chloe's mother?" she heard herself ask.

"I'd have to check," Detective Gordon said, referring to his notes. "We understand from the neighbor that her mother is currently out of town."

"Yes. She's in Las Vegas. On her honeymoon."

"Chloe's mother got married?" Joan Hamilton exclaimed.

"Her mother's name is Jennifer Powadiuk. Is that correct?" Detective McMillan asked.

"Yes. Someone should call her. I'm sure her number is in Chloe's phone."

The detectives moved just out of earshot to confer.

"I wondered why Chloe was cleaning out her mother's apartment," Joan remarked.

If only Jennifer Powadiuk hadn't gotten married again. If only she hadn't called Chloe and asked her to pack up her things. If only she hadn't been such a selfish, narcissistic bitch, maybe Chloe wouldn't have married a man just like her. She wouldn't be lying on an operating table with three bullets in her body. She wouldn't be clinging to life.

We go with what's familiar, Paige understood, no matter how unpleasant. We're always seeking to make things right, to find that elusive happy ending.

Looking for Mr. Right.

Finding Mr. Right Now, she thought, a sound halfway between a laugh and a cry escaping her lips.

"Did you think of something?" Detective Gordon asked, returning to her side, notebook and pencil poised and ready.

Paige shook her head. "Did you get ahold of Chloe's mother?"

"She's not answering her phone. We've left several messages, informing her there's an emergency and asking her to get in touch as soon as possible."

"Don't hold your breath," Paige said.

The detective raised one bushy eyebrow. "Well, if you think of anything else, no matter how insignificant it may seem, please don't hesitate to let us know."

"And if there's any news about . . . anything," Paige said, "we'll be right here."

The detectives retreated down the hall as Paige and her mother resumed their seats, their hands interlocked, their fingers intertwined.

"Thanks for being here," Paige said, leaning her head against her mother's shoulder.

"No thanks necessary."

"Do you think Chloe will be all right?"

"I don't know, darling," her mother said, hugging her daughter tight. "I just don't know."

CHAPTER FIFTY-FIVE

Heather stood in the middle of her aunt's kitchen, trying to make sense of what had happened, replaying in her mind the one-sided conversation she'd just overheard. But it was difficult when you were only privy to half of what was being said. And you were stoned. She tried taking it apart, piece by piece, then filling in the blanks.

"What's the matter, Mom?" she heard Paige say. *"What? No! Not again."*

Okay, so it had initially appeared as if Paige's mother was in some sort of trouble, and it wasn't the first time.

"I don't understand. Has something happened to Harry?"

Who the hell was Harry?

"In Cambridge? What are you doing there? Oh, God. It's Chloe, isn't it?"

Okay, so Auntie Joan was all right, and so was this Harry, whoever the hell he was. It was Chloe. Something bad had happened to Chloe.

So, not so bad after all, Heather thought.

"*What? What?*" Emphasis on the second *what. "How is that possible? Who . . . ? Oh, God. Is she . . . Is she still alive?*"

So, whatever had happened to Chloe was not only bad, it was life-threatening. It was so serious that Paige had grabbed her purse and torn out of the apartment like it was on fire, leaving Heather without an explanation or a second thought.

"What's happening?" Heather had called after her. "Where are you going?"

But the only response she'd received was the sound of a slamming door.

So rude, Heather thought now, as she'd thought then. And what could be so terrible, so urgent? It had to be an accident of some sort. Maybe Chloe had been hit by a car while crossing the street, or been involved in a head-on collision with a Mack truck. Maybe she was the victim of a purse-snatching gone bad, or a break-in at her home. Maybe she'd been attacked, beaten, maybe even raped . . .

Whatever, Heather thought, suppressing an unexpected twinge of concern. She wasn't going to waste time worrying about Chloe. Not after the little stunt she'd pulled, making her drive out to Cambridge in the middle of a workday, only to be humiliated and sent packing, which made her at least partly responsible for Heather losing her job. It would be silly to waste her tears on such an undeserving friend, she thought, impatiently wiping away the few she felt forming.

Whatever had happened, no matter how bad it was, Chloe would pull through. Despite her delicate exterior, the woman had a core of steel. She'd survive. There was no reason for concern. There were more pressing things to worry about.

Heather felt her stomach rumble, reminding her that she hadn't eaten all day. She'd fled her parents' house almost as fast as Paige had fled the condo, if you didn't count the five minutes it had taken her to smoke a joint, leaving most of her belongings behind. What the hell, she'd thought as she was backing her car out of her parents' driveway, narrowly missing smashing into the ornate wrought-iron fence surrounding the front lawn. She'd get her mother to cart over the rest of her things after she'd settled in somewhere. Or better yet, she just might treat herself to a whole new wardrobe at Daddy's expense.

After all, how could she be expected to make a good impression on prospective employers without the proper wardrobe?

And while Ted Hamilton might be a heart-less jackass, when push came to shove, he wasn't going to let his only daughter live on the streets. His pride, his good name and reputation, would never allow that.

Neither would her mother.

If and when Heather ran short of money, she knew she could count on her mother to persuade her father to give her more.

So, she thought, walking to the fridge and opening it, *not so dumb after all.*

There was a big bowl of fresh, plump blueberries and another one of luscious-looking raspberries on the fridge's middle shelf, and Heather brought both bowls to the counter, eating the berries with her fingers, until there were none left. That should keep her for another hour, she thought, until she figured out where to spend the night. Maybe she'd go back to the Four Seasons, order room service, have a much-needed massage. It was almost six o'clock. She'd spent half the afternoon aim-lessly driving around, trying to decide her next move, before stopping on a side street somewhere in the city's South End and smoking some more weed. Which had led to the dubious decision to have it out with Paige. Which led to her spending the better part of an hour freezing in the overly air-conditioned lobby of her aunt's building, waiting for her cousin to come home. She was exhausted. Tomorrow would be soon enough to start looking for an apartment.

The more immediate worry was where the hell she'd parked her car.

Maybe instead of looking for an apartment, she'd visit a travel agent, inquire about that trip to Europe she'd tossed at Paige earlier. Not that she'd ever had much curiosity about Europe, or any burning desire to go. The truth was that she'd rather go lie on a beach somewhere, but God, the look on Paige's face!

"You don't think you should start looking for an apartment and another job?" she'd asked, sounding every bit as tight-assed and judgmental as Heather's father. *So maybe we really were switched at birth,* Heather thought.

"I'm sorry you're hurting," she heard Paige say.

"Sure you are," Heather said now, hearing the ping of a text message come through on Paige's cell. "Well, what do you know? You took off so fast, you forgot your stupid phone." She sidled over to where it lay charging on the counter and picked it up, then stole a glance over her shoulder, as if

Paige had snuck back into the apartment and was hiding in the corner, watching to see what she would do.

"No need to hide," she said out loud, as if Paige were in the room. "I'm happy to show you." Heather checked the phone to see the beginning of a message from someone calling himself Mr. Right Now.

Hey, Wildflower.

Mr. Right Now? Wildflower? "You've got to be kidding."

No problem. And no rush. I'll be waiting at Anthony's Bar whenever you . . .

If there was more to the message, Heather couldn't get at it. In order to access her cousin's message page, she needed to know her password, and while it was tempting to spend a few minutes experimenting — her own password was the year of their birth — she could almost hear her father's snide comment that Paige would never choose anything so obvious.

Talk about obvious. "Wildflower," she scoffed. "Mr. Right Now." Clearly their online aliases. So, Paige's big date was someone she'd met on a dating site, someone it appeared she was meeting in person for the first time tonight.

Heather reached into her pocket for her cell and quickly connected to Match Sticks, the most popular of Boston's online dating sites, scrolling through the seemingly endless number of male pictures and profiles until she found the one she was looking for. "Wow," she said, staring at the tiny photo of the man calling himself Mr. Right Now. "Aren't you the handsome one." No wonder Paige had been in such a hurry.

"Oh, well. Too bad, so sad." Paige wouldn't be able to make their date after all. Nor would she have any way of texting the poor man her predicament. He'd be left to cool his heels, figuring he'd been stood up. Although it was safe to assume that any man who looked like that wouldn't be alone for long.

Heather smiled, the beginnings of an idea taking shape in her admittedly addled brain.

People were always saying she and her cousin looked enough alike to be twins. She was familiar with Anthony's Bar, and it was relatively close by. Assuming Mr. Right Now looked anything like his picture, she'd have no trouble spotting him, and with the bar's dim lighting, she'd have no trouble passing herself off as her cousin. So, all she had to do was introduce herself as Wildflower, and see how things progressed from there.

She laughed out loud. What could be more perfect? She couldn't have scripted this any better.

But first, of course, she needed something to wear. Couldn't very well meet the potential man of Paige's dreams in shorts and an off-the-shoulder blouse. Besides, she was still chilled to the bone from the air-conditioning in the lobby. "I'll be lucky not to catch my death from the cold," she said out loud, and laughed. *Catch my death,* she thought. What a strange expression! How did one "catch death"?

Yes, she definitely needed something to wear. But there was no time to go shopping, and besides, why go shopping when there was a whole closetful of clothes down the hall? She and Paige wore the same size and had similar taste, even if Paige generally favored more conservative fare. She was bound to find something.

Heather floated out of the kitchen and down the hall to Paige's bedroom. "This must be the place," she giggled, crossing to the small walk-in closet and opening the door. "Well, well. Let's see what we have here." Her hand rifled through the various clothes on the hangers, passing up the silk blouses, straight skirts, and cotton dresses she pictured Paige wearing to work. "God, you're even more boring than I thought." Did her cousin not own anything with a plunging neckline? Did all her dresses have to reach her knees? "Surely to God, you have something you wouldn't feel comfortable being buried in," she said, dissolving in a fit of giggles.

Which was when she saw it — the perfect outfit in which to meet Mr. Right Now. A pearl-gray dress trimmed with lace, with a V-neckline that, if it wasn't exactly revealing, at least hinted at cleavage. Sexy without being slutty. The kind of dress that said "maybe," not "you bet!"

Heather slipped out of her shorts and top, then wiggled into the dress. "Perfect," she said, going through Paige's shoes, and selecting a pair of high-heeled black pumps. "A little tight, but manageable." She ran into Paige's bathroom and helped herself to her cousin's blush and mascara, then fluffed out her hair before borrowing one of Paige's lipsticks. "Hmm. Good color. Think I'll keep this one."

She took one last, satisfied glance in the mirror over the sink. "Okay. Looking good." She laughed, a feeling of pride surging through her body, like an electrical current. *Score another one for Heather,* she thought. "Mr. Right Now, here I come."

CHAPTER FIFTY-SIX

He spots her the minute she walks through the door.

Something is off, he thinks from his hidden vantage point at a table in the corner of the crowded room, although he can't put a finger on what it is. She looks much like he remembers: the dark, shoulder-length hair, the slim build, the pretty face. More makeup than the last time he saw her. A little fuller in the chest. Not quite as sophisticated-looking as he'd been expecting, despite the obviously expensive dress she's wearing.

Has he been kidding himself, thinking she was different from the women he usually "dated"? Did the fact that she had an actual career as opposed to just a job, that her messages made her seem genuinely smart as opposed to passably clever, fool him into thinking that she had greater depth than she did, and would prove a more challenging, more satisfying kill?

Clearly, he's read too much into her messages.

Clearly, he's been expecting too much.

He takes a deep breath, hoping to quell his disappointment. Maybe he's just pissed off about her being so late, despite her promise to be there at "six on the button."

Or maybe he's just nervous.

Which is strange, because he's never nervous. Oh, he gets a little anxious, but more from anticipation than fear. Usually he can't wait to get this show on the road, which is, of course, where he'll be taking it after tonight's final Boston performance. So maybe that accounts for his slight case of jitters. The fact that he'll be closing up shop, moving in the morning to another city, in another state.

Buffalo, he's decided after much consideration. He's heard that the city has improved greatly in the last few years, become much more cosmopolitan. It's also close to Niagara Falls, where, surprisingly, he's never been. And the Baseball Hall of Fame is only a four-hour drive away, and might be worth a visit. Always nice to include a few touristy things into the program. So, a few months there shouldn't be too intolerable before he crosses over into Canada in time to take in the magnificent dying of the leaves.

He spent the day packing. Not that he has much to pack. Just one suitcase for his clothes and a few boxes, two of them still empty, awaiting his good china and cutlery, his wineglasses, his fine Irish linen table-cloth, and of course, his envious collection of knives, all of which can't be tucked away until they've served their purpose. Nor can he load anything into the trunk of his car before morning. Other than Wildflower, of course. He snickers inwardly, his face remaining an immobile mask that reveals nothing beyond its handsome features. Judging by Wildflower's slim physique, he doubts she'll require much space.

But he's learned through experience that dead bodies can't always be depended on. For one thing, they usually take up more space than one thinks they will, their stubborn limbs often refusing to bend or co-operate, and he hasn't got much time to fiddle around. He's decided it will be best to dispose of Wildflower's body in the early morning hours, while it's still dark, before rigor has a chance to set in, or Jenna Lebowski comes snooping around to check that he's vacated the premises as promised. He'll get rid of the rope and handcuffs at a rest stop along the highway tomorrow morning, en route to Buffalo and the tiny bungalow he's rented through Airbnb.

The changes to his dating profile will be made once he's settled in. He'll have to pick a new name, although he's grown rather fond of his current moniker. Mr. Right Now has served him remarkably well these last months in Boston.

Still, it's never a good idea to get too attached to anything — person, place, thing, or name — and a new city deserves a new online identity. He already has a few handles in mind. Hamlet is one. Prince Hal is another. A nod to his high school English teacher, the glorious Miss Brenda Williams. She of the long red hair and coral-colored lips, the mellifluous voice and love of all things Shakespeare. *"Isn't that splendid?"* he can still hear her sigh after reciting several lines of the Bard's poetry to a roomful of indifferent teens. He'd often go to sleep dreaming of making her recite those lines with his hands around her throat. *"Isn't that splendid?"* he'd ask as he choked the life right out of her.

So, maybe Hamlet or Prince Hal. Or maybe something simpler. Something like Miller or Smith. Yes, he thinks, deciding on the latter. He likes Smith. It has a nice, clean ring to it. So, Smith he will be.

"Hi," a voice chirps from somewhere

beside him.

He jumps at the sound.

"Sorry," she says, the word accompanied by an annoyingly girlish giggle. "I didn't mean to scare you. Mr. Right Now, I presume?" She cocks her head to one side, like an inquisitive puppy.

Is it possible she really doesn't recognize him from their previous encounter?

"Wildflower?" he asks, further surprised she has managed to sneak up on him this way. He notes that her voice is coarser, less tentative, more openly flirtatious than the voice he heard on the phone last Saturday, the voice he was looking forward to hearing tonight in person.

"That's me," she says, accompanied by another annoying giggle. "Have you been waiting long?"

He checks his watch. "Forty-five minutes."

"Yeah," she says. "Sorry about that."

You don't sound sorry, he thinks. *But you will be.*

"My cousin dropped over unexpectedly, and she wouldn't take a hint. I practically had to shove her out the door."

That's it? he wonders. *That's your lame excuse for making me cool my heels for the better part of an hour?* "Well, you're here now. That's what matters. What are you

541

drinking?"

"Champagne?"

"A glass of champagne for the lady," he calls to a passing waitress, suppressing the urge to shout, *Why the question mark? Do you want champagne or don't you?*

"So," Wildflower says, settling into the seat beside him, "what do you think? Am I what you expected?"

"Even better," he lies. "Your picture doesn't do you justice." No point in mentioning that they've met before, since she obviously doesn't remember.

Her smile indicates this is exactly what she was hoping to hear. She leans forward, allowing him a slight peek down the front of her dress. He's furious to find her so obvious. She's proving to be a major disappointment, and she will be punished severely.

"What about me?" he asks.

"Much, *much* better," she says, another giggle following. "I think you know you're pretty hot."

He glances toward the floor, as if embarrassed by the compliment.

"So, Mr. Right Now," she says, taking the lead. "What is it you do?"

The question catches him off guard. He's already told her what he supposedly does

542

for a living, and the fact that she doesn't remember means she either has a very poor memory or he's just one of many men she's been meeting online and it's hard to keep track, which again, is as infuriating as it is unexpected. Not that it matters. He intends to be the *last* man she meets, online or otherwise. "Stockbroker."

If that rings any bells, she gives no such sign. "Must be challenging."

"It has its moments. And you? Heard back about your interview yet?"

The expression on her face freezes, almost as if she has no idea what he's talking about. It makes him wonder how much of what she's told him is true. Perhaps she's as good a liar, as skilled a game player, as he is, an unexpected twist he finds exciting.

Because this is a game where there can be only one winner.

And, Wildflower, he says with his eyes, *you're looking at him.*

"Nothing yet," she says, recovering. "Hopefully soon. But let's not talk about work. It's too depressing."

"Fine by me. What would you like to talk about?"

"How about you start by telling me your name. I mean, I can't keep calling you Mr. Right Now."

"It's Smith," he says, deciding to try it out. What the hell? It's not like she'll get the chance to tell anyone.

"That's your first name? Smith?"

"It was my mother's maiden name," he says. Another lie. His mother's maiden name was Ukrainian and virtually unpronounceable.

"I like it. It's very sexy."

"Glad you approve. And you?"

She hesitates. "It's Heather," she says finally.

Heather? Why, you lying little bitch, he thinks, deciding she might make a worthy adversary after all. "You don't sound sure," he says with a smile.

"Well, it's . . . complicated."

"I look forward to hearing why," he says, as the waitress approaches with the glass of champagne.

"Maybe later. After I know you better."

"To later." He clinks his glass against hers.

"To later," she repeats, taking a long sip. "Hmm. Good stuff. But I warn you, this is probably going to go straight to my head. I haven't eaten all day."

"You're not on some crazy diet, are you?"

"God, no. *No* . . . it's . . ."

"Complicated?"

"A little." She giggles, then takes another,

longer sip of her champagne.

"Looks like we'll have lots to talk about . . . later," he says. "If you haven't eaten all day, you must be very hungry."

"Starving."

"Do you like steak?"

"Love it."

"Because I happen to know a place where they make the best steaks in town."

"Seriously? That would be absolute heaven. But do you think we'd be able to get a reservation this late?"

"No problem at all. The chef happens to be a great friend of mine."

Heather downs the remaining contents of her glass and pushes herself to her feet. "Then what are we waiting for?"

He laughs, his hand curling around her slender waist. "My sentiments exactly."

CHAPTER FIFTY-SEVEN

She looked so pale, so small, so vulnerable, lying there.

Paige shuddered as she approached the bed, her eyes searching for signs of life. It took a moment, but eventually she was able to make out the subtle rise and fall of Chloe's breath beneath the stiff, white hospital sheets.

She'd come so close to dying. The doctors said it was a miracle she'd pulled through. They'd given her only a slim chance of surviving the six-hour surgery, and less than a fifty-fifty chance of making it through that first critical week, and yet here they were, fifteen days after the shooting, and Chloe was out of the ICU and on the road to a full recovery. There was even talk of sending her home next week.

"Hi, you," Chloe said, eyes still closed.

"How'd you know I was here?" Paige asked.

" 'Cause you're always here for me," Chloe said, eyes fluttering open, her lips quivering into a smile.

"Did I wake you?"

"No. I was just resting my eyes. What time is it?"

"Almost one o'clock." Paige reached for her friend's hand beneath the covers. "How are you feeling?"

"Pretty damn good, considering. How are the kids?"

"Wonderful. My mother is absolutely adoring playing grandmother. You might have a hard time convincing her to give them back."

"I can't thank you both enough . . ."

"Oh, please," Paige said. "The fact that you're alive is all the thanks we need."

Josh and Sasha had been staying with Paige and her mother since their father's arrest. The Amber Alert had led to a flood of sightings, and Matt's car had been spotted in the parking lot of a motel on the outskirts of Pittsburgh at around ten o'clock that night. Fortunately, the children were asleep and unharmed. They'd been returned to Boston, where Matt was currently in jail, being held without bond, awaiting trial for kidnapping and attempted murder.

The phone on the side table rang.

"Would you mind getting that?" Chloe asked.

Paige reached past the beautiful arrangement of white and yellow roses her mother and Harry had sent over the previous day and picked up the phone. "Hello. Chloe's room, Paige speaking."

"Paige, how are you?" There was no mistaking Jennifer Powadiuk's distinctive growl.

"It's your mother," Paige mouthed. "I'm fine, Mrs. Powadiuk. How are you?"

"I've been better," came the answer. "And it's Mrs. Girard now. How's Chloe doing?"

"Why don't you ask her yourself?" Paige handed the phone to Chloe.

"Hi, Mom." Chloe held the phone out so that Paige could hear her mother's side of the conversation. "How are you?"

"About as well as can be expected, I guess. All this worry about you has taken more than a few years off my life."

Paige rolled her eyes. It was so like Chloe's mother to make her daughter's shooting all about her.

"How are things going in Miami?"

"Still settling in. It's dreadfully hot here. Gerry says it's much better in the winter months, but I don't know . . . We're heading to Chicago next week for a competition,

so that should be a nice break from everything."

You should only break a leg, Paige thought.

"Anyway, I'll get going and let you rest.
How are the kids?" she asked, an obvious
afterthought.

"They're doing great. Paige and her
mother have been looking after them —"

"Yes, well, you know I would be there if I
could," Jennifer interrupted. "It's just that,
well, the timing couldn't be worse."

As if there were a good time to get shot,
Paige thought.

"Things are so hectic, what with the
honeymoon and the move and preparing
our routine for the competition . . ."

"I understand."

". . . plus you know how much I hate
hospitals."

As opposed to the rest of us, who love them,
Paige thought.

"And once I knew you were out of danger . . ."

"It's okay, Mom. Really."

"Yes, well. I should go, let you rest. Wish
me luck in Chicago."

"Good luck," Chloe obliged her by saying. "Oh, and Mom?"

"Yes?"

"Maybe when I'm better, the kids and I

could come see you dance."

There was a moment's silence.

"That would be very nice," her mother said.

Another silence.

"Okay, well," Chloe said. "Thanks for calling."

"Take care."

"Wow," Paige said as Chloe handed her the phone to hang up. "That was pretty generous of you."

"I'm not under any delusions here," Chloe said. "I know she's not going to change. But, what the hell? Life's too short. Gotta watch your mother dance when you get the chance."

Paige laughed. "How'd you turn out so great?"

"It's a miracle," Chloe said.

"*You're* the miracle."

Chloe smiled. "Yes, well, enough about Miracle Woman. I want to hear about you. Are you all excited about your new job?"

"So excited," Paige said, thinking ahead to next week. "And a little nervous. It's been a while."

"Don't be nervous. You'll be great. They're lucky to have you. And speaking of being lucky to have you, anything happening with you and Sam?"

Paige smiled. "I took your advice."

"You called him?"

"I called him."

"And?"

"We're going out this weekend."

Chloe smiled. "That's so great."

"Well, it's early days. We'll see how it goes."

"Knock, knock. Can we come in?" Joan Hamilton poked her head in the doorway. "I have some people here who are most anxious to see you."

"Mommy!" Josh and Sasha shouted together, racing for their mother's bed.

"Careful. No running," Joan cautioned. "No jumping on the bed."

"Oh, my sweet angels," Chloe cried, as they clambered into her arms.

"Careful," Paige and her mother urged, their voices overlapping.

"The doctor said they could visit for a few minutes," Joan explained, "providing they're very gentle with Mommy."

"Are we gentle, Mommy?" Sasha asked. "Are you okay?"

"I am now that you're here."

"When are you coming home?" Josh said.

"Soon, I hope."

"Paige and Nana Joan are taking good

care of us till you get better," Sasha told her mother.

"I'm so glad."

"Why isn't Daddy taking care of us?" Josh asked, hazel eyes narrowing.

"We weren't sure how much to tell them," Paige whispered under her breath.

Chloe nodded. "I think this is a job for Miracle Woman," she said. "If you could give us a minute."

"You're sure you're up for this?" Paige asked.

"I'm sure."

"We'll be in the hall," Joan said.

"Your daddy did a bad thing," Chloe began as the door closed after them.

Paige leaned against the wall as her mother began pacing back and forth in front of her. "Problem?" Paige asked.

"I don't know."

"What do you mean, you don't know? Please tell me you're feeling all right."

"I'm fine, darling. It's Bev. She called earlier . . ."

"And?"

"Have you spoken to Heather lately?"

"Not since the day Chloe was shot. Why?"

"Neither have Ted or Bev," Joan said.

"Well, they kicked her out of the house, so they shouldn't be all that surprised.

Heather's pretty famous for holding a grudge."

"I suppose."

"And remember, she told me she was thinking of taking a trip, maybe going to Europe."

"I told Bev that, but she can't imagine Heather just taking off without letting her know, no matter how angry she was. She doesn't think Heather even has a passport."

"Well, there's a lot about Heather her mother probably doesn't know. I wouldn't worry too much."

"I told her that, too. But then she said that Ted called the bank this morning and found out that Heather hasn't touched any of the money he transferred into her account. Bev said if they don't hear something by the end of the week, they're going to call the police."

Paige shrugged. "She probably just met some guy. She'll turn up when she's good and ready. Oh . . ."

"What?"

"I just had a thought. No, it's too crazy."

"What?"

"Well, remember that guy, Mr. Right Now, the man I was supposed to go out with the night Chloe was shot . . . ?"

"The one who's disappeared off the face

of the earth?" her mother asked.

Paige nodded. She'd tried both calling and texting him to apologize, but the number he'd given her was no longer in service and his profile had been removed from all his dating sites. "I'd left my phone charging on the counter," Paige continued, thinking out loud. "When we got home, I saw that he'd texted me to say he'd be waiting. Maybe Heather read the message and decided to go meet him herself."

"You're thinking she ran off with your Mr. Right Now?"

"I wouldn't put it past her."

"Me neither," Joan agreed. "I'll tell Bev and Ted. Who knows? If she doesn't call them soon, it might be worth mentioning to the police."

Josh pulled open the door to Chloe's room. "Mommy says you can come back inside now."

Joan took a step forward.

"Mom? Wait." Paige took a deep breath. "I was thinking that maybe we should invite Harry over for dinner one of these nights."

"Really?"

Paige slipped her hand through her mother's arm. Harry had put the spark back into her mother's eyes. Chloe's words echoed in her ear. *"Life's too short. Gotta watch your mother dance when you get the chance.*"

"Really," she said.

"I'm sure Harry would be delighted."

"Then it's settled."

"Thank you, darling. This means a lot to me."

"*You* mean a lot to me," Paige told her. "And just in case I don't say it enough . . . I hope you know how much I love you."

Joan leaned over to kiss her daughter's cheek. "I know, darling. I love you, too."

ACKNOWLEDGMENTS

This is probably the hardest part of writing my books: trying to remember — and properly thank — all the people who have helped shape my efforts and supported me through periods of doubt and general chaos. As always, I want to thank my family: my husband, Warren, of (gasp!) forty-five years; my beautiful daughters, Shannon and Annie; my son-in-law, Courtney; my two glorious grandchildren, Hayden and Skylar; and my sister, Renee. I love and appreciate you all.

As always, I have to acknowledge my stalwart first readers: Larry Mirkin, Beverley Slopen, and Robin Stone. Your advice has once again proven invaluable and I'm honestly not sure what I'd do without you.

Thank you to Tracy Fisher, my wise and beautiful agent at William Morris Endeavor, and to her assistant, Alyssa Eatherly. Thanks also to her previous assistant, Fiona Smith.

557

Heartfelt thanks to my editor at Ballantine, Anne Speyer, who is patient, tactful, and a real joy to work with. I knew from our past experience on *The Bad Daughter* that we'd make a good team, and I'm happy to say my instincts were correct.

I'd also like to acknowledge the team at Ballantine that has worked so hard on my behalf: Jennifer Hershey, Kim Hovey, Kara Welsh, Cindy Murray, Allison Schuster, Steve Messina, and Scott Biel. (It was Scott who designed the gorgeous cover.)

My gratitude to everyone at Doubleday, part of Penguin Random House Canada, for their constant support over these many years. In particular, I would like to thank Amy Black, Kaitlin Smith, Val Gow, Robin Thomas, Susan Burns, and Emma Ingram. Also a shout-out to Kristin Cochrane and (the now retired) Brad Martin for their unwavering loyalty over the years.

Thanks to my various publishers all over the world — I will dearly miss you, Georg — and to all the translators who do such a good job of interpreting my stories.

Thank you to Corinne Assayag, who is responsible for designing and running my website — joyfielding.com — and to Peter Baraian, whose name was misspelled in my last acknowledgments — so sorry! — for coming to my frequent rescue when I'm having a meltdown over problems with my computer.

Finally, thanks to Aurora and to Mary for making my life easier.

And, of course, my thanks to my readers. What can I say? You're the best.

ABOUT THE AUTHOR

Joy Fielding is the *New York Times* bestselling author of *The Bad Daughter, She's Not There, Someone Is Watching, Charley's Web, Heartstopper, Mad River Road, See Jane Run,* and other acclaimed novels. She divides her time between Toronto and Palm Beach, Florida.

joyfielding.com
Twitter: @joyfielding
Instagram: @fieldingjoy
Find Joy Fielding on Facebook

The employees of Thorndike Press hope you have enjoyed this Large Print book. All our Thorndike, Wheeler, and Kennebec Large Print titles are designed for easy reading, and all our books are made to last. Other Thorndike Press Large Print books are available at your library, through selected bookstores, or directly from us.

For information about titles, please call:
(800) 223-1244

or visit our website at:
gale.com/thorndike

To share your comments, please write:
Publisher
Thorndike Press
10 Water St., Suite 310
Waterville, ME 04901